Daylilies And Nightshades

by
Deborah Bowden

"Daylilies and Nightshades"

Written by Deborah Bowden

rosemarycoven@yahoo.com
www.deborahbowden.com
www.amazon.com

ISBN: 978-1958792209
Edited by EBowden
Cover Design by Donna Cook

A Note from the Author

This manuscript disappeared from Indiana to Texas with parts scattered and nearly lost. It took six years to compile all the pieces. Therefore, I dedicate this anthology to Thoth, Sekhmet, and Bastet. Without their intervention, this compilation would never have found fruition. Thanks also to my talented son, Trevor Mason who encouraged me through the many dark days this writing cost me. I could not have continued without his strong shoulders.

A special thanks to Debi Stanton, Michelle Barron, and Tabitha Morley who helped type this book from my unedited, hand-scribbled notes – all that was left of the manuscript. Theirs was a monumental task.

My first anthology, *Dandelion and Other Weeds*, had a lighthearted tone. In this companion book, I have chosen to explore darker themes and memories as well as lighter ones. Hence the name: *Daylilies and Nightshades*. I hope you enjoy the duality.

Table of Contents

Section 1

A Taste of Belladonna

The Tarantula

Everywhere we went, Dad wanted me to learn new experiences. If there was a factory, ship, or anything else that caught his eye, he'd locate an owner or manager, and get a guided tour. He would tell the folks that he wanted me to learn about whatever they did. I, of course, did my best to look wide-eyed and adorable as a youngster and very interested as a teenager. It always worked.

In Louisiana, down on the docks, Dad managed to get us on board a banana boat. Most of the crew only spoke Spanish, so Mom and I wondered around looking at the large crates holding the bananas which were about to be hoisted off onto the docks for distribution. Most all were green—this kept them from damaging during the trip; they would ripen by the time they were delivered to stores or restaurants. There was one big uncrated pile of ripe, yellow ones just lying on the deck. Maybe they were destined to travel only a short distance, maybe a crate broke, or maybe they were too ripe to ship and were culled out. They looked delicious to me. There was no one who spoke English near us to ask. Dad was off somewhere talking to the captain; so it was just Mom and me. She wanted to take a picture of my sitting on that big pile, so she got the attention of one of the men, and pointed to the camera, the pile of bananas, and me. He nodded, "Yes."

She had me climb up a ways and sit down. She snapped my picture with an old-fashioned box camera which she'd had for most of her life. It always took great pictures she said, and preferred it over any of the newer models. The camera was a bit slow to use, so I had to sit still. Then she turned to take pictures of the boat and a couple of the sailors as I climbed down. Some of the banana bunches were dislodged from the pile and rolled down to the floor. Out came a huge spider. I'd never seen anything so gigantic—it was a tarantula. I was too stunned to say anything.

Just then, Mom turned my way, and she saw it too. Now she was deathly afraid of spiders and snakes. Black widows, copperheads, and water moccasins were very common in Kentucky, and she'd learned at an early age to be cautious. I never did understand why she was so extremely afraid, however she let out a garbled gasp that would have been a scream if it hadn't caught in her throat. I saw that my mother was scared to death—she couldn't move. I grabbed a couple of bananas and threw them at the big hairy creature. I missed, and it ran back into the pile.

Mom took off looking for Dad, leaving me behind. She insisted we leave the boat immediately. We did after he thanked the captain for allowing us on board. He explained to her when she was "safely" on the dock, surrounded by crates of bananas, that tarantulas are often found in the banana bunches. They eat bugs and bugs are attracted to the sweet fruit. So when the fruit gets picked, the spiders get carted along also. The boats and docks always had some crawling around; some probably even made it to shops.

It was awhile before she would get near any bananas in the grocery stores. Me? Well, I was too stunned to be scared. The fact that I was sitting on top of that pile while my picture was being taken, and that the tarantula could easily have crawled out on my leg at any time while Mom fiddled with the old camera, didn't dawn on me then. But I've never liked any spiders since.

Of course, my brother-in-law, Steve, just had to get one for a pet. "Gerry" was always getting loose and hiding behind a chair or couch; it would be weeks sometimes before she was caught and returned to her aquarium.

Then, oh joy, Steve was taking a vacation and wanted me to feed that ugly fuzz ball crickets while he was gone for two weeks. I did it, but I wonder if she came over on a banana boat and was sold to a pet shop. What do people do about all those wild tarantulas arriving here? Men running around wielding rolled up newspapers, smacking them right and left comes to mind.

Spiders and Snakes with Other Critters

Brown County, Indiana has copperheads and some rattlers, and a goodly collection of spiders. Kentucky, being a little farther south, has even more of the above. Dad was always showing me critters of all kinds both when we lived in Hartford and in Beaver Dam.

I collected locust shells many afternoons when we took a walk. Once he lifted me up on his shoulders to pick a locust shell off a tree trunk, and it still had the bug inside. I touched it, and it flew right by my ear. Dad then taught me to check for a split along the back. If it had one, then the shell was empty and ready for my collection.

We gathered butterflies that were already dead, and he used a magnifying glass to show me the scales on their wings. We studied ants

3

and again used the glass. (I accidentally roasted one on a hot day when I was studying it.)

He showed me the fat black and yellow garden spiders and their webs, the brown "tobacco juice" from grasshoppers, the bubbly "spit" from aphids, and praying mantises stalking their supper. I learned to play with daddy-long-legs and listen to the buzzing of the green bottle flies.

He took me to Green River to look for crawdads and minnows. He dug up fishing worms for me to play with, and caught June bugs on the door screen at night. They had scratchy feet.

Stag-horn and snap beetles entertained me. I listened to cicadas and katydids songs and the chirp of crickets. Frogs, toads, and turtles were temporary playmates.

He caught two black widow spiders and locked them tightly in a small jelly jar for me to examine. He warned me not to open the jar for any reason, and to make sure the lid stayed tight. He said the spiders might be able to unscrew the top so I needed to constantly check it. That probably wasn't true, but to this day I believe they might.

Then Dad found two garter snakes in the flower garden around the foundation of our rental house. (Now would probably be the time to mention that Mom was still driving during that time period and wasn't home when Dad found the snakes. Also Mom was absolutely petrified of any snake!) On that fateful afternoon, I was playing with my jar of black widows when Dad called me over and wrapped the snakes around my wrists. I had quite a time pretending I was Cleopatra with my snake jewelry. I had put one around my upper arm and let it unwrap itself and crawl up around my neck or down to my hand. The other I placed in my hair like a crown. I played with them long enough that they were tired and not moving very fast.

Then my mother pulled into the driveway. The car windows were down. I ran over to show her my snakes and spiders. She quietly examined the spiders but refused to hold the jar. She was used to my little Daddy souvenirs by this time and tried to pretend an interest although most gave her "the willies." She knew my father was teaching me about nature.

Then Mother noticed my two bracelets. One snake was quietly wrapped around my wrist, but the other slowly started to unwind and slither up my arm. Mom's eyes widened as large as golf balls and she yelled, "Bradley!"

Dad came running. My petrified Mother sat in the car watching what she probably imagined to be a fifty-foot anaconda with poisonous fangs slowly crawl up my arm and wrap around my neck. I began to take the other snake off my wrist, not knowing Mom's fear, and hand it to her.

4

She was able to say, "No thanks, Dear," before positively screaming "Bradley!!!" again.

Dad arrived immediately after the second scream and unwound the two tired little 10" or 12" snakes from around my neck and wrist. He quickly released them in the neighbor's bushes. He then had to help my weak-kneed, half-hysterical mother into the house. I didn't know what all the excitement was about, so I just took my spiders into the back yard, and looked for Sago Dingo, my dog.

I have no idea what went on in the house; all was quiet. However, Dad fixed dinner that evening for just the two of us--fried potatoes, lima beans, and pork chops. My mother wasn't hungry; she stayed in the living room, watched television, and furiously embroidered a dresser scarf with cute kittens on it.

Don't Fence Me In

There wasn't much grass in Papa King's immediate backyard-- it was mostly gravel. There were fenced-in areas to the left of the meat house which held a garden and a chicken pen. That left the front yard for me to play where my mother could watch me from the windows or porch. Of course there was the street out front and a shallow drainage ditch between it and the sidewalk.

Mom was afraid I'd run into that road, so Papa and my dad surrounded the left side of the yard with a wire fence. The metal poles holding it were not down too deep in the ground as it was only a temporary playpen for me until I got older.

At two years old, I was tall enough to look over the top of it, and old enough to work out a plan to get out. I began leaning on the fence. I would back up to it, lean, and bounce. That part was fun; it was my own personal ride. I'd push on it, and it would push back. In a few days, the posts and fence were leaning, and my ride was more fun as I could bounce even higher.

When the playpen was leaning over enough, I crawled over it and started down the sidewalk. The Bennetts, our next door neighbors and relatives, saw me and got my mother. She and Papa straightened the fence, and put me back inside. However the ground was loose now around the posts, and only a little leaning and bouncing each playtime gave me an escape route. I was out every other day. They realized that

5

they weren't going to be able to keep me fenced in. I figured I had won. Or so I thought.

Papa went out to the barn and returned with a small diameter rope and a concrete block-- the type with three large square holes in it. He put the block in the middle of the fenced area and tied one end of the rope through a hole. He tied the other end around my waist over my clothes. Then he straightened the battered fence and poles as best he could— again. That worked for a while.

Then I discovered that if I pulled on the rope like a horse pulling a wagon, I could drag that block with me. Then there was the problem of the fence. How could I get that block out with me? I couldn't lift it.

However, first things first. I dragged that chunk of concrete over to the fence, backed up and began leaning and bouncing as usual. It went down easily enough, and I started climbing over. That block got stuck, of course. I was on one side of my playpen and the block was on the other. I couldn't climb back in because of the angle of the fencing, and no matter how hard I pulled, I couldn't move that heavy concrete chunk up the incline. I was stuck! I kept trying, and all I did was put rope burns on my hands and stomach. I started crying.

Papa found me that way and untied the rope. Peggy, my babysitter, was there, and both of them put medicine on my hands and tender bruised tummy. I received a milk and cookie snack. Then both sat with me on the front porch swing and rocked until I fell asleep. They put me to bed. When I awoke, I went to the locked screen door and looked out. Papa King was dismantling that fence.

From then on, I played out back with Papa sitting outside watching me. Now I don't have many memories of my first two years except for Jit-it Bear, a few others, and that fence-- especially being tied to that concrete block. It left an impression on me which I think helped to shape my personality. Never again would I allow my freedom to be curtailed-- no concrete blocks would ever hold me back ever again, thank you!

My Little Yellow Chicken

Everyone who has ever lived has had a few regrets about things they have done. Some of mine were about pets; one in particular involved a little baby chicken. We were living with my grandfather, Papa King, in Hartford, Kentucky. He raised chickens for eggs and meat; my father

6

gave me a newly hatched chick as a pet. I was only two or three at the time.

Peep was yellow, fluffy, and very round; he followed me everywhere. I adored him and was very careful not to hurt his tiny legs or wings when I carried him close to my chest. I watched him attentively as he ate the food I constantly gave him so that he wouldn't choke. I made sure he didn't fall into his water dish or wade in it. I carried toilet paper around to clean up his poop before Mom could spot it and get angry. All went well for a few days. Peep was growing fatter by the hour.

Then I made a fatal mistake. I had a doll crib with a slide down gate and long wooden slats which ran head to toe rather than left to right. I decided to put my pet on one side of the crib and sit next to him on the other rather like on a couch. I found a piece of cardboard to cover the slats so Peep wouldn't fall through the spaces between them. It was only long enough to cover about two thirds of the length.

I gently put my pet in the crib close to one end and I carefully started to sit down on the other end. I put my hand on the cardboard to hold it, but it slipped up and Peep fell underneath just as I sat. I jumped up quickly before all my weight hit the crib's bottom, but it was too late. I gently lifted Peep out from under the cardboard. He looked fine, but he didn't move. I tried to stand him up but he fell over. I held him and pushed his legs, but he didn't respond. I must have broken his neck. I became hysterical and began screaming, "Mamma, Mamma!"

My mother came running from the kitchen. I asked her what was wrong; why wouldn't Peep move? She said he was dead. She wanted to throw him outside, but I wouldn't let her. I sat on the floor holding him and rocking him and crying the rest of the afternoon.

Papa put Peep in a little box and tucked him into bed with me that night. I carried him around in the box with the lid off all the next day. That was Friday, and my dad was due to come home before sunset. (He traveled all week for the health department.) I was sitting on the front steps when he arrived. I showed him Peep and started crying again.

I said, "I'm sorry, Daddy; I'm sorry. I killed Peep. I didn't mean to. Will you forgive me?"

Dad sat down next to me and held me. He took his bag inside and I followed. Mom had dinner ready, but he just looked at her. Then he looked at Papa. Papa King said he'd get the shovel, and the three of us plus Peep went out behind the meat house. Daddy dug the hole, and I put Peep inside. Papa said a few words, then I scooped some loose dirt inside, and my father shoveled in the rest. Afterwards, Papa and Dad took me out to the front porch swing; I squeezed in between them.

Mom stayed inside the house and ate alone. She was angry because we hadn't eaten first, and the food was cold. A little later when we came in to eat, Mom glared at Dad, then at me.

"You and that damned chicken!" she said to me.

"Mildred!" Papa said rather sternly.

She stormed out and sat in the swing. Papa, Dad, and I ate a cold supper in more ways than one. I think Mom was simply hurt. She had waited all week, just as I had, to see Dad, and she had had to wait an extra hour before she could get his attention because of me.

After we ate, my father went outside, and I helped Papa clean up the kitchen. I think my parents had a slight argument over my having a chick as a pet. Papa tried to keep me occupied, but little ears can hear very well when they are straining to.

Mother said something like, "You should have known she'd kill it. Why didn't you give her a dog? Why the big funeral? I had to eat a cold dinner alone."

I felt very guilty when I went to bed that night. Even today I occasionally relive the trauma of Peep's limp body held in my hands. I was too young to have such a tiny pet, but regrets die hard. Peep is a reminder of how fragile life can be and how precious. So if you see my car stopped on the side of some winding country road, and me carrying a turtle out of the middle of that road, you'll know why.

Mom's Naugahyde Couch

When my parents moved back the second time into Papa King's, we lived in the two rooms he allotted for himself because the other side of the house was rented. The cold room was both our bedroom and living room while the other was Papa's bedroom, living room, and kitchen.

It was called "the cold room" because it was only heated by a fireplace when necessary. Both rooms were very large. Papa had a big rocking chair next to his fireplace. The only other seats in his part were 4 black-varnished, spindled kitchen chairs with replacement bottoms. They were not comfortable enough to relax in.

There were no chairs in the cold room at all. The only furnishings were the radio and my crib, Papa's two iron beds, lamp, trunk, and one large square table. Later Papa moved an upright piano in there with a hard bench. We needed a place to sit.

I'm not sure of the circumstances, but somehow we acquired a used Naugahyde couch. It may have been given to my parents, or Dad may have paid a nominal price at a used furniture store. It was an ugly thing- -big, boxy with squared arms and back, and covered with mottled grey Naugahyde which was supposed to faintly resemble grey leather.

Naugahyde was one of the first plastics used on furniture. And just like today's plastic, it was hot, and skin stuck to it. It was also very hard— there was no softness in the cushions. Whatever it was stiffed with was more like shredded corn cobs with a thin layer of cotton than anything else. But it was a place to sit none-the-less.

Mom was proud of it, as it was the only piece of furniture other than my crib and the old radio that we owned at the time. At least here was a place to sit if we had company, and the weather was not suitable to be on the porch.

Mom gave me strict orders about that couch. I could not have any items on it that might puncture the Naugahyde. That included buckles on my Mary Jane shoes. I usually didn't sit on it at all because little girls wore dresses, or in the hot summer just underwear; bare skin didn't work well with plastic. I know I left the top layers of skin from the back of my thighs on that bench-like seat. I had to peel myself off that thing like one peels off tape or Band-Aids.

The old hardwood floor had a worn wool rug covering most of it. That too was uncomfortable—scratchy, itchy, and dirty. I usually played on Papa's bed or linoleum floor.

I was only in the cold room to sleep or do something quietly such as play dress-up in any old clothes or shoes of Mom's. I had a purse and an old pair of high heels, and leftover scraps from some drab-green, loose-weave curtains to wear as clothes. I was very inventive.

I also wanted to use Mom's make-up which she kept on the table in a closed box; however, that was taboo as she couldn't afford to buy much. If I played with it, I would use it up and be in big trouble. Once in a while she would powder my nose with her Merle Norman face powder and apply lipstick. I thought that was grand.

She also had a bottle of red fingernail polish which totally fascinated me. I often watched her paint her fingernails, and she would paint mine sometimes when she did hers. I had a Honey Walker doll by that time and a Betsy Wetsy. Mom painted my two dollies' fingers and toenails for me. I received a promotional doll out of a Fab detergent box and my mother polished her fingernails also.

I wanted so badly to paint my own myself, but Mom wouldn't let me. She said I would spill the polish and ruin something. I, of course, said I'd be really careful, but I didn't get anywhere. If she would have let me try it with her supervision, even outside in just underpants, I would have been content. But her usual daily order of, "I said NO," to most any ideas of mine, by this time only angered and hurt me. I plotted. I was going to prove to her I could do it without making a mess.

One afternoon when Dad was still gone during the week and Mother wasn't home, Peggy had left early, and Papa was taking a short nap in his rocker, I had my chance. I got the polish from her box and sat it on the flat square arm of the couch. I got a Kleenex from Mom's table to use to wipe around the edges of my cuticle as I had seen her do. I opened the polish, laid my hand flat on the couch arm and began painting my left hand.

I did a fairly decent job of keeping it on the nails and not the skin. I carefully wiped off any mistakes. All went well until I began painting my right hand with my left. I hadn't moved the polish over, so the angle was bad. I decided to climb up on the couch and rest my left hand on the arm to steady it while painting my right.

The couch was high enough that I had to crawl up on my hands and knees, then turn around and sit down. I put the cap on the bottle and held it in my hand while I climbed up. However I had not screwed the top on. It had a high pointed top, and I bumped it as I climbed up. The top popped up but didn't come out as the attached brush held it in. The polish had sloshed all over the brush and wand.

I grabbed at the top thinking it would come out. Since my arms were on the couch seat and one knee was also on the seat (I used my knee to push myself up) I actually caused the lid to come off. It fell on the cushion and left a glob of red polish.

I slid back off the couch, picked up the brush, and screwed it back on the bottle. I wasn't worried at this point. If I had let it dry, I could have picked it off and all would have been well. I thought, however, that I could wipe it off as I did my cuticles. I used the Kleenex, but I only smeared it. Now I was a bit worried.

I put the polish back, got more Kleenex and the polish remover. I got the polish off with no problem; however that remover took the mottled gray finish off the Naugahyde. Only the plain gray under color remained wherever the polish remover touched. I put the remover back and threw away the Kleenex. I didn't know what to do.

Just then Mom came up the front steps. I jumped up on the couch and sat on the damaged spot, hoping she wouldn't suspect. However, the minute she came in, she must have seen the scared look on my face. She came directly over to me and demanded to know what was wrong. I tried to tell her nothing, but I'm a terrible liar. She saw my one painted hand and the other only partially painted. She became very angry because she knew I had been into the polish.

She grabbed my right arm and yanked me off the couch to spank me; she saw the damage to the couch. Mom whirled, grabbed me, and demanded to know what had happened. I told her that I had tried to clean up my mess. The damage was about ½ inch wide and perhaps 2 inches long where I had wiped the remover on.

Now my Mother has always had a hot temper and this day was no exception. She slapped my face several times, then really spanked me hard. I was hysterical; Papa came rushing in to see what was going on and had to physically grab her hands to stop her as she was out of control. Bruises began to appear on my face and legs.

She sat on the couch and started crying. I know now the reason was that the couch was the only furniture other than the baby bed, and radio that Mom and Dad owned. And now it was ruined in her eyes. I think she felt defeated by life at that moment. I was totally confused. I couldn't understand why she took it so hard. I tried my best to cheer her up, but it wouldn't work. She pushed me away for the rest of the week.

Friday night Dad came home from his job with the health department, and she promptly showed him the damage. She hoped he would punish me too. He didn't. He said he could do touch-up painting on it to hide the light grey streaks—after all he was an artist and painted beautifully. He patched it up so it really didn't show. But Mother never accepted it. It was ruined in her eyes.

We used it when we rented Papa's apartment next door, as it was a hide-a-bed. But then we were able to rent a house in Beaver Dam in 1954 because both of my parents got teaching jobs there—a whole $3000 between them. They could only afford that place for one year, but she got rid of the couch.

Deever

When Mom and Dad lived in Beaver Dam, Kentucky, they needed a babysitter while they taught school. They found one—Mrs. Deever. She was an older woman and rather fat. It was hate at first sight on my behalf.

My father wasn't too fond of her either. I remember his telling me that each morning when he kissed me goodbye, I would tell him to, "Kiss Deever too, Daddy." Then Dad would give her a peck on the cheek just to satisfy me. When he reminded me of that in later years, he always said, "Ugh!" and closed his eyes while scrunching up his face.

I think part of the reason I disliked her was because she wasn't Peggy or Papa King. No one had ever taken care of me except those two, and I resented that woman to the max. Also she was authoritarian rather than loving in her methods, and that did not go over well with me at all.

I remember one big argument between us. It was a warm fall day in early September, and I wanted to go outside to play. She insisted that I wear thin cotton gloves, a coat, and a head scarf. I wore them outside, but became very hot. It was in the mid 70's, and no one had ever made me wear gloves and a coat, let alone a scarf tied in a big knot under my chin on warm days.

I went inside and took all three off. She allowed me to leave the coat and gloves off, but she ordered me to put the scarf back on. I refused, saying it was hot. It kept sliding off backwards with the big knot choking me, or forward, catching on my ears and acting as a blindfold.

She said young ladies always kept their heads covered when outside in the hottest weather to prevent headaches, or sickness in the cold weather, or earaches in windy weather. She also pulled that scarf out over my forehead much like the bill on a baseball cap. She said it protected the eyes from wind, cold, or sun so weather wouldn't cause blindness, sunburn, windburn, or a chapped forehead. I was too young to realize that she was very old fashioned in her beliefs.

I know now that she was trying to protect me according to how either she was reared or how she reared her children. However I was four and saw no reason at all in what she said. And, I was very stubborn by this time.

I defied her; as fast as she put that scarf on me, I yanked it off. Finally she took a pair of my underpants and stuck them on my head. She then pushed me outside and locked the back door. I was humiliated but not crushed. I took the underpants off and left them in the yard; she saw me and came out. She forced those things back on and partly rammed my head through one leg opening. Then she dragged me inside and shoved me into my room.

Deever must have tied a heavy string to the doorknob and then to something else because I couldn't get the door open. I was so angry, frustrated, and humiliated that I took my little hard rubber ballpien hammer and kept pounding on the door. I was determined to hammer a hole to get out. The door was solid wood rather than the hollow core ones of today, but I splintered it in several places. I kept it up until I was exhausted and fell asleep leaning against the splinters.

When my parents returned around 4:00, I was sleeping on the floor and the door was open; I heard them and woke up. Deever was gone. I told them what had happened. Dad called the woman on the phone and fired her. There after the lady next door who had a daughter—my playmate, a year older than me, became my babysitter. She was great!

The following spring when we were packing to move back to Papa King's, Mom discovered what I had done to the door. She showed Dad, but he said he couldn't repair it. We just didn't mention it when we moved out; Dad screwed a cork board onto it to hide the damage. After all, most children back then had some sort of bulletin board in their rooms to display their artwork. That wouldn't work now because the refrigerator has become the bulletin board of yesterday.

I didn't get punished for the damage, but I did have to explain why I did it. I guess I forgot to mention the hammer part to Mom and Dad the day old Deever got fired. All my father said was, "Well, Millie, she has your temper," and Mom just rolled her eyes.

Water and More Water

My mother's philosophy on raising children involved a tight routine. She felt such structure made a child secure. Mom had been raised as a spoiled, only daughter, because her sister was grown and out of the house. She had never been around children. Her ideas were based on her military training as a Tech Sergeant during WWII.

On school days, I was up at 6:00 to dress; I had one egg, one piece of toast, a small glass of orange juice, and an 8 oz. glass of milk at 7:10;I brushed my teeth at 7:25 and walked outside to wait for the bus at 7:30. I returned from school at 4:00, had ice cream with chocolate syrup and cheese crackers while watching the TV until 4:30. This was my time to relax.

Mom and Dad arrived at 4:15, and Mom lay down until 5:00. I did homework from 4:30 to 6:00 while she fixed supper; we ate at 6:00. At 6:30, I helped clean up and dry the dishes. I then was back on the homework at 7:00. I took my bath at 8:00 and was in bed by 8:30. I followed this routine through six grade.

Bedtime was changed to 9:00 then 9:30 as I began junior high. Then to 10:30 or 11:00 my sophomore year, depending on how much homework I had. Weekends and summers were slightly different, but it was still a tight routine.

When it came to the meals, I could have as much as I wanted as long as I had a little of everything. I had to eat all that was on my plate and finish all of my drink before I could be excused from the table—no exceptions. To this day it's still hard for me to leave any food on my dish, even if I'm so full, I am about to pop. Such was my training.

I remember one time when we were traveling, that that "no exception" rule caused me some problems. We had gone to a good restaurant for a hot meal after having eaten deli sandwiches out of our cooler or hamburgers for days. The food was delicious, and our waitress was very conscientious. Since the meal was more expensive than the hamburger drive-ins, Mom strongly cautioned me to eat everything and finish my drink.

Given Mother's order, I dutifully downed all the water as well as my milk. However the waitress kept refilling my water glass. As soon as I drank it, she filled it again. After 3 glasses of water and a forth refill, I said, "Momma, do I have to drink all my water?"

I think it finally dawned on her what was happening—she had been talking to Dad about our trip and hadn't noticed all the refills. When she discovered that I had already finished 3 glasses, she started laughing. "No," she said, "water doesn't count; that's extra if you want it."

I was very grateful, because my eyeballs were floating by that time. Dad had to stop twice by the side of the road on our way back to the motel so I could frantically potty. Back in our room, I dashed three more times.

Mom made sure the next day that I knew I didn't have to drink all my water when we ate out. I think she suddenly realized just how literal-minded a child can be. From then on, I only had to eat or drink what I had asked for or whatever Mom or Dad put on my plate. No more extras!

Toot, Toot, Tootsie

Like all little girls, I dreamed of being a ballerina. When I was seven, Mother enrolled me in a dancing school. Because of my age, the instructor started me out tap dancing to strengthen my legs and ankles. I was hooked, forget the tights and tutus. I could make rhythms and clacks with my feet. That was much more fun!

I had class each week, and Mom helped me with the steps and rhythm at home. She made me practice on the kitchen linoleum because my heavy steel "taps" would easily tear up her hardwood floor's finish.

When spring came, we girls were going to be in a recital at Memorial Hall. The month before, I met my partner. I didn't know it, but she had learned the same routine, and now we had to synchronize our steps as we were to be billed as "Two Girls in Blue," dancing to "Toot Toot Tootsie." We even practiced on the auditorium stage. The sound of our clicking heels and toes was very loud because of the acoustics; it was wonderful noise to my ears.

Linda's mother and my mom made our outfits. Each was a one-piece light blue satin with a short pleated skirt. The underside of the skirt and the shoulder straps were pink. We had pink hair ribbons and pink ribbon laces. Everything had silver sequins sewn on. Even our shoes were spray painted silver.

The week before the recital, my school had a spring talent show, and my mother had signed me up to perform. Since elementary, junior high, and high school were all in one large building, performers were all ages.

Mother hadn't spray painted my black dancing shoes yet, so she bought wide red ribbons for laces and to tie my long hair in a ponytail. I had tight black dancing shorts, and a long sleeve white blouse complete with a red tie with two black horizontal stripes. I even had a pair of skin-colored tights with tiny sparkles woven in. I liked that outfit more than the pink and blue one. (Pastels weren't my style; I liked bright, bold colors. I guess they fit my personality better.)

The two weeks before the talent show and recital, it seemed that all I did was practice, not only at home but also at Linda's house and in the studio or the auditorium. I could have done my routine solo or duo in my sleep.

However, my mother was a nervous wreck. She was sure I'd freeze up in front of the large audience, or that I'd forget and break rhythm and sound terrible with the music. She didn't know that I'd picked up some extra steps from my dancing instructor.

I have forgotten my teacher's name, but she told me I needed to do extra since I wouldn't have a partner. She taught me a different opening and finish, then she added two new combinations where I'd turn a circle and stay in rhythm and another which was a cross between jumping and almost doing the splits. I can't describe that last one, and I certainly couldn't demonstrate it after all these years; I'd fall on my bottom.

Mom only found out about the extra parts two days before the talent show, and I thought she was going to collapse. She told me not to try the new steps as I'd probably forget.

The night of the show, she again told me not to try the new stuff. I looked up at her just before the music started, and said, "Don't worry, Mommy, if I forget, I'll just make it up. No one will know."

With that, the opening notes of "Toot Toot Tootsie" started, and I tap-danced my way onto that large stage. The lights were very bright, but when I could look, I saw the place was completely filled with people. That didn't scare me at all—I thought it was wonderful to have so many folks watch my performance.

I did my new steps perfectly and even added a couple of double-time parts that I had only seen done by one or two older tap-dancers when we practiced at Memorial Hall. I was disappointed when my routine came to an end, but I was also very pleased with myself. The huge applause thrilled me when I came back on stage to take my bow.

After the show, many people complimented Mom and Dad about my act: I received lots of praise also but I enjoyed seeing Mother beam with pride. She had been so sure I couldn't do it, that it felt great to prove to her that I could.

I stuck with Dad during the refreshments afterwards—I knew he'd let me have anything I wanted, and if I didn't like what I chose, I could throw it away. Mom would have only allowed me one or two items and made me eat it no matter how nasty it tasted. Luckily, she wasn't checking as she was talking to others; she was laughing and happy.

I stuffed myself on goodies and smiled proudly and said, "Thank you," when people flocked to Dad to praise him. He always told them to direct the compliments to me, as I was the one who did the dance, not him. I was on top of the world that night.

The next weekend Linda and I performed together in Memorial Hall. Afterwards, a photographer from the newspaper had us strike a pose by the marble columns in the lobby. He put it in the paper. He sent each of our families an 8 x 10 black and white picture. I still have it, as well as my old pink and blue costume. The only part I have of my red and black outfit is the tie.

TOOT, TOOT, TOOTSIE!
(GOOD-BYE)

by
GUS KAHN
ERNIE ERDMAN
and DAN RUSSO

Yes-ter-day I heard a lov-er sigh, "Good - bye_____ oh me, oh
When some-bod-y says good-bye to me,_____ I'm sad_____ as I can

my"._____ Sev - en times he got a-board his train_____ And
be,_____ Not so with this lov-ing Ro - me - o,_____ He

sev - en times he hur-ried back to kiss his love a - gain, and tell her:
seemed to take a lot of pleas-ure say-ing bye-bye to his treas-ure;

17

Linda and I had a lot of fun at our recital and couldn't wait to learn a new dance for our winter show. I wanted to do two—a duet and a solo. Unfortunately, that fall I didn't get to go to the studio. I turned eight in October and was in bed with rheumatic fever for the next year.

After that, the doctor wouldn't allow me to dance or even climb stairs, for that matter. Mom stored my costume and even my shoes in her large steamer trunk saved from WWII. I kept my woven red tie with its two black stripes—and remembered.

Lestoil Dolls

In the 1950's, an all-purpose cleaning product was popular on the market—liquid Lestoil. In 1958, the company began a big advertising campaign to push the cleaner. They especially got the little girls involved by offering Lestoil Dolls of all Lands. These were hard plastic 7 1/2-inch dolls with moveable arms, heads, and eyes. There were thirty-two dolls, each dressed in "authentic" outfits from different countries.

All a little girl had to do to get one was to send a Lestoil label and a dollar to Lestoil, Holyoke, Massachusetts, and in about two weeks, she would get one of the dolls advertised on television. She could even specify which country she wanted.

When the doll arrived, there would be a black and white pamphlet and order blank so that more could be purchased. Since television was black and white in those days, the costumes had to be outstanding to even show up on the screen, and those dolls were certainly that.

The idea was, of course, that the mothers had to buy the cleaning product so the daughter could have the label. It was a great way to gain new customers. Thousands of these beautiful little dolls were sent out over the next year, and the Adell Chemical Company prospered.

I was seven at the time, and I fell head over heels for those beauties. I wanted all of them. My mother, however, used Spic and Span, a powdered cleaner, or liquid Lysol, and had no intention of switching. She might have tried it, if I hadn't asked her, but she knew I wanted those dolls badly.

She decided this would be another good way to teach me hard work, saving, and goals. She refused to buy Lestoil, but said I should go door to door in the neighborhood asking folks if they used Lestoil, and if they did, would they save me the label.

There were only four other girls in our subdivision and one was a much older teenager. None of the other three my age seemed to want the dolls, so their mothers saved me their labels. Out of approximately 25 houses, ten housewives collected for me.

Then there was the problem of the money. I was no longer getting a quarter a week allowance, so I had to find a way. We had had a bumper crop of strawberries that spring, so Dad allowed me to pick the ones left in the garden to sell. I filled the quart containers, put them in my wagon, and traveled door to door. I priced them for less than the local grocery, so I sold all I had in one day. I didn't know that I should have charged more than a quarter a quart.

19

I helped my Father wash the car for $2.00. I did other odd jobs for the neighbors such as sweep their driveways, bring in their clothes off clotheslines and fold them or clean up the neighbor's dog poop. They paid me 10 to 25 cents.

Every time I got a label and a dollar, I sent for a doll. The promotion lasted quite a while, and I managed to collect 8 of them.

By 1959, they had added some new choices. Miss Russia, Miss China, Miss Lestoil, and Miss India were new as well as some male dolls, such as an army, marines, air force and a Dutch boy in blue velvet bloomers – approximately a total of 42 dolls.

I spent a year in bed with rheumatic fever during this time, and could do little even when allowed up, so working for those dolls was difficult. I only was able to get two new ones and a duplicate. I have protected those dolls for over 50 years, and kept a sharp eye open at antique stores, flea markets, garage sales, and on eBay.

So far I've picked up about 24 more—some duplicates but wearing different materials in their costumes. These were the only dolls I ever collected and am still looking to fulfill my long-held dream of owning all of them. I have written a book called *Little Lestoil Ladies* but, I would still buy another Lestoil doll if I can find one. Got one for sale?

Mom's New Shoes

My Mother always said that the feet are the foundation of the body, and if the feet hurt, the whole body hurts. She should know - she had foot problems her whole life. Mom had an extremely narrow foot—a 4A with a 6A heel. Also, as an adult, she took a 9 ½ length—which was very hard to find.

From the time she was little, the hunt for even one pair of shoes took all day and often nothing could be found. Papa and Mama King took Mom to Owensboro twice a year to shop for shoes. They would go from store to store trying on any pair even remotely close to her size. Papa would ask the owners for their catalogs, but nothing could be found that way.

Papa even tried to have a cast of her foot made so shoes could be custom formed. That proved to be impractical as a new one would have to be made for each shoe style and size as her foot grew larger. Before one cast and shoe could be designed, her foot would grow longer.

All of Papa's money couldn't buy my mother a single shoe that fit. She would get one pair each half of the year and had to stuff cotton inside to keep them on. Shoe choices had to be ones that buckled or had laces which could be tightened as much as possible even after getting the narrowest in any store.

When Papa bought that red roadster, Mama King and Mother had been shoe shopping. Mom sat in the rumble seat on the way home holding her precious one pair of shoes.

When Mom started working at a bank in Cincinnati before she joined the Army, no shoes for her could be found in that city. Even the Army couldn't help her.

Because of the poor fitting shoes she developed several foot problems which affected her knees and back. Her 2nd and 3rd toe on her left foot became hammer toes from scrunching them to hold her shoes on. And she developed a nasty callous on the ball of each foot that eventually went almost to the bone. Her feet always hurt, so the rest of her body did too.

In 1955, my parents moved to Union City, Indiana, to teach in the Jacksonburg High School close by. The ladies would talk in the teachers' lounge, and the subject of shoes came up. Apparently one lady there had a hard-to-fit size 5.

She told Mom that Crawford's Shoe Store in Dayton, Ohio specialized in sizes for the hard to fit. This teacher bought her shoes there—they were sample shoes from factories made in sizes 4 and 5 and sent to stores to show-case their products. These weren't meant for retail sales, but Crawford's ordered many to have on hand for small feet. They also had extremely narrow and bigger sizes, as well as half-sizes.

Since my parents were now making $11,000 between them instead of the $3,000 in Beaver Dam, Dad said he would take Mom in hopes of finding a pair to fit. She put the trip off for a while with several excuses— no time, too far, needed the money for other things. In reality she was afraid of being disappointed again. It was easier to dream about going and finding shoes than to accept what she saw as reality—not finding any. Finally Dad talked her into going.

When we arrived at Crawford's, Mom just sat down. She wouldn't even look at the shoes displayed. She glanced at the many shelves holding beautiful pairs in all styles and colors, and shook her head, "Not for me," she sadly said.

Dad and I looked at a corner unit displaying about 4 pair per shelf with 5 shelves. All of those beautiful flats and dressy heels were sized 4 and 5. I was 6 yrs. old, and those tiny women's shoes would have fit me!

One pair had four tiny straps, three-inch stiletto heels, and was in turquoise. I adored them and took them over to my Mom. I said, "See,

Mommy, you can find shoes here. Aren't they pretty?" Mother just looked away, and said nothing.

Soon one salesman was free and came over to help; he was one of the store's owners. Mom could barely speak. Mr. Crawford asked her if she were left or right-handed. She looked puzzled. He told her that the foot opposite her dominate hand was usually the larger. He measured both her feet and found that her left foot was indeed larger. That was the foot that had the hammer toes.

He brought out a pair for her to try on. She was surprised—they fit! Then he brought the same style out in two more colors. Mom was overwhelmed. She tried them on also. These shoes were nothing special—just a flat comfortable shoe to wear to work. But they *fit*, were stylish, didn't have laces or buckled straps, were comfortable, and she had a choice of black, brown, or camel. Mom was like a kid in a candy store for the first time. It took her a while to decide on the brown.

Then Mr. Crawford said something that I will never forget: "Now then, Mrs. Patrick, what other styles would you like?"

My mother half-raised herself out of the chair with her elbows, leaned forward, and with the most shocked expression on her face said, "You mean you have more?"

Mr. Crawford smiled and asked me to help him. He took me into the back room where shoe boxes were stacked to the ceiling on long rows of many shelves. Each type was in a different section, and that section had many sizes and colors.

He put 4 different boxes in my arms and selected 7 more for himself. I proudly carried my four to my mother and saw her eyes widen. But when 7 more styles were placed at her feet, Mom started trembling. Eleven more styles in addition to the one she already had tried.

There were dressy and dressier shoes in several size heels. There were casual ones, and sandals. Some were piped in a different color, some had front bows, some had side bows, and all came in more than one color.

Tears started sliding slowly down my mother's face. Dad and Mr. Crawford looked at each other and both headed back into the storeroom to bring out the other colors. The floor was piled with shoes. Mom tried on all of them.

We were in the store several hours before Mom finally chose 5 different pairs. Those leather shoes were quite expensive for the year 1956, twenty dollars apiece. Dad only had $100 to spend, but he made arrangements for 3 more pair to be sent the following month when he got paid.

That day began a life-long friendship between the Crawford brothers and my mother and father. She was even sent monthly flyers over the next 40 yrs. showing her the new styles in her size.

But *that* day, my mother walked out of a shoe store with five pairs of colorful, stylish shoes that actually fit—no more cotton stuffed inside. She cried all the way to the car, and held them, boxes open, on her lap all the way back to Union City. It was the first time she had had shoes to fit, and the first time she had ever had more than one pair to wear. She was 35.

I guess that's where I got my fascination for shoes. I also had a 9 ½ 3A foot that was hard to fit. Mom and I never had less than 35 or 40 pairs of shoes at any one time. When my mother died, she still had many pairs, some not even worn.

I didn't know who I could give them to. Then one of Mom's best friends, Norma Spar mentioned a lovely lady whom she knew in Nashville, Indiana who wore 9 ½ 4A. I was very glad to give Mrs. Markley, on Artist Drive, all my mother's best shoes.

The Night My Mother Cried

When my parents and I moved to Union City from Papa King's in 1955, we moved into an older farmhouse within walking distance of town. Mr. and Mrs. Snyder, our landlords, lived right behind us; in fact, we shared the same back yard. This retired couple was very friendly and kind.

They made the transition from the culture of the south to the north much easier, and they treated me as if I were their granddaughter. Mr. and Mrs. Snyder became my adopted grandparents as I was so far away from my own. I was constantly at their house, and they at ours. We remained there for 1½ years before buying a house in Greenville, Ohio.

This larger town was only approximately twelve miles from Union City, and we often drove over to visit Charlie and Marie on Sundays after church. We three were very lonely at our new location. For some reason, perhaps because Greenville was larger, the people there were not as friendly. In fact, they were mostly cold and indifferent. This was not expected at all. My father could make a rock smile, but even he seemed perplexed.

We lived at 807 Daly Road, and the subdivision in which we lived had 25 houses at that time. Some of the inhabitants had children at home, and some were empty nesters. Since my parents were older when they had me, they were close in age to most of the neighbors.

None of these folks, whatever their ages, came over to say, "Welcome to the neighborhood." The only individual who was friendly was Mr.

23

Fansler--this was the Fansler Addition, and he was the contractor. However he lived at the entrance to the long row of houses that made up our subdivision, and we were near the other end. If the two men wanted to talk, one had to drive to the other's house. There was no gabbing over the back-yard fence.

I sometimes wonder if it was our Southern accents which put the neighbors off. Maybe we were just too strange or too friendly, but Southerners are friendly people and gracious also. I heard it said many years later that Southern folks are gushy and insincere, and therefore not to be trusted. Whatever the reason, the coldness we felt in that place was almost arctic.

Somewhere along the line, Mother decided to throw a large party, and invite the whole neighborhood over to our house. I guess that since no one had invited her over, she felt that it was up to her to break the ice—that this was the proper custom here.

Mom was determined to make the party a success. She sent invitations to every family on the block and waited for responses. Having received none except from Mr. Fansler who couldn't come as his family would be out of town, she called or walked house to house and asked if each would be attending.

Some said yes and some gave nebulous answers. I would have thought that such a chilly start would have triggered warning bells, but Mother had never met with a failure. She didn't anticipate one now.

My parents were only earning eleven thousand dollars between them as teachers, but my mom was able to stretch the money fairly well. She juggled the budget and had enough to buy paper tablecloths, and all the necessary items for an outside summer party. She bought all the food and prepared salads, arranged cold cuts, made dips, and in general, had quite a large spread.

Dad was given permission to bring four long folding tables and some fifty chairs from school to their house for that weekend. It took him two days and several round trips to the Jackson High School near Union City to get everything home. It was a forty-minute drive one way, and he had no one to help him load or unload all the chairs and tables.

Mother cleaned the house until it squeaked, and Dad cut the grass and trimmed the bushes. They even bought new potted flowers to decorate the grounds and set on the tables. The whole preparation took nearly a week. They both worked very hard to make a good impression and to make everything seem inviting and cheerful.

The party was set for the late afternoon, near four o'clock, I think. We were dressed and ready to receive our lovely guests. I was stationed in the front to welcome the people as they arrived and to usher them into the back yard. I waited and waited. Finally I went to the back and sat down.

Mom had covered the tables with cloth to keep the bugs off, and was sitting in one of our own lawn chairs. I remember the way she was sitting-- with her legs crossed, and one leg swinging. She was slumped down in the chair as if totally relaxed. But, her swinging leg belayed that impression. Dad just stood around or paced, not talking.

I think it was around five that she started calling neighbors up the street, and dad went to the ones close by. If they answered the phones or doors, and most *were* home, they gave indifferent excuses such as, "It was today?" or "Something came up." or "Just didn't feel like coming." Not one single person out of 25 families came to the party!

In dead silence, we took all the food inside and refrigerated it. We gathered all paper items and packed them away. I helped Dad fold and stack the chairs. He loaded the tables into the station wagon to begin returning the school's property the next day.

Mom took off her pretty summer frock and put on one of her usual house dresses. She sat inside staring into space. When Dad and I joined her, she started crying.

Then she got this determined look on her face and said between clinched teeth, "I will live here and take their money. When I retire, I will leave. I will never associate with anyone in this damned place for as long as I live. To hell with them all." Then she put her face in her hands and sobbed. Dad just stood helplessly beside her.

I sat quietly in a corner chair trying to be as invisible as possible. I was afraid that she might lash out at me if I did anything wrong; I didn't understand exactly what was going on. I had never seen my mother sob before, and to this day I can only remember two occasions when she cried that hard—when Papa died and when Daddy died.

Her heart must have broken that evening. When it repaired itself, she was hardened and there was a steely glint in her green eyes. She took an oath that evening and never relented.

Over the years Dad made friends in town who had some association with his teaching or with the church, but Mother remained aloof from all but a select few. They found their close friends in nearby towns.

When they retired, they sold their properties, and moved to Florida. They made good friends with most of the folks at Lake Arrowhead and socialized constantly. Mom lived in lonely isolation in Greenville—she wasted no time correcting that after the move. The rest of her life there was very happy. I guess you could say she was making up for lost time.

The Rat Catcher

My mother was deathly afraid of snakes; big spiders, mice, and rats weren't high on her list either. But she learned when she married my father that she was going to have to become more stoic. The fresh, jumping frog-legs in her frying pan gave her an early clue. Then I came along; between Dad and me, poor Mother was constantly surprised. I have many stories of critters that tested her endurance, but I think this was one of the best.

I was in high school when Dad brought home eleven white rats—pets for me. Someone had taken them to the school where he taught and given them to him. They were fully grown; so from nose to tail, they were very long. They came supplied with a large cage, three water bottles, cedar mulch, food bowls, and a bag of food.

I kept them on a long work bench in our attached, heated garage. They were very tame and cuddly, and liked to be held. I always had three or four hanging on my sweaters or shirts like jewelry when I was home, maybe one riding my head, and several snooping around my bedroom or the TV room.

Mom learned to tolerate eleven loose rats running around, but she didn't want me to sit next to her on the couch when we watched TV. My babies had a habit of scampering over to her lap or across the back of the couch to climb up her shoulder and into her hair. She'd shriek, shiver, and move to the chair.

Dad was usually curled up on the rug in front of us, holding a cat. He'd be wearing a jacket and stocking cap, and be fast asleep, so he didn't mind if a few rats crawled up and lay on him. The cat didn't mind either. Once Mama Kitty used a rat for a head pillow; both were white so I couldn't tell whose fur was whose.

Mom would try to watch *Gun Smoke* or *Perry Mason*, but sometimes she just couldn't. Even sitting across the room from me, a rat would scamper over and try to climb up her stockings or inside her pants. She wouldn't touch them, so I'd have to keep a sharp eye cocked to make sure I knew where all my pets were.

My little darlings were very well behaved, but one was much smarter than the others. They were all albinos and all boys, but I knew each one by his personality or face. Fluff Ball had the longest whiskers and the brightest eyes. His little pink nose was always twitching, and I could see the wheels turning in his head.

In less than a month, he learned how to open the door on top of the cage, and he was constantly escaping and trying to get his buddies to follow. I finally had to wire the door shut. Fluff would try to open the door, encounter the wire, bite it, and then sit below staring at it.

One Saturday morning he figured it out. Saturdays were always wash day, and Mom would pile the dirty laundry on the floor next to the washer and dryer in the garage. The clothes were separated by color, and she discovered some white rats mixed in with the white clothing.

Maybe Mother had begun to lose her fear, or else she was exasperated beyond all caution. She had never touched my pets before. I must have been sick because I was in bed rather than up cleaning.

Mom came in holding two rats by their tails with her left thumb and index finger and two rats by her right two fingers. I remember her exact words. In a teacher - like authoritarian voice, she quietly said, "Deborah, your rats are loose. They are under and in the washer, come get them." Then she put the four on my bed and left.

I hung them on my pajamas and headed for the garage. My mother was sitting at the kitchen table with a cup of coffee, and just looked at me with unreadable eyes as I passed. My pets were really scared. I fished a couple out of the clothes in the washer and put those six back in their cage. Fluff was sitting on the red laundry pile, but scampered up my leg while I was getting the other two free of the machine.

The last four were underneath the washer and were afraid to come out. I used Fluff as bait. I held him by his tail and let him crawl under to them, then I pulled him out—one of his buddies would be holding on to him for dear life, and I would grab my poor scared darling. I did this four times, and got all safely back in their cage. They never tried to escape again; either Fluff was scared of that washer too or the other ten voted him out as their leader.

A couple of months later, they all became ill. I never knew why or how. I forced food and water down their throats with a small eye dropper and added a tiny shaving of a penicillin pill to each once a day.

Since it was late summer and school hadn't started yet, I was able to keep the feedings up 'round the clock for several days. I managed to save two; the rest I tearfully buried in the flower garden as each died. (After Mom dug one up while planting fall flowers, she made me move them to the beds by the fence.)

Fluff Ball and Fuzzy lived until Christmas vacation, when I came home from school to find both dead. Maybe it was just their time; I have no idea how old they were. Maybe they were sick again, and I didn't know it.

I was a sophomore and was studying biology. I decided to take them to school to my teacher. I think I wanted him to do an autopsy to see why they died. There was some white plastic-lined freezer paper in the trash that had been wrapped around pork chops from the butcher. I rinsed off the paper, wrapped up my two dead pets, and stored them in the freezer until vacation was over, and I could take them to school. As teenagers do, I forgot they were in there.

Sometime in late February, Mother pulled out a package marked pork chops from the freezer and set it on the counter to thaw while we were all at school. That night we were going to have pork chops, potatoes, lima beans, and Jell-O for supper. That is until she discovered she had thawed out my two rats! The howl from the kitchen and Mom's, "Mary Deborah!" clued me in. I re-wrapped them, and put them in the refrigerator for the next day when I could take them to school.

We went down the road to a local restaurant for our meal. Mom wouldn't touch anything except a large salad; she gagged at the idea of meat. Dad giggled at both of us while he and I enjoyed pizza. I didn't dare let Mother see me giggle, or I might have been wearing her salad.

From then on, nothing except human food was allowed in the freezer. Even my golf ball and baseball sized hail stones were tossed out, as well as Dad's frozen grasshoppers for fishing bait. No arguments accepted!!!

A Past Remembered Darkly

In September when I was still seven, I spent a weekend at a girl friend's house. When my mother came to pick me up, Mrs. G. told her that I seemed weak, I tired easily, and I wouldn't eat. Mother just laughed and said that I had never been a big eater and that I always played hard, so when I plopped, I plopped. She thought nothing of it.

However when my 3rd grade teacher sent me to the school nurse and both reported the same findings to my father, my parents took me to a doctor. He sent me to a Catholic hospital in Dayton, Ohio for observation and tests. I was there for two weeks.

This was quite a distance from Greenville, Ohio where we lived. Mom and Dad worked at the Jacksonburg high school near Union City, Indiana and couldn't come see me until the following weekend.

It was a lonely, scary time in a strange place with strangers performing tests on me. I was in a private room and saw no one. I had no toys—not even my Jit-it bear to comfort me. There was no TV, radio, or telephone as I was supposed to rest and stay in bed except to use the bathroom.

The only people I saw were black-clothed nuns who were cold, grim-faced, and disapproving. They never had a kind word for me. Instead they constantly told me to be quiet because children were neither to be seen nor heard. That was the week that played a pivotal role in my changing from an outgoing, confident, happy child into a silent, shy, and thoughtful one.

I went in on a Sunday, and it was the following Saturday evening that my parents came to visit. They didn't bring me my bear or doll, and I asked for something to play with. Mother wasn't happy that I asked, but Dad sent her to the hospital gift shop to find me something cuddly.

I guess the toys were too expensive because she bought me a small package of pink plastic silhouetted ballerinas. These six, each in a different poise, were embossed on one side and fitted into little slotted stands.

My parents only stayed two hours at most before Mom said they had to go. They didn't say much to me; I guess they were worried and didn't know what to say. I begged them to take me home, but Mother was very stern; she also didn't believe me when I said the nuns were mean, and called me a liar.

The little dolls were all I had to entertain myself for the next week, but they were more than I had had the week before. I hid them under the covers if I heard footsteps because the nuns would have thrown them away.

The next Saturday, my parents arrived after lunch. They stayed only a few minutes and then left to talk to the doctor. While they were gone, one nun whom I had not seen before came in and told me there was nothing wrong with me.

She said that I was just a sinful child trying to get attention. She continued to lecture me on how bad I was, and that I was a "brat who didn't deserve such good parents." She ordered me to get up and get dressed. I asked where my clothes and parents were. She told me to shut up and do as I was told, and then she left.

When the coast was clear, I ran barefooted in my nightgown up and down the highly polished hallways looking for Mom and Dad. I had no idea where to go or where to look; mostly I was just trying to escape.

I heard talking and then recognized my mother's voice. They were coming out of an office followed by a doctor. He was horrified that I was running around. All three took me straight back to my room.

They told me that I had rheumatic fever and that my heart was damaged. There was evidence that I had had the disease earlier, but the doctor couldn't say if that "earlier" had damaged my heart or whether I'd been born with the damage.

I was confused and said a nun had told me that nothing was wrong, and that was the reason I was looking for my parents. The doctor seemed angry and left for a while; I think he was looking for that nun.

Mother told me that I was going home, but that I had to stay in bed for a least a year, and I couldn't get up even to use the potty. She said it was my choice—I could obey and be up in a year and have a normal, healthy life, or I could be a bad child who wouldn't stay in bed, and be an invalid the rest of my life, and that life would be short. Then she handed me some clothes from a bag she was carrying. The doctor returned to apologize to my parents for the nun's behavior; she had been reprimanded he said. Nothing was said to me, and her words still echoed in my head.

I was silent on the way home, and neither parent spoke to me. Mother told Dad not to talk, hug, or kiss me; she wanted her words to "sink in." She didn't allow the radio on either.

When we reached home, I was sent straight to bed. She put a bed pan on a chair by my bed and told me to go to sleep. That evening when she brought in a tray of food, she asked my decision. At that point, she was as cold, hard, and distant as the nuns. I promised to obey.

She said, "Good," and left to eat with Dad in the kitchen—the entire length of the house away. She forgot to turn on a light so I ate in the darkening gloom which matched my thoughts.

When I finished, I played with my ballerinas by the light of the neighbor's outside lamp before falling asleep. Sometime later, either Mom or Dad must have removed my food tray.

I kept my promise and stayed in bed for a year. No one was allowed to visit for fear of exciting me. Each morning, Mother would set a tray of food on a chair by my bed before she and dad left for work. Dad always hugged and kissed me before leaving, but Mom didn't return.

A long string of older women (the state paid for my medication, bills, and care givers) would exchange my breakfast tray for a lunch one, while the bed pan sitting on the chair next to my food chair filled up until my parents returned; the room stank since my "care giver" didn't change it or remove my lunch; in fact the tray exchange was the only time I would see any of them. They spent their time watching television or talking on the phone. I could hardly eat lunch.

When Dad returned, he would remove the tray, empty the bed pan, and open the window when it was warm outside. Then he would bring me the books he picked from the school's library and read one or two to me or get me my toys which I wasn't allowed to get for myself. Later he would bring my supper, remove it when I had finished, and turn on the light. He'd at bedtime to either read or tell me a story. This was the time I began creating little stories in my head as I didn't have paper or pencil.

I wouldn't see Mother except when she brought in my breakfast tray. Since Dad was the one who cooked breakfasts, often he would bring it instead of her.

Someone donated a small TV which Dad hooked up next to the bed. There wasn't much on except soap operas, but it was better than staring at the ceiling or out the window all day. I read a lot and my father kept me in books of all sorts.

Later, tutors came three mornings each week so I had homework to occupy my mind. My favorite tutor taught me crafts, so then I would have things I could make from paper, cloth, beads, or yarn. That's when I developed a love of making jewelry. She even got my mother to teach me how to embroidery a few stitches. Later, Dad taught me how to paint pictures with watercolors.

I saw very little of my mother that year. Since she was the one who managed the family budget, and was the department head at school, she was always busy when she came home. The only emotional support I had, came from my father. It was a rough year.

During the summer I read any book I could get including the Bible (I read it five times). Many were way beyond my age as time crawled on. I read mysteries, philosophies, the dictionary, encyclopedias, and Dad's textbooks.

The lack of emotional support and the loneliness that year affected my ability to laugh or feel; I did a lot of thinking instead. Intellectually by the end of my "incarceration" I was much older than my eight years. I was writing poetry and short stories, but I never showed them even to my father.

I became introverted, shy, and cynical. I developed a deep inferiority complex from feeling rejected by my mother and seldom smiled or laughed. I lost the ability to socialize with anyone and put up a wall that allowed no one inside except my father and Papa King who wrote me letters twice a month.

Mom never understood my increasing coldness toward her, and I couldn't accept her rejection of me. I loved her so much, but feared to show it. She wasn't much for children as she never wanted a child, and she couldn't cope with sickness. That bed pan was beyond her abilities.

She gave me the occasional order like the tec-sargeant she had been, but couldn't get near me even to hug or kiss me. I did understand her behavior in retrospect, but that was after her death when I had a discussion with my much older cousin who knew Mom well.

I finally came out of my "shell" when I entered college, but that wall never left. It affected my developing close friendships for many years out of fear of rejection; that's mostly gone now.

On a happier end note, that was the year I developed my own love of writing which continues even now. I occasionally still paint in oils and acrylics. I used my embroidery and jewelry making skills to earn extra money in college and to make presents for my daughter and friends. I also made stained glass items and started an antique business. My love of learning stemmed from that time and has stood me in good stead all my life. I've made lots of lemonade over the years from that lemony time. And, I'm healthy!

Mother and Me

My mother had had to endure much in her role of motherhood. She never wanted children because of her age—she had been in the Army, then college, and marriage at 26. In the 1940's ladies married early and had their children early. Since she hadn't yet achieved any success in these roles allotted her, she probably felt too old to start a family. She was opting for a good career as a CPA. Then I came along when she was 28.

Being reared basically as an only child, since her sister was 15 years older and soon out of the house, Mom had no idea how to deal with a new life which had a "clean slate" on which she had to imprint everything necessary for it to grow emotionally, logically, and physically. She received quite an education in her own right!

Once she got past the diapers, colic, and basic baby stage, and I began talking and walking, she may have felt as if she were being dragged behind a greyhound bus or dog. Papa King, Peggy, and my father often contributed to this—compliant little baby doll I wasn't. I was full of ideas and ways to accomplish those ideas; I was stubborn, determined, and individualistic.

When I was four, we moved to Beverdam; Papa, Peggy, and Dad were not there to help her care for me. My father worked eleven months at school and Papa and Peggy were 12-15 miles away. That summer she resorted to the army boot-camp style of discipline.

Daily she broke an extra thick yardstick over me, folded it, and then continued. Then I'd get a half hour in my room in a corner. She spanked me for just a certain look on my face or the fact that I'd stare her directly in the eyes rather than take a submissive role.

When I was sent to my room, I had a musical rocking chair that I sat in. The music was triggered by a long rod that continued through the rocker and protruded out the bottom—pushed in, a jingle played; released, and it stopped. The faster one rocked, the faster the jingle. I would ferociously rock that chair to show my anger, or defiance.

Mom couldn't avoid listening to my musical message of thumbing my nose at her. She became very intolerant out of frustration and jealousy. When we lived at Papa's, Peggy took control of the discipline.

Papa pampered me, and took me everywhere with him. He often blocked mother's methods of control and daily routine. My father adored me, and I could do no wrong in his eyes. Since my mother had always been the spoiled younger child and center of attention everywhere, she found it hard to take a back seat to her daughter—especially, she thought, in Dad's and Papa's heart.

It became a life-long battle between us. I did not know why Mom did what she did until my cousin who was only 10 years younger than my mother, and her confidant, sat me down after Mom died, and explained.

Mom did not like sharing center stage. She constantly vied for my father's attention, but Dad and I were too firmly connected. Still there were times my mother tried hard to accept me and understand.

Thanks to Dad, who grew up on a farm, I was always learning about insects and snakes, animals, and natural phenomena, and doing or collecting a variety of pets. This was not anything she had encountered in her upbringing, as she was a town kid.

I have to give my mom credit for great patience and the ability to cope with a one-of-a-kind, too-smart-for-her-own-good, spoiled daughter. She endured spiders in bottles, and others pinned to cork boards. She dusted around collections of discarded locust shells, and tried not to panic when I wore garter snakes as jewelry. I collected stamps, postcards, coins, Lestoil dolls, shells, fossils, leaves, and anything else that struck my fancy; she had to maneuver around all of these things. Books were everywhere.

I created a tree-house world for the dolls she got for me out of Fab laundry boxes. I had walk ways made of string and cardboard, and houses also. All were connected to my 4 poster bed. Then needing a ladder, I cut holes in a leather belt of Dad's for my dolls to insert hands and feet to climb. She kept running into the string when changing sheets or putting me to bed. (She did finally tear all the tree houses down and spank me for protesting. Then, I got a second spanking because of that damaged leather belt.)

She tried hard to get me to love dogs and train them to do tricks; she did not like cats. I liked the many dogs she got me, but loved on every cat I could find until Dad got me one. She got to clean the fur off my clothing. I ate the Milk Bone dog biscuits, but sneaked the canned salmon, tuna, and milk to the cat. Then she had to go to the store because her planned dinner was missing; she'd try to reward her dog but had no treats.

Mother put up with putrid smelling water or milk in cartons that I was testing. Often this was sitting all around my room. My praying mantis which had complete freedom in the house would fly around her or fall off the curtain onto her head.

I collected newspaper, wire, Styrofoam balls, paint, and dried grass to form papier-mâché´, life-size squirrels for a class project. These items covered the garage floor. I worked on many Girl Scout badges on my own and all the stuff needed for those projects was in piles everywhere; I did the work for 15 badges all at one time. Mom liked everything in its place, but those 15 separate stacks of completed and partly finished work littered the kitchen, family room, and my bedroom.

We had quite a hail storm once. Some of the hailstones were golf ball size and a few were baseball size. I had a variety of these stones in the freezer in her kitchen containers. She had none for storing left-overs or freezing foods.

Dad had eleven white rats which he brought home to me. Mom was afraid of all such rodents. Once she couldn't use the washing machine because all had escaped and were inside, or under the appliance or in the laundry. She grabbed four of them by their tails and brought them to me, simply saying that they were loose. I give her credit for courage on that one.

Later my two biggest rats died, and I wanted to take them to my biology teacher for dissecting. I wrapped them in some discarded white paper used to wrap meat from the butcher and froze them. Mom thought she was thawing out pork chops until she opened the package to start supper. There were the rats, freshly thawed.

I had Tid Bit, the squirrel, and Sweetie, my guinea pig, in the garage. Sweetie always squealed when I was around, demanding my attention. She tried to bite Mom. There were albino and brown hamsters, birds, rabbits, and fish all mixed with the usual dog, and by now, several cats.

A professor from Thailand gave me a Siamese cat that acted like a goat. He could jump six feet straight up to get on dressers. Vichy especially liked to hide under furniture, give a loud squall, dash out, and butt the back of the victim's knees almost knocking him or her down—usually Mom. He didn't like her any more than she liked him.

34

Then there was Flower, my opossum. I was helping dry dishes with her sitting on my head. Mother looked my way just as my pet put her prehensile tail up my nostril. She left the kitchen on that one, and Flower had a new home the next day.

I tried to climb a water tower, taught myself to ride the neighbor's bicycle so my parents would have to get me one of my own, covered my car with plastic bathtub flowers, changed my politics and religion, told my piano teacher I was quitting because I didn't like her choice of music.

I listened to the Rolling Stones, "I Can't Get No Satisfaction," rather than songs like, "My Boyfriend's Back" or "We're Going to the Chapel and We're Going to Get Married." She couldn't understand, "Lucie in the Sky with Diamonds" or psychedelic art. When Mic Jagger wore wide bell-bottoms with a long matching over-tunic and conservatives were screaming. "He's wearing a dress," Mom bought me one such outfit and made me another. I was in college then, and she was trying harder to connect with me. We did for a while before her old jealousies returned.

I tried to please her, but never seemed to be able to do so. I was my own person; she wanted me to be like what she imagined herself to be, but wasn't. Perhaps she decided it was a safer way for me to live. Sometimes I believe that she wanted me to change myself so radically that Dad would love me less.

She even tried buying me clothes including flat, sensible lace-up shoes with rubber soles which were much too old for my twenty-some years. She would argue with me if I wouldn't wear them. During those times, I imagined that her getting me such outfits was a way of keeping potential boyfriends away and keeping me for herself out of love. But, I really didn't ever know why.

As for my Father's love, she never figured out that we both were equal in his heart. She confused me; I didn't understand her or her motives, and she could change very quickly.

But in all fairness, she didn't understand me either. If she could have looked in a mirror with unclouded judgment, Mom would have recognized that so much of me was just a carbon copy of herself. I loved her so much. She died in 1997, and I miss her terribly still today. In retrospect, I was and still am the more conservative of the two of us. I suspect she knows all this now, and we will talk about it when I cross through the veil; maybe we can reconcile then.

Puff-Puff

Mom was a heavy smoker. She started when she was in the Army and refused to quit. Dad had also smoked, but he stopped back in the early '50's. From then on, it was a battle between them. It's said that a person who quits smoking can no longer stand being around the smell. There must be something to that because my father tried for the rest of his life to get Mom to stop too.

However, my mother was very stubborn; the more you'd try to get her to do something, the more she'd do the opposite. In a way, I guess, I could see her point; Dad was relentless. Although some of the things he did to her were really funny.

Dad brought home a huge industrial fan he'd scavenged somewhere. He had got it to dry the garage floor whenever he washed out the dirt and oil. The garages on the houses in our subdivision were heated and plastered so that their owners could easily convert them into family rooms.

Most of the neighbors had done so, and my parents were considering it before they added on to the back of the house. Dad hadn't wanted oil to soak into the concrete floor in case they did remodel the garage. The fan would prevent moisture from getting to the plastered walls. It had a lot of wind speed and worked *really, really* well.

One summer afternoon, my mother had washed her hair and was in the bedroom rolling it on curlers. The door was closed. As usual, she was smoking and drinking a Coke. Dad and I were in the garage putting the fan away after drying the floor when he got one of those gleams in his eyes. I knew he was cooking up something. He had me hold open the kitchen door while he picked up the huge, heavy fan, and carried it into the hall outside the bedroom door. He plugged it in, opened the door, and turned it on.

A hurricane wind exploded behind Mom. Her hair flew straight up and moved like snakes around her head; the curlers in her hair and on the dressing table shot around the room like shrapnel. Her cigarettes went flying as did the ash tray and ashes. Her Coke glass and the water glass (She used the water to re-wet her drying locks before rolling.) slide up against the wall but luckily didn't turn over. She came out of her chair shrieking, "Bradley Patrick!" as she fought her way toward the fan.

Curtains tried to leap out the window; the bedspread started flapping and attempting to leave the bed. Even the rug started sliding around on the floor. Pictures swayed on the walls, and her chair exited to the left.

36

Everything in the room suddenly was alive and moving, and trying to prevent her from getting to the doorway and that fan. She managed, however, and turned the off switch.

She glared at Dad, but he was laughing so hard with tears running down his cheeks that she started laughing also. They both cleaned up the ashes, picked up the curlers, and straightened the pictures. Then as he started to take the fan back to the garage, she thanked him for drying her hair then said, "I'm still not giving up smoking!" and quietly shut the door.

She must have been nervous or absent minded after all that because she used her Coke instead of the water to wet her hair. Later, she ruefully said the soda was better than hair spray for holding the curls.

That was only one of Dad's tricks. Others included using an animal syringe to squirt Mogen David blackberry wine into her cigarettes' tobacco and opening the bedroom windows in the dead of winter— supposedly to air out the room. Unfortunately, that trick froze them both, and they slept on the hide-a-bed in another room for the night. Mom just calmly bought an electric blanket that weekend in case Dad opened the window again.

As for the wine-laced cigarettes, she tossed the whole pack and opened another one. The rest of the wine in the bottle she used to cook a duck. She said she had wanted to try a new recipe she saw in a magazine, and now she had the chance. I admired her for that come-back. My mother didn't like to cook, and seldom tried anything new. Using recipes from magazines never happened, but she must have hunted for days to find something, *anything*, to cook in wine. The meal was a success.

In later years, she did compromise by going out on the enclosed porch to smoke rather than in the house. That way Dad didn't have to breathe the smoke or the lingering odor. Then he only put a clothes pin on his nose when he kissed her. She never got mad at his pranks. She just got even--like when she heavily starched his underwear. But that's another story!

My Bicycle

I lived in a fairly large neighborhood with other subdivisions close by, so there were lots of kids. By some luck of the draw, most were near the same age. It took two buses to load all of us for school. However, in our subdivision, there were only five girls with one being a senior in high school; the rest were boys.

Everyone had a bicycle – except for me. It was hard to socialize without one. It wasn't cool being fourteen and having to hoof it to the other end of the road to see a friend. The bicycle gave everyone some freedom. Most had had one since grade school.

Whole groups would ride up and down together, then stop in someone's driveway, lounge on the bikes and talk. Many conversations centered on bike chains, handlebars, seats, brakes, makes, and colors. The boys were always showing off with fancy tricks or racing each other. The girls were adept at getting the boys to examine their attributes as they rode; they could show off their long toned legs clad in shorts when gliding past the appreciative males.

If you didn't have a bicycle, you were out of the group. During school days, I came home, and started homework soon after. I wasn't allowed to go anywhere. Saturdays were for cleaning, and Sundays we went to visit the Snyders after church.

When we returned, I did homework or read. I had a tight routine during the school year, but I didn't mind the isolation too much; I saw my friends between classes.

It was in the summers that I felt very lonely. With Dad working during the week and using our one car, I could only visit the girls in my neighborhood, but they were gone on their bikes. I did have one friend, Sally, who lived three doors up.

Sometimes the boys and girls congregated in her driveway to pick up her and her brother. I could walk up there to do some quick socializing. Sometimes they'd be there a while and sometimes everyone wheeled off almost as soon as I arrived.

Sally agreed that fourteen was too old to be without "wheels". Bolstered by her urgings, I decided to do something about it since my parents didn't seem to notice those bicycles all over the place and my lack of one.

I knew I couldn't approach my mother because she didn't permit me to ask for anything unless I needed it for a class and had a teacher's note as proof. I decided to talk to my dad. He would understand.

I waited until he was home from work which was usually around two o'clock. Before he could go inside, I pointed out the problem. He saw all the bicycles traveling up and down our street, and he agreed that I was long past due for one. Then he said some chilling words, "I'll talk to your mother about this. Money is tight, but we'll see."

Mother controlled the money with an iron fist; even Dad had to ask if he wanted to buy something. Usually he used his G.I. disability check for "frivolous things" rather than listen to mother's howling over money not growing on trees. (She had wanted to be a CPA and had worked in a bank until the War. Managing money was her forte.)

At supper that evening, I knew my father had mentioned the bicycle to her. She looked at me and said, "What good is a bike to you? You don't know how to ride."

I told her that I could learn if I had one. Then she laughed and said, "When you learn to ride, I'll consider getting you one, but not before." Then she changed the subject.

That did it. She had thrown the gauntlet into the ring. I know she thought she could get out of buying me a bicycle, at least for a while. Maybe she was figuring that she could find me a good used one for Christmas. But I'd be fifteen then, and I would have a driver's license at sixteen. (I was definitely wrong on that notion!) I needed a bicycle this summer. I plotted.

The next morning, I slipped out after doing the breakfast dishes and ran for Sally's house. I explained the dilemma. She wanted to know how I was going to learn to ride if I didn't have a bike to learn on. She saw the look in my eye, and said, "Okay, what are you thinking?" I reminded her that she had a bicycle. She became my teacher. We practiced all morning in her driveway.

Later in the afternoon, my parents went grocery shopping, and I stayed home. While they were gone, we sneaked Sally's brother's bike out of the garage. (He was sixteen and cruising in the car. He never missed it.) She perfected my skills by riding with me up and down the entire street for over two hours. Others rode by and found out what I was up to. They cheered me on and promised not to mention that Sally was using her brother's bike in our plot.

I wore my poor girlfriend out, but I wouldn't stop. She went home, but let me keep her bike for more practice. When I figured it was about time for my parents to arrive home, I parked Sally's bicycle in the front yard and sat outside on the steps.

I didn't have to wait long. They pulled the car into the driveway and opened the garage door to begin unloading the supplies. Before they could start, I jumped on the borrowed bike and started riding around them. When I stopped, Dad was wearing his signature silly grin. He looked at my mother and said, "Well, Millie, I guess she knows how to ride." Mother wasn't amused, but she knew she had been out-maneuvered.

I returned Sally's bicycle while they took the groceries inside. They must have talked while I was gone. When I returned, Dad laughed and said, "I thought I had a couple of weeks to get the money together. I guess I was wrong. Let's go get that bicycle."

Either he got "Millie" to hand over the cash, or he used his G.I. check, but we went to the hardware store right then. One hour later, I was the proud owner of a brand new blue and white Schwinn complete with a built-in horn, lights, and a front basket! Daddy splurged – fifty dollars' worth!

The Prize

When I was in high school, there was a goal I had set my hopes on: a new set of encyclopedias. This prize was given to all graduates who had perfect attendance during their last four years.

I worked hard for that one. I had always missed quite a bit of school in the past because of rubella, chicken pox, recurrent strep throat, rheumatic fever, and a variety of other lovely diseases. It was a double goal for me—to stay well and not get tons of make-up assignments added to my already heavy homework load (so I could enjoy a social life at school), plus new reference books for college. My old World Books were dated from the early 1950's.

I endured colds, flu, cramps, and grand-mal migraines just to name a few "nasties" determined to keep me away from school. I took a variety of medicines and ignored my doctor's and parents' pleas to stay home and get well. I suppose I infected a few fellow students, but I'm the sort of person who sets her mind on something and does it.

My parents had long since figured that out when I was much younger. Mom said the only creature more stubborn than a mule sitting in the middle of a road was me. It wasn't always meant as a compliment, but I did win their admiration.

So after four years of such determination, I had won my goal. On the day of awards assembly, the superintendent named the four of us who had had perfect attendance for all our high school years: the valedictorian, the salutatorian, myself, and one other. He said that in the past, there had never been more than one or two who had accomplished this feat. Because there were four of us that year, the school board had decided not to award the encyclopedias because of cost. Instead, we four received only a certificate of perfect attendance. We didn't even get an apology.

The decision had been reached a couple of weeks earlier, and no one thought to tell us four. We had even foregone our Senior Skip Day to make sure we didn't lose the prize. We really felt cheated.

When our parents asked the superintendent about it, all he said was that encyclopedias were costing over a thousand a set, and it was felt that the money could be *better* spent. That loss was a crushing blow to us, but I guess it was a learning experience—our first dose of the real world.

Honor Society

When I was in high school, there was an organization called the National Honor Society; I don't know if many schools still have this group anymore, but I really wanted to be a member. You had to be a junior or senior and be chosen by other members and faculty based on "character, scholarship, leadership, and school/community service."

I was bitterly disappointed my junior year when my boyfriend got in and I didn't. We had been in friendly competition with each other since seventh grade, and I figured we'd get in together. He couldn't figure it out either; he had been in baseball for three years, science club one year, and "G" association two years.

I had been in science club three years, French club two years, hall monitor two years, and had attended JESSI at De Paul University. I'd also done water purification tests at Bears Mill which had helped their state lawsuit. I had fit all the criteria.

My father contacted our neighbor Corney Cornett who was the principal and on the nominating committee. He told my father that the other teachers didn't feel I had enough leadership ability.

When my dad told me that, I was angry. My boyfriend had coached a Little League team which gave him the leadership requirement, but some faculty didn't think my work with Dad on the Bear's Mill project counted.

True to form, my teachers had put what I considered a challenge at my feet, and I was determined to prove them wrong. I was never one to accept "no" as a permanent answer even when three years old. They didn't know what they had stirred up.

The Tap Assembly, where past members wander through the students selecting the new members by surprise, occurred in February. It was the following week when I began my assault. I became a lab assistant for my biology teacher. I ran for and became secretary of the science club, and when I discovered the lead hall monitor position was open, I grabbed that job.

When our French teacher wanted to add a third year class to the curriculum, I helped organize that. I really didn't want a third year of

French, but anything for leadership qualifications. None of the other students wanted one either, and the school didn't feel it had the money; I lucked out of that one!

That lead hall monitor job didn't carry a lot of additional responsibilities over a regular hall monitor. The difference was that I was stationed in the front corridor by the main door and the superintendent's office; it was centrally located so I could see the entire first floor. I had to see that all monitors were at their stations both downstairs and up, and to go get the fill-ins if someone was absent.

I also had to help visitors and run notes to teachers from the office. All monitors had to keep a log of who went where or did what to protect the students from thefts, vandalism, and possible fights. We were the protection and surveillance system on the campus.

Ours was a big high school, but there were almost never any problems. The job basically gave us all a quiet place to study, sleep, read comics hidden in our textbooks, use the bathroom, get a drink, or go to our lockers with no supervision but each other. It was a "cushy" job.

Well, almost. The lunch room food started getting worse and worse. We were getting peanut butter and honey sandwiches three days a week. Our vegetables were carrots and olives—raw or steamed and sometimes mixed together, sometimes separate, sometimes ground into a paste, and sometimes one or the other or both were ground up and put on sandwiches—with or without the peanut butter and/or honey. Sometimes we had mystery meat patties burned so badly that the outer charcoal layer could be cracked open and the dehydrated insides scooped out for eating.

Everyone was complaining and finally the straw broke. Student council and we monitors secretly spread the word. On a chosen Friday, the school revolted. The home-economics department opened its kitchens so students could come in and cook their own food. The rest brought lunch from home. Students and some teachers spent the entire lunch period (all four lunch groups—freshmen, sophomores, juniors, and seniors) outside together. Many carried large signs protesting the food.

Only fifty students were in the lunch room that day and our school had well over 1,000 kids—our class being the biggest in the town's history. We all went quietly back to class after the final lunch period. No one got in trouble.

Things improved a little that next Monday—we got hot dogs and lumpy boxed mashed potatoes with Jell-O containing olives and carrots.

That afternoon when I was at my post, I again watched the cafeteria workers carrying several large metal containers out the far corridor to their cars. I had watched this scenario for several weeks, but hadn't known what was being taken out; I assumed the workers were doing their jobs. This time the wind blew the smell toward me—warm baked steak. That hadn't been lunch that day.

I went to the superintendent's office and told him about the food leaving. He and the principal weren't fast enough to catch them that day, but did so a couple of days later. We were getting bad meals because the workers were stealing what we were supposed to be eating. They all were fired and substitutes from the other schools filled in for the rest of the year.

Mr. Cornett came down to our house and told Dad about it— everything had been kept quiet to avoid a scandal, but I did get a personal thanks. Then I found out that I was supposed to have been "tapped" at the assembly for Honor Society--there had been some mix up. I've always wondered about that considering what I had been told earlier, But I wasn't about to challenge that "mix-up."

I got tapped the following February, but my yearbook says I was a member both my junior and senior year. I was able to participate the rest of that year and my final year before I was "official." I had a smirk on my face the rest of my junior year, I'm sure.

Row 1, left to right: Coney Cornett, Dianna Wiles, Delores Stubbs, Doris Stubbs, Carol Young, Jo Ann Brubaker, Susan Eikenberry, Mary Brinkman, June Sanders, Debbie Huffman and Beryl Hensel. Row 2: Ruth Yocum, Carol Potter, Mary Gibbons, Cynthia Morton, Vicki Katzenberger, A l i c e

Browne, Linda Eaton, Carol Mason, Donnita Robinson and Barbara Turner. Row 3: Vicki Whitesell, Kathy Rhoades, Sandra Armstrong, Linda Gibson, Debbie Patrick, Nancy Westfall, Roxie Eyler, Debbie Locke and Betsy Nealeigh. Row 4: Roy Nixon, Charles Labig, Terry Cassel, John Ackley, Joel

Loy, Fred Dohse, John Hawley, Jack Farnham and Jerry Bish. Row 5: Kent Bowers, Bill McVay, Bill Raudabaugh, Ron McLear, Doug Wetzel, Brad Malcolm, Bob Prophater and Dave Shoemaker. Row 6: Kerri Kohli, Philip Blocher, Ken Sechler, Alex Warner, Edwin Randall, John Moore and Tom Gueth.

Thirty-Nine Top Scholars Chosen At Annual Honor Tap Assembly

Thirty-nine top seniors and juniors were elected to membership in National Honor society at the surprise tap assembly February 20.

Without any announcement tapping began while Miss Elizabeth Hill, vocal music teacher, played the school alma mater. New members were introduced by Beryl Hensel, superintendent of schools by present active members. After receiving congratulations from Mr. Hensel and principal Coney Cornett and after receiving the traditional green and white stole and pins, the newly elected members took their seats on the stage and received the oath which was administered by President Debbie Huffman. Mr. Cornett then introduced William McPherson who was the guest

speaker.

Seniors who were tapped are: Betsy Nealeigh, Cynthia Morton, Phillip Blocher, Jerry Bish, Bill Raudabaugh, Carol Young, John Ackley, Charles Labig, Vicki Katzenberger, Mary Gibbons, Edwin Randall, Susan Eikenberry, Carol Potter, Kathleen Rhodes, Ruth Yocum, Terry Cassel, Kerri Kohli, Barbara Turner, Mary Brinkman, Deborah Patrich, Joel Loy, Roy Nixon, John Hawley, William McVay, Donnita Robinson and Deloris Stubbs.

Juniors tapped are: Tom Gueth, Linda Eaton, Linda Gibson, David Shoemaker, Brad Malcom, Ron McLear, Roxie Eyler, Doug Wetzel, June Sanders, Jo Ann Brubaker, Deborah Locke, Fred Dohse and Kent Bowers

MENU

February 27
Cold meat sandwich
Cheese wedge
W. K. corn, milk
Potato Chips and Apple Sauce

February 28
Barbecue sandwich
Green beans
Creamed rice and milk
Ice cream & cookie

March 1
Wiener sandwich
Baked Beans and fruit
Cole slaw and milk

March 2
Hot chicken sandwich
Creamed peas
Stuffed celery
Upside down cake and milk

March 3
Fish sandwich
Succotash and milk
Pear and cottage cheese
Carrot sticks and ice cream

Hurt

It was my senior year and the day of the Tap Assembly. At this ritual, teachers and members of the National Honor Society "tapped" new nominees in a silent gymnasium filled with all four grades. It was considered quite an event, ranking up there with graduation.

Only juniors and seniors were picked. They sat in chairs in front of the stage while sophomores and freshmen watched from the bleachers. I knew I would be going in this time as I was already on the acceptance list as a junior but was not yet an "official" member.

I assumed my boyfriend Bill who had been "tapped" the spring before would be the one to take me to the stage, but it was my senior English teacher Mrs. Schmidt instead. Bill later said she pulled rank on him.

Mothers and Fathers were usually notified a week ahead of time so they could plan to be there at 2:00. Parents were not allowed to tell their hopeful teen if he or she was accepted; it was to be a big surprise.

Actually, at least one parent was expected to be there, but hopefuls did not get a chance to see if a family member was present until after they were "tapped." Then the parent would step forward as their 17 or 18 year old crossed the stage and received a white banner across his/her shoulders.

At the end, the new members were presented to the entire school including the superintendent and maybe a board member, plus all the parents. A photographer would be on hand from the town newspaper to take pictures. A large banquet would be held that same week to celebrate the new members and present each with an honor society pin.

When I was tapped, I looked around. I was surprised to see Mrs. Schmidt rather than Bill because we two had agreed that he'd be the one, when my time came, to escort me to the front. Instead, he was waiting on stage for me, and I stood beside him.

I looked out over the audience expecting to see Mom and Dad. I didn't see them. Throughout the next hour, I kept watching for them; I was hoping that they were late. When the assembly was over and we got our things from our chairs, I was still looking for them.

Everyone else's parents were there. Where were mine? The other initiates went out with their parents to celebrate or receive flowers or small gifts. Bill helped me keep watch for either my mom or my dad, surely my dad, to arrive, but they never came.

My boyfriend had to go to ball practice, so he couldn't drive me home, and Mother wouldn't have allowed him to anyway. He squeezed my hand and said, "Sorry," then left. I went to my locker for my things, and boarded my bus.

When I arrived home, I figured my parents would show up to take me out to eat or bring flowers or something. Instead, they were late, and nothing was even mentioned. Mom knew how much it meant to me to be chosen to join, especially considering what I had done to get nominated the year before, but I didn't even get a congratulations.

She took her usual 30 minute nap, and then announced she was too tired to cook. I thought that meant we would go out to eat, but that didn't happen. She told me to throw three TV dinners into the oven. I reminded Mom that I had been "tapped" that day, and asked why she and Dad didn't come. She shrugged and said she had known, but had to work. She refused to say more.

I went outside to talk to my father who was piddling with something in the front yard. He had been waiting to talk to me away from my mother, but I didn't realize it until I went looking for him.

I knew that we only had one car and both my parents worked in Bradford High School at the time, which was about 30 or 40 minutes from my high school. I also knew that they would have had to come together to the assembly, or else one would have had to return to pick the other up at their school.

But teachers are allowed two personal days during the school year to use for any necessity. My parents had never used any of theirs over the years and could easily have got the afternoon off. If they had left at 1:00 to attend, only two and a half hours would have been lost, and Mom's last hour was her planning period; she would only have missed her typing class.

I told Dad all this when he said that Mother stayed to work; she was even in her room an extra half-hour. He had nothing to say about the personal days. I asked why he didn't come, and then return to get my mother. He said he suggested that, but Mother refused—it was a waste of gasoline she said, and she'd have to stay in Bradford until at least 4:00; she wanted to come home.

I went into the house to my room and shut the door. I'd long since learned not to cry over disappointment, but I was deeply depressed for days. I just got out my physics book and started my homework. Nothing more was ever said. Bill took me to the banquet that Friday night; I sat with his parents. Mom didn't feel good, and wanted my father to stay with her.

Over my childhood years, my mother and I had grown more distant. However, her pronounced coldness toward me seemed to have started when I was around seven years old. Maybe it was my illness, maybe it was my strong attachment to my father and he to me, but my mother

46

took no pride in any of my accomplishments. My cousin, who was only ten years younger than my mother and who was her confidant, told me after my mother's death that Mom had been jealous of me.

Was that the reason she bitterly let me down when I was so excited that senior day? Was that the reason my father didn't attend—to keep the peace? Was that the reason she interfered with my working on my doctorate? Was that also the reason she sneered and called it a "con" when I was accepted into Who's Who Among American Teachers twice?

A counselor said my mother exhibited growing emotional problems and some paranoia as she got older. I knew that she hadn't wanted me, but maybe she never got over the post-partum blues. Some women never do, and in the late '40's and '50's, I don't think they diagnosed for such things. I've tried to rationalize the times she seemed to delight in hurting me, but I still wonder.

I loved my mother very much and would like to think she was just mildly ill rather than accept other possibilities. Even so, that feeling of excitement and pride followed by hope, anxiousness, and deep disappointment is hard to forget—especially when my hands were shaking so badly that I kept dropping things as I got ready for the bus that afternoon long ago.

Back Row *Papa King/Mama King; Uncle Claude/Aunt Hula; Eunice/Uncle Herbert/his wife; Aunt Sally*

Front Row *Great Grandpa King, Edith (daughter of Papa and Mama King), Frank/Pauline (Sally's kids); Great Grandma King; Uncle Erten*

Grandma Patrick

Grandma Nora and Grandpa Garrison Patrick still had their farms in Tennessee when I was little. We lived at Papa King's house in Kentucky, but went down to stay with them for a week each summer.

Dad would help Grandpa outside and Mother was put to work inside. They had a bungalow style house and Grandma was a fastidious house keeper. She made me come in the back door, never the front, after playing outside.

There was a sink there on the enclosed porch with usually cold, soapy, and slightly dirty water. I had to wash my hands in that water before going inside. Everyone used the same wash water but Mom did not appreciate it. I remember her grumbling that she and I shouldn't have to use dirty water.

Grandma had handed Mom five dresses to iron. That was a little different from the way she was used to being treated, as Papa had always had "hired help", and my mother never had to do any housework. So, ironing her own dress was quite an adjustment for her, let alone being asked to iron someone else's. I guess she thought it was demeaning.

She packed her bags and told Dad to take her to the bus station. She gave him an ultimatum; he could stay or return to Kentucky with her, but she was leaving. We left that day for Harford. It was just a different lifestyle, and my mother had trouble adjusting.

After that, I would go with my Father to my grandmother's, and Mother stayed back north. Often, and I don't know why, she wouldn't let me go down with him; therefore, I only know there were huge arguments over if he could take me. Whether I went or not, they fought when Dad returned. I didn't get to know my Grandma and Grandpa Patrick very well. Still when I was there, they tried hard to make me feel comfortable.

Grandma would fix purple-hulled peas and cornbread for me because she knew I really like that meal. She also had chess pie waiting when Dad and I arrived. No one could make chess pie like she could, and I usually went through two or three during our week there.

Grandma Patrick just didn't know how to talk to me like she did to my cousins, Andrea, Janice, and Robert. They lived on a farm also while I was a town kid. She often told Dad (Dad told Mom, and Mom told me) that I was so smart for my age that she was at a loss as how to get close to me, and Grandma didn't talk a lot—maybe because everyone else did. She'd sit quietly while other family members yakked on and on.

So she tried in her own way with the cooking and laundry. She showed me how she washed clothes in an old wringer washing machine, and she would let me feed the clothing through the wringer to squeeze the soapy water out. Then she would drain the tub, refill it with clean water, and put the clothes in to rinse; I'd run to the machine when she called that it was time to squeeze out the clean clothes. Sometimes she'd let me turn the crank on the wringer. However, that was also around the time she purchased a washer with an electric wringer, and she didn't let me near that one for fear it would have been my hand that was squeezed instead of Grandpa's shirts.

Then I took the bag of clothes pins outside while she carried the basket of laundry to be hanged. I'd hand her each shirt or towel and try to find each sock's mate so she could pin them together. Since I helped Peggy, our housekeeper, back home, this was familiar and fun. Then we'd go back inside for home-made biscuits and honey (Grandpa had bees at one time but later he bought large half-gallons from locals.)

After a snack, if there were clothes to iron, I would get a Coke bottle, fill it with water, add a sprinkling top, and shake water over the starched shirts or dresses and roll them up. Grandma would then start ironing when the water had soaked in. She would lower the wooden ironing board to its sit-down level so I could reach it, and let me try ironing once in a while.

That was only after she bought an electric iron. The older type she used had a wooden handle and iron frame with several smooth iron bottoms which she heated on the gas stove. She'd take one off when it cooled down too much, put it on the stove, and fasten in a hot one.

That was too heavy for me to manage, and Grandma didn't want me to burn myself. She watched me like a hawk when I used the electric one too. That's how I learned to iron. (When Mother found out that Grandma had taught me to iron, she put me to work ironing on weekends and dismissed the ironing lady. That wasn't much fun.)

Another time when I visited, I watched her sew on a treadle machine. She made me a pillow with strips of red and green plaid with a blue back. It was just out of scraps, but it's the only gift I remember her giving me. Usually she sent a five-dollar bill in birthday or Christmas cards so I could get what I wanted; she had no idea what would please me.

My mother would take the money away from me and put it in "savings." I have no idea what she bought with it for me or even if she did buy anything, so that pillow was rather special. It remained on my bed for years before it fell apart.

Grandma had an upright parlor clock with an alarm on it. One of the first of the alarm clocks, I guess. It fascinated me so much that when I was five, she promised it would be mine someday. She also had two large cedar hope chests which she filled with home-made linens and mementoes.

In her will, Andrea was to get one chest, and I was to get the other, both filled to their tops. It was up to us to choose which one we wanted. In addition, I was to get Grandmas favorite watch and the clock. Dad was to get the big round antique dining table and chairs.

When we went back north after the funeral, the clock and my watch were in the trunk. Dad was going to come back with a truck to get the dining room set and my filled chest.

His only living sister Gertrude was "something else," and she caused all sorts of trouble over the table and chairs. Mom and Dad really didn't have a place for the set so he let her keep it—she sold it. Then I don't know what happened, but my chest and items simply disappeared. Uncle John was to have taken care of Andrea's and mine too.

I overheard a conversation about Uncle John catching Gertrude going through things when he went to check on the house. I guess Aunt Gertrude simply took my chest and Andrea's as well. There's one in every family!!

I have the watch, and Dad gave me a real tortoise-shell comb with NORA written in gold—it was large and would fit in a hair bun rather like a Spanish lady would wear. I took it to Donnas frame shop to get it put in a shadow box, but it was so fragile and old that it disintegrated into many tiny pieces, impossible to repair.

Dad, later on, also gave me two necklaces—one he had given Grandma during or right after WWII, which was shaped like a book and would open to hold two tiny pictures and the other was a beautiful cameo with "Nora" written in the back in pencil.

Mother wouldn't give me the clock; I think it was because my father got nothing of his mother's except a covered clear pressed glass candy dish and a fruit compote (Mom just slipped those out of the house at the time because she wanted them. I don't think they meant much to Dad.) Then Erin, as a three year old, broke the candy dish lid. Mom was furious with her and me.

For years my Mother dangled that clock in my face, and said she was giving it to my maternal cousin Shirley. I just kept my mouth shut. When Mother died, the clock was still in her house, and I finally have the only item of my grandmother's that I ever wanted. It was a bond between her and me, two people who loved each other, but never got much time to be together.

Grandpa Patrick

I didn't get to spend much time at my Grandma and Grandpa Patrick's place because my mother didn't like Grandma and wasn't too keen on the rest of Dad's family. However, once every couple of years when my Father would go to visit, Mom would allow me to go, mostly at Dad's insistence. It usually involved long arguments before we went and after we returned, with my mother slapping my father's face many times.

When I was very young, Grandpa and Grandma owned a couple of farms and a bungalow near Bolivar, Tennessee. Their house was very modern for its times—hot and cold running water and a full bathroom inside, rather than an outhouse and only cold water like Papa King's. Papa's lighting consisted of bare bulbs dangling on long cords from the ceiling in his half of the house. But Grandpa had regular ceiling fixtures. Papa didn't care about such things after Mama King died in the early 40s, but Grandpa Patrick did.

I loved taking a hot bath at Grandpa's every night. That tub would be filled with lots of bubble bath, and my inflatable black cat floated on top; its body was flat and round like an inner tube and its center was made to hold the soap. Dad would have to empty the tub and refill it to rinse me off because the water would be white from so much soap. I was definitely the cleanest kid around.

After my bath, I got to stay up, rather than be put to bed. I would be shy around Grandpa at first since there were long intervals between visits. He, Grandma, and Dad would talk, and I would want Grandpa's attention, so I'd back up to him. He knew I wanted my back rubbed—Papa King always did it, as we lived with him in Kentucky; I figured I'd put Grandpa to work also.

He always laughed and would stand me between his knees and start rubbing or scratching. When I got tired of standing, I would sit on his lap still with my back to him. Sometime later, relaxed from my bath and less shy, I'd curl up with my arms around his neck. He'd hold me, and I'd fall asleep. He wouldn't let my father put me to bed. I'd sleep on his lap until everyone headed upstairs, then he'd tuck me in. Maybe he thought I'd be afraid if I waked up alone in a strange bed during the evening, but I suspect the real reason was just so he could hold me. Grandpa was very much like my daddy, and since I adored my Dad, I also loved him very much; I just had to re-acquaint myself each time I visited. Once those introductions were over, I'd be Grandpa's side-kick. All the parts that made up my father, I found double in him.

51

Like my Dad, Grandpa didn't talk much about himself, but I did get a little information over the years. The Patrick family was pure Irish from Dublin, Ireland and worshiped at St. Patrick's Cathedral. It was my Grandpa's grandfather who had brought the family over to America, and all had flaming red hair.

My Grandpa had an identical twin, but I can't remember his name. His brother had a daughter, Kathleen, who had a boy and a girl. Jerry was my third cousin and my best friend—he'd come by Grandma's and Grandpa's town house in later years and take me for motorcycle rides, hence my love of motorcycles.

All family members lived very long lives—the men in their 90s and the women somewhere around 100. I met Kathleen's mother when she was 103. She invited Dad and me out to her back porch while she shelled beans.

In his younger years, my grandfather had owned a store in Ft. Smith, Arkansas and sold provisions to the Indians and early settlers. That's how he made his fortune. He was also an undertaker and would joke about the number of times he'd have a body lying on the table, and it would move.

I remember his telling Daddy during dinner one afternoon about this. It seems Grandpa had an assistant who didn't know such things. The gases in the body released through the mouth and activated the vocal cords. The lessened internal pressure allowed the stomach muscles to contract and the corpse moaned and sat up.

My grandfather said his assistant thought the body was coming to life. The man's eyes got very wide; he jumped and shrieked, and flew out the door. Grandpa started laughing so hard at the dinner table that he got the hic ups. He said he had lost a couple of assistants that way. He learned the undertaking business from his aunt and uncle who lived in Bolivar, Tennessee and owned a mortuary.

I know almost next to nothing about his adventures while Indian trading. All I know is that he would return to Tennessee every year, and on one trip home, he met Nora. Grandma said he was very dashing and quite rich. She envisioned living a wealthy southern life with him, but made him give up his trips west to trade, which was the source of his money. He did as she asked, took his money and invested it in farming. Grandma thought she'd be living in town with a social life and servants.

Ruefully, she said she had envisioned being a socialite rather than a farm wife, but admitted it had been her own fault. She wouldn't move west with him and didn't want him gone for long stretches of time. Obviously they weren't poor.

In later years, I remember my Uncle John showing Dad and me one of the old remaining slave quarter houses still standing on one of the farms that Grandpa sold. No Grandpa didn't own slaves; that was before his time. He was born in 1882. But the land may have been part of a plantation. Possibly a farm worker's family lived there in years past.

Grandpa, Garrison Mears Patrick, was Catholic, and Grandma Nora was Baptist. They reared four children—John Robert, Vernell, Gertrude, and Bradley Garrison in that order. Vernell was married but had no children because she was killed in an automobile wreck when she was 24; she hadn't been married long. Since there was no Catholic church nearby, all the children including my father went to the Baptist Church. All remained Baptists except my dad who became Methodist when he married my mother.

Most all the Patricks were red-haired, but Nora was blond with blue eyes. So my father had blond hair with red undertones and the blue eyes. That's where I got my blond-red hair, instead of my mother's black hair from her Scottish ancestors.

That's about all the history I remember. There were few stories told as my father didn't reminisce around the supper table. The here and now occupied the conversation or else Mother talked about her past. Uncle John always had Grandma and Grandpa over to his house for Sunday dinners—which was always quiet a feast.

Once Uncle John and Grandpa told how Uncle John had put my father as a little boy, on a horse. Supper was called, but the animal wouldn't let Dad off, or else my father was afraid to try. It was a long way down. John didn't tell what he had done or where. Daddy sat there a couple of hours before my grandpa found him. That's how I know there were horses on the farm at one time.

So what little I knew about the Patrick family centered around the few times I was there. I did get my love of television wrestling from Grandpa, to my mother's horror. Dad bought Grandpa a small television as a Christmas present sometime after we got one. He and I would sit together watching men in tight pants roll around on the floor of a rink. Mom said it was all fake and low-class, but it was something Grandpa and I did together, so I loved it.

Often he'd pull a pouch out of his left pocket while holding me. He'd open it with his teeth, pull out a packet of papers and take one out. Then he'd hold the paper between his 3rd and 4th fingers and tap loose tobacco out of the leather pouch onto the paper with his thumb and index fingers. Using his teeth again, he'd pull the drawstring closed and put it in his pocket. Then still only using one hand, he'd smooth out and roll up the tobacco in the paper and wet the paper in his mouth to make it stay together. He leave it in his mouth, slide open the match box, take out the match, strike it on his shoe, and light his cigarette. He'd either blow out the match while the cigarette was in his mouth or pinch it out with his left thumb and finger. He had done this for so many years that his left thumb was stained deep yellow brown from the tobacco.

It always fascinated me to watch him; he said he learned it out west. I never saw a television cowboy roll cigarettes the way he did, and I was extremely impressed.

When they sold the farms and moved into town, he had little to do anymore. Every afternoon, he'd walk down to the local gas station, (Back then they also fixed cars there as well as pumped gas.) and buy a Coke. He'd spend several hours there talking to folks and watching them work on tires or transmissions.

Tires had inner tubes at that time, so Grandpa was my source of such "floaties" for swimming in the local creeks or ponds. He'd take my cousin Andrea and me down to places near bridges where he said the best swimming was. He didn't come in with us but would keep watch as sometimes quick sand was nearby. We'd be forbidden to go into that part.

Later such places became very polluted. Chickasaw Park's swimming area became that way, and Andrea got a bad ear infection from there. That's the last I remember of any swimming in Tennessee. But I did have a selection of Tennessee inner tubes for many years.

When Grandma Patrick died, Grandpa moved himself into an assisted living nursing home. He didn't need to, but he was lonely at his house, and didn't know much about cooking and didn't like what he did cook. Many of his friends were there, and as this was, in his opinion, a good place to meet folks his own age since he didn't go to church, he had a busy social life.

He'd still walk to his favorite gas station each day for a Coke and maybe a game of checkers. Then sometimes he'd go to his house for a pair of socks or a shirt he wanted, and to see that everything was alright there.

It was odd, but when Grandma died, there was no mention of Grandpa in the will. Everything was given to the family with nothing for him. Uncle John and Dad gathered everyone together for a conference. By putting all the facts together, they figured out why.

A few years before Grandma died, Grandpa Patrick had been very ill—a bleeding ulcer and some heart problems. He could have died. Grandma had been afraid he would die before her so she changed the will—they only had one. She never changed it back, and she never told him that she had changed it. Then she died first.

The family decided not to tell him about it considering Aunt Gertrude's tendency to be greedy; it was quite an accomplishment to get her to go along with the decision. (She later prepared a bill for sitting at the hospital by his side when he was so sick, and she wanted payment from the estate!)

So the house remained as it had been—even Grandma's effects were left untouched. Sometimes Grandpa would stay the night there or putter around, but that wasn't too often. He preferred his new location. He did stop driving sometime after Grandma died as he liked to walk, and it was good for his heart.

His car was still in the car port in back of the house; he kept it licensed and in good working order in case he wanted to go somewhere. Usually, Uncle John would come get him if he wanted to go to the cemetery or shopping, and always for Sunday dinner. Grandpa was tall, thin, healthy, and quick witted even at 94. Then one night at his new place, he went to sleep and left us.

Because I was not given a past history of the family, I have never known where the Patrick members all went when they came from Ireland. Dad located a family in Ohio, and it's possible some of the Patricks' around Brown County, Indiana are distant relatives, but I have no way of finding out as yet.

I'm not as close to those still living as I would like, thanks to my mother. Many are dead that I did know, but Robert O'Neal Patrick lives in Georgia and has an International Harvester dealership. Maybe if I can locate his address, he might have some genealogy information that could get me started. It would be wonderful if I found out that some of my ancestors called Indiana, especially Brown County, home as I do.

Papa's Romance

Sometimes after supper when we were still sitting around the table and didn't have to hurry—me to do homework, and my parents, who taught school, to do their paperwork, my mother would reminisce about her past. One time she told Dad and me about how Papa and Mama King began their courtship. Some of the facts may be a little wrong, but since she only told it once, I'm telling it the best I remember.

Papa was a good looking young man in his early twenties. He had finished college and was already working in the oil fields. He didn't own his own company yet, but was doing well working for another. He was what folks called "up and coming." He always wore a suit and white shirt with replaceable collar and cuffs, a fashionable hat, and his silver tipped leather cane.

Mom never knew what accident had caused his need for a cane—one story was about getting into some mischief with other boys concerning a girl, dares, and an apple orchard. The one I heard the most, however, involved a horse falling on him or a horse and buggy with the horse falling on him near railroad tracks. Perhaps the horse spooked because of the train whistle. There is no one left who could tell me, so that story will remain a mystery. Although my cousin Shirley says she believes the tree story, that he fell out of an apple tree, broke his leg, and it wasn't set right.

The Kings were a very respectable upper middle class family who believed in educating all their children and had done so for generations. Papa was one of four boys—Herbert, Claude, Erten, and Moten D., and one girl—Hula.

Hula was educated in business and had gone out west to work. She became engaged to a doctor, but when her mother—my great-grandmother King became ill, she called off the engagement and returned home to nurse her. She then became the branch manager of the local bank, but never married.

Uncle Claude had a farm and raised race horses. He dated a lady named Pearl for many, many years, but also never married. Herbert or Uncle Hub had 6 children with his wife. Erten was a master welder and married Sally (I don't know her maiden name.) They had two children, Pauline and Frank.

Papa or Moten King was neither the oldest nor youngest of the five, but was doing well enough that he could afford to marry if he found the right lady. I guess he was considered an eligible bachelor in the late 1890's. Several mothers found ways to present their daughters to him - some at church socials, others at "coming-out" parties, or invitations to tea. They could be seen dragging their girls with them when they called on Great Grandmother, knowing Papa was home, or just stopping him on the street in town. I'm sure he found all this attention rather nerve-racking as he tried to be the perfect gentleman toward the determined mothers.

Papa was a man who preferred to do his own looking, and no young lady had caught his eye. Actually he was more interested in doing well at his job at this time than courting someone. That is until he met Mary Parks.

County fairs are great social events even now. I think they were more so back then. There were rides, games, food, and horse races. Judges picked the best pies, relish, preserves, cookies, flowers, crops, and animals just like they do today. Of course they didn't have motorcycle races or demolition derbies or electric bands, but there was music, and, of course, a queen contest. If grandparents are around I'm sure they remember the fairs when they were little and could tell all about them.

Hartford was the county seat of Ohio County in Kentucky just as Nashville is of Brown County, Indiana. Both were about the same size, so use your imagination.

Papa escorted Hula and his parents on that important day. The rest of the family members were there also. Sometime during the afternoon, Papa was off on his own when he saw a young lady and her older brother walking the grounds. If there truly is love at first sight, Papa fell hard. He located various family members and asked who she was. Hula knew her because she occasionally came to the bank. She said her name was Mary Parks and that she was 15. Hula also knew her family was equal in class status to the Kings which, I guess, was important back then.

Mary's family also believed in educating all the boys and girls, and Mary was going to milliner's school after she finished high school. According to my mother, Mary was one of the prettiest girls in Hartford, and several world-be suitors were waiting in the wings until she had her formal coming-out party at 16.

Papa insisted Hula introduce him. So Papa, Hula, and my great grandparents all casually placed themselves in Mary's path. Papa was properly introduced to her and all walked for ice cream. Papa paid for every one's, which was his way of showing that such things were well within his means.

Soon all six headed for the grandstand for the races—Uncle Claude had a horse entered. Papa was allowed to sit by Mary and they had a chance to talk. I have no idea what was said, but the next day Papa went to Mary's house and asked to speak to her father. He asked permission to court her with the intention of marriage.

Mr. Parks was not shocked by Papa's declaration of love, so Mary must have spoken to her parents that evening when she returned from the fair. Papa was told that she was too young, and he would have to wait until she was 19. Papa agreed and left.

Mary had her coming-out party at 16, finished high school, and went to milliner's school. Papa spent the 4 years working hard to rise with the company, set aside money, and start his own oil company called Sunnydale.

Mom didn't say but I'm sure Papa and Mary occasionally dated during that time—chaperoned of course. I have a picture of Mary in a tight striped Victorian dress and wide hat, sitting with my Uncle Hub in his open carriage drawn by 2 matching black horses with white feet. Papa was taking the picture. They were out for a ride, and my married uncle with 6 kids was the chaperone. (Papa had a rival. I have one picture of him, but not his name. I don't believe that Mary was interested, only polite.)

On Mary's 19th birthday, Papa went to her house and formally asked her father for her hand in marriage. Mr. Parks accepted. They were married April 25, 1906, and my Aunt Edith was born in October 20, 1907.

Papa bought their last house in 1919, and Mother was born there on March 12, 1921. My grandmother died sometime during WWII of a perforated colon or perhaps colon cancer.

According to Mom, after Mama King died, Papa dated a lady who had a daughter for a short while. (Mother said the girl broke her China dish set, and she wasn't happy about that. I'm not positive, but I think Mom had a hand in breaking up that relationship.) At any rate, he wasn't serious. Not long after, he sold his oil business, donated his eleven natural gas wells to the city, retired, and remained in the house. It seems he just quit after that. He died in the late 1960's of prostate cancer. Papa and Mama's was truly a happy Romeo and Juliet story.

Not A Good Place

In my book *Dandelions & Other Weeds,* I introduced my readers to my grandfather Papa King with whom I lived until Aug. 1955. He was a wonderful second father to me during those years when my Dad traveled working with the health dept. Now I will tell another story not so pleasant—about the end of his life.

In the middle of the 1960s, my parents and Aunt Edith discovered that Papa was failing and decided that he could no longer live alone in Hartford. They could have hired Peggy or one of her family members to keep an eye on him because he didn't want to leave home, but my mother decided without considering his feelings or the consequences of her decision, to move him to our house.

She put an iron bed frame and mattress in the corner of our dining room, but did not move the table out. That dining room had been a bedroom at one time and had been converted years before. It had three doors—one to the kitchen which now had western-style swinging bar doors, one into the hall leading to the bathroom, and a large sliding glass door going down two steps to the family room. He had no privacy as everyone went through that room to get wherever they were going.

My parents were going to Ball State to finish their Masters and Doctors degrees during that time as well as teaching school full time. I was in high school and didn't get home until 4:15. He was alone all day.

In Hartford, he had many friends and his brothers to keep him company, but he had no one where we were. There was only the television or radio, and as he never cared to have either at his home, preferring the local newspaper, he never turned them on.

Mom didn't get the paper and he wouldn't have cared about information containing nothing familiar anyway. We were in the country, and he was used to a front porch. We didn't have a front porch—only a back patio enclosed on 3 sides. So he just sat inside and waited for me to get home.

I didn't know how to cook; Mom had never let me in the kitchen when she cooked, and now that she was in school, the refrigerator held frozen TV dinners and weekend left overs. Dad would cook Papa the same breakfast he cooked me, but he had to fend for himself until I got home. Then we had TV dinners.

I remember one evening I only had one turkey and one fried chicken dinner left to fix. I gave him the turkey as it was the better of the two— the fried chicken was always soggy and certainly not what he was used to fixing himself. He kept looking at my chicken as I ate, and I figured out that he would have preferred what I had.

Since I had started eating it, I couldn't trade with him, but I've always felt guilty about that meal. Dad fixed him lots of pancakes with syrup on weekends and for supper during the week when he was home. Papa loved it, but all that sugar lead to his having a minor stroke. That's when we discovered he had diabetes and prostate cancer. After that during the day he wore a urinal—a cup with a long tube that traveled down the inside of his pant leg.

Mom had never been good at nursing anyone—even me when I was bedridden at 8 with rheumatic fever. I seldom saw her. She never changed my bedpan which sat on a chair by my bed, and she certainly wouldn't help Papa. She avoided him as much as possible; evening talks with my father couldn't compensate.

Being a shy teen with lots of homework, I didn't have a lot of time to spend with him, and I didn't know what to even talk about except school. I only had a couple of school friends, and my mom never allowed them over. I only saw them between classes, so I had no stories to tell him when I got home.

I would tell him about my worm or frog dissections or a chemistry quiz, but that wasn't very interesting, I'm sure. Then I had to start my homework. When my parents got home, Mom would take a half hour nap and maybe fix supper or TV dinners.

59

If Papa had had an accident in his bed, she would complain or glare at him and change the sheets. Wash day was always Saturday. Dad took over the bed changing; Papa was so embarrassed and even ashamed as he had always been a proud and independent man. Papa began avoiding my mother altogether or was shy and withdrawn when she was around. Finally the bed changing became too much for mother, and she called Aunt Edith to come get him.

Now Aunt Edith lived in an upstairs efficiency apartment in Cincinnati, Ohio. The streets were noisy and the space was small. She was a widow who lived alone and worked a 9-5 job before eating out with friends. She only had a hide-a-bed to sleep on. She dutifully took Papa to her apartment and installed the twin bed. Now Papa was even more isolated as he didn't have my father as a companion now.

The apartment high rise had no elevator so he was stuck in the room. Aunt Edith tried, but even she had to go up and down the stairs to do laundry elsewhere in the building, and she had no one to help her with Papa at all.

I don't know the circumstances, but she lasted less than my mother did in caring for Papa. She and Mom got their heads together and put him in a nursing home in Covington, Ky. I thought the place looked a bit seedy, but it had a screened-in sitting room; Papa could make friends there. I hoped he wouldn't be lonely. We didn't get down to visit very often, and I'm not sure how often Aunt Edith visited. She didn't own a car and had to get public transit to go.

Then things went bad. Over the next year when we visited, we noticed Papa vomiting and passing some black blood. Once we found him strapped to a chair. Dad started going a bit more often when he had some extra money for gas. He didn't notify the nursing home that he was coming. He found Papa in bed with his arms strapped to the bed rails. Now my father loved Papa very much and was furious.

He began an investigation and discovered that a nurse there was mistreating patients. She would get mad at Papa for some reason, or maybe it was just for some perverted fun on her part. She would yank out his catheter, still inflated. I guess the blood backed up and came out black. I'm not sure if the blood he spit up was connected to that particular torture or to some other. Papa's wrists and arms were bruised and lacerated from being tied down and his struggling to get free. Then they drugged him to keep him quiet.

When Daddy discovered all this, he, Mom, and Aunt Edith moved him to another nursing home out of Covington. He received much better care, and a closer watch was kept to protect him from any such happenings again.

Still Papa was a broken man. I think it was the summer after my freshman year in college that Papa began slipping in and out of a coma. Family gathered for the final vigil. Three times he stopped breathing and three times he gasped and started breathing again. The last time he stopped for good. The prostate cancer finally won.

My father deeply loved and respected my grandfather. When Papa died, Daddy began shaking so much that he asked Mom for a cigarette. He hadn't smoked in 10 yrs. or more. When Mother refused, he broke down and sobbed. I had never seen my father cry before. Mom just sat there. Then she asked for scissors and cut a lock of Papa's hair as a remembrance. It was a traditional family thing she did.

White-Washed Trees

Before my Uncle Claude moved into town, only a few blocks from Papa King's, he owned a farm. He raised horses there and raced them at the Kentucky Derby. By the time I was born, he was winding the farm down. I only saw a few horses there (possibly some were being boarded,) but he still had one jersey cow which I knew well—I got to ride her. My uncle would lift me up and set me on her neck.

She would follow him into the barn to be milked. I'd climb off her and onto the stall rails, then watch the whole process. Uncle Claude did the milking by hand; he had none of the machine-operated equipment that some large dairy farms used. I think he sold her milk, but kept some for himself.

One summer when my uncle still had the farm, Papa, Mom, Dad, and I were sitting outside in the shade of a grove of trees to the right of his house. We were drinking ice tea as usual. Uncle Claude's trees were white-washed up to the first branches.

Folks back then usually did white-wash all the trunks of trees which surrounded their houses, but not elsewhere. It was considered attractive and classy. My uncle said his were about due for a new coat. I asked if I could help paint when he was ready; he smiled and nodded, "yes."

Papa never white-washed his trees that I remember, so, this seemed like fun to me. Mother didn't think too much of my helping. She figured I'd be wearing more white than the trees, and she'd get to wash me, but she shrugged and asked when she should bring me over.

When the day arrived, I came early, dressed in my oldest clothes. Mom wasn't going to help, but she said she'd fix lunch. Uncle Claude wanted

61

to work before the noon day sun got too hot, so we started immediately. He handed me a big paint brush.

He had already mixed the lime, powdered chalk, glaze, and water before we came. He may have mixed other things in it; I don't know his recipe, and Dad only mentioned the ingredients listed. The mixture was thick, but drippy.

I dipped in and started painting a tree, beginning with the base and any exposed roots; I had to use both hands to hold the heavy, loaded brush. Uncle Claude said I could skip the roots as I'd get dirt on my brush and in the bucket of wash, and I was already painting enough of the grass as it was. It only took one coat to cover the smooth bark of the trees I was given to paint. My uncle coated the rougher barked ones. I reached as high as I could while the white-wash dripped off my elbows. It dried my skin and made it itch; I scratched and coated myself more.

When I was too tired to continue, Mother took me inside for a bath and a change of clothing. She put me in a dark grey short set which she had made, and sent me out to play away from the newly painted trees and the buckets of white wash. I climbed about the old white-washed trees and rubbed up against them while circling around and around. The old wash rubbed off on my outfit and skin; I was very dusty and white, again. Mom just rubbed me down with a dry towel and sent me outside, this time to the grass or gravel driveway. She said to stay away from all trees.

Uncle Claude had done this job for many years, so he was a fast worker. Most trunks that were marked for painting were done by lunch time. We ate outside well away from any trees which could coat me for a third time. I thought everything was bright and pretty; the newly white-washed trunks had that effect on the whole yard. When I think back on it, I'd say the look was "stately" or "elegant."

Although coating the trees seemed just right for the times, I can see why the practice isn't continued today. It takes a lot of upkeep and rubs off on any hands or clothing which touches the trunks. That means lots of cleaning.

No one has enough leisure time to spend this way, and I doubt anyone younger that me ever saw it done, and I was only four. Still, surrounding one's pretty flower gardens with white-washed trees was beautiful; the colors really stood out. Maybe someone caring for a historical house will bring that old practice back again. I'd like to think so.

Samuel

Samuel was chained by his ankle to a tree on the courthouse lawn. His church elders and the sheriff, after much debate, removed him from his home as he was a danger to his family as well as to the townspeople. He couldn't just be shot, which is what folks would have done to a dog, because such a merciful action would be murder; whoever pulled the trigger would have to be tried, convicted, hanged, and his immortal soul sent to hell.

You see, Samuel had been bitten by a rabid animal only a few days before. There was a vaccine in the 1920s, and terrible as it was to take, it could have saved his life. It wasn't given to him. Maybe there was none available; maybe his family didn't have the money for it, and no one would help out; maybe it was too late to administer the vaccine; maybe folks hoped he wouldn't get the disease.

Whatever the reason, he was chained and left to his fate. His family brought him food and water. He had a pillow and a couple of blankets, but no shelter from the weather except the trees' leafy branches overhead. Southern summer heat and some rain were his to endure. Friends came by and talked, but were careful to stay beyond the length of the chain. He was soft-spoken and polite to all, but he seldom smiled even to his family. Did he tell anyone his thoughts? Folks didn't say.

Within a few days, less than 10, he began to have a burning and numbness where he was bitten. Then he complained of headaches. Town folks noticed he was restless; they heard his chain rattling as it dragged across the ground at night as he paced, unable to sleep.

During the day, his nervous family pushed a water bowl and a plate of food toward him using a forked stick or broom. He complained that his throat felt swollen; he began having trouble eating food and swallowing water. Soon even the sight of water agitated him, and he would throw the water at whoever brought it to him. He would scream at his tormenter; just seeing the water caused painful throat contractions.

He became more agitated, and he paced constantly or yanked at the chain. Family and friends abandoned him, and all the towns' folk stayed away. The chain rattled day and night, giving many folks nightmares for years to come. Then the convulsions started, and no one would go near that side of the courthouse.

Everything seemed to anger him as the days progressed. Then he became quiet; he just sat staring at the ground between his legs or pulling idly at his chain. Other times he leaned against the tree or lay down, no longer using the pillow or blankets. It was a day or so before anyone noticed that he was unconscious.

It was the flies on him, which signaled folks that he was dead. Even then, their fear kept them away. They poked him with long sticks or threw rocks to see if he really was dead. When he didn't move and they were sure, they wrapped him in the blankets he had, and put him in a casket right there.

Here the story ends; I don't know if he was cremated or buried. You see, this story was told to me by my mother. It happened when she was a child somewhere between 7 to 10 years old, so her memory wasn't perfect nor did she want to remember. The horror was too real. She didn't even remember his name, so I called him Samuel; after all, he was a human being.

The Game

I like to play checkers. Maybe chess and backgammon are classier, but I don't mind. Checkers fits me.

My invitation to the game began in late summer when I was five. My mother and father had taken new jobs, so we moved from Papa King's in Kentucky to Union City, Indiana. Everything and everyone I had ever known were far away; I was a lost little girl badly in need of a substitute grandpa. I found Charlie and Marie Snyder.

We rented their farmhouse on South Stateline Rd. Their newly built ranch was back to back with our house, so it was one big back yard. I was constantly outside playing and climbing the willow tree that grew in the middle of the open space.

The Snyder's had a grandson, but since I was always underfoot, they "adopted" me. Every day, Mrs. Snyder had me over for either lunch or snacks, and my mother's perpetual and half-hearted fussing that I was bothering them did not affect my new grandma or me. She cooked and I ate; we were happy.

One day after lunch, Mr. Snyder set up this checkerboard. He had played for sixty years and was a champ. Mrs. Snyder wouldn't play with him anymore. His grandson and two daughters had no interest, so I was drafted.

It became our daily ritual. We ate lunch, then played from 12 o'clock until 2:00 when his favorite show, *As the World Turns,* came on. We would play several games as each was over quickly. I was no match for his skills. Once or twice he showed me a trick of his; I would also watch him intently to see how he beat me.

Some evenings I would get my father to play a game, and he would teach me new skills. I wanted to be a good player so that my new grandpa wouldn't get tired of winning so easily; I didn't want to lose his attention. Gradually the games took longer to play before Mr. Snyder won.

Then just before I started third grade, Mom and Dad bought a house in Greenville, Ohio, which was twelve miles away. We came to visit most Sundays after church as they missed Papa King also; the Snyder's were a good substitute. When Mr. Snyder saw us, the checkerboard came out. One Sunday I actually won a game. After that day, we always had to play best-two-out-of-three to find the winner. We played many Sundays over the years, and Mrs. Snyder said he really looked forward to my visits and our games.

When he died, I quit playing checkers. No one wanted to play. That is, until my daughter was born. We started playing when she was about five, and it's still her favorite game. Maybe someday she will teach her own children to play. If she doesn't, I will.

Here I Come

My father worked in a men's clothing store on the weekends while he and mother were going to Murray State-- that's how he bought her a radio for Christmas. The two owners really liked Dad and asked him to buy into the store. Both were older and one wanted to retire.

If my father had had the money to buy the one partner out, he would have been half-owner. The store was doing well and both partners were comfortably well-off. Papa King would have loaned my father the money, but Dad didn't feel he could do that. I guess it was his pride that made him want to work out a way himself. My parents were both twenty-seven and wanted to be independent.

Then mother became pregnant. The G.I. Bill and Dad's weekend job supported them marginally if they lived in married housing, but there was no room or money for a baby. Mom was planning to become a CPA, and Dad was studying to be a veterinarian. Neither wanted children as they considered themselves too old-- this was 1949. They wanted to finish college and establish themselves in good careers. Becoming a partner in that clothing store was a very good start.

However, sometimes the "cookie" doesn't crumble just right. Both were flabbergasted. They saw their carefully planned futures swirling down the drain. Now, there was no possible way to buy that partnership. They quickly came up with a new plan; both took education courses that spring so that they could teach in the public schools if necessary. Then they quit college and went to live with Papa King. Mom's extended family could help care for her during the pregnancy and after I was born. Dad began selling cows and hogs; then cured hams and sold them.

Pregnant women couldn't get jobs in 1949, so my mother tried selling World Book Encyclopedias from door-to-door. She wasn't very good at it. She told me later that she only sold one set other than the one she purchased herself at a discounted rate. She really didn't have much time or energy to devote to walking door-to-door; I was due soon.

On Thursday, October 6, she went into labor. Papa and Daddy rushed her to the Owensboro Hospital, but it was a long wait. She spent twenty-two hours in labor and didn't dilate. Dr. Parker arrived at the hospital in a tuxedo, and was very unhappy with his staff for allowing her to go so long. He hadn't been notified. His staff gave mother a spinal and prepped her for surgery. The doctor cut her wider, and pulled me out with forceps. It was 8:22 PM, Friday night, October 7.

Mom said I was the ugliest baby she had ever seen. I had 3-inch black hair all over my head. That stands to reason as mother's hair was black, but they both had hoped for my dad's mane of curly blonde. The nurse took me out and cleaned me up. She put spit curls all through my hair before bringing me back. Mother said the hairdo didn't help; it only made me look worse.

She was disappointed that I wasn't a boy, but Dad wanted a girl from the beginning. He was happy when he heard the news-- black hair and all.

The hospital staff wouldn't let him see Mom that night because she was exhausted, especially after they stitched her back together. A nurse told Papa King and my dad to go home and get some rest. They could see her in the morning; he and Papa left.

Saturday morning, Daddy went to a floral shop to buy flowers. He found a tall pink Hull vase which cost $15 without any flowers. That was expensive back then, but my father was determined to buy it. He has always been good at haggling for his price. He found a glazing flaw on the top rim and talked the owner down to $12. That was all the money he had. Since he had nothing left to buy flowers, he picked them from neighbors' yards, and added wild ones to the grouping as he drove to the hospital.

Mom loved the flowers and vase, and Dad loved me. She got to come home a week or so later, and soon my black hair fell out. White-blond hair came in behind it, and mother decided I was much better looking. I guess those spit curls which resembled a 1920's flapper-style must have been awful! There are certainly no pictures of me with them.

My mother kept that vase closed by all the rest of her life. Often it was filled with red roses. It stayed in a prominent place in her corner cabinet, and was still there when she died. Now I have it. A couple of antique dealers have offered to buy it over the years, and they have offered a very good price. Not a chance!

Broken Things

When Mom and Dad were teaching in Beaver Dam, Kentucky, they made a whole $3,000 between them. They were able to rent a house there for a year and move from Papa King's. They didn't have many furnishings, but they had managed to pick up a few pieces.

First they got rid of the gray Naugahyde couch which I had damaged and replaced it with a beautiful tapestry covered Dunkin Phyfe style. They bought it from someone who no longer wanted it. It did have a broken back leg, but Dad repaired it.

We had that television set that Papa had helped buy—luckily the Beaver Dam house had an antenna. We had a metal kitchen table and chairs with Naugahyde seats which Orela's family gave us. And, of course, Mom and Dad still had the radio from their college days.

Dad bought Mom a singer sewing machine with lots of attachments, and they had bought a new chair to go with the couch at a close-out sale in Owensboro. They paid for it in full and were to pick it up in 3 weeks as it was to be upholstered in a coordinating color.

When they went back, their chair was sitting in the window but the store had gone bankrupt. They tried several times to get the chair, but the bank said it was now part of their assets and wouldn't give it to them. I don't know which bank it was, but an officer there said it wasn't the bank's problem, and it didn't have to honor any receipts. I remember Mother saying that never again would she pay for something in full until it was delivered to our house and we were satisfied.

She held to that vow her whole life, and could be very inflexible. I don't blame her because we needed a chair, and the one we bought took all the extra money we had. Now we had no money and no extra seat. I

67

never heard them speak about that chair again, but I know it bothered Dad.

A few months later when he was making his rounds of local farms checking on his students' projects, someone offered him a beautiful antique chair which was stored in the barn. It actually was very similar to the one they lost.

He was so excited when he brought it home, but Mom wouldn't let it in the house. It was covered in pigeon poop, and a nest, complete with a mouse, was inside the bottom of the seat. Mouse poop and fly specks also decorated it. However, it was solid walnut with not a bit of damage, and very sturdy.

That weekend Dad cleaned it up with Spic and Span and got the nest out—the mouse had already escaped. Then he put it in the living room. The upholstery was really ugly but in good condition. All it needed was to be reupholstered, and it wouldn't even take much material—just a seat and back. The little arm pads could be covered with left-over scraps.

Mom found some gold damask and matching braid at an upholstery shop. It was the end of the bolt, so the store owner sold it to her at one-third the price. One of Orela's relatives could re-cover chairs, so he got the job. The stuffing was in perfect shape except around the mouse nest. He cleaned that all out, and put in new batting. The chair was beautiful when he delivered it about a week later.

Mom was so proud when she sat it in the living room, that there was a tear in each eye. She wouldn't let us sit on it for over a week. Mom contacted Mrs. Tarter, her antique dealer friend, who came to see it; she was impressed.

The gentleman who upholstered it wouldn't take any money except for the extra stuffing and tacks. So Dad helped him out on his small farm—either he trimmed the mules hooves or gave his few pigs some shots. That chair cost almost nothing, and made up for the one lost.

Then Papa King got into the act. Beaver Dam was more or less as far from Hartford as Morgantown is from Nashville, 15 or so miles. We still went to Hartford for church on Sundays, and after chicken at Casebier's, we would go to Papa's for the day.

One Sunday, Papa was so proud of himself that mother said he was about to pop a button. In someone's old chicken coop, a very large, ornate gilded picture frame had been stored, and he bought it for my mother.

It had an inner frame with an oval opening for the picture. We went out to the meat house where he had stored it to see this prize. Some of the plaster designs were missing and so was the glass. The inner frame was separated from the outer and the whole thing was splattered with chicken poop and old stuck feathers. Mom smiled bravely and thanked

Papa over and over as she knew how proud he was. We took it home in the trunk of the car that evening.

Mom didn't know what to do; she didn't want to hurt Papa's feelings, but she didn't think it could be restored. But Dad said not to worry. He used Spic and Span, a basting brush, and a toothbrush to gently clean the crud out of all the little decorative plaster scrolls. Then he used tooth picks to get the really tiny openings and comb-work clean. When it no longer smelled like a chicken coup, he brought it in and put it on the kitchen table. We were eating our meals in front of the television, so he was free to use it as a work bench.

First I watched him carefully glue the oval inner frame back into the outer part and reinforce it with brackets. Then each night over several weeks, he worked on the frame to restore the plaster work. He used the old type of children's modeling clay—the type that got hard when it wasn't being played with and had to be softened by kneading.

Dad would get it very soft. He would use a tiny bit of car paste wax brushed onto the plaster designs so the clay wouldn't stick. Then he would push this modeling clay onto the frame. Being soft, it conformed perfectly to the design. He allowed it to harden overnight. Then he would peel the newly formed mold off and fill it with plaster of Paris.

When it hardened, he gently removed the plaster cast and cleaned it up if needed. He used his pocket knife to trim the edges to fit where the missing designs had been. Then he would smear a layer of household glue to the back of the plaster to seal it. When that dried, he used more glue to attach it to the frame.

He'd smooth it out or fill in any cracks with thick plaster or spackling compound or even wood dough. When the entire frame was repaired, he re-gilded it and cut a piece of glass from an old window he found somewhere. The frame looked as if it had never been damaged.

Mom got an art print catalogue and ordered "The Southern Bell" to put in it. She proudly hung it in the living room in Beaver Dam and in every place we lived after that. I still have it. Dad did an amazing job of repairing it, and I learned from him how to do the repair and how to cut glass. I used his technique to repair old frames I have bought over the years.

I also discovered I could use the same process to repair missing wood decorations by using wood-dough in the right color as it doesn't stain well. This served me well when I started a small antique business.

It's hard now to get that old modeling clay. Most is the non-hardening type. Play-do works but not as well because it won't conform to the decorative work. So, I don't do much frame or furniture repairing anymore. However Dad's glass repair was the start of my making stained glass objects.

I still make stained glass items, even today. I learned from him that if someone says it can't be done or will be extremely labor intensive and expensive, it only means a creative method hasn't been found yet. Mom and I firmly believed Dad could fix anything, and he always did.

A Hot Dog, a Coke Bottle, and Toothpicks

My father was always making little things for me. Often, he'd stay up late, after I'd gone to bed, to make some little surprise for me to discover when I woke up in the morning. His tools often involved just glue, toothpicks, or other odds and ends, and his imagination.

One morning, when I went into the kitchen, I found a wiener dog sitting on a plate on the table. He had taken a hot dog, strips of cheese, two cloves, a stuffed olive, and toothpicks, and fashioned a dog sitting on his haunches. The cloves were its eyes and the big olive was its head. He reinforced the cheese with toothpicks to form the legs, tail, and ears.

I thought it was wonderful and wanted to save it, but such items won't last. I ate it for my lunch that day. I wish someone had taken a picture of it because the one I attempted to make for Erin years later just didn't look as realistic. It sagged in the middle; maybe Dad's did too, but I thought it was a work of art.

Another time he made me a 3.5 inch cricket cage out of flat toothpicks. It had a gabled roof and a door that slid upward. When a visiting friend nagged at me to give her the little house, and I did, Dad used toothpicks and made me a small Chinese-style house with a sliding door panel. He glued it to a wooden base and made hedges out of a fibrous material and colored it green with markers. I had two little Chinese people inside made from the tops of clothespins and then painted.

But one of the funniest creations of his came after I received a Barbie doll for Christmas. When those dolls came out in the late '50's, people howled. Her shape was very different from any doll ever seen before, and people said she wasn't normal.

The only problem I saw was that I couldn't put any of my other dolls' clothes on her--they didn't fit. Mom did buy me a couple of Barbie outfits, but they were expensive for the time period. She had always made my dolls' clothes from patterns purchased at the fabric shop. There weren't any Barbie patterns at that time--the doll was too new. My mother had become a good seamstress, but she needed to use those patterns, and trying to just "eyeball" it wouldn't work.

Even my father tried his hand. He wanted to surprise me, but since I usually had a death grip on that doll, he couldn't get it secretly away to make the clothes. So, he used a coke bottle. He knew the bottle and the doll had curvy shapes, but he didn't consider how tiny Barbie's waist was. He too was used to seeing other dolls which had regular sized torsos.

He spent hours each night for two weeks making all sorts of dresses, blouses, hats, skirts, a coat, and a nightgown. It was all handwork--buttons, hems, elastic; he didn't use the sewing machine. I didn't know my father could sew so well! I loved the clothes.

Of course, they didn't fit my Barbie, but I didn't care. I played with my Coca-Cola doll for months. Dad even glued a ping pong ball on top of the bottle for a head, so she could wear her hats. We painted on a face and glued yellow yarn to the ball for hair.

That "doll" was a favorite of mine for a long time. It became Barbie's companion since I didn't get a Midge doll, who was supposed to be her best friend. I still have my Barbie, but I have no idea what happened to Miss Coca-Cola or her clothes, and that's one item not found on e-Bay.

The Midget Wedding

I remember going to two nuptials when I was a small child. Both gave me the Cinderella idea of a storybook wedding to Prince Charming and the "happily ever after" romantic life, which was to follow. So much so, that my mother bought a whole bridal doll kit of sew-your-own outfits for me one Christmas. It consisted of the dolls with their bride, maid-of-honor, and the bride's maid costumes. Mom was sewing for a while just so I could constantly play wedding.

One of those nuptials involved my much older first cousin. It was an elegant Catholic version with much ritual, and very impressive. However, it was the other one, which I remember the best. This involved a good friend of my father. Some of the particulars, I never knew because grown-ups in the early '50's didn't explain in great detail to children. I will relate what I do remember being told and observing myself.

My parents and I, their only child, lived with Papa King, my grandfather, in Harford, Kentucky. My father traveled during the week, working for the Health Department. I do not know whether he met the

71

gentleman during his travels or if Dad knew him from college days. I do know that the two were good friends.

My father was six feet two and his buddy was a midget just a little taller than I was. It is possible that the man worked with animals and Dad treated those animals. It is also possible that he worked as an actor or with a circus. As my dad had friends from all over, from deep sea divers, to Romas with small circuses, I might have the how of the meeting entirely wrong.

I had never met the bride although I imagine my mother knew her. Dad, of course, did. The lights were dimmed so that the multitude of candle flames shimmered in the sanctuary. The members of the wedding party were also midgets, most likely family. One bride's maid, however, was average height. Everyone wore variations of silver and white. The bride was entirely in white satin with a satin trimmed veil. Her bouquet was silver and white with tiny blue flowers.

I sat next to the aisle when the bride with her ladies slowly marched from the back of the church to the altar. Her reddish, light-brown hair was short; she looked like a child just my size. I was so excited because I saw that she was little like me, and so were her maids or "playmates." I assumed the taller maid was her mother. I thought that Daddy's friend was marrying a little girl my age, which meant that whenever they came over, she would bring her maids, and I would have several playmates. I would no longer be sent to play alone in my room when grownups came visiting. Such was the case in those years when children were to be "seen and not heard."

Because I was watching a wedding of "little girls" my size, I fantasized that the bride was me. Every romantic fairytale, which Papa or Daddy read at nightly story time was traveling through my brain. I was so happy to "know" that such dreams could come true to a lonely child such as me. Being cloistered all of my short life, I didn't have any playmates, but I was sure some would be provided so I could have a boy and several girls as friends as soon as I got married.

Weddings were relatively simple affairs during that time period, so the reception was punch and cake in the church basement. There was no formal dinner or dance. After eating my piece of cake, I ran up to the newly married girl and asked if she wanted to play…I suggested either hide-and-seek or tag in the empty hallways, which led to the school rooms and meeting areas. I received quite a shock. She had a grownup voice, not a child's. And she spoke to me as if she were an adult and I, a little girl.

I was confused and hurt. However, as my mother had trained me well, I didn't make a scene. I politely said I was sorry that she couldn't play, told her how lovely she looked, and escaped. I walked to my father's side and stayed glued to him until he figured out that something was wrong.

As soon as he could, he walked me aside and asked what the problem was. I told him that I had thought she was my age, and had asked her to play, and that she talked adult-like to me. I also said that I didn't understand. He kindly reminded me his friend was a grownup, of which I was well aware. Using this man as an anchor point to guide me through my confusion, he soon had me understanding that the bride was really an adult also. His midget buddy hadn't married a three year old.

The reality didn't stop my day dreaming about weddings and the "happily-ever-after." As long as I played with dolls, their wardrobes had to have bridal and bride's maid dresses included. My mother dutifully made sure that Santa hand-sewed such clothing for each doll, be it Barbie, Renewal Jolly Twins doll house dolls, or Betsy Wetsy.

A Romantic Return

My mother's maiden name was King, and she ran around the University with a male buddy whose last name was also King. Dad had spotted my mother around campus and thought she was good looking, but he assumed she was married--a Mrs. King. So, he didn't pay attention to her. Mom had flirted with him, but because all he ever said was, "Hump,"-as she remembered, she didn't like him. She thought he was stuck up. Imagine their surprise when both wound up together on a double date.

Dad discovered she wasn't married; her companion for the night was a different man entirely! She discovered he wasn't a snob, but actually a nice guy. Everyone was having a great time; sometime during the evening, my parent's dates left with each other. I think Mom and Dad were a little surprised at the rudeness, but they got over the awkwardness very quickly.

They headed for a ride on the Ferris wheel. When they started talking (and probably flirting), the night went too quickly for both. It was long past dorm curfew for my mother when he brought her back, but she and her pack of girlfriends always used a first floor window after hours. A special rap on the glass notified the girls inside to take out the screen. Dad helped my mother climb in. That was it; he was in love.

It was a couple of months later that he planned to propose. He took her to a small seafood restaurant and got them a table near the back by a window. After a romantic dinner, he proposed; she said, "Yes," and they were married at Papa King's house in Hartford on September 6, 1947.

Now Marvin Parks, my mother's uncle, lived in Bowling Green, a short distance from the college. My parents often visited them, and I remember Uncle Marvin and especially Aunt Rosie to be wonderful people. Later, when we moved to Ohio, we still dropped by for overnight visits while on our way to see other family members or to vacations in other states.

Then sometime in the early 1960's, Mom and Dad decided that while they were visiting my great uncle and aunt, they would go back to that little seafood restaurant—yes, it was still there because Dad had checked. We spent time with Aunt Rosie and Uncle Marvin, and then went to explore the college campus. Around six or seven, we headed over to "their restaurant."

Somehow, my dad managed to get the same table by the window where he had proposed; he had his ways of getting what he wanted. Maybe he had reserved it earlier with a small tip to the manager. Or maybe he just told them about the proposal in 1947. At any rate, the table was waiting and we were ushered directly to it. It was covered with a red checked tablecloth.

I ordered shrimp, and I think my parents ordered what they had back when they were single. That made it seem more romantic to them. It didn't seem so romantic to me—the place was very full, and I was squeezed against the wall. Mom had shrimp and scallops, and my father had fish and clams.

I'd eaten in better restaurants by then, but I don't think my parents would have noticed if they had been served horseflies and dried leaves. They were holding hands, smiling, and staring into each other's eyes. They definitely were back in the past.

I ate my shrimp but skipped the nasty tasting cocktail sauce. The tartar sauce wasn't any better. I also kept quiet and ignored my love-struck family members while being bumped by a loud fat man at the next table. I kept telling myself that things would have been different here in 1947. We stayed quite a while; it was getting dark as we left and headed back to my aunt and uncle's house.

Dad wasn't feeling too well as he drove back—he was getting sick to his stomach, and turning white. His forehead was clammy. Mom asked if he had noticed if his food tasted odd or maybe the tartar sauce. He said that he didn't think it did, but as I said, they were more into each other and the past, not their meal in the present.

Either the clams or fish fillets were spoiled, because my father now had a strong dose of food poisoning. When we arrived at Uncle Marvin's, Dad had to be helped inside; his legs were rubbery. He started to lie down on top of the bed, but had to quickly stagger to the bathroom close by.

Mom was scared and Aunt Rosie offered to take him to the hospital or call an ambulance. Dad said, no, he would be alright. But he wasn't. He was sick many times throughout the night; he became so weak from vomiting that Aunt Rosie put a large bucket beside the bed. He couldn't make it to the bathroom anymore.

We stayed there for a week while Mother and my aunt nursed him around the clock. I spent my time out in the back yard. The entire area was one big flower garden with paths winding throughout; I loved the hollyhocks the best. It gave me something to do as Uncle Marvin was at work during the day, and the women considered me to just be in the way—or, at least, Mother did. She kept telling me to go outside and stay there. I was allowed to look in on him from the door, but I was not allowed in the room.

Later in the week, he sat on the couch in the living room, wrapped in a blanket, with his feet propped up on a foot stool. Over Mother's protests, he wanted me to sit next to him. We even played a few card games like "Go Fish" or "Old Maid" when he was stronger and feeling well enough to be fidgety and bored.

He was still weak, but said he was very tired of chicken broth and dry toast, and being fussed over; he flashed me his silly big toothy grin. Yup, Dad was getting better! I may have been 13 or 14, but my daddy was still my whole world, and my not being allowed near him had made me worry more than if I had been given the chance to help.

Finally, Dad was much stronger, and he wanted to get on with our vacation plans. We thanked my great aunt and uncle for their care and hospitality, packed up the car, and headed out of town. They certainly were *not* stopping to eat when they passed that restaurant.

My father sheepishly grinned at Mom and said, "They say you can never go back again." She started laughing until tears rolled down her cheeks. Then she said, "And we're *never* going to either." She was very relieved that her husband was back to normal as she had never seen him so sick before. That restaurant and his food poisoning were not mentioned again. So much for their romantic return to the past!

The Ice House

Ice is something very common. Whenever a person wants it, the refrigerator is close by. But when I was little, not everyone had an electric refrigerator to make ice. Some folks had big chunks of the cold stuff brought to their house in a truck. Then the driver would get in the back and use large ice tongs to carry in a 25-pound or bigger block to put in someone's icebox. A card in a front window told the iceman if or how much ice was needed that week.

I had never seen an icehouse, so one winter evening, my father took me to the one by Hartford. Being around three, my memory of its location is faulty. We were down by Green River, and I watched men dragging blocks of ice as big as end tables. The ground was wet and slippery; it had to be or the wooden skids or sleds the blocks sat on wouldn't have moved. Men hauled them up ramps into the icehouse for storage until summer. Dad told me the large blocks were cut from the river when it froze over.

Inside the icehouse, the blocks were covered with straw or sawdust to help insulate and slow down the melting. I remember the place was cold and damp, and even though the men were dressed warmly, their clothes and shoes got wet.

Dad's shoes and mine were very wet from just walking around. My feet hurt from the cold. My father offered to let me sit on one of the ice blocks, but I was cold all over, and sitting on ice would have made me colder still. I remember wanting to leave, but my dad wasn't ready to. He had some business with one of the men there-- maybe he was looking for work.

He put me in the car, and turned on the motor. I was shivering, and the heat felt so good. I fell asleep quickly, and don't remember the ride home or being put to bed. I just remember the greenish cast of the dim lights from lanterns and bare light bulbs, the chilling dampness, and many men talking and working quickly.

It looked like rough work when I think back on it. The men had to wait until the winter temperature was cold enough for the river to freeze hard and thick--enough to walk on and hold the sawing equipment. I don't know if they cut the blocks during the day or just at night. I also don't know if they moved the blocks to the icehouse by day or only by night.

Dad did say that it was colder at night and there was less melting to work then. But what I did learn from that visit was an appreciation for how easy it is to get ice today. I push my glass up to the door dispenser and push; out comes either crushed ice or cubes-- my choice. Sometimes though, I think about what I saw as a child in the 1950's. It was a cold job I wouldn't have wanted.

The Black Widow

My father was always warning me to be careful of black widow spiders; he said their "bite" was very poisonous. There were always some in Papa King's outhouse up high in the corners, and my father kept the place sprayed so that Papa, Mother, Peggy, and I wouldn't have to worry when we needed to "potty." Mom especially feared having those spiders drop down on her head; she was more afraid of them than of snakes. Dad was very protective of us, but he should have been more careful of himself.

The summer we moved to a house in Beaver Dam, he was working outside in the garage. Mom and I were inside when he came in holding his left eye. Somehow a black widow had landed on his face and bit him right in the fold on the outside of his eye. Mom rushed my father to the doctor.

Doc did what he could, but this was 1954. He did say Dad had been lucky. The skin was thin and the fangs had gone in deep to inject the poison, but none had got in the eye itself. Otherwise, Dad might have lost his sight. Still my father wasn't over the worst yet.

He spent the next week and longer in a lot of pain. I mostly remember him lying down with a cold ice pack on the side of his face to keep down the swelling. He didn't eat much and tried to sleep most of the time. Dad said he hurt all over. We tried to be very quiet around him because his head hurt so much he couldn't take the noise. As he got better, Dad still didn't move very fast.

The poison seemed to have affected his whole body. It was about three weeks before he was up and flashing that silly grin of his again. After that incident, he always had two scars near his eye the size of small round pin heads. That's where the spider's fangs penetrated his skin.

I learned right then to have a hardy respect for black widows and to stay well away from them. Even when Dad later that same summer put two such spiders in a tightly fastened jar for me to watch, I knew not to open the lid. It was his way of teaching me exactly what they looked like close up. I've never forgotten.

Leaf Raking Day

In the autumn, I couldn't wait for the golden leaves to start falling. When enough were on the ground, Dad and I would grab rakes and start heaping those crunchy cracklies into two large piles--one for each of us. Then we'd lean the rakes against a tree and dive in. We would throw handfuls at each other or tunnel inside.

Sometimes I'd stuff some down Dad's shirt. When we tired of such games, Dad and I would rake all the scattered leaves into one big stack and lie down. If Mom came to check on our progress, we'd tell her we were resting. Sometimes Dad and I would talk, but usually we just looked at the clouds. I'd spot a cat or elephant shape and show him. Then it would be his turn to find something and show me.

It wouldn't be long before I'd hear a snort and a buzz-saw noise and know my father was asleep. The leaves would be soft, the temperature mildly warm, and a bright sun would add extra heat through our clothing. I'd put my head on Dad's stomach and nap too for a short while. Then one of us would wake up and shake the other, and we'd head inside for hot chocolate and maybe a bologna sandwich.

After our snack, we would go back outside and start piling our leaves into the wheel barrow. I'd hop on top, and he'd wheel us out to the now bare ground in the garden. I'd get out and toss the leaves over the side. Then we would go for another load.

We had tarpaulins, but neither of us suggested raking all the leaves onto one and pulling it to the garden. It would have saved us some work. Maybe it was just more fun our way. I was ten or eleven before he stopped giving me rides in the wheelbarrow. I'm sure I was getting very heavy by that time, but he never complained.

When all the leaves we had raked that day were heaped in the garden, Dad and I would put branches on top to keep the pile intact. We collected those branches all spring and summer and stacked them behind the garden next to the farm fence just for this purpose.

Next, he would cut three green branches from one of our maple trees while I dragged three folding lawn chairs from the patio and arranged them around our soon-to-be bonfire. Dad would alert my mother that we were ready, and I would bring out two trays--the type used to hold a Banquet TV dinner while watching television.

All three of us would then grab hot dogs, buns, marshmallows, mustard, relish, napkins, plus a butter knife and spoon for the condiments. Mom would get the bottle opener and three bottles of Coke. Everything fit on those two trays. Dad would light the fire, and we'd all sit up close for warmth; by then the air was chilly. When the fire was just right, Dad would pass out the green, sharpened branches, and the three of us would each grab a hot dog, impale it, and start roasting.

Mom liked hers evenly browned, Dad cooked his different ways, and I liked mine with some charred spots for taste. I didn't use relish or mustard; I preferred the smoky flavor all by itself. I'd wrap the bun around the dog while it was still on the stick and pull it off. Extra black got on the bread that way.

In my opinion, no wiener ever tastes as good as one cooked over a bonfire on an October evening. The smell of the meat mixed with burning leaves and twigs adds a smoky perfume to the air, hair, and clothing. I've always liked that smell; it seems so warm and peaceful--a smell of home.

After sitting awhile, we would open the marshmallows and roast them. I liked mine charcoaled on the outside and melted into a cream inside. I'd set several on fire and watch the flames shoot high like a torch before blowing them out. I'd pull them off with my fingers and gingerly savor each one so as not to burn my tongue. Dad wanted his evenly toasted, and Mother's had to just be warm.

The magic of the happy evening would die with the fire. Mom and I would take the trays and food inside. I would take the chairs back to the patio, and Dad would spread the coals and spray water to make sure the fire was out.

When my father and I went inside, Mom would be watching *Gunsmoke*, *Rawhide*, or *Perry Mason*. Dad would bring in the family cat who was only allowed in if someone held him. Then, still in his jacket with a stocking cap pulled down over his ears, Dad would lie down on the large braided rug in a fetal position, hold the cat, and fall asleep. The cat would purr in harmony with Dad's snores.

Shortly it would be bedtime for me. I didn't mind. I'd be under the warm covers and could breathe the smoky-hot-dog, sweet-charred-marshmallow, leaf-fire smell still lingering in my hair. I'd fall asleep with a full stomach and happy dreams of that Saturday and of the next leaf-raking day to come.

The Lawnmower Accident

As most children do, I thought of my parents as invincible--incapable of being harmed or getting really sick. That notion was badly shaken when I was somewhere around nine years old.

Dad had not yet bought a riding lawnmower for our new place and was using a push one to do our acre yard. He'd always warned me not to get close while he was using it, because it would throw rocks. I didn't pay much attention because I didn't think we had rocks in our grass. I just wanted to be close to him when he mowed. Dad would keep warning me to stay clear, and I would for a short while.

Then one afternoon, the unthinkable happened. He was mowing the back yard when an inch-long piece of heavy wire flew into his lower leg, cutting an artery. He fell in the grass, calling for help. Our neighbor, Mr. Marsh, was working his garden; he heard the cry and ran to Dad. His wife Ginny called an ambulance while he lifted my father up and half carried him toward the front yard.

Mother and I were inside our house when the commotion began. We ran out the garage door, which was attached to our kitchen, just as my father collapsed on the sidewalk; Mr. Marsh tried to lift him up. Mom started hopping in circles around them. She was frantic and mostly in the way. I just stood watching. I wanted to get Mom back because Dad said, "Millie, let him do it." But seeing how upset she was, I was afraid to pull her hand or even touch her. So I just stood there feeling helpless.

Dad couldn't get up again, he was too weak, and so Mr. Marsh dragged him into the front yard. There was a trail of blood all the way. The ambulance arrived just then. The paramedics tied a tourniquet around my father's leg, rushed him onto a gurney and into the ambulance. They headed for the hospital.

There wasn't room in the vehicle for Mother--although I suspect they didn't want her in there with two men working on Dad and one driving, plus she was rather incoherent. She was trying to push everyone away so she could get to Dad.

Mrs. Marsh was there and took control. She told her husband that they were taking Mother to the hospital. They all three rushed next door to the car. Ginny held onto Mom in the back seat while Mr. Marsh drove.

I just stood there watching as my dad, covered in blood, was taken away, and my mother, seemingly insane, was physically held and dragged to a car and also taken away. I was left behind. No one remembered I was there in all the chaos. I wasn't old enough to understand fully what had happened, and no one told me anything.

I went back to the side garage door and sat on the stoop. I saw the trail of blood which led from the back yard grass to the sidewalk. I saw the bigger pool where Dad fell, and then the blood trail where Mr. Marsh dragged him into the front yard and onto the paved driveway.

Mom had taught me to wax, polish, iron, scrub, and clean since before we had purchased the new house. Helping her was something we could do together, and, by that time, that was all we had in common. In my young mind, I thought there was something I should be doing to help; Mother might be angry with me if the blood were left there. I think I was in shock too and needed some physical activity to keep me from thinking. I hooked up the hose and began washing the driveway and sidewalk. I used a scrub brush in some places.

Then I washed the grass all the way back to the mower. When all the blood was gone, I pushed the mower into the tool shed and shut the door. I knew Mom wouldn't want to see that either when she came back.

Since I'd seen lots of cowboy shows on television where the bad guy is shot, falls down, and dies, I think I believed that's what had happened to Dad--the mower shot him, he had fallen down, and the ambulance had taken him away to die. I didn't expect him to come back, but I figured Mom would sometime. How she would behave when she returned unnerved me. Strong emotions caused her to lash out either verbally or physically, and I had never seen her so upset. Dad wouldn't be there, only me.

I fed and watered Champion, our Boxer, and the cat. Then I made sure the house was straight and that I had nothing of mine out. I ate some cold black-eyed peas and cornbread. Mom and I often ate cold leftovers when Dad was working at school or on farms; there weren't any microwaves back then. It was one of my favorite leftovers. Then I washed my dishes.

I went back outside and turned Champion loose. He had been my companion for years--I had shared my ice-cream and cereal with him at Papa King's. I was feeling lonely and playing with him helped. When it got dark, I took him inside with me to watch television. He and I shared a couple of Milk Bone dog biscuits while watching Perry Mason, Mom's favorite program.

Mrs. Futrell came to the door right as the show was ending. She came inside and told me Mrs. Marsh had called her. Dad had been operated on and was doing fine. Mom would be home after he woke up. I asked if my father would be coming home too, and she said not for a while.

She cooked me a TV dinner that she found in the freezer while we watched another show. After eating, I fell asleep on the floor holding

Champion. I wouldn't go to my room, so she gave me my pillow and blanket and let me sleep there; then she left.

When my mother returned many hours later, she put Champion back on his chain and sent me to bed. We were up early the next morning; after cereal and milk, my mom took me with her to the hospital.

Every day for what seemed like forever, we went to see Dad. Children weren't allowed in the hospital rooms back then or even in the waiting area unless accompanied by an adult. Mother found a couple of bricks somewhere and put them underneath Dad's window.

Luckily he was on the first floor. I had to stand on my tip-toes, even with the bricks; only my eyes could see above the sill. I'd jump and wave and my father would wave back. That's when I knew the mower hadn't shot and killed him like in my Lone Ranger shows. Until I actually saw Dad, I didn't believe he was alive.

When he finally got to come home, I wouldn't let him out of my sight. I'd just sit quietly nearby so not to disturb him if he slept, and when he needed anything, I'd run to get it for him.

Sometimes I woke up at night and checked on him. Then I'd get my pillow and blanket and sleep on the floor next to his side of the bed.

As soon as he was up and well, he bought a riding lawnmower. I had learned my lesson; I stayed well away from it when he was mowing, but close enough to make sure this mower didn't shoot him.

Fishing

One of the times my parents and I vacationed in Florida, Dad wanted to go deep sea fishing. He quit fishing before I was born, so it was a bit of a surprise. Anyway, we joined a group going out in the Atlantic for that purpose. Most folks didn't catch anything, me included.

Dad was "lucky"; he hooked an octopus. Each arm was about a foot long and that unhappy critter was pink. It crawled up the line and started down the fishing pole. Mom screamed, "Bradley, drop it, drop it!" My father dropped the pole on the deck and one of the crew members grabbed the creature. He put the octopus in a box-type refrigerator.

The only other catch in the box was some type of fish about 3 feet long. We didn't get to keep the octopus, but that was okay by me. The way it started down that fishing pole said it meant business, and I think it was mad. I don't believe octopi turn pink when they're happy! No more fishing for me. That was too fresh.

Tid Bit

My father loved to hunt, fish, and frog gig which was only natural as he grew up on a farm during the 1920's and 30's. He stopped gigging when some fresh frog legs attacked Mom from her frying pan. After that, she refused also to fry fish; she stuck to salmon or tuna from a can. Anything else had to be frozen and breaded so she could bake it in the oven.

So, Dad stopped fishing as well. He did try to interest me in the sport when I was 10. We went to a large, deep pond fed by the river below our house. In the hot summer, the channel would dry up, and the fish would be trapped in the pond until heavy rains would flood the whole area. There were lots of different fish in it, both big and small. Sun fish probably were the most prominent.

We took two bamboo poles and a can of worms, climbed the farm fence, and walked around the cows and cow patties to the only tree in the pasture. It was a huge dying elm right next to the pond. It didn't give much shade, but we could lean against the trunk.

I didn't like sticking hooks through wiggly worms because of the black muddy stuff that would come out on my fingers. Also I was sure that the sharp point hurt them, and I felt like a torturer. So Dad baited the hook for me. I learned how to flip out the line and sit watching for the bobber to go under. I had trouble sitting still and not talking. That part was boring.

When the bobber went under, Dad showed me how to bring in the line. I had caught a pretty little sun fish. He tossed it back in after removing the hook which it had swallowed. I had wanted to take it home to put in a fish bowl, but my father said it would die because of swallowing the metal hook.

Today hooks are made of something that will disintegrate if they are swallowed, and supposedly the fish will be all right. At least, that's what I have been told. Not so back then. I didn't want to fish anymore that day because I knew I'd caused a fish to die. He took me one other time, but we didn't catch anything; I'm glad we didn't. Then I told him I didn't want to fish anymore. He said OK, and we went home.

I don't remember him ever fishing again, until we went out on the ocean. Maybe he saw fishing through my eyes or figured there wasn't any reason to go if Mom wouldn't cook or eat it, and I wouldn't be his fishing buddy. He just packed his poles away.

Then one squirrel season, he decided to go hunting. Wild rabbits had some disease and couldn't be eaten, but Dad wanted us to try fried squirrel. He came back home late that Saturday afternoon with five dead adults and a tiny live baby. He seemed very sad.

He had shot a squirrel going into a hole in the tree. When he climbed up to get it, he discovered that he'd killed a momma and two of her babies. He brought the third one home to try to save it. We had fried squirrel for Sunday dinner and it was good, but he put his guns away after cleaning them just like he did the fishing poles.

Dad and I concentrated on saving the baby whom we named Tid Bit. He checked some of the books he had and called a friend in the forestry service. It's called the DNR today. We took one of my doll baby bottles and fed little Tid Bit a milk formula round the clock and kept him warm on a heating pad. That little scamp knew he was special; and as he grew, he got into everything.

He usually ran loose in the house except at night when we kept him in a large bird cage in the heated garage. That was for his protection and to ensure we got some sleep. During the day, he liked to climb up our legs to the table or counter and beg for dog or cat food. Tid Bit knew we always had *something* he'd want to eat.

He would sit on my shoulders or head when I watched television and chatter at the cat through the window. My father adored him; Tid Bit could do no wrong. Dad taught him to walk a clothesline and laughed when he knocked things off shelves.

Mom wasn't too thrilled when our "baby" as she called him, opened the talcum powder in the bathroom, played in it with his little hands, pushed the box from the counter to the floor, and then rolled in the stuff. He smelled great, but Mom got the job of cleaning up the little white footprints all over everything and the places where he shook his powdered tail. Also the bathroom floor was a mess.

I carried him around like a baby, and often would wrap him in a doll blanket or towel and put a little bonnet on his head. He would chew off the ribbons that tied under his chin and remove the hat. Then he'd proudly chatter at me.

He was very smart and figured out all sorts of trouble for us. That little brain of his was always thinking and his twitchy tail let us know when he had an idea. Those were little hands he had, not paws, and if he could get a grip, he opened just about everything.

He and Dad had a special bond. Tid Bit would sit on the round table in the living room picture window and watch for my father to come home. As soon as he saw Dad, he'd start chattering and run to the kitchen or back door.

When my father came inside, "baby" would run up his pant leg and ride on his shoulder or cling to the back of his shirt. If Dad sat down, Tid But would often sit or lay across his head. He also loved the riding lawnmower. Tid Bit always rode Dad's shoulder when he mowed the grass. As long as Dad mowed, that squirrel would sit and ride. I have some old pictures of them riding together and Dad laughing.

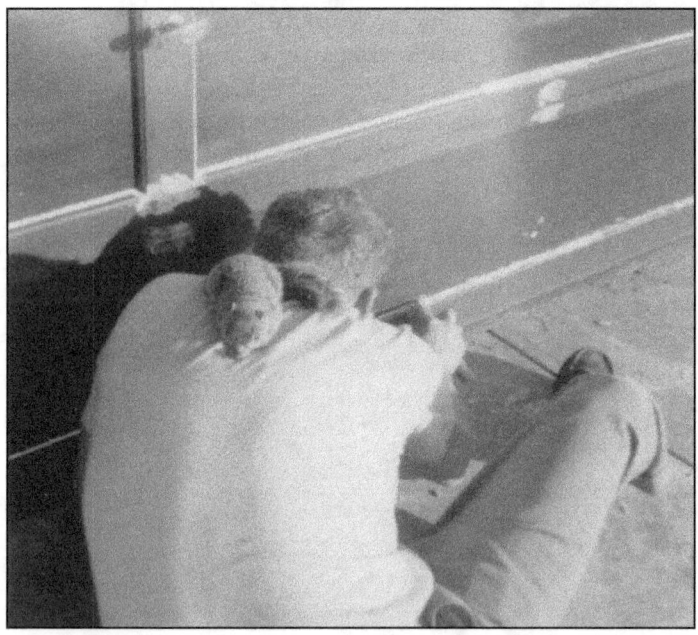

Sometime after that next winter, when I came home from school, Dad said Tid Bit was irritable and snappish. He had refused to come out of his cage that morning when Dad tried to get him to come to the table for breakfast. I was told to leave him alone as he might bite me.

I could tell Dad was worried, because he found reasons to putter in the garage where he could be near him, and he didn't take his usual evening nap on the family room floor with Tid Bit in tow. My father tried to coax his "baby" to eat or come to him to be held, but he wouldn't move off the floor of his cage.

The next morning Dad found him dead. He had tears in his eyes and didn't fix breakfast for me as he had every school morning of my life. He was outside digging a little grave in the garden instead. That evening he spent his time putting Tid Bit's toys and cage in the attic and hanging outside near the garden, We all missed that little scamp, but Dad most of all. We had him nearly two years. That was the only time I'd ever seen my dad cry until years later when Papa King died.

Sour Cherries

I've never really liked sweet cherries. My Dad had two sour cherry trees in our back yard, and that's what I got used to. Every year he was careful to spray them to keep the bugs off—no worms please. Then I'd help him cover the trees with a cheese cloth netting when the little green "balls" appeared. That kept most of the birds out unless a smart one got under the net.

Because of our cats and two dogs, most other hungry critters didn't get to them either, although an occasional raccoon or squirrel did try when temptation became too strong. Of course, that rule of no birds, bugs, or beasts in the two trees didn't apply to our pet squirrel Tid Bit.

When it came time to harvest the fruit, I'd get the lower limbs, and Dad would use a ladder for the higher ones. Tid Bit, our pet squirrel, would climb up on my father's shoulder or head, and jump to the highest branches—he could have as many cherries as his little tummy wanted.

We would store several days pickings in the refrigerator until it couldn't hold anymore, then my parents would set up the cherry pitter outside. We all took turns feeding the machine, turning its crank, dumping the pits, and replacing the full bucket of pitted cherries with an empty one. Tid Bit helped by crawling all over us and stuffing himself.

It was a sticky job requiring showers afterwards. Even our pet was coated. Mom burned citronella candles nearby because our juicy bodies were a tasty treat for many hungry insects. We would repeat the process until most of the fruit was harvested or all three of us were sick of even thinking about cherries. That usually happened first. The rest were left on the tree for whatever winged or four-footed "person" was hungry.

Mom packed most of our efforts in quart containers and froze them for later use. Many became pies or cobblers, but occasionally we used the juice in home-made ice cream.

We had a bumper crop a couple of years in a row, and couldn't eat all of the last year's cherries when the next was ready. My parents decided to make cherry preserves. Neither of them knew how but they had books on the subject. Also Grandma Patrick and Aunt Louise were only a phone call away.

Armed with information, equipment, determination, and motive, they spent the day working in a hot kitchen. (We didn't have air conditioning.) I went to the swimming pool with a friend. I knew if I didn't, I'd be drafted for some KP duty.

When I arrived home around six o' clock, they were finished and exhausted. Everything was cleaned-up, and TV dinners were in the oven. On the counter sat forty-some quart jars filled with still-warm cherry preserves. The metal lids had already "popped," so they were sealed properly. My parents figured the juice would thicken when it cooled to room temperature. After dinner, I got the job of hauling the cherries out to a garage cabinet for storage. I left two quarts in the kitchen.

The next morning, none of us could wait. Dad opened a jar at breakfast. The juice hadn't jelled. It was more of a cherry-fruited syrup, but absolutely delicious. None of those quarts of fruit ever did jell. Mom and Dad checked and double checked their recipe to see if they had missed something. Dad even called Grandma and Aunt Louise for advice. No one ever figured out what went wrong unless the gelatin was defective. But it didn't matter. We enjoyed our syrupy cherries on Dad's homemade biscuits or toast for years.

My parents never again attempted making preserves so when the last jar was gone (I was home from college), we paid a final farewell to that last spoonful. They figured there was too much time and work involved to make more. Mom just bought cherry jelly at the grocery store. It isn't as good because sweet cherries are used rather than sour ones, so the taste is rather bland. I never buy it.

Last week I was at the IGA and discovered that a local company makes a tart cherry preserve. It's not as good as I remembered Mom and Dad's recipe, but I'm enjoying eating my words along with the sour cherries on biscuits.

Wings

Dad loved to fly. He was a radio man on a B26 during WWII. Later, after he married my mother, he planned on getting a pilot's license, but Mom talked him out of it. I think he was in the reserves, and the Korean War was kicking off. She was positive that if he had his license, he would be called to active duty. I also know she was scared of flying and refused to get on a plane to anywhere for many, many years. Perhaps she didn't want Dad to fly because she refused to. At any rate, he never did get that license which he wanted so badly.

He compensated by getting to be friends with crop dusters and accompanying them whenever he could. He met other pilots at airfields who enjoyed pleasure flying and often invited him to join them. Dad seldom mentioned any such trips to Mother. The men who used planes for dropping fertilizer, water, or pesticides were sometimes daredevils; my father loved that! They'd sweep down as low as possible over a field and spread their load, then fly upward rapidly.

Mom had given strict orders that I was not to go flying. She was afraid I'd be killed or even worse, love it. Then she'd be outvoted and her protests ignored. But Dad got around that edict with the idea that what she didn't know before-hand, couldn't stop either of us. He made plans, but didn't tell me; it might have slipped out to Mother.

During the summer, I often went with my father when he traveled to farms or worked in his school's industrial arts shop. When he made home visitations, I could be with my dad and away from my mother's perpetual work plans for me. Weekends and most summer days, Mom was under the impression that idle hands got into trouble, so she kept me busy starching laundry, ironing, dusting, vacuuming, waxing, or cleaning the oven.

Dad was gone every day as he worked eleven months rather than the usual nine. So in the summer, I'd slide into the car when he was leaving the house. Sometimes he'd drop me off at the swimming pool in the park, but often he'd take me with him.

Everything seemed as usual that particular day, except we went to an airfield rather than to school. A two engine plane flew low overhead and waved its wings. Dad waved back. It landed and we walked over to the emerging pilot. Dad and he laughed and talked. Then the man asked me if I was ready for my first airplane ride. I was excited.

When the plane was refueled and some tanks filled with something, we took off. Dad rode next to the pilot, and I sat behind in a third seat.

When we taxied for take-off, I could feel every bump on the runway. Then we were in the air. The engine noise was very loud, and the wind buffeted us. It definitely wasn't like riding in a car. I think the guy flying was showing off. He flew straight up, then swooped down, then back up again.

When the farmer's field which he was to "dust" came into view, this wild man dived down toward the ground. I was sure he planned on dusting while riding along on his landing gear. Suddenly he flew upward again and circled the field. Down we went, dusting again, then up. I guess the pilot was now out of whatever it was he was paid to spread on the field.

Now it was party time in his eyes. Perhaps this would be a good time to mention that I get motion sickness very easily. Even an elevator going down or a Ferris wheel going around mildly nauseated me. That day was no exception. He swooped to the left; then he swooped to the right; then he waved his wings, and came back around. I was beginning to think he was doing an aerial dance with an invisible partner.

He flew straight for a few minutes, and I thought things would get better. Oh no!!! Next he rolled the plane upside down—twice. All this time he was talking ninety-miles-an-hour to my dad, who was very attentive. Then this ace flyer circled us round and around, sort of in a spiral.

Finally, an eternity later, and a few more tricks, he came in for a landing. I had to sit for a minute to keep my stomach down; then I staggered off the plane like a drunk. I almost sank to my hands and knees on the runway, but I fought that urge with all my willpower. I wasn't about to let that jokester see how nauseated I was, or maybe disappoint my dad. My pride was at stake. I looked him right in the eye and said, "Nice ride, thanks," and walked to the car with what I hoped looked like a normal gait.

I was never so glad to sit down on something unmoving. I leaned back and waited for my father. Luckily, by the time he returned, I wasn't so green and shaky. Dad loved the ride and was very happy that I seemed to also. Actually, once I got over the shock of the noise and vibrations, it was quite an experience. I'm really glad I went as I've never had such a ride ever again. I just wish now that I'd had some Dramamine—if they made it back then!

The Kentucky Dam Elk

My father didn't let me get my driver's license until I was almost 21. I must have held the world's record for most permits back in the 1960's. He wanted to make sure I could handle just about any situation he could think of before he "turned me loose." I drove on two and four lane highways and country roads. I drove on hills and curves. I drove in sunshine, driving rain, sleet, and snow. I drove with wind gusts blasting me from all directions.

I learned about snow and ice covered bridges, and hydroplaning on water-covered blacktop. I learned to watch for black ice. I learned how gravel could cause sliding at stops and around curves. I learned nothing about unpredictable animals in the road until I was 20. That was one thing Dad didn't think of.

Now either my father had nerves of steel, or else he was able to hide his fears when he took me driving. He was quiet and patient; he never raised his voice in case it might rattle me. But, I finally saw that veneer crack the time I drove over the Kentucky Dam.

It was during my college spring break. We had been visiting a girlfriend of my mother's; she and her husband had a beautiful home overlooking Kentucky Lake. My father was never one to sit still for very long, so he decided to take me sightseeing and let me do the driving.

We had a great time, and I was doing quite well until what I thought was a very large deer with an equally large rack of antlers showed up on the side of the road just as we were heading over the dam. He decided to run right out in front of us. There were cars coming toward me and cars behind me; but none in front of me.

That "deer" ran into the next lane but dodged a car and jumped back in front of our green Chrysler. There he proceeded to hop back and forth like a rabbit dodging a hound dog. Luckily he kept moving forward and didn't turn around to charge at us. We would have been wearing him as a hood ornament if he had.

We were going about 45 to 50 mph. I couldn't hit my brakes because of the cars following close behind me, so I took my foot off the accelerator and just coasted. Dad was yelling "slow down, slow down," so I kept lightly tapping the brakes to gently slow down and to warn the unobservant driver tailgating behind me. Cars in the on-coming lane were trying to slow down or move to the side as best they could.

There was nowhere to go; on either side of the metal railings was just water. That "deer" kept bounding on ahead of us until we reached the

91

other side of the dam where he could get away from all the cars and humans. He took off to the right side.

My father quietly asked me to find a place to park. There was a scenic over-look with parking to the right and I pulled in. During the whole ordeal, I hadn't become nervous at all; I couldn't allow myself any thoughts. I just watched that "deer," the traffic, and our car. Even when we stopped, I was calm. All that training Dad had put me through since I was 16 paid off.

Now my dad was a different story. We got out of the car, and he walked very unsteadily up to the railings and held on tight. He was shaking badly and sweat was pouring off his face. He kept saying "Whew," over and over for several minutes. All he finally said when he was able to talk was, "That elk could have jumped back into our windshield." He sat down on the hood of the car, took out his handkerchief, and wiped his face. Then he looked me in the eyes and quietly said, "You did a good job." I smiled back and sat on the hood with him.

We looked at the water, and he told me some facts about the dam. In about 30 minutes, we got back in the car; I drove, and we continued sight-seeing. I don't think Dad ever told anyone, maybe not even my mother (at least she never said anything to me), about that incident. He never mentioned it to me either after that.

However, that summer when college was out, he started looking for a car for me. He brought a green GMC Opel from a neighbor's missionary daughter and worked for two months to get it ready for me to take back to Ball State my senior year. That's how I got "Flower Baby." I guess after that elk, Dad figured I was ready to solo.

The Judge

My father had always wanted to be a veterinarian, but when Mom became pregnant with me, he quickly changed to agriculture. He had grown up on a farm so it was an easy switch. In August of 1955, we moved to Union City, Indiana, and Dad began working at the Jacksonburg (now Mississinawa) High School. He taught shop and was the FFA (Future Farms of America) leader/advisor.

He was often out on some farm inspecting a student's project. One boy was raising worms for human consumption--his father had a worm farm and was selling his "crop" to a restaurant chain. He declined to say which chain was buying the worms. My dad said that was the most unusual project he had ever inspected. He also sheered sheep, castrated hogs, examined cows, gave animals shots, and trimmed horse/pony hoofs.

Because he was very knowledgeable, he was given the job of judging crops at the Darke County Fair in Greenville, Ohio. This fair is advertised as the largest county fair in the world, and it really is huge. He also had to be there every day to man the FFA building. I always went with him.

Year after year, I watched my father judge everything from tobacco to corn and soy beans. He also judged apples, cherries, grapes and turnips. I never did figure what he looked for or the criteria he used to make his decisions, but for nearly 30 years he was the sole undisputed choice of the fair board.

His helpers would lay out the many entries in a category, and in less than five minutes, he would make the decision, the ribbons would be placed, and he would be on to the next group.

The entries were housed in the basement of the large grange hall while the upstairs held the vendors. There was even a concrete ramp to the upstairs so that cars or trucks could be driven in. The two long vendor's tents at the Brown County fair could easily fit inside with another one besides. This should give an idea of how much space there is. He also had the projects in the FFA building to judge.

Then one year, he was asked to judge the food as well as the crops. He agreed, not knowing what he had got himself into. For two days, he tasted batches of cookies, an assortment of cakes and breads, quarts of pickles and pickle relish. Next he judged hard candy, soft candy, jams, jellies, and preserves; then came the fudge and brownies. The pickled eggs and quarts of tomatoes, peaches, and a variety of juices were followed by the dried fruits and trail mixes. He judged cream pies and fruit pies; squash, yam and pumpkin pies; and almond, peanut and pecan pies. Then he judged persimmon puddings and bread puddings.

Dad was looking very green when we went home both nights, but he was extra green that second evening. He couldn't eat any supper; in fact, he had trouble keeping down the day's judging.

The next year he begged off, and never judged the food again. He said the different varieties and entries were too much, such as tasting four bread puddings after 10 different relishes. Then he told Mom and me the reason he was barely keeping his stomach together that second day—he had to judge several pies and puddings made with pig, cow, and sheep blood. All he would say was that the tastes were "very unique."

Banana Trees

My father and his brother, Uncle John, were very close even though John was the oldest and Dad, the youngest of the children. The older girl, Vernell, had been killed in a car accident when she was in her early twenties. I think that brought them even closer.

One time when Mom, Dad, and I went to their home in Enville, Tennessee, to visit, Uncle John was growing several banana trees. A friend of his had brought them back from Florida, and he was experimenting with them on his farm to see if they could flourish in the cooler climate. It seems those trees were all they talked about the week we were there.

We took off on our vacation to Florida after that and Dad picked up three banana trees himself while down there and brought them back home to Greenville, Ohio. Both being farm boys, Dad couldn't resist the challenge. They were going to compare notes and perhaps write an article for a farmer's magazine.

Back then the interstates weren't completed. There were just sections that were 4 lanes then back to the 2 lane state highways. Dad packed the three trees, now planted in 10" inch pots, on the floor of the back seat where I sat, and I got the job of keeping those three-foot plants upright.

Banana trees are still a type of palm tree which meant very shallow roots, and very large leaves. They didn't like standing up, and I liked taking naps. For much of the trip, I had leaves in my face if I lay down or sat up, and in my lap if the pots tipped over. I think I threatened Dad with eating those leaves for a salad.

The interstate highways were originally built to move troops and weapons in case of a war with the U.S.S.R. As we traveled, we passed several convoys of troops going our way and even a flatbed semi carrying a missile the other way. We would wave at the men, and many did double takes or laughed and pointed to the trees engulfing me in the back seat. The guys were young and, I thought, good looking. As a typical pre-teen, I was mortified. All I felt I needed was a banana in my mouth to complete the picture.

I was very glad when we reached home, and was sick of those trees. My dad, however, was happy they survived the trip; they showed no sign of stress. He moved them to the back yard close to the house because the bricks on that side absorbed heat during the day and radiated it at night.

94

BANANA TREE IN GREENVILLE

Trees are no rarity in this part of the country, but a banana tree is! Bradley Patrick, 807 Daly Rd., Greenville, is shown above with his banana tree, which is bearing real fruit. The tree was growing in the backyard of the Patrick home, but it was dug up and lodged in the garage after the hard frosts came. Patrick pur- chased the tree in 1963 while in Florida for $4. Each year he plants it in the back yard and then moves it inside when cold weather hits. However, this was the first year that about one dozen bananas. He noted that the tree is still blooming, in spite of the cold weather. (Advocate staff photo)

*Article states one tree, but there were two trees.
The second only had a small bunch of four or five.*

When it got cooler in the fall, he brought them into the heated garage, and babied them all winter; one died. They grew slowly
but they did grow. The next summer, he planted them in the ground. They continued to grow, so he had to get larger pots when he dug them up that fall. This became a yearly routine.

Eventually, the second one died after producing a few stunted bananas, and the other was as tall as the house. He and Uncle John kept in contact and exchanged information. Dad had some horticultural friends examine the trees. Then the newspapers got the story and came to take pictures.

Banana trees die after producing fruit, and new ones come up from seeds. Uncle John's never did bear fruit and died during one winter. The last of Dad's trees produced one stalk with ten or twelve bananas the year of the newspaper story. The bananas were not as big as those in the grocery store, but they were good eating.

This news not only hit the local papers, it was also on television across the state. My father later wrote a magazine article about raising the trees, and how it could be done in colder climates.

The trees slowly died after bearing their fruit, but it was a fun experiment for Dad, and he was proud of what he accomplished. I have one of the newspaper pictures showing one of the two trees with my father standing beside it. It was almost ten feet tall at the time. I don't have the article he wrote, but I guess the memories are more important.

Shrimp and Cyprus Trees

Sometimes traveling the old back roads can be more interesting than taking the interstates. Often back in the '60's when Mom, Dad, and I took a vacation, my father would enjoy getting away from boring long straight strips for a while. That was fairly easy to do as the four-lanes weren't always finished. We'd be on those for a while then back on two lanes. The only interesting part about those interstates was the many Jeeps and military men traveling in convoys. I'd wave and some would smile and wave back. Once we saw a rocket being transported in the opposite direction. Now that was impressive. I'd never seen anything so big!

One of the times a four-lane highway ended, we were in Tennessee, and we decided to stay at a motel near Reelfoot Lake. We arrived in the afternoon and took a drive. The lake had lots of Cyprus knees sticking up and wasn't too deep. Those Cyprus "stumps" fascinated me as Mom and Dad had a red table lamp made from one.

While we were driving, we saw a ramshackled restaurant which advertised shrimp. My father and I thought that would be a great place for supper. Mother said nothing. Then we saw a place where we could rent flat bottomed boats with small fishing motors. We stopped to check the cost and decided it would be fun.

Mom wanted nothing to do with that boat or the lake. She said that lake was more like a swamp and probably full of snakes which she was very afraid of. Also, the boat was too close to the water and too slow; a snake could crawl in.

We dropped her off at the motel and returned to rent the boat. Dad got oars too. He took me right up to the Cyprus trees so I could reach out and touch them. It was fascinating. Then we heard singing coming from the shore. Dad quietly rowed up and we hid behind a clump of trees and watched.

It was a baptism. There were about 20 people on the edge of the lake singing. A preacher, dressed in black, was holding a young woman's hand up in the air. She was in a white dress and both were standing in the water. He was praying over her rather loudly. When he finished, he tipped her backwards and totally submerged her in the lake. She rose back up and began jumping up and down, splashing water with her hands, and shrieking.

Now since the baptisms in my church involved dipping a rose into the font and sprinkling the person, this was very new to me. I didn't know it *was* a baptism until my father told me. I thought the lady had been bitten by a snake or at least had been scared by one. We slipped away quietly, and Dad explained it all to me. He even told me that when I had been baptized as a baby, I had tried to eat the rose!

We had a great afternoon, and I didn't want to get off the water. We decided that definitely we were going to the restaurant we'd seen earlier. We returned the boat and drove back to the motel to get Mother. She was angry because we had left her in the room when we went boating, and she flat refused to go to that "dump" to eat. She said the place looked dirty, and the food probably was greasy or would give us food poisoning. My parents had a bit of an argument.

Mother said she'd rather eat out of the cooler. We carried food in a Coleman chest in our car whenever we traveled; it saved money and we liked the picnic style of eating. Dad said we were going whether she went with us or not. We left.

That restaurant was one of my favorite memories. It was getting dark when we arrived. The Cyprus trees were silhouetted against the moonlit sky and the trees and water sparkled. The restaurant had several windows which were all lit up with a yellow glow. The small building had sunk over time and leaned a bit. The paint was gone. The screen door didn't fit into its frame very well, and the main door was propped open with a rock. Inside were a few tables and a bar area.

Everything did look a bit seedy, I guess. At least Mother would have thought so. But to me, it was picturesque and wonderful. We sat at a rough table in mismatched chairs, and the waitress brought water and menus. She had a southern accent which was deeper than what my family and relatives had. I loved to hear her speak. She was very friendly, and as usual, Dad struck up a conversation. She said to get the shrimp, so we did.

Oh my! Those plates were the size of small turkey platters —oval and over 12" long. Each was mounded high with popcorn shrimp--maybe 2 lbs. each. The French fries came on a separate dinner plate, and the slaw came in cereal bowls. Dad and I looked at each other. No way could we both eat all the food on one platter let alone one each.

So we ate slowly and enjoyed the atmosphere. We listened to the folks banter back and forth. Dad talked to some of the men there, and I just listened. There was lots of gentle laughter. I felt so comfortable and happy. The place was full, but no one was in a hurry--everyone moved slowly as if time were only creeping by. We sat there nearly two hours just eating, talking, taking it easy, and enjoying the gentle fellowship around us. To our amazement, we did almost finish the shrimp. We were relaxed and very content. Dad said he hated to go back to the motel and listen to Mom "bitch".

So we stayed a little longer and nibbled at the slaw, shrimp, and fries. Then we got pie just to stay longer. Both meals only came to six or eight dollars with drinks and dessert. Of course, that was the '60's. Still, the shrimp was cheap even for those days. We reluctantly left and went back to the motel.

Mother was in bed reading. I excitedly told her how great the place was. She no longer seemed angry, but said she was sorry now that she hadn't gone. We also told her about the boat ride and baptism. I think Mother realized that she had missed out on a good time and meal. All she had to eat was a bologna sandwich.

My parents talked in low tones after I'd gone to bed, and they thought I was asleep. I heard my mother say next time she'd give things a try and not pass judgment so quickly. I think she also realized that if she didn't join the two of us, she'd get left behind. We wouldn't change our plans just because she would throw a fit.

So from then on, on vacations at least, she was very flexible. We began traveling more back roads and wondered where they would take us. We followed no schedules and stopped at many interesting places on the spur of the moment. Those were happy times.

Traveling

After Mom loosened up a bit on our vacations, we really had some interesting experiences. We went to Gatlinburg one year. That place was like an Eastern Las Vegas. There were advertising signs on top of advertising signs. One sign touted 21 hotels in a single block.

When we walked down the streets, there were open air stalls selling every "Indian" artifact imaginable such as rubber knives and tomahawks, plastic beads, plastic headdresses with multicolored turkey feathers--you get the idea. There were even "Indians" in costumes that tourists could have their pictures taken with--for a fee. That place was definitely over the top!

Another time we were in Cherokee, North Carolina. We sat on a hillside and watched a passion play. It was a history of the Cherokee nation and the time period when the people were forced to walk all the way into the West. The path they walked was called "The Trail of Tears." Later my father struck up a conversation with a Native American and we learned more. Then the gentleman put on a real outfit and performed the Eagle Dance for us. That was amazing!

On another vacation, I remember staying at a motel by the Atlantic Ocean. There was a back door to our room. Mom opened it, and we looked down onto stretches of sand--we were right on the beach. We decided to take a walk out our back door the next morning. We got up early, opened the door, and saw seawater about four feet straight down; the tide was up. We were not just on the beach; we were in the tidal zone. I wonder if that place is still there, or if the ocean claimed it.

We went to Niagara Falls. I wanted to take the walking tour going behind the waterfall, but both parents said no because of slippery rocks. We took the boat "Maid of the Mist" instead which went very close to the bottom of the falls. The thundering power of the water was deafening, and scary. Then we went into the museum which showed sections of crafts and people who had tried to go over the falls. There was a barrel there from one such try. The before and after pictures of a bunch of big inner tubes strapped together still sticks in my mind. I guess only one man at that time had successfully gone over the falls—he lived to tell about it anyway.

We followed the gulf coast from Florida over to Texas. A hurricane was only a day or two behind us. Corpus Christi was very soggy when we arrived in the late afternoon. We walked out onto a pier and later talked to a bait store owner nearby. We were in a lull between the big storms.

When we reached Laredo, Texas, we visited some acquaintances Dad had met on another vacation. The man had caught some baby skunks. They were very tame and adorable, but they were not de-scented. All four were in a large cage *in my bedroom*. There was a lot of squabbling going on, and one or more of the babies started spraying in the middle of the night. The noise and odor waked me up. However, I discovered that one's "smeller" can even became numb to that perfume after about half an hour. Or maybe I just passed out from the smell.

The next morning, Mother immediately sent me to the shower which was in the basement. The tub in the bathroom upstairs was filled with dirty cloth diapers, so I couldn't use it. I had to share the stall with a dog, but even wet, he smelled better than I did.

Mom had the foresight to keep my suitcase and next day's outfit in her bedroom. We left these people as soon as was polite, and located a laundromat. Mother washed all my clothes that had been in the bedroom just to get the odor out. Luckily no spray was on them, or my pajamas and dirty laundry would have been trashed.

After cleaning my clothes, we parked and walked over a long wooden bridge to Nuevo Laredo, Mexico. We sat in an open air restaurant and drank Cokes. Dumb me! I didn't know people outside of the U.S. had Coca-Cola. We went shopping, and Mom bought some silver earrings with the Aztec calendar on them.

I wanted an armadillo purse I saw very badly, but didn't have enough money. After we left the store, Dad told me I could have haggled with the lady over the price. I didn't know that and was too tired to go back and try. To this day, I wish I had.

On other vacations, we traveled to many areas in the South. Often, people had roadside stands selling souvenirs. Many clotheslines next to houses had quilts for sale hanging on them. One pattern that seemed popular was a peacock; the head, turned sideways, was at the top of the quilt and the rest was taken up with an opened tail. The quilt contained lots of pieces. Some lady spent many long hours making that work of art, and sold it for a very low price. It was a poor area.

The strip mines were quite a shock. All I saw were black land and black hillsides. Soil and vegetation had been scraped off so that the coal could be shoveled up; that area didn't seem like planet earth. I even got to see the world's biggest steam shovel used to scoop the coal. I forgot how many cars it could pick up on one load. I have a picture of my sitting in the shovel, and I look very tiny.

We went down into the everglades on another trip. I remember it was late afternoon and the sun was sinking. Mom spotted some fruit bearing trees to the side of the road. It was about 50 feet off into what she thought was just grass. She asked Dad to stop so she could go pick a couple of the fruits for me. My father did *not* stop the car. I remember his saying, "Millie, that's all swamp over there. You'll be walking in water with snakes and alligators." She changed her mind really fast.

Later we took an airboat ride; it was just a short tour over the grass-- we didn't go deep into the everglades. I did learn that the Seminoles never signed a peace treaty with the government and were technically still at war. The folks we saw were pretty peaceful.

About every place we traveled has a story to go with it, and Mom became even more adventuresome than Dad. Sometimes he had to slow her down. She kept her word about trying new things after that Reelfoot Lake incident. However she always insisted on carrying sponges and a large bottle of Lysol. Every motel we stayed in had its bathroom fixtures (floor too) disinfected before Dad and I were allowed to use them. Also, we were required to wear shoes at all times on the carpet. Considering some of the places we stayed, that was a good idea.

The Breakers Hotel

One summer around 1959 or 1960, my parents decided to travel to Sandusky, Ohio, for a vacation at the lake. We had heard that the Breakers Hotel was an elegant place to stay, so my parents decided to treat themselves.

The hotel lobby was very beautiful although a bit run down at the time. I've heard it's been magnificently restored since, but not then. We gasped at its splendor—then we checked into our room.

I didn't think anything had been done to that room or any of the others since the place was built. The walls were a dirty yellow, and the space was not much bigger than the double bed. There was a small cloudy window on the right side of the room which had a noisy air conditioner stuck in its bottom half and a rusty heater under it.

The old wooden floor was scratched and scarred from years of use; it squeaked and groaned when we walked on it. The double bed had seen better years, and my bed was just a fold-out cot. There was only an overhead light and a single table next to the bed.

Mom looked up at the ceiling and her eyes widened—spider webs with their owners lowering themselves on long silk threads were right over the bed and cot. She said she was going to have nightmares about them crawling into bed with Dad and her. My father got a towel from the bathroom, stood on the edge of the bed's frame, and flipped them down. Then he killed them. He called downstairs for a few extra towels.

After a light lunch, we changed into our swim suits, grabbed our beach paraphernalia, and headed for the water. We had a great day. Dad and I found several trampolines that were suspended over rectangular holes in the sand. He and I had great fun jumping on those things. I went back several more times to jump throughout the day.

There were hot dog vendors set up on the beach, and we ate afternoon snacks there. Later, we headed back to the hotel to change into casual clothes and had dinner. We did a little sight-seeing and returned to our rooms for baths and bed.

That's when we discovered the wonders of our bathroom. It had a toilet, sink and metal shower. A single, ugly, bright light was glaring from the ceiling, very similar to the one in the bedroom. Mother stripped off her clothes and climbed into the small enclosure. Only then did she discover there were no handles to turn on the water. She stepped out, looked around, and discovered two pipes running up the wall and over to the shower nozzle. The spigot valves were on those wall pipes.

She had to turn each one on, walk over to the shower, check the temperature, walk back to make adjustments, check again, and if a satisfactory temperature, step in to bathe. Of course, the small floor tiles were soggy, and we had to protect ourselves from falling by putting our swim towels down to walk on. Each of us had to perform the same water ritual to get a shower.

After we were all clean, Dad tucked me into my cot. It was narrower than a twin bed with a metal frame surrounding it. I'm sure the thin, old, stained mattress was filled with rocks rather than stuffing. It was miserably uncomfortable. The metal frame pushed against me no matter how I lay. If either parent would have allowed it, I'd have slept on the floor, but ground-in dirt, uneven boards, and splinters ruined that idea.

Mother sat down on the edge of the mattress to take off her slippers while Dad turned out the light. He walked over and climbed into bed. Suddenly, I heard my mother let out a loud squawk which shocked me. I'd never heard her make *that* noise before. Then there was the sound of squeaky bedsprings and what I thought were my parents wrestling.

No, they weren't loving on each other—the mattress and springs were only suspended from the head and foot of the bed frame, sort of like a hammock. Mom had been pitched bottom over head when Dad climbed in. They crunched together in the middle with Mom's legs over Dad's neck. After bouncing around each other in the dark, Dad managed to hook a leg over the side of the mattress and draw himself to the edge.

He had to battle the bed and gravity to get all of him out of there. He dropped to the floor on his knees, muttered something I probably shouldn't have heard, and headed for the light switch. From the looks on both faces, Mom's curlers falling out, and their disarrayed pajamas, I think the bed won the battle.

Dad discovered there were no slats under the springs to keep the whole thing from sagging when any weight was applied. He appeared stumped for a minute—just looking around the room aimlessly. Then his eyes focused on our suitcases. Back then, everyone had luggage made of lightweight wooden frames.

That gave my father an idea. He pushed our three pieces under the bed to keep it from sagging as much. It was a bit lumpy, but it worked. Still they rolled together in the middle all night and endured each other's knees, elbows, and flying arms.

Mom said the next morning that neither could turn their backs to each other. Dad's hand had been over her face, and he said her elbow had wacked his Adam's apple more than once. None of us had slept well. We were stiff and cranky.

However, another fun day at the beach and a couple of naps on our blanket in the sand, covered by towels, soothed our moods and muscles greatly. Later, we went shopping downtown. Mom bought me a shorts outfit, herself a beach bag, and a shirt for Dad.

We ate supper in town, and went back for a late stroll on the sand. The lake by night with the stars and moon reflected on its water was a beautiful and restful sight. We took off our shoes and let the water splash over our ankles and calves. It was a wonderful time. I suspect we all were trying not to think about another night in our hotel room from hell, but there was no way to avoid it. We had paid for two nights.

Finally, we had to go back inside. At bath time, we decided to have one person adjust the hot and cold water while another was in the shower. We figured the tiles wouldn't get wet and slippery that way. It was a great idea *in theory*. But the one manning the valves had no idea what the water felt like on a bare body inside the tiny stall. The hot water was boiling, and the cold icy. Mom was inside, and Dad was outside.

Her howls of protest while she alternately boiled and froze nearly started a fight between them. Finally, she told him to stop—she'd do it herself. The floor became wet and slippery as before, but none of us fell down.

Mom *was* a bit snappish with Dad for a short while but forgave him. He talked her into lying on the bed while he put a nickel or dime in a machine attached to the mattress. The "gentle" vibration was supposed to "sooth away the aches and cares of the world."

Maybe it would have if the mattress and springs were firmly attached to the frame. Instead, it shook Mom as if she were in a paint mixing machine. She yelled for Dad to turn it off, but it was on a timer—it couldn't be shut off. He pulled her off the bed to the tune of her chattering teeth.

I asked if I could try it, and hopped on. Bad decision! I was bouncing since I jumped into the bed, and that "soothing" machine shook me mercilessly. I stayed on until the timer ran out, but all that vibration made me sick with a headache and upset stomach. It gave my mother a headache too. So bedtime was another joyous memory.

That next morning, we packed as fast as we could to get out of that hotel; you would have thought the place was on fire. Our house never seemed so sweet or so far away. We homing pigeons didn't stop 'til we hit the driveway.

Maybe someday I'll re-visit the Breakers Hotel to use the restroom, but stay there? Possibly, since it has been restored. Still, I'd want to see my room first. Old memories die hard.

The Camping Trip

My parents loved to travel. As soon as they started making enough money to take vacations, around 1955, we were gone every summer. Three hundred dollars allowed us to roam anywhere we wanted for two weeks. For the next seven years, we stopped at small motels along the way, and Mom repeatedly swabbed everything she could in those rented rooms with Lysol before we settled in for the night.

Then when I was around 13, friends from our church started a side-line business in a lot by their house. They rented small travel trailers and pop-up tent campers. My parents held a dinner-table discussion and decided that traveling with a camper might be fun.

Mother had never done any sort of camping in her life, but talking to her friend Glenna must have convinced her that pulling a small clean house with a kitchen was better than Lysol scrubs and soggy food carried in a watery ice-filled cooler.

She had looked inside several of the trailers that were for rent and was impressed with the organization. I think my mother was more excited about vacationing with a trailer than Dad was. He realized that there was much to learn and a lot involved.

First, he paid to have a trailer hitch bolted or maybe welded to the frame of the car. Then he had to have wiring and plugs installed so that the trailer's running and brake lights would work because the car's lights would be blocked from view.

Glenna's husband convinced my father to have sway bars installed to keep the "tag-along" traveling behind and not beside them as they wandered down the highways. Also, since cars at the time often only had a driver's side mirror, Dad took the car to our dealer to have a matching one installed on the passenger side. He didn't tell Mom about the expenses involved in getting the car ready to pull a camper; he just saved his monthly GI disability checks and used them to pay for the additions.

The day my father picked up our trailer, he had to practice turning, backing, and driving around the rental lot and streets before he slowly drove from Arcanum to Greenville, and home. He said it was hard to get used to using the side mirrors. He kept trying to look out the rear-view mirror, only to see the camper's front window framed in it.

He thought he could teach Mother to maneuver the two piece rig; but she was too scared to even try. She was *positive* that she would jack-knife, roll over, or back into something.

Dad discovered very quickly that the driving was going to be all up to him. As he always drove on other vacations, he resigned himself easily enough. We packed the cooking and eating utensils in the cupboards and clothes in the cabinets. Mom loved putting food in a real refrigerator where it wouldn't get water-logged. No more ice chests for her!

We left the next morning as planned. Mom's job as navigator included locating suitable campgrounds as listed in her AAA books. Because of Dad's preparations, he found that pulling the camper was actually easy. He drove 50 mph and let others pass him. (He hadn't let on that he had been worried.)

When we reached our first destination, Dad maneuvered the rig into the appropriate site, stabilized and leveled the trailer as he had been taught the day before. I helped him as much as he asked; we made an efficient team. We hooked up the water and electricity at our site and turned on the bottled gas.

Then we stayed out of Mother's way as she cooked a respectable supper in the tiny kitchen. I received the task of doing dishes afterwards while my parents sat at the picnic table outside and talked. It wasn't long before my father met our neighbors and invited them over for ice tea. That was the icing on the cake. They never had the opportunity to have neighborly evenings at the motels, but RV travelers turned out to be friendly folks. There were even teens my age.

All in all, things were working out well. The only problem my parents had was figuring out how to lower the table to convert it into a bed later that night. After a couple of smashed fingers, they figured it out. They had the same problem the next morning when trying to return it to a table. It was a re-occurring problem the whole trip, but my parents decided it was a design flaw and not something that we were doing wrong.

Dad had picked a site close to the bathrooms when he registered; so it was an easy walk to showers, sinks, toilets, laundry facilities, and vending machines. There was a well-lighted, graveled road leading to the buildings; we didn't need flashlights. After taking showers and brushing teeth, we headed back to sleep in clean beds with our own pillows and covers.

Following breakfast the next morning and friendly chats with other families nearby, Dad and I removed the leveling jacks and drove over to the dumping station to let out the grey water from our holding tank. Mom couldn't believe it—she didn't have to pack up and lug big suitcases to the car, drain and re-fill the ice chest, or check for items left behind. No more Lysol scented hands and rooms to make our cold suppers unappetizing. She even had her kitchen organization perfected by that first breakfast, and getting dressed out of drawers and closets certainly beat rooting around in bags for wrinkled clothing.

All was rosy in her eyes, and a happy Mom made for a happy trip. It really was a great vacation and Mother discovered that we actually had saved a little money when we returned home.

Over the next six years, my parents rented a camper for most of our summer vacations. A couple of times one wasn't available when we wanted it; then, our trips were not as enjoyable. We had definitely become travel trailer lovers. Then I headed off to college in August of 1967.

Soon after, Dad thought it might be fun to try camping in a tent for one weekend. He felt that it would be a romantic get-away for just the two of them now that I was out of the house. I think he believed it was just what both of them needed as they were having an empty-nest attack. Mom took a lot of convincing. She was skeptical of the whole idea, but she finally agreed, and the date was set for Labor Day weekend.

She had no idea what tenting was about, or she would *never* have agreed. Possibly she thought it would be similar to their travel trailer vacations.

106

Remembering his joyful camping trips as a boy near Bolívar, TN, Dad was as happy as a kid in a candy store holding a five dollar bill in his hand. He whistled for days as he made a camping list and purchased two sleeping bags, two air mattresses, an air pump, a tent with a vapor barrier, a Coleman lantern with neon tube lights and a Coleman stove with propane cartridges, two 5-gallon Coleman water coolers, two long handle Coleman flashlights with extra batteries and bulbs, and whatever else he thought they would need.

Mom bought lots of bug spray, poison ivy spray, stop-itch spray, Calamine lotion, sun block, rubbing alcohol, band aids, and any other sprays or lotions her nightmares convinced her to get. To her horror, he told her to buy some blue-jeans and heavy tennis shoes.

She had never owned a pair of jeans in her life and had never allowed me to have any. Only farmers and other hard-laboring men wore those "things," not women, or so she believed. The only tennis shoes she had ever had were little white flats with four holes for laces and she wouldn't have ever had those except they became stylish for me along with poodle skirts and pony tails. She had thought they looked cute and bought herself a pair when she bought mine.

She purchased the items requested and discovered that while the sneakers were heavy, they were comfortable. She just walked oddly as if 10 lbs. were attached to each foot until she became used to them. Dad said it was pretty funny to watch as she kept lifting her feet up too fast, and often got one foot tangled with the other in the process. He didn't dare let her see him chuckling, or he would have been in deep trouble.

The one pair of jeans she bought was very stiff and didn't fit—maybe because they were men's. She returned them to the hardware store and packed polyester slacks instead. She took nylon knee-high hose instead of socks. At least she didn't pack dresses as she did on the summer vacations--just a nightgown and robe.

That appointed Friday morning, Dad lowered the back seat of their green station wagon, and literally crammed it full, even the nooks and crannies, with all the gear and extras Mother wanted along. These included pillows, blankets, sheets, hair curlers, lotions, make-up, electric toaster, electric hair dryer, and electric razor. Then with the car's shocks groaning under the weight, they headed cross country to a state park not too far from my college.

A couple of hours later, they arrived. Dad went to the park office, paid the fee, and bought some fire wood. He had a map showing where their campsite was. She navigated and he drove. When Mom saw the sign which said *primitive* camping and an arrow pointing left, her eyes grew very wide. The RV camping went to the right.

107

"What does *that* mean," she nervously asked. Dad cautiously explained that all tent camping was primitive which meant no water. They would have to walk to an outhouse when the urge arose. There was also no electricity so lanterns and flashlights were needed at the campsites and to walk to the outhouses.

How was she going to take a shower or brush her teeth and where were the vending machines, Mom wanted to know. Panic was edging into her voice. My father told her that those were in the RV area which was quite a walk away, but they could driver over, if necessary.

Mother was *not* happy, and she said so. Dad persuaded her to give it a try by saying that the outhouses were well cleaned and wouldn't stink. He also reminded her of the two 5-gallon water coolers which could be used to wash hands, brush teeth, and cook.

She wanted to know if they could set up the tent on the RV side instead of the primitive side. Dad told her that wasn't allowed. By this time, he had located their campsite and pulled in. It was a grassy place surrounded with trees and packed dirt. The grass needed mowing, and there was some poison ivy nearby. A picnic table and garbage can stood on the grass. The fire-pit ring was on the packed dirt. The outhouse was a distance away and upwind.

Mom could just barely see the lighted bathhouse over on the travel trailer side. She got out of the car and sat at the picnic table; I think she was in shock. Dad set up the tent, pumped up the air mattresses and put them inside. He laid the sleeping bags on top and did everything else needed to prepare for a comfortable evening.

She didn't help until he started moving the cooking equipment to the table. Then she arranged things to suit herself. Dad put the wood in the fire ring for later and set out two folding chairs nearby. She wanted to put the food and ice chest on the table, but my father nonchalantly said, "We can do all that later. How about a walk to the lake? There's a beach and some walking paths." (He refrained from calling those walking paths what they really were--hiking trails. Some trails more challenging than others, according to the back of his map.) I imagine that Dad was beginning to think that his camping plan was a bad idea, but was determined to be optimistic, for now.

Just then she slapped at her first mosquito, jumped off the table's bench, and agreed to the walk. She rooted around in the side of the station wagon and located her tennis shoes or "brogans", as she liked to call them, and tied them on.

Dad suggested that Mom take her swimsuit and a towel, but she wouldn't. She said that she wanted to see how clean the water and beach were before deciding. It would mean a trip back to the car if she wanted to swim, but Dad was patient. He tucked his suit under his belt, and waited until she was ready. He led the way.

Mother was still clumsily walking in her new thickly-padded shoes, and she occasionally tripped over a mossy clump on the well-trod path to the water. She saw a beach house with showers, sinks, toilets, and changing booths. Now she felt better, and Dad sighed in relief.

She decided the beach looked all right but asked a lady there with children how clean and deep the water was. The woman told her everything was great, but mentioned that the bottom was mud and not sand. That stopped Mother cold; the idea of ooze squishing up between her toes turned her off. She shuddered, remembering another mud bottomed lake where she dislodged a fish's backbone still with eyes attached. It had floated to the surface near her face.

Swimming was out for her. Dad changed, put his pants and shorts on the ground by a tree, and went in. Mom rolled up her pants, put her shoes with his clothes, and waded in the shallows where the sand was. Splashing children didn't bother her, but her pant bottoms did get wet.

Dad returned shortly and said the mud wasn't bad. She wasn't interested. They just walked and sat on a picnic table watching the water and the people. When Mom's pants were dry, Dad changed into his clothes, and they walked back to the tent.

Both were hungry, so out came the food. Mother couldn't figure out the Coleman stove. She pumped too much air into the gas cylinder. When she turned the gas valve and put the lighted match to the burner, flames shot up nearly a foot. She singed the hair off her right arm. Mother shrieked and swerved sideways, knocking my dad off-balance. He staggered, got his feet firmly re-planted, and grabbed the stove's knob to turn down the flame.

They cooked together, and their early supper went well except for the lake breezes wafting the odors from the privies toward them. Mom wasn't too hungry because of that. My father just pretended he couldn't smell very well because of his swimming.

The mosquitoes were moving in fast so Mother grabbed the bug spray. After dousing herself, she started cleaning up from the meal. That's when she found out that all the food and utensils had to go back into the car to keep the raccoons and other night creatures from scavenging. Before Dad could stop her, she had dumped the scraps, and paper plates into their site's trash can. It couldn't be moved because it was chained to a post. That way, animals couldn't turn it over and roll it around at night.

Since he couldn't move the can away from their tent, he just hoped the animals would stay away during the night; he didn't tell mother.

Instead he decided to build a long-lasting fire which might keep the hungry scavengers away.

While he was starting the fire, Mom decided to go to the beach house to clean up for the night. She wanted a shower to wash off the lake water and bug spray. She figured that no one would be there, and she would be safe to take her nightgown and robe, and to wear her rubber flip flops. She used the water bucket to carry her curlers, lotions, and other necessities. Her clothes took up her other arm, so Dad hooked the Coleman lantern handle over her wrist.

She made it there safely, washed off all the bug spray, put on perfumed deodorant, perfumed lotions, and perfumed hair setting gel. She smelled wonderful as always. Unfortunately, she smelled just as wonderful to mosquitoes, and all sorts of other insects, and she walked back to camp in those flips flops while wearing a night gown and summer robe. The chiggers came running as mother clomped through the grass and poison ivy. A cloud of mosquitoes followed her scent.

She returned to the car, stored her stuff, and sat down on a lawn chair beside my father. Luckily the smoke from the fire kept most of the mosquitoes at bay *after* she reached the campsite, but not the collection of chiggers she had already picked up on the way back. She started itching in short order and flip-flopped her way to the station wagon for her stop-itch spray.

She almost reached the vehicle but then let loose with a blood-curdling scream. Dad came running, flashlight in hand. Mom was sure she saw a snake glide under the car. Dad didn't see anything, but he stood guard while she used her spray. She stayed close to the fire and the packed dirt around it until bed time. He had to do some convincing to get her to crawl into the tent after her snake scare, but finally she did.

She crawled back out, rear-end first, very quickly. It seems that all that aromatic gas from the outhouse had collected through the side screens into the tent. Somehow Dad convinced her that the smell would keep insects and snakes out, or maybe he just thought he had, and she just pretended to believe him since she had nowhere else to sleep. Maybe she hoped it was the truth. At least she crawled back inside and on the air mattress.

She had never slept in a sleeping bag before, so my father had to crawl in and help get her into it. Her nightgown got caught in the zipper but neither noticed as he tucked her in. She tried to roll over to get comfortable, but she rolled off the mattress. Dad grabbed the sleeping bag and rolled her back on.

Then she tried scooting around inside the bag. She got wound up in her nightgown as she maneuvered because it stayed firmly fastened to the large metal zipper. My father had already zipped himself in and was sound asleep.

Now when Dad falls asleep, especially after a long hard day, nothing short of an air horn blasting right next to him has any chance of waking him. So, knowing that she couldn't get him awake to help, and not being able to unzip the sleeping bag enough to release herself, she tried to make the best of it. After a while she could no longer smell the outhouse.

However, her anti-itch spray had worn off, and the heat of the bag made the itching unbearable. And she itched in places she had never itched before. Her efforts of squirming to scratch and get comfortable without rolling off the mattress finally wore her out.

She was almost asleep when she heard noises outside. It was a variety of night creatures looking for anything available in the quiet campsites. Mom had never heard such sounds. Travel trailers had air conditioning going, were made of insulated metal, and were off the ground. This tent had none of these qualities.

Something landed with a plop on the tent's fabric. She didn't know it was a tree frog. Possibly; she thought it had to be a snake. Little shuffling feet and grunting noises scared her stiff. Then the trash can lids began banging.

It was only a family of raccoons making their nightly rounds. They had found the leftovers Mom had dumped into the trash and were busily feasting and scrapping with each other as loudly as any human family. My mother was positive some homeless person, possibly a criminal, was rummaging around their camp and would find them any minute.

Then she saw a flash through the canvas wall. A flashlight? But a distant rumbling told her it was lightning. She tried to relax. She hoped the thunder would drive away the sounds, and it did. She fell asleep exhausted, not realizing that thunder could mean rain.

Now Dad was a good outdoorsman, but over the years he had forgotten a few things, especially since his last camping trip was over thirty years earlier. The grass was in need of mowing where they had camped; it hid a small depression in the ground. My father had set the tent over a nice shallow bowl where water could collect if a heavy rain came. And it came....Hard!

Wind blew a fine spray through the window flaps and into Mother's face. She rolled over sleepily to avoid it, and her arm flopped out of her partly unzipped bag and off the side of the mattress.

Her hand landed in water. She partially awoke and splashed her hand around in the water. Then her bed moved because of her hand movements. She began sinking back to sleep when somewhere in her brain, alarm bells went off; her eyes shot wide open. She moved a little too fast, and her bed began rocking. She rolled off into the water. She

111

thought she was drowning, but, in reality, it was only about six to eight inches deep. (I'm guessing at the depth as no one said.)

She clutched at Dad, causing his mattress to rock. He rolled off, still asleep, on top of her. She started screaming, "Bradley! Bradley!" which must have been as loud as an air horn near his ear because he did wake up. Now both my parents were flopping like fish and getting wetter each moment. The two air mattresses tried to slide over the top of them.

Considering that these items were fairly lightweight, resembling the type used in swimming pools, Dad, still bound in his sleeping sack, inched like a caterpillar toward the door, unzipped its flaps, and tossed the mattresses out. He extracted himself through the bag's top; the thing was so twisted that he didn't bother to get out the normal way.

He scooted around in the water facing Mom, and pried her zipper part-way down, releasing her, but not the nightgown. It decided to remain firmly locked in the zipper's teeth; she squirmed her way out through its neck. She just sat in the water, naked, and said nothing. She wasn't angry, just miserable, wet, and sleepy. Dad, however, thought she was.

He rushed out of the tent, into the rain, and began moving everything that could stand to get wet out of the car and onto the now muddy ground around the fire pit. The rest he crammed into the front seat. Since the air mattresses had built in pillows, the extra ones Mom brought weren't useful before; now they came in handy, as did the extra sheets and blankets.

My father dragged her out of the tent, and pushed her in the back door. He stripped and climbed in the other side. They dried off with one sheet, and since the carpeted floor was scratchy, they covered it with the other sheet. The blankets warmed them up. My parents fell asleep, dry, safe, and listening to the rain hypnotically drumming on the roof. Both were totally naked in a fairly crowded camping area.

During the evening, the campers had kept pretty much to themselves. Now it was morning and everyone was awake, moving around, and talking; kids were running and playing. It was as if the rain had energized them all. The paths around my parent's camping area were now heavily traveled.

One man, seeing the disheveled mess their site was, knocked on the car's window to see if Mom and Dad were alright. The sudden noise startled them. They banged their heads together as they shot up out of bed; then they hit their heads on the ceiling. They forgot that they were naked, and I guess the poor man outside got quite a view.

He covered his face quickly and apologized while backing away as fast as he could. Mother was certain she saw a smirk on his lips as he turned to flee. "Dirty old man," she said. However, my father just grinned as he looked at her. She rolled her eyes, and blushed.

Keeping covered with the blanket, Dad reached over the front seat and opened his suitcase. He grabbed some clothes and dressed under the blanket. Then he got out and brought Mother's case back to her. He handed her what she asked for, and she too dressed under the blanket. She climbed out of the car, carrying extra items, and walked toward the beach house to finish putting herself in order.

While Mom was gone, my father wiped things dry and began packing them in the car. The wet sleeping bags went on the car's roof to dry out somewhat. He figured his wife wouldn't want to stay another night, and he was right.

When she returned, covered in bug spray, poison ivy spray, and dotted with fingernail polish on the chigger bites, she slathered the Calamine lotion over all parts of her body, beginning at the knees and moving downward.

Unfortunately she sat down on the woven seat of the lawn chair to coat herself with the medicine. The seat still held water between the webbing despite Dad's best efforts, and she soaked her bottom.

Dad fixed breakfast. She had no intentions of helping him. She was in a better mood after eating, and my father was able to joke with her about the man's knocking on their window earlier. She started laughing, and soon the misadventures of the previous night seemed equally as humorous.

They packed the food, coolers, and lawn chairs away. The sleeping bags were left on the roof as they slowly drove to the bathhouse where they found washers and dryers. Anything wet that could be washed and dried went into the machines. Soon everything was re-packed for the trip home.

Dad went to the park office and wangled a refund for the second night. Then since they were close to Ball State, my parents decided to come see me on their way home.

Over a late lunch, I got the entire story before either could forget any details. Mom even raised her pant legs to show me her polish-dots. She confided that the coated chiggers continued the rest of the way up, and then some.

I decided that I had had enough information on that subject, and my parents decided that tent camping was no fun. Even my dad had had enough. "Leave it to the younger folks," he said.

Later that fall, they found a 30-foot Yellowstone travel trailer on summer clearance. One year after that, my parents purchased a small motor home to pull it. Since I was at college from August to May and not able to go with them, they would take the combination on winter vacations, park the Yellowstone at a campground for several months, and use the motor home for short excursions.

They definitely preferred to take the comforts of home with them— no tents or motels ever again. Mom and Dad routinely traveled the roads of America for twenty more years before settling in North Fort Myers; even then, they kept the motor home. They just couldn't stay put— roaming was in their blood!

The Yellow Corduroy Skirt

After I finished college, my parents traveled a lot. We seldom were near each other during Christmases, Mothers' or Fathers' Days, other holidays, or birthdays. It wasn't long before they bought a place in Florida and sold the old homestead.

They did keep a summer house on Indian Lake in Ohio, and would come back north when the summer's heat was too much down south. In time, they sold this house also as it was too much upkeep, and they were no longer interested in the necessary long distance traveling needed to maintain both places. Traveling to distant locations to sightsee was by far more fun.

Our "togetherness" was now limited to short phone calls because the long distance charges were rather high. Thank goodness now for modern technology; those hurried, condensed conversations were not very satisfying or fulfilling.

Writing letters really wasn't an option as the mail would pile up for weeks when they were traveling. If I had written, the news would have been long out of date when they read it. Then too, my mother wasn't fond of writing; she simply didn't.

She also told me not to send letters as she couldn't read my handwriting. Any short letters I received came from my father, although he usually sent me postcards. Often I'd have one a day during their vacations, and at least one a month from Florida.

As technology got better and phone calls became cheaper, I'd call quite often. Mom usually answered, and she would tell me all about what she had been doing. When I did get to talk to Dad, he didn't have much to say—"Mom said it all," he would respond.

If Mother didn't cut the call short saying it was costing money, I might be able to get Dad to talk about the men's group he helped organize, or

114

the articles he had been writing for the home association's biweekly newspaper. He was proud of such "doings."

Christmases were hard; I missed not seeing my parents, especially Dad. I had neither the time nor money to take trips or cruises with them. I was teaching school, and my vacation was too short to fit into their schedule; being retired, they were not so limited.

Usually I'd send them presents early so that they'd have them before they left. My mother would inform me in advance what she wanted. Most of the time, Dad wouldn't have a suggestion.

She'd ask for an expensive Hull vase (I was a part-time antique dealer) or some such item, and then she'd tell me to get him something utilitarian like socks or a silk tie, maybe to go with a new suit she had purchased. That didn't seem right. I had to be creative to make the gifts equal.

I bought things I thought he might like—books, music, tools, movies, a painting. He was an avid fan of Zane Gray's novels, so I'd try to get him several for his birthday and Fathers' Day as well as Christmas.

One year during the time I had a stained glass business, I made him a large piece featuring a Mallard duck lifting off into the sunset. He really, really liked that gift. (I think I upset Mother with that one because Dad wrote in January to ask me to make her three door panels containing bluebirds. Neither he nor I ever heard the end of that gift.) Any book about birds, animals, or plants he especially enjoyed as well as wood carvings. Elephants were a favorite.

Mom would send a card with five dollars for my birthday or ten dollars for Christmas and a note saying she didn't have time to shop for me. I don't know what she told my father about this. He never asked and I never said.

One Christmas they were staying home, and I flew down. She had surprised me earlier by asking what I wanted since we could finally open gifts together. I had been planning to purchase a yellow corduroy, eight-gored skirt from some catalog. It had almost three yards of material in its design as it was mid-calf length and cost 30 dollars including tax, shipping, and handling.

I could make five different outfits using that skirt, both for work and for play. I thought the item was practical and the price reasonable. Most winter skirts were costing fifty dollars or more. So when Mother asked, I mailed her the catalog as a suggestion. I should have known better.

While growing up, I had learned never to ask her for anything unless it was something needed for school, and I'd had a paper from the teacher listing the supplies. I still remember a 15-minute tirade about money not growing on trees when I had asked for a nickel ice-cream cone. I didn't get that cone, either.

115

As a sort of defense, I did tell her about how useful the skirt would be, but I thought because she had asked, I was safe. She really caught me off guard, and I made a very stupid mistake.

I got the skirt. However, for the rest of my stay, she let me know how angry she was over being tricked into purchasing such an expensive gift. Unfortunately, the remarks didn't stop after Christmas.

Over the next several years, she'd ask if I had been wearing it—when and where and how often. Then she would remind me of how much she had paid and how upset she still was.

I began to dread talking to her on the phone, and every time I put on that skirt, her words would ring in my ears. Still, I wore it until it became frayed. When some printing ink dripped on the bottom front, and the cleaners could not remove the stain, I finally retired it.

After I gave the skirt to Goodwill, figuring someone could shorten it, and, thereby, cut off the stain, I made the mistake of telling Mom what happened when she again asked if I had been wearing it. I should have said yes. But, hindsight is twenty-twenty.

That fateful Yellow Corduroy Christmas was in the late seventies. When she came to stay with me for two weeks in the spring of 1996, my mother again berated me for asking for such an expensive item. She added a new twist—she said I had hardly worn it, and then had just given it away. In her eyes, I had added insult to misery.

Is it any wonder that when we shopped downtown during her visit and she offered two separate times to buy me a waffle cone with hand-dipped ice cream, I refused? I finally learned my lesson.

Section Two

Buds from a Tomato Vine

Initiation

You haven't really been initiated into early childhood until your mother washes your messy face or mouth with her well-used, soured kitchen dish rag.

Grits

I was complaining to a Southern buddy about my ant problems. She told me that her family put a trail of grits wherever the little beasties roamed. Ants take the grits into their hill, eat it, and die. I hate to use poisons because of my pets, so I tried it. It seemed to work. I have no clue why.

Jumpers

Another thing I learned about ants is that they don't like whole cloves. I scattered some on my kitchen counter, back near the wall, and the ants left. Just for fun, I surrounded a black ant with a circle of cloves. It ran around looking for a way out, but couldn't find one. Suddenly it reared up on its back legs and jumped right out of the circle. I'd never seen an ant jump like a frog to get where it wanted to go. It surely surprised me. I guess I'll have to give those critters a little more respect!

To Tell the Truth

A while ago I read in the Herald Times that the IU psychology department released these findings: when people are angry or drunk, they say what they really mean. When calm or sober, manners or social mores prevent them from doing so.

They did state that perceptions of what another is saying could be clouded by the alcohol. I guess if you really want to know what a person is thinking, invite him or her over, get out the booze, wait until they are feeling no pain, and ask. It won't be tactful, but you'll find out what you want to know. Ouch!

Now We Know

In my opinion, our government often spends money on the oddest things. In the 1990's, someone or some group was given a grant to study the length of American men's penises. Their findings stated that the average size was six inches. Now figuring that just asking a random sampling of men what their lengths are won't work as many or most will exaggerate at least a little, how did these folks get their exacting laboratory statistics? Many unwanted pictures come to mind.

Family Remedies

Mama King made my mother drink cod liver oil when she was little to keep her healthy. Mom swore she'd never do that to her children. I got mineral oil instead. Gee, thanks a lot!

Pin Worms

When I had pin worms as a little girl, Mother fed me a teaspoon of sugar with turpentine in it. It got rid of the worms all right, but it was the nastiest tasting stuff I've ever had to swallow.

Head Lice

It's a good thing I never had head lice as a child. Soaking the hair and scalp in kerosene was the usual remedy. It worked, but was extremely hard to get the greasy stuff out of the hair, and the smell would nearly asphyxiate the victim.

Good Teeth

My mother never did have very good teeth. She took excellent care of them, but they were just soft. She had several pulled. The dentist had her bite on a wet tea bag to slow down the bleeding after each tooth was pulled.

Baking Soda

When we ran out of tooth powder or toothpaste, Papa King would grab the baking soda. Worked fine, but I didn't like the taste much.

Split Ends

When my hair had split ends and was dry and brittle, Mom's old hairdresser glopped mayonnaise on my hair and left it there for 20 minutes. She said that was the best remedy.

Dandruff

Mom always had me rinse my hair in vinegar. Then she sent me out into the sunshine. She told me that red vinegar gave red high lights and white gave blond. It also gets rid of dandruff problems better than any shampoo can.

Migraines

I used to get lots of migraines up through my 30's, and the doctor gave me a prescription drug that helped. Before I had the medicine or if I didn't have any with me, my mother would fix coffee with a heaping teaspoon of sugar drowned in it. That concoction learned from Great Grandma Parks stopped the headache. That's the only time I'll drink coffee with sugar thanks to my dad's method of fixing instant Folgers. It does need to have caffeine in it or it won't work.

Green Onion Teether

When I was a teething toddler, my Papa King would give me a green onion coated in salt. The bulb was too big to swallow, but I got lots of chewing exercise and the salt helped too.

Whiskey Teether

A family friend used to dip his finger into whiskey and rub it on his grandson's gums when he was teething. It numbed the pain. The baby didn't seem to mind; I think he liked the taste. Just don't use too much if you try this because you don't want an alcoholic baby!

Tangled Locks

Coca Cola works very well for setting your hair. Just pour the Coke in a glass, dip in a comb, and drag it through your locks. Then roll on curlers and let dry.

Cigarette Ashes

Mom was a heavy smoker, but a friend of hers taught me a use for the cigarette ashes. Mix them with mineral or cooking oil and rub the mixture on those white water rings left on a wooden table from a wet glass. It also works on white spots on wooden floors left from wet shoes.

Easter Shoes

My mother used to polish my patent leather Easter shoes with a wadded up piece of fresh bread. It seems to work on other smooth leather also.

Icebox Lard

Grandma Patrick kept her lard in the icebox and later in the refrigerator. She said it made better pastries if it were cold. Also, if any family member sprained an ankle or wrist, she would glop that cold stuff all around the hurt to reduce swelling. I'll take an ice pack, thanks.

Fertilizer

Papa King always saved our stale coffee and iced tea plus the grounds and dumped them on the plants outside. It helped them grow. I pour my pasta water on house plants for the same reason. (I hate to waste water.) A lady who lived in the county went one better. She had men urinate on her lilac bushes or saved the urine from the slop buckets to pour on the plants. Supposedly the testosterone made the plants grow healthier and produce more flowers. You might try it if you can find a willing volunteer, and you don't live right downtown. I wouldn't want to explain the situation to a policeman.

Death to Fleas

Folks with floor coverings are plagued with fleas unless lots of pesticides are used. One old remedy was to take a shallow dish like a saucer, set it on the carpet or rug, and put soapy water in it. Shine a light directly on the water during the night. The fleas will be attracted to the light and jump into the water and drown.

You have to do it several nights in a row. At first, there will be many dead bugs, but there will be fewer and fewer each night until they're gone. If many rooms are plagued, use a saucer and light in each. This method will have to be repeated whenever more fleas are spotted—it's not a one-time deal. It *is* cheap however.

Super Cleaner

Mom used toothpaste for many things when I was growing up. She cleaned her rings with it, and scrubbed the mold off grout around the ceramic tile in the shower. She cleaned her silver plated cutlery and sterling silver jewelry. For me, toothpaste was an all-purpose, wonder cleaner. It even worked on some laundry stains.

So when a dermatologist couldn't clear up my acne, I resorted to toothpaste. I washed my face with it daily and used it as a face mask weekly. Maybe the fluoride in it did the trick. Whatever, it worked for me. The only problem is that the stuff is strong. It made my eyes water and my nose run. I recommend no company while indulging. A nose leaking its contents down through a toothpaste mask is not a pretty sight!

Merthiolate

I've never had my tonsils removed; whenever they became inflamed, the doctor and my parents would swab them with Merthiolate. It worked really well. Overnight the swelling and soreness would disappear. However since Merthiolate contained mercury, it's not on the market anymore.

I use Ever Clear now because of the high alcohol content. It works. Trouble is, your breath smells like you've been drinking. Since I don't want a DUI based on my breath, and my daughter didn't want to be sent home from high school under suspicion of drinking, I swabbed our sore throats at night.

For some reason, our cats won't let us kiss or even breathe on them. I guess they don't like our breath either. I also recommend using a Q-tip for swabbing rather than my dad's invention—a wad of cotton wrapped around the end of a tooth brush. Sometimes that cotton came off and got stuck half way down the side of my throat. Fishing that out was fun.

Pennies from Heaven

This old home remedy came from a nurse who said that to get rid of the pain, swelling, and reaction to insect stings, especially hornets, tape a copper penny over the puncture wound and leave it on for a while. The copper leeches in and neutralizes the venom.

I keep spare pennies nearby all during the summer months, and I've used this remedy many times. Just make sure the penny is dated before 1964. Newer ones don't have copper in them.

Once when I was away from home, a yellow jacket flew up my skirt. Not knowing the critter was there, I sat on it. In retaliation, it stung me. I dug a penny out of my purse, put it where I was stung, and proceeded to drive home.

The pain was soon gone and no after effects. I've use this remedy on my daughter, who is still slightly allergic to the venom. Trouble is, most folks today jeer and say it won't work and refuse to try it.

This remedy might not work as well for highly allergic folks, but for average people, it should work just fine. I'd suggest the others not throw away their Epi-pens.

The old cure my mother tried was a mustard plaster, but those never worked well on me. So Dad started handing me the pennies, and I got to keep them afterwards. Five would get me a dip of ice cream. No, I didn't try to get stung for the money, in case someone is wondering.

FYI

Florence Nightingale started a cosmetic company under the name Elizabeth Arden. I remember Mom using those cosmetics. It seems strange because I read about her in my history books. I guess it wasn't ancient history after all.

A Christmas Gift

In my Dandelions book, I wrote about bad ideas for Christmas gifts. I now have a new one for the list as I received this awhile back—a size 5X tie-dyed union suit complete with a buttoned flap. No such gag gifts accepted. I may roll the giver in skunk spray.

Brains

I was sent an e-mail that said intelligent people have more zinc and copper in their hair. I guess I need to go to the vitamin section of the local pharmacy.

Tea

I read somewhere that Earl Grey tea gives some folks migraines. Also, green tea slows down the early effects of Alzheimer's disease. Now when I make sun tea, I mix half green with half black. It makes "good for you" taste better.

A Touch of Trivia

Kirlin photography can photograph auras of people. Some folks with E.S.P. can see auras naturally. That's how halos used in paintings got started. They were partial depictions of whole body auras.

The gold color surrounding a person seems to show that the individual is getting inspirational ideas or is intuitive. He or she is a natural leader with lots of energy, charisma, idealism, and a strong sense of responsibility. I guess that's why only gold halos appear around religious figures in much of the world's art.

Thunder Bird

The thunder bird is actually the condor. These large scavengers ride air currents to save their strength when flying. They especially use the large currents that come before a storm. Observant people could tell when a thunder storm was approaching by watching these huge birds.

Iris

The "fleur-de-lis" is an iris.

Carter's Little Pills

Back in the 1950s or early 1960s, there used to be a product called "Carter's Little Liver Pills." It was heavily advertised, especially on television. Suddenly the ads stopped and the pills were off the shelves. The government went after the company because of false advertising— the medicine did nothing for the liver.

The product is back on the market now, only it's called "Carter's Little Pills." That's how the expression, "He has more excuses (or whatever) than Carter had liver pills" got started. During that time, the company would have had lots of pills in their store rooms that they couldn't sell.

The Boogie Man

Boogie Man came from Bog Man—the people ritualistically killed and buried in the bogs of Europe. The tannin in the water perfectly preserved (tanned) their flesh but not the bones. I guess a body with no inside support could be really scary. It would have to slither across the floor like a snake if it were alive. That would make a good horror movie.

Cleaning Copper

My friend Vicki told me the easiest way to clean copper was to use ketchup. I tried it on my Revereware copper pots. It really worked!

Bonfire

Bonfire was originally bone fire. The bodies of Bubonic plague victims were often burned in large piles to try to stop the disease. The nursery rhyme "Ring Around the Rosy" was also about the plague.

Barbie Doll

I found out that the Barbie doll was originally designed and sold in Europe as a man's toy. She often came with a drink in a bar. Maybe that's why the doll looks so deformed.

Phoenix

The phoenix was really a stork; it symbolized re-birth. That's where the idea that storks bring babies originated.

Dodman

If your name is Dodman, you might want to know that "dod" meant "dead." Deadman would be an unusual last name.

Pygg

"Piggy bank" comes from orange clay called "pygg." It was originally used to make jars for holding money.

More on Sweets

Egyptians used sugar to cure meats. I've eaten sugar-cured hams, salt-cured, and smoked. Then I found out that if you have an infection, you can pack it with sugar rather than salt to kill the bacteria—the Egyptians did. It might not hurt as much as salt. I haven't tried it, but I guess our body parts aren't much different from those hams.

Cherry Juice

Some cherry juice cuts the pain from osteoarthritis of the hip joint and some say gout too. My dad grew sour cherry trees, and we made lots of juice and preserves. He had five hip replacements before the doctors finally fixed him. He seldom took pain medication. Now I know why. That homemade juice cut his pain in half. Great tasting too!

Sugar Water

When babies get shots, giving them sugar water to drink cuts their pain. It's like chocolate for us gals. Let's hear it for sweets.

More Remedies

Mom said chlorine bleach will take the sting out of fire ants. She and Dad lived in North Fort Myers, Florida where lots of these nasties crawl. They got bit more than once while walking around their yard, so I guess they knew it worked.

Jellyfish

Vodka takes the sting out of jellyfish venom (except for deadly box jellyfish). Apply it straight. I don't think the proof matters unless you want to drink what's left in the bottle to help get over the trauma.

Deodorant

I was told that the aluminum in my antiperspirant may have contributed to my breast cancer as the limp nodes under the arm also go into the breast area. I've had a hard time finding brands which don't have this metal as an ingredient. It's not found in deodorant however.

A friend told me to use magnesium hydroxide, commonly known as Milk of Magnesia. I've drunk it before, but never worn it. No jokes please!

Lemon Juice

I knew that rubbing lemon juice on the hands removes the smell from chopping onions. Then I discovered a lemon wet nap removes the smell of gasoline on the hands after filling up the car at a station. I always did think gas made a poor perfume.

Plaintain

An old friend of my grandpa said to chew the flower stalks from plantain as a medicine. I'm not sure what it protects against, but I do still munch on them when I think about it.

Plastic Tablecloths

At Papa King's house, butter, red-eye gravy, and some foods would be left on the table all day. He just covered everything with a plastic tablecloth to keep flies out. That worked just fine, but not for the ants. He sat the table legs down in short tin cans and added water with a little soap in it. No more ants on the table. Kerosene worked too, but the smell...not so good.

Camphor Oil

Camphor oil soaked into a small piece of paper and put in with the silver will keep the pieces from tarnishing. Just be sure to wash the items before using them or everything will taste like camphor.

Oil of Mustard

Dad used to put oil of mustard on the plant leaves outside to keep animals away. I deliberately smelled some when I was about 12 just so I'd know what it smelled like. That's an experience I don't want to relive. It's not harmful, but my eyes and nose ran for several minutes.

Witch Hazel

Witch hazel is great for stinky feet. Just use a cotton ball and swab it on each tootsie especially between the toes. Rub it around in the shoes too. Now my dogs don't pass out when they sniff my feet.

Soaked Cotton Balls

Mom whispered to me that if I ever developed hemorrhoids because of pregnancy or had a sore rectum, to soak cotton balls with witch hazel and wipe the affected area. It stops the itch. Not exactly a conversation to have around the dinner table.

Pimples

If you have a pimple that just won't come to a head, put a piece of plastic tape on it overnight. It should be ready by the next morning.

Seasick

My father got seasick only once. We were on Lake Superior; the day was cold and windy, and the water was very choppy. My poor dad was turning almost green. As usual, he had struck up an acquaintance with the captain. So when he saw how nauseated Dad was, he gave him ginger. It stopped the seasickness. It's supposed to work on any nausea.

Oops!

I made my mother a hot toddy to calm her bad cough. I used hot tea, honey, lemon juice, and two teaspoons of whiskey. (Thyme, ginger, and sugar can be substituted, but keep the whiskey.) I used too high of a proof, and Mom got sleepy.

I'll check the percent next time I make a cough medicine because my concoction stopped her cough all right. She told me that she finally got a good night's sleep, but couldn't figure out why she had a headache that next morning. I didn't have the nerve to tell her she had a hang-over.

Insect Bites

Ammonia stops the itching from insect bites.

A Light Bulb Moment!

A bit of trivia I picked up said that men can read smaller print than women can, but women can hear better. That's not exactly a light bulb moment. I taught school for 25 years, and I've had several husbands and boyfriends in my lifetime. I had no trouble figuring out that *all* males practice selective deafness when women speak to them. However their ears work just fine all other times—especially if there's gossip to be heard. And, yes, guys do gossip more than women.

Original Coke

Would you believe that Coca-Cola was originally colored green? I'm glad the company changed the color. Somehow drinking green Coke doesn't seem appetizing.

More Trivia

"The rule of thumb" was based on an English law passed sometime in the 15th century. It said that a man could only use a stick as thick as his thumb to beat his wife. Did someone say divorce?

Bedding

Mattresses and beds weren't as comfortable as they are today. Instead of bed slats, ropes were used, and if you wanted a firmer bed, you had to tighten the ropes. That's where the phrase "sleep tight" originated. And the second part—"don't let the bed bugs bite" had a bit to do with the stuffing used in the mattress—grass, straw, corn cobs. Bedbugs could hide very well in that stuff. You get the idea.

Wet Your Whistle

In English pubs, the mugs had built in whistles. When a customer needed a refill, he blew on the whistle. That's where "wet your whistle" started. I can just see a lady bartender or waitress responding to that. It could get ugly.

Paint

My father taught agriculture in schools and was often visiting his students on the farms. He also grew up on a farm near Bolivar, Tennessee. He was a wealth of knowledge for me.

One day we were talking about the old milk paint found on antique furniture. With his signature silly grin, he asked me if I knew why barns were traditionally painted red. Of course I asked why. It seems that nothing ever went to waste on farms. The blood was saved from slaughtering hogs or cows in the fall and used for making blood pies and other baked foods. It was also used as paint for the barns. It was very durable. Makes me contemplate the smell.

Section Three

Bittersweet, the Climbing Nightshade

The Trainor Horror

The Trainor mansion at 200 Vine Street was erected in 1863 for John Devor. This plush Civil War era house was said to have represented American architecture at its opulent best. The three stories consisted of 15 rooms and cost $50,000 to build.

The main and second floor had iron and wood fireplaces in each room. Brass chandeliers and fixtures were used everywhere. Deep relief sculptured ceilings, ornamented window frames, and overhanging bay windows added to its beauty. Above the front entrance was a dark blue skylight which cast blue light and dark shadows on the winding staircase.

Martin B. Trainor was born in Tyner, Indiana, and later served in the Civil War. He had enlisted in Company H., One Hundred and Fifty-fifth Volunteer Infantry from Indiana. After being honorably discharged at the end of the war, he attended the university at Ann Arbor, Michigan.

There he met Katherine Kecklider, a native of Darke County, Ohio. After their marriage, the couple bought what was to be known as the Trainor Mansion in Greenville, the county seat. They had a son, Morgan D., and two daughters, Mabel and Agnes.

Judge Trainor was one of the county's wealthiest residents. The railroad tracks ran near his house with a diverted track directly on the back of his property where his personal Pullman car sat. Whenever he traveled on business or took his family on outings, the train would back onto the side tracks and attach the Trainor's car.

Judge Trainor died of "acute indigestion" at his home in November of 1927. His daughter Agnes married John M. Keehan and lived at 212 Vine Street, only two houses up from the mansion but still on part of the family compound.

Mabel married a man named Johnson—first name unknown. A matching house at 208 Vine Street was used by them until they divorced. Mabel then lived in the mansion where her mother died in 1929.

These are the basic facts that can be found in the county records. I have included them because most folklore experts, whom I have encountered, consider this story (if they are familiar with it) to only be an urbane legend. I know the following events to be true because I was there.

My family moved from Hartford, Kentucky in 1955 to Union City, Indiana. Then in 1957, my parents purchased a house at 807 Daly Road in Greenville, Ohio. The Trainor compound was only three miles, at the most, from our house. We passed it many times each week, both day and night, as we traveled into town.

My girlfriend Ann lived only two blocks from the compound. I visited her often and there were times we walked by the tracks behind the mansion or strolled the sidewalk in front. We were typical nosy youngsters.

I do not know when Mabel Trainor Johnson divorced her husband, but as divorcees were not thought well of in the early 1900's, I do know she was a recluse for many years living on the last of the family money.

When we moved to Greenville, the Trainor Mansion had long since fallen into disrepair and the Pullman car was a rusty metal box disintegrating on its rails out back. It had not moved in a very long time, perhaps not since the mother's death. Sometime before the mansion was torn down, I noticed the car was gone altogether—perhaps sold or simply towed away.

The main entrance to the house was up steps to the second floor, but I think they were too rotted to be used by 1957. Mabel lived on the ground floor even after the house was condemned.

I remember traveling by the mansion at night and seeing the first floor's bay windows lit up. If there were any curtains, they were never closed. Perhaps that front part was a library because I saw many shelves lined with books.

It is possible that Mabel had moved things down from the upstairs because the lighted part that I could see was filled with things stacked and piled around; it resembled a warehouse. A table sat among this clutter perhaps 12 or 15 feet from the window.

In early 1957, I saw Mabel sitting at that table talking to a man. Whoever he was, I couldn't say, unless he was her lawyer; it wouldn't have been a family member.

She seldom permitted anyone to enter her house; all her business was conducted by telephone. Even the groceries were brought to her kitchen door. She never left and seldom ventured outside.

No green bushes or lovingly cultivated flower gardens were there when I lived on Daly Road. The grass was cut, but in time, only tangled stalks of dead plants surrounded sections of her house.

When Mabel was finally forced to leave her condemned home, she moved back into 208 Vine Street. Her house and Agnes' were either mirrored images of each other or exactly alike. My memory fails somewhat here although I do remember one place was yellow and the other grey in later years. There was enough space between them for another house and yard.

For company, Mabel kept cats—thirty-five of them at least and perhaps five or ten more. It was generally known that the grocery boy only delivered cases of cat food to her house. The grocer said that was all the food she ever ordered, and there was no information concerning anyone taking human food to her. Many speculated that perhaps she also ate cat food because of her dwindling bank account.

She was not on speaking terms with her sister or brother-in-law even though they lived side by side, and Mabel made a will dated May 20, 1957, leaving money to Agnes and to eight distant relatives in other states. Agnes could offer no information as to her sister's habits or pets. I doubt she knew of the will.

At the end of December, 1961, neighbors saw piles of newspapers outside her house. The grocery boy, making his usual two week delivery, saw his last order still sitting outside the back door; he left, leaving the groceries. Perhaps he reported to someone about the possible problem.

Whatever alerted the family, Mabel's brother-in-law, John Keehan called the police at 1:30 to report that water was running from the back door of #208. He did not bother to investigate as the rift was deep between Mabel and the Keehans.

The local newspaper reported that the police found two or three inches of water covering the kitchen floor and a faucet running. The body, covered by a blanket, was found lying on cushions on the floor of a downstairs bedroom. A floor lamp was on.

A document stated that she was buried in January, 1963, but I believe this to be a typographical error. Since the newspaper article I found was dated January, 1962, I doubt there was a year's delay in burying her.

The article did not state the facts about the over-two-weeks of newspapers or what the grocery boy witnessed. This and the following information is what my father received from his friend at the Greenville Police Dept. I believe he was one of the men who investigated.

The officer informed my father that when they entered, the place was filled with cats on furniture, on window sills, on a mantel or shelf, and even one on a hanging lamp. These cats had water from the running faucet, but nothing to eat. They were mad from hunger and ran at the investigating officers, perhaps hoping for food. A cat jumped onto one man's shoulder and so startled him that he shook it off and shot it.

The odor from the cat's urine and feces was overpowering as the animals had not been cared for at least during the last two weeks. The stench of death also filled their nostrils. Mabel was partly decomposed and the starving cats, having nothing else to eat, had been eating her. Her bodily fluids released in death had soaked the blanket and cushions, and had leeched into the floor.

The cause of death for the 67 year old lady was reported as "natural causes" but exactly what that meant was never disclosed. The coroner estimated that she may have died around December 16 to possibly December 22. However, some of the piled newspapers outside had earlier dates than the 16th. Also the cases of cat food still sitting outside when the grocery boy came again were delivered before the 16th.

It is possible that she couldn't get up to get the papers or the food and died later. Who turned on the faucet? Did Mabel forget the running water because she was not feeling well? Did the water pressure turn the handle as sometimes happens? Did a desperate cat manage to turn on the water? (I know that can happen as I owned a cat with a habit of pulling or pushing any lever—toilet, faucet, or door, which he could reach.) How long had the water been on? Had another person been inside? Also nothing was ever discovered as to why she was on cushions on the bedroom floor and covered with a blanket. Whether she had a bed or not wasn't ever stated. She was simply buried January 1st.

The animal warden with the help of the police shot the cats in the house. They did not try to rescue or feed them. He stated that the animals acted "very wild." Their blood was splattered where each of the

35 was killed. The warden assured folks that all the cats were "disposed of" but my father's source of information said that some may have escaped when officials were going in and out because no one knew exactly how many Mabel owned.

This created a scare all over town. Parents told teenagers not to go around the old Trainor Mansion or the compound for fear of man-eating, crazed cats which would attack and give their victims diseases or tear out their eyes. Of course, telling kids not to only meant they definitely would. Whether any additional Trainor cats were ever identified, I don't know. The fear and rumors continued for several years.

Some brave school mates of mine reported seeing feral cats hanging around the mansion and tracks, but whether they were descendants of Mabel's starved pets or not, no one knew. It was fun tip-toeing around there on Halloween. The half-crazed, attacking-cat stories were scary at bonfires and pajama parties and good for many screams.

The old mansion was dilapidated and stood empty and forlorn before it was finally torn down. A realtor purchased Mabel's house, cleaned it up, and attempted to sell, then to rent it. No one ever moved in. It was said the smell could never be removed, and I believe it. I used to drive past 208 Vine Street when I came home from college, and the windows on the left side were always open. The place was reported to be haunted also.

Finally Mabel's house too was torn down. Some rather ugly rentals were built over the site of both places. Agnes' house is there. It has been refurbished and altered, but I can still recognize it. When I returned to Greenville in 2002, I took my 13 year old daughter with me.

We visited the historical museum where my past English teacher was curator. She helped me dig up some official reports and find pictures of the old Trainor Mansion for my daughter to see. Then we traveled to Vine Street to locate the compound, railroad tracks, and Agnes's house. She discovered that the location existed and the events really happened and are still remembered around town. She even read the newspaper articles saved on film at the library.

The tale of the man-eating, insane cats has since joined the annals of modern folk tales, categorized as an urban legend. I know because a folklorist mentioned it at a Halloween event in the Bloomington Library in Bloomington, Indiana where I had taken my daughter. Erin and I both tried to tell the lady that it really happened.

She brushed us off saying folks often think the legends are real, but there is no hard evidence to support any of them. Too bad she wouldn't listen. That's why we went to Greenville, Ohio—to get the hard evidence.

Hello

She hadn't felt well all day. Even though her pregnancy leave had begun four days before, she had promised to accompany her students on their field trip to the caverns. She had called in that Friday morning to say she wasn't able and to apologize. The principal wasn't pleased; now he would have to go instead. He told her so.

She spent the day in the recliner, feet up, resting or sleeping—the bed was no longer an option; the toxemia prevented it. She watched the Rolling Stones' Steel Wheels Concert that she taped off TV a while back, but had not yet seen. Hungry, she pushed her cat off her lap. The huge white Maine Coon looked up quizzically as she raised her bulky body out of the chair.

Her water broke, flooding everything, even the cat. She was shocked; the baby wasn't supposed to come for another month. She didn't know what to do. She called her doctor and asked if she should come in the next day. The doctor chuckled at her ignorance.

"Get to the hospital now; I'll meet you there," he ordered.

There wasn't enough gas in the car to make it to the hospital—a 45 minute drive. She hadn't filled it since she visited her cousin, two hours away, earlier in the week. *Stupid me*, she thought.

She called her parents for a ride and for support. Her mother answered, "Sorry but there won't be enough time for me to get my make-up on. Find someone else."

"Could I talk to Daddy?" she begged. "No, he's busy; I'll tell him you called."

The receiver went dead.

She had thought…but it didn't matter. She was alone, and it was up to her. Her "significant other" had left four months before to go out west. He wanted to persuade his old girlfriend, who had dumped him over three years earlier, to take him back.

Actually he had run from responsibility. She had known this and accepted his fear. It had hurt, but life went on, and she was a survivor.

Doubling over each time the contractions started, she forced her jelly-like legs to the car, and drove to the station for gas. She covered her mouth and nose so not to breathe the fumes—it could harm her baby. Then she began the long drive to the hospital. The contractions were 3 minutes apart. She timed them as she drove. When she reached the hospital they were less than two.

She had to put the car in the long-term parking area which was quite far from the emergency entrance. She parked and sat there shaking. She didn't know if she could make it, but she had no choice. Her legs were so weak; she staggered, but used the other parked cars to help herself.

The wide-open emergency area was the biggest challenge. It took forever to reach the entrance. Inside was a wheel chair. Holding on to the wall, she reached it, and collapsed. Holding back her tears of relief, she tried to wheel herself to the desk, but couldn't. A passer-by saw her problem and flagged a nurse. She smiled gratefully, but couldn't speak - maybe she passed out.

She found herself on a gurney in a hospital gown. The room was dim. The wall clock said 8:30; it had been 6:00 when she left the gas station. The contractions were constant now.

A nurse entered. "The doctor is prepping. I'm here to take you down. Too bad you're not getting the epidural; it would be a lot easier for us. You haven't dilated."

"I can't," she mumbled, "genetics." In the operating room, she was surrounded by people, some watching, one putting in an IV, one holding a syringe, two doctors; the one with the scalpel she recognized—her doctor.

He said chuckling, "Don't you know that when your water breaks, you should head for the hospital, not call to see if you need an appointment?"

She smiled back, "I do now."

"The anesthesiologist is going to use that syringe to administer the anesthesia into the IV. When she does I want you to start counting backwards from 100. We will have only a little over 30 sec. to get your baby out before the anesthesia hits her. Ready?" Her doctor nodded to the woman who pushed in the syringe and opened the IV valve.

She began, "100, 99, 98, I'm scared." The room spun around.

Sometime in the middle of the night, she partly awoke. A nurse was pushing on her abdomen.

She screamed, and her torturer said, "Sorry, Dear, I have to do this to make sure you aren't bleeding to death. Do you want your baby now?"

She saw no bedrails—just two bars, "No, I'll drop her or she'll roll off if I pass out," she tried to say, as she blacked out again.

Two nurses brought her new-born in the next morning. Tiny eyes focused on her mother's bigger ones.

"Hi there, look at your long eyelashes. You have your daddy's eyes," the new mother smiled, and her little girl smiled back. The baby book she had read said an infant can neither focus nor smile for a while, but little Bradleigh could, her mother was positive of that.

"It's just you and me, kid, in this crazy world. You didn't come with an instruction booklet, but I'll do my best. Just know I'll screw up sometimes, and you'll have to help me make it right. I'll always love you and stand by you. I'm not perfect—just a scared little girl in a mother's body. Hope it's good enough, Bradleigh, I named you for my father," she said.

Bradleigh raised her arms as if wanting to hug, and her mother hugged her.

Odd that the chart at the foot of the bed stated clearly, "Mother hasn't bonded to child." It must have been because of the night before, and was probably why the nurses had been so churlish toward her that morning. But that didn't matter; she had Bradleigh, and the world was waiting.

The Daughter

"**H**ello, no one is available to take your call. Please leave a message."

"Hi, its Dad. Sorry I didn't make it over yesterday; I was busy. My girlfriend Roxanne's son's girlfriend needed us to babysit her little girl. She's the cutest little baby doll I've ever seen; I just adore her. Hey, uh, maybe we can go out for supper tomorrow. When is school out? I'll be free after 5:00. I don't have much money right now. I took Roxanne out to dinner yesterday and breakfast today, but we could split a burger and fries. I'll call if I'm not too tired. You understand. Leave a message on my machine."

The daughter deleted her father's voice. Yes, she understood. She heard the slurred words. She had waited all day Sunday for him to pick her up. He'd missed the week before, so she had been sure he would come. But the long day had worn on, and he hadn't shown up or called.

She had cried Saturday night. Part of her had been afraid that he might not come after all, and part of her had been afraid that he would ignore her for others if he did come. She was afraid to tell him her feelings. He might stop coming all together.

Now she cried again because he had disappointed her *again*. So many times he had promised then said he was too tired or too busy.

So many times she had said, "That's ok, Daddy, I understand. I'm cool."

Many broken plans and broken hopes. She cried harder because she had always been his Baby Doll. She loved him so much, and she hurt so badly.

"I guess I'm not his Baby Doll anymore," she sobbed.

When she couldn't cry anymore, she put on her head phones and listened to her music.

Her heart still bleeding, she shrugged, "I'm good for his image; he'll call when he wants to parade me around, and I'll smile and say, "Yes, Daddy."

Then she started singing along with her Bon Jove CD, "Struck through the heart, and you're to blame; you give love a bad name."

The Christmas Gift

He called to say he wasn't coming by that Christmas Day; he was spending his time with his girlfriend instead. His daughter begged him to at least come over and get the presents she had bought for both of them.

She had saved her allowance and done odd jobs to get enough to buy two nice gifts—ones she hoped would please. Grudgingly he said he'd stop by to pick them up, but he couldn't stay. She waited all morning and into the afternoon, before he and his girlfriend arrived.

He wanted to take the gifts at the door and leave, but his girlfriend went inside and sat down. There was nothing he could do but follow although he fidgeted the entire time. They opened their presents and thanked her. Then he gave his daughter two presents—a harmonica and a mug with cute kittens on it. She didn't know how to play a harmonica, and she nearly cried when she saw the mug. But she said nothing. They left soon after.

Her father came back to the door after helping his girlfriend into the car. He asked to "borrow" the harmonica, and his daughter returned it to him. "Thanks," he said, and left.

She closed the door and went over to her mom; she wanted to be hugged. As her mother held her, she felt her daughter trembling and knew her teen was close to tears.

"Mama, why did he take the harmonica back?" she asked, knowing the answer, but hoping she was wrong.

Her mother said nothing, but looked over the teenager's shoulder at the mug, hoping it wasn't what she thought; hoping her daughter wouldn't recognize it. Hoping, but knowing it was a false hope.

She'd found that mug at a local used clothing store months before, and brought it home as a little surprise. Her daughter used it often, and then it disappeared. She assumed it was up in her teen's bedroom. Now she knew she was wrong.

Her ex-husband had been in the house. He came over to feed the pets when they were gone, and did his laundry there rather than spending his money at the laundry mat.

Casually the mother checked the kitchen cupboards, praying to find that mug somewhere inside.

"You won't find it there, Mom," her daughter said, coming up behind her, and carrying the mug.

"Maybe it's one just like yours. They make thousands of those things. Now you'll have two," her mother smiled.

"Mom!" was all her daughter said, as she turned the mug over. On the bottom, written in black nail polish were her initials "E.B."

A Haunted Tale

The old farmhouse was attractive. It was in good shape, and the rent was affordable. What pleased Sue and John were the big windows and wide doorways; light traveled from room to room easily, creating a cheery atmosphere. The layout was unique in that it was four squares with a connecting rectangle in the middle.

Between the twin front parlors was an enclosed staircase which led to the second floor and on to the attic. The door opened into the dining room. It appeared more like a closet than as a way to reach the bedrooms above.

The two older sisters who owned the house had recently moved elsewhere and had decided to rent the old homestead; it had become too much for them to maintain. The Schultzes signed a short lease and moved their two young children, cat and dog, and belongings in the following week.

They had come from a small apartment, and didn't have the furniture to fill the spacious rooms. The dining room was empty and served as a play area. Only one parlor had furniture in it. They had splurged and bought another used bed and dresser so that their boy and girl could each have a bedroom upstairs. Sue and John had the adjoining room and used the fourth bedroom to store extra clothing. No one went into the attic, or even the basement; there was no reason to do so.

John worked a lot, and as they had only one car, Sue was mostly home with the children unless friends or family dropped over to visit or take her out. She discovered over the weeks that she was reluctant to go upstairs by herself, and Annie and JJ refused to go up even for a favorite toy unless Sue went with them. They took their naps on the floor or couch in the parlor.

John couldn't understand why his children cried when put to bed in their rooms, saying they were scared. He figured it was because they had slept in the same room before. Lights were left on in the bathroom, bedrooms, closets, and center room, but still the children begged to sleep downstairs. Often he and Sue would wake up at night to find Annie and JJ sleeping on the floor next to their bed.

Sue tried to explain her uneasiness during the daytime to him, but John just scoffed. He said he didn't sense anything unusual. His wife reminded him that he wasn't home until late and was so tired that nothing "sank in." She told him that a train could go right through the house, and he wouldn't notice. He laughed and agreed. He told her old houses have their own personalities and as they'd never had a second floor before, the enclosed stairs probably seemed like a cave.

John told her everything would settle down as they got used to the place. He also said that the windows weren't as large upstairs so the rooms were a little darker, and that the bare, dark-painted pine floors didn't help. He promised that they would get some carpet remnants, white curtains, and white paint to brighten things up. They went shopping that next weekend.

John took a few days off from work to paint the floors and walls white. After hanging some cheerful prints found at a thrift store and Sue's counted cross stitch samplers, they put down the carpet remnants—red for JJ's room, pink for Annie's, blue for the master bedroom, and white in the bathroom and long center room. Now the upstairs was more inviting. Even the enclosed staircase looked better painted white. The creaks and groans of the house weren't scary anymore.

The children liked their rooms better but still wanted the lights on at night. One of John's buddies joked that the second floor looked like a lit up Christmas tree. John smiled and said whatever it took to get the kids into their own beds was better than tripping over them in his room.

He even let Annie keep her cat and JJ keep his dog on their beds. It worked for a couple of weeks. Then the children were back to begging and sleeping on John and Sue's bedroom floor.

Again they wouldn't go upstairs during the day. Sue's uneasiness grew daily. Several times when she carried laundry to the bedrooms or was cleaning, she saw that the children's doors were shut. All doors were usually open to allow extra light to flow inside. She knew neither Annie nor JJ had shut them.

When she told John, he said the shifting of houses from weather changes often made doors off center. Sometimes they'd close on their own, and sometimes they wouldn't stay closed. Sue agreed, but said something still didn't seem right. John told her that her imagination was working overtime.

Then she began finding the bedroom doors locked. They were easy enough to unlock with the old style keys, but both children denied playing with the locks. Sue began checking each morning; she used doorstops to hold the doors open and made sure the locks were unlocked. Then she deliberately checked several times a day. Each time they were closed and locked.

A week later, still checking the children's bedroom doors, Sue began hearing noises in the attic which sounded like wheels rolling. She opened the door to the attic and listened, but the noises had stopped. Taking a deep breath, she climbed the dusty steps and peeked over the top of the floor.

The attic was one large room with windows on all sides. The front wall had a three-sectioned window with a triangular glass like a hat above the middle part. The two outer windows were shorter than the center one. All three could be raised; they had screens. This large window allowed sunlight to stream in and offered quite a view of the countryside. Sue was surprised as she had not noticed it from the outside. Then she smiled, thinking to herself, "Of course I didn't notice it; I go in the kitchen door all the time."

Dirty curtains covered all the windows. The lacy panels on the large one allowed light through, but the others were thick cotton. There were some boxes, two trunks, a wardrobe, and a couple of side tables with lamps. A dismantled bed was propped against a side wall.

One section of the room resembled a kitchen of sorts. There was an unusual appliance that had a refrigerator below with two electric burners and a sink on top. It ran on regular 110 current; Sue could see the plug snaking around the front. Next to it was a Hoosier Kitchen and its matching tall cabinets, one on each side. A small wooden kitchen table was nearby, but no chairs, just a wheel chair instead. A television on a swivel-top table sat in the center of the room with two comfortable loungers nearby. There was even a toilet and shower.

The attic appeared to have once been a stark one-room apartment; it wasn't overly inviting. Everything was very dusty, especially the floor.

Nothing had been used for a long time. The only object which could have caused the sound of rolling wheels was the wheelchair, but the dust on the floor was undisturbed.

"Well," she thought, "the house's shifting could have slanted the floor up here, but that wheelchair didn't roll." Sue didn't like the atmosphere either; it was oppressive. She felt as if she were intruding. She hurried back down and shut the door. Then on impulse, she turned the lock and almost ran down the steps to the first floor, and locked that door too.

Sue spent the next hour looking over her shoulder, feeling as if someone were watching her. Finally not being able to withstand her growing unease, she took Annie and JJ outside to read books and play ball. She only went back inside to fix an afternoon snack for the three of them, but felt such fear that her hands shook as she made peanut butter and jelly sandwiches.

She quickly grabbed the milk from the refrigerator, but when she turned around, three glasses were sitting by the plate of sandwiches. Next a bag of chips slid towards her. Sue quickly put everything on a tray and fled outside. She tried to pretend that everything was fine, and thought she was succeeding.

Then Annie asked, "Why are your hands shaking Mommy—you almost spilled my milk?"

She tried to find an excuse, but JJ turned to his sister and said, "The house scares Mommy like it scares us."

Sue passed around the sandwiches and milk. She had forgotten the plates and napkins, but was not going back inside for them. She opened the chip bag so they could just reach in.

Trying to appear calm, she asked, "JJ, how does the house scare you?"

JJ shrugged, "The doors open and close by themselves; the house doesn't like Annie and me."

Annie said, "I didn't unroll all that toilet paper; it unrolled itself. I tried to roll it back, but it unrolled again and wrapped around my neck. I was afraid to tell you because I didn't think you'd believe me. I told you Tippy did it. Then I said I did it so you wouldn't make him stay downstairs. He protects me—he meows and growls and claws at the bad things in my room at night. They go away."

"Yeah, and I wasn't teasing Molly," JJ said. "She was barking at my closet door because it kept swinging wide open, then almost closed, then opened again. It didn't make any noise so you didn't hear it. Daddy said he'd spank me if I didn't stop making her bark. That's why I took her and my pillow and went to your room to sleep."

Annie said, "Our doors close at night and lock. We can't get them open. We can't see the light in the bathroom or center room."

"And the lights go off in our rooms," JJ added. "And there're sounds like a wagon rolling."

"And someone's talking."

"Yeah, it sounds like a man saying, 'Get out! Go away; I hate you," JJ said.

"I see a white thing in my room—like smoke. It doesn't say anything bad to me, like it does to JJ. I can't understand the talking except it likes Tippy. It said, 'Nice kitty,' but I know it doesn't like me either."

Sue asked, "Are you scared in Mommy and Daddy's room?"

"No, it's safe there," JJ said.

Annie agreed, "That's the only safe room upstairs. Can we please have our bedrooms downstairs? It won't bother us there."

Sue's sandwich felt like concrete in her stomach. Trying to remain calm, she said, "Ok, Daddy and I will get your bedrooms down in the two front parlors this weekend. Until then, you can sleep in our room."

When John arrived home that evening, he found supper outside on the picnic table. Chips, ham sandwiches, ice tea and carrot sticks weren't what he was hoping for—a cold meal in the chilly night air. He looked confused, but smiled and said, "Oh, a picnic, what's the occasion?" Four sandwiches later he knew the answer.

He said he'd stay in JJ's room the next few nights, and if anything happened, he'd move all three bedrooms downstairs.

"The children are still young enough to share the one parlor for a bedroom, and we can use the other one," he said. "I know you won't want to be upstairs and have the kids downstairs—too far away."

Sue felt relieved, but didn't feel he believed all that he was told. She also knew her husband. All he wanted when he got home in the evening was a filling hot meal and a chance to relax. He'd do anything to prevent loosing either one of these.

That night Annie slept in bed with Sue, and JJ had a sleeping bag on the floor. The night was uneventful for them. John was so tired that he figured nothing would keep him awake. He fell asleep immediately, but a short time later he felt a hard bump.

He awoke to find himself on the floor. He was surprised because he hadn't fallen out of bed since he was a child. He just told himself that he wasn't used to sleeping in a twin bed. Groggily, he crawled back into bed. His pillow was gone; he found it under the bed.

Now that he was up, he decided he'd use the bathroom. The door wouldn't open. No matter how hard he turned the knob and pulled, nothing happened.

Must be dreaming, he thought. *Work too much, need to cut back, hire some help, so tired.* He staggered back to bed, and pulled the covers up to his chin. Something yanked them off and threw them over the foot of the bed. Then all the lights in the room came on.

John yelled, "Enough!" He got up, took the pillow and blankets and started for the door. It opened by itself. "Thanks," he mumbled and stumbled to his room. He gently put Annie on the floor with the pillow and blankets, and climbed into bed.

Sue woke up. "What?" she asked.

"Go back to sleep. I'll stay home tomorrow and move the rooms," he mumbled.

Sue thought to herself, "I guess he's had a rough night."

After breakfast when the children were busily playing in the dining room, John told her what had happened.

"Maybe I should have been scared, but I was too tired; I was just angry at not being allowed to sleep. I'm still worn out, but I promised."

Sue said, "You go back to sleep for an hour or so, and I'll slide the living room furniture into the dining room. The space is big enough to separate into two parts; the kids will still have a big play area."

John agreed and dragged himself up to bed.

When the dishes were done, Sue asked JJ and Annie to move their toys to one side of the room. They immediately did so, and then asked if they could help her move things. She was very surprised.

They really want to be downstairs. I've never seen them help like this without orders and complaints, she thought. JJ even helped slide the couch.

Two hours later, Sue had the new living room/ play room just the way she wanted it. She thought everything looked better and warmer than before. She lay down on the couch and fell asleep. The children played quietly; then they also took naps.

John came downstairs around 11:00. He was impressed at how fast everything had been moved, and how inviting it looked. He tip toed into the kitchen and fixed cheeseburgers for lunch.

Actually he had some help. The buns put themselves on the plates when his back was turned, and the cheese slices separated themselves from the package and lay neatly on the counter ready to be put on the meat. He was startled by the buns before he even saw the cheese, and he dropped a glass he was carrying towards the table. It stopped just before it hit the floor, then landed safely.

John felt a little spooked, but mumbled, "Thank you." The cheeseburgers and milk were all he could manage as his nerves were on edge. He woke the family for lunch.

While JJ and Annie were getting the chips out of the pantry and dividing them on four plates, John drew Sue aside and told her what happened.

"It's like we got help when we decided to move the kids. Something here doesn't like children upstairs."

Sue agreed. "Let's eat and get started," she said.

It took the rest of the day to move all the furniture downstairs and arrange each room. JJ and Annie had the right parlor; Sue and John had the left. The children were very good about helping carry the lighter belongings to their new room; they were even laughing.

Supper that night was pizza—ordered in. Everyone was too tired to cook anything. Annie and JJ went to bed and fell asleep immediately. John and Sue collapsed on the couch in the new living room, too tired to move. She told him about the attic and the bad atmosphere she had felt up there. He suggested that they should talk to their two old landladies. Sue agreed to call them soon.

All seemed well for many months. She kept the door to the upstairs locked unless she needed to get something stored in the fourth bedroom. Sue never got around to contacting the two sisters; she just mailed the rent.

It was nearing late July when Sue invited two girlfriends over for lunch. One was almost seven months pregnant. During dessert, she told the women all about the happenings that past year. Both wanted to see the bedrooms; they begged until Sue reluctantly agreed.

As she unlocked the stairway door, she asked them to be respectful and quiet, hoping the ghost wouldn't become angry.

"We have to live here, you know, and I don't want it doing things to scare us after you leave," she said.

They didn't listen. The two friends bounded ahead laughing and joking. "Come out, Mr. Ghostie, if you're really here," Ellen called as she climbed. Louise whistled as if she were calling a dog.

Sue followed slowly. She realized her friends thought what had happened to her family was more like fun at an amusement park haunted house than the fear found in a real one. They looked all around the upstairs. Ellen examined every closet, and Louise checked the door locks.

Ellen said, "This is a totally boring. There's nothing here." Both were noisy and disappointed.

Since no ghost had jumped out at them and nothing had floated through the air, they insisted on going up to the attic. Sue felt the atmosphere upstairs grow more ominous by the minute, and was positively petrified at their insistence.

The girlfriends didn't seem to notice anything unusual. Louise located the attic door in the center room, opened it and yelled, "Ready or not, ghost, here we come." Both started laughing at her little joke and began climbing.

Sue pushed them to the side of the stairs and led the way up. Maybe she thought she could act as a guard between her two friends and the attic. They didn't even get to the landing. A feeling of pure hate slammed into all three, and Louise, the pregnant one, screamed.

Off balance, she grabbed for the handrail and slammed her back into the wall. Her legs slipped down the steps; one landed her on a knee as the other continued sliding, hitting Ellen below her.

Sue, in the lead, grabbed Louise's arm and blouse. She fell up the stairs and landed on her bottom. Bracing herself with her legs, she pulled against Louise's fall. Her pregnant friend stopped sliding which gave Ellen time to catch her balance. If Sue hadn't grabbed Louise, her two friends would have tumbled down together.

Both girlfriends sat down on the steps, hysterical and crying. Louise kept screaming that someone had pushed her backwards, trying to knock her down the stairs.

Sue, closer to the attic landing, heard something rolling and looked up. She saw a man's face surrounded by medium-length white hair and beard. His eyes glowed red and his face was contorted in murderous rage. The apparition only flashed in front of her face for the shortest of seconds, but it was enough. She ordered everyone downstairs.

Louise was sobbing, "My baby, my baby. It tried to kill my baby!" Ellen was white faced and silent.

Only Sue saw the ghost. Her hands shook as she locked the door to the stairs after they reached the dining room. She led the others into the kitchen and slowly calmed them down.

She had to forget her own fears for the time being. No one was hurt. They refused her offer of ice tea and left soon after.

Sue sat down on the couch. As she thought about those red eyes and the terrible anger on the ghost's contorted face, she began shaking violently. She thanked God that her two children were at their cousins' house for the day; the ghost might have vented his rage at them.

And he still might, she thought. Getting up, Sue ran to the phone and called John at work. "Come home now," was all she said.

He left immediately. When he arrived, Sue was sitting at the kitchen table, clasping a full glass of tea in hands so shaky that the liquid sloshed over the top. She couldn't talk—her teeth just chattered.

He pried the glass loose and set it on the counter. Then he led her outside to the picnic table. The sunshine helped, and the shaking stopped. Still, it was close to an hour before she could explain what happened.

"I'm calling the landladies right now," he said. "We're going over there. I want this straightened out today. We're moving out. Stay here."

Within the hour, they were sitting in the two sisters' apartment across town. When Sue and John explained all that had happened over the past year, the women pulled out a family album.

"Look through the pages and see if you recognize anyone," they said.

Several pages in, Sue saw a man with a beard and a pony tail; he was sitting in a wheelchair. "That's him," she said, "only his hair isn't white. But those eyes are definitely what I saw. They are so intense!"

One sister, Opal, said, "I suspected it was him from your description. Edward was injured in WWII, and was very bitter. He insisted on living in the attic even though he had a lovely room on the second floor. So we converted that area into an efficiency apartment for him. He spent a lot of his time just staring out that big window up there. For some reason after he was wounded, he positively hated children, and babies, and even pregnant women."

Abigail added, "He didn't like children much before the war, saying they were noisy, demanding, and always crying, but he couldn't stand to have any around when he got home. We never knew why. He died in that room; we found him just sitting in his wheelchair in front of the television. I guess we can't rent to folks with children from now on. Sorry. Your lease was only for a year, and the time's up. I suppose you will be moving?"

One month later, the Schultzes moved into another house—one with no ghost.

This being a true story, I have changed the names so that the family won't be bothered by curious folks. Sue was a close friend of mine, and I visited her only two days after the final incident occurred. She and I had been neighbors just before they moved into the haunted house, and she knew that I had some slight paranormal abilities. (These are gone now.)

Wanting to know what I thought about her problem, she explained everything to me in depth. The children were living with relatives until she and John could find another place. With Annie and JJ out of the house, the atmosphere was cheerful and cozy downstairs. She wouldn't unlock the stairs so that I could go up. I really didn't want too anyway as the air near the stairs seemed odd.

This happened in Kenton, Ohio during the 1970's. When I visited her in the 1990's in Columbus, Ohio, she still was having occasional dreams about the red eyes and contorted face. She said it was not something she could ever forget. She didn't mention her two girlfriends—I don't think they kept in touch. As for the house, I have no further information.

155

Who's on the Phone?

In 1976 when I was teaching in Ohio, I met another teacher who had just transferred into my building. C.W. was assigned to teach social studies at the junior high where I was teaching English and science; her classroom was very close to mine.

As we were both single and about the same age, it wasn't long before we were great friends. It turned out that she only lived a block from my apartment. So naturally we were constantly at each other's place. It wasn't long before I noticed that she had an unusual, but very handy talent. She knew who was calling before the telephone even rang.

She was eating supper at my house one evening when she looked at me rather matter-of-factly, and said, "Your mother's calling." Then she continued eating. I remember beginning to say, "How do you....," when the phone rang, and it was, indeed, my mother on the phone. After the call, she explained that she had always been able to do this. I asked why she hadn't told me before this time.

"I usually don't say when I know a call is coming; I just keep quiet. I never know what the reaction will be," was her answer.

"Why did you decide to tell me now?" I asked.

Her response was, "Yeah, well, you're different."

"Wow, thanks," was all I could think to say, and we finished supper.

C's talent became so normal that I didn't think anything about it. Actually it was handy. This was a time before message machines and the only way to know who wanted to borrow your time was to pick up the receiver. When she was around, I could decide if I wanted to talk to the person on the other end of the line before the bell began ringing. If not, I was forewarned.

I never told anyone about her ability—it just didn't seem any more unusual than having a friend who breathed air. However I was wrong in that assumption. Somehow others found out about this and were afraid. They were determined to take action.

Late one evening, I received a frantic call from C. asking if she could stay with me for the night. Of course I agreed. When she arrived, she looked scared. She told me that two other teachers, one from the junior high and one from the high school, both of whom I knew and will not here name, invited her to join them for dinner—a girls' night out. All three were to meet at one's house before going together to a restaurant.

Whether they went out to eat and then returned to the house or not, I don't remember, but the two women tied C.W. to a chair and told her they were going to beat the demons out of her no matter how long it would take. Because of their religion, they were certain that her talent could only be the work of the devil.

How they planned on explaining her absence from work or whether they had even thought that far ahead, I haven't a clue, but they did plan to keep her tied up and locked in a room until they accomplished their mission. They wanted to save her soul.

How my girlfriend managed to loosen her bonds and escape, only she knows. C.W. was a tiny little lady, but strong. I believe she said that the ties used weren't tight enough or that they stretched when she exerted pressure. Somehow she got loose and ran to her car. She drove straight home and packed an overnight bag.

She had planned to go to a motel if I wouldn't take her in. How could I refuse? Of course she stayed the night, and she moved in with me over the next week.

I told no one that she was living at my apartment; however, those two women found out. I can only guess that they themselves or others were watching my girlfriend's movements. One evening, C. informed me that one of them was calling. She advised me not to pick up the phone when it rang. I chose to answer.

The caller said, "We know C. is living with you. You need to give her up. She's a demon. If you don't, we are coming for you too."

I responded, "I don't think you'll want to do that." Replacing the receiver, I turned to my friend. She looked very relieved and smiled at me. I think that she believed I might actually toss her to those "wolves" to save myself. Not a chance!

The one teacher who worked in my building tried to "talk some sense into me," but failed.

I simply told her, "I don't appreciate threats. Leave me alone." I'm not sure why there were no further problems, but all ended after that conversation.

C.W. lived with me until the end of the school year. Then she moved to San Francisco, and I traveled with her. We had lots of fun and escapades during our trip. However, that's another tale.

Letters To Mildred

Based upon letters Grandma Mary Parks King wrote to my mother which I found among my mother's effects after she died. I claim poetic license in the writing.

Sept. 15

Dear Mildred,

How do you like your new job at the bank? You must write and tell me all about your responsibilities, the people there, etc. Have you met any friends as yet? How do you like Cincinnati? Is it confusing to get around the city by bus or by car? I hope you and your sister are tolerating each other well enough. I know you two don't get along, but be patient; it's only a temporary arrangement. You will soon save enough for your own apartment, I'm sure.

Your puppy Champion is so sweet and into everything. I caught him chewing on the kitchen table leg. He looked so innocent of wrong-doing that I just couldn't bring myself to swat him with a newspaper. Instead, I took him outside to the swing and just held him. Your Papa says I'm spoiling him rotten, but I just can't help it. He's such company now that you are off on your own. I miss you even though you only left in July. He gladly tolerates the hugs I wish I could give you. What will I do when you are able to take him with you? He's eight months old now and growing fast.

We are getting rid of the chickens. It has just become too much for me to take care of them. I'll get my eggs from the grocer from now on. I know I will probably miss the company when neighbors drop over to get a dozen or two, but I am sure my work will get finished quicker. I have been passing a little blood this week. I think my hemorrhoids are acting up. Another good reason to sell the chickens. However, I will still have fried chicken on that table when you come home.

Will you be coming home for Thanksgiving? Let me know when you write.

Love,
Mama

Nov. 8

Dear Mildred,

Your pup Champion is 10 months old and looking so handsome—his fawn colored coat just shines. Our friends love on him when they come over as he is so very friendly. I'm certain all the female dogs on the street have their eyes on him—he maybe siring their puppies someday. Oh dear! He is very attached to me and protective; I don't have to worry about safety when he is near. I have been training him to walk beside me on a leash. He has learned so fast and so well that I can leave the leash off and he obeys as if he were wearing it. He follows me wherever I go and just watches me. I had heard that Boxers were excellent dogs, but I think this one is exceptional. The name "Champion" certainly fits him very well. You won't recognize him when you come for Thanksgiving.

Write quickly to tell me if and when you will be home. I've invited your Aunt Sally and Uncle Erten as well as Uncle Claude for dinner. We will be having a large turkey, corn-bread stuffing, green beans, a cranberry salad, and mincemeat pie. Aunt Sally will be bringing food also. She is bringing a pumpkin and a lemon pie for certain and potato rolls. Whatever else she hasn't decided. We will be eating left-overs for days, and there will be plenty for you to take back with you.

The chickens are all gone now; I did put a few in the freezer. Mr. Duke bought them and he took the chicken coop also. He and a couple of extra men hooked a wagon to his truck and loaded it on. He will be coming back for the fencing tomorrow. There won't be much cleaning up for your Papa to do, fortunately.

I am still bleeding some off and on. I figure it will stop soon since the chickens are gone. I won't be lifting heavy water buckets, bags of feed, or egg baskets. I know that I didn't have to, but I didn't want to bother others to do it for me. Miss you. Write.

Love,
Mama

Dec. 12

Dear Mildred,

Papa and I had hoped you would make it for Thanksgiving. I wish you had written me to say you weren't coming. Everyone asked about your accounting position, but I could not tell them much as you haven't told me. All I could say was that you were well and working hard.

Christmas will be here soon. I haven't heard from you, so I don't know if you are coming. Surely the bank will give you two days off—Christmas Eve and Day. If you can't afford the gasoline for your car, Papa will drive up to get you and take you back. Let us know.

I'm planning to have fried chicken and a ham, candied yams, potatoes, creamed peas, chilled whole cranberries, oyster stuffing, biscuits, and you favorite, gooseberry cobbler. We will eat around 1:00 PM, after church on Christmas Day.

159

Papa is putting up the tree sometime this week. He and Uncle Claude have picked a nice one on his farm to cut. Wish you would be here to help decorate it. I am still feeling somewhat weak and am still bleeding. I haven't felt like popping corn and stringing it for the tree. Instead, I bought some garland and tinsel at the hardware store. It will be very festive, I am sure.

I have put fresh sheets and quilts on your bed in anticipation of your being here. Everything is ready or will be soon. Papa is fine. He took me to Owensboro to shop for gifts on the 9th. I hope you will like your presents. They are all wrapped already and waiting to go under the tree. I can't wait to see you!

Have you found an affordable apartment as yet? Or are you having trouble finding one which will allow you to have Champion? He is eleven months old now and very strong. He is quite the companion, and I will miss him when you take him to Cincinnati. I brush him every day and his coat just glows.

I am counting the days until I can see you.
Merry Christmas!

Love,
Mama

Jan. 15

Dear Mildred,

I am very upset with you. Edith wrote to say she was not coming as she would be with Bob's family. That's understandable as they are married, but I heard nothing from you. Papa took me for a drive after Christmas Eve services because I didn't want to go home.

We opened our gifts when we returned; I couldn't bear to open them Christmas Day and have Uncle Claude watch just the two of us. I put your presents on your bed. We tried to be cheerful for Christmas dinner, but it wasn't the same. I wasn't hungry—Champion had plenty of leftovers so he was a very full dog.

Would a letter have been too hard? What did you do for Christmas—please write. I will be mailing your gifts to you this week. I hope you will like them.

Papa is getting someone to help me around the house. Orella is still doing the cooking, but I just can't seem to do all the things I want to. I'm bleeding more, and it seems to be making me weak. I assume I have colitis rather than the hemorrhoids. I had it once before. I'm going to see the doctor next week for an examination. I may ask him for some penicillin. Papa is well but as hungry to hear from you as I am.

Love,
Mama

Feb. 10

Dear Mildred,

Would you believe Champion is over a year old now? He poses just as a show dog would. He is very strong, not to mention, bull-headed. I have had to knock him over the head with a newspaper several different times to make him mind. He thinks he should dig holes in or trample on my flower bed, then sleep in it. He also won't stay in the yard. He has broken his chain just to get to the neighbors female; she isn't in heat yet, luckily.

Did you receive your presents? I hope the blue suit fits correctly. It is appropriate attire to wear at your bank, isn't it? Your Aunt Hula, who manages the bank branch here, told me it was suitable. She also said the white blouse would not be too frilly to wear either with the suit or another outfit and could work well for casual gatherings. I wanted to be sure you had new clothes; I didn't know if you could afford any as you are saving for an apartment.

If you do not like the clothes or they do not fit, return them and I will send you the money to buy something else. If they are acceptable, send me a picture of you wearing the pieces—I am sure you will look both professional and lovely.

I am bleeding constantly from the rectum now. The penicillin that Doctor Parker gave me has not helped. He gave me an iron tonic to help with the weakness. Oh, it has a __nasty__ taste. It has helped some, but not enough, he thinks. I saw him again yesterday, and he wants me to see a specialist in Owensboro. He seems to believe the bleeding might be a symptom of something worse—perhaps a perforated colon. Papa insists that I make an appointment—I will set it up for the end of this month or March 1st. Papa sends his love.

Love,
Mama

March 1

Dear Mildred,

Papa gave me the money to see the specialist today. I could not tell him how afraid I was to go. I skipped the appointment and went shopping instead. I bought a cute hat, matching purse, and shoes. I also purchased a pair of gloves for you.

Papa won't be pleased that I didn't keep the appointment. I'm not sure what to tell him when he returns this evening. He is very worried, but I just couldn't face that specialist. Maybe I will make another appointment for later this month.

I have to get this in the mail before I return home. I am still in Owensboro at the moment. I picked up this stationery in the front of this little drug store soda fountain. I am trying a "Black Cow" which is made with coke and vanilla ice cream. Very tasty.

I am very weak after shopping, but this drink is a quick "pick me up."

Hope to hear from you soon.

Love,
Mama

April 8

Dear Mildred,

It has been over a month since I wrote you last. I guess your letter to me got lost, so write me again. I hope you will like the gloves I bought you last month. They are short, black satin with a small bow at the wrist. Maybe you could pick them up if you came for Easter. I'd love to see you, as would Papa. It has been nearly a year.

Papa is doing fine, although he sprained his ankle last week and is temporarily using a cane. He says it is feeling better each day; but I see a grimace each time he bends it. He has it taped.

I'm weak—still losing blood. I have not made an appointment for the specialist as yet. I keep putting it off for various reasons. I tell Papa I will, but that I'm busy right now. He thinks I am doing better because I keep saying the bleeding is getting less. I picked up some iron pills at the drug store, and Dr. Parker gave me some new medicine also.

Please write; I miss you so much.

Happy Easter!

Love,
Mama

May 11

Dear Mildred,

Papa is still limping. He has his ankle heavily taped. It is swollen and he walks stiffly. Possibly he has torn a ligament. He finally admitted that he only told me it was feeling better as not to worry me. A fine pair we are. I keep telling him my bleeding is getting less and less because I do not wish to worry him. Still I see the concern in his eyes.

I am so very weak now and seem to be getting weaker, but I smile and try not to show it—I pretend I am getting stronger when he is home. The extra effort only compounds the problem. I spend much time reading out on the front porch swing when he is home and in bed when he is gone. The new help is doing all my chores now. I don't even help Orella in the kitchen.

Papa is worried and getting most impatient with you. He is threatening to come to Cincinnati to see you if you do not write soon. We have heard nothing from you since you left last July. You know you have always been Papa's favorite. Won't you please write him, if you won't write me?

Edith did write to say you were still at her and Bob's apartment. If it weren't for her few letters and slight mentions of you, we would not even know if you were still in Cincinnati or alive. Your Uncle Claude is thinking about selling his racehorses, and farm, and moving into town. That was quite a shock! He does get lonely out there.

I keep hoping he and Pearl will get married someday. She can't spend her entire life caring for her parents, I hope. Could it possibly be an excuse so not to marry at all? Neither she nor Claude is young anymore. It is none of my business, but I really doubt that Claude will sell the horses or farm anytime soon. I think he wants to be closer to Pearl, that's all.

Edith mentioned that you received a raise. Did you get a promotion? How do you like your work? You aren't over-working are you? You need a social life. Are you dating? You know that Papa will send you the money to help get an apartment if you want, and you need not pay him back. Or you can work it out as a loan, if you prefer.

Your brother-in-law is a lawyer, you know, and he probably knows people who would rent to you and allow you to keep Champion. I'm just trying to help. I do know how independent you are, but Edith accepted our help, can't you? Just a mother's concern and interest. Write!

Love,
Mama

June 20

Dear Mildred,

Congratulations! Your Champion sired three puppies on the neighbor's chocolate poodle. She is standard size, so the pups will grow large. They are so cute and fuzzy; they have poodle fur but look like a boxer.

Papa is much better. He discovered that the ankle was cracked. Dr. Parker was not pleased that Papa hadn't come to see him sooner. He is still using the cane as the

163

ankle is stiff, but the pain and swelling are gone. I can tell because he is smiling again. He thinks I am improving too.

I'm making a red velvet cake for the Fourth of July and icing it in red, white, and blue. Hopefully, I can do it all by myself, but Orella seems doubtful. I told her I wanted to do it to convince Papa that I really am better. She says I am being deceptive, but I do so want to keep him smiling.

I know that you probably will not be able to get off work to come home, so should I mail the gloves I bought? They are out of season right now as they are black and June has turned hot. However, you could use them come September.

I keep checking the mailbox for a letter. Your bank must be keeping you very busy. Hope you are well.

Love,
Mama

January 2

Dear Mildred,

I am sorry that I have not written for so long. Writing has become difficult for me. We just had our second heavy snow fall yesterday. Since you are farther north, I know you have had more than we.

We missed not having you here for Thanksgiving or Christmas. I bought you a pretty dress and a black hat to match the gloves. Papa will be mailing them to you shortly.

Orella is now making out the food lists for the grocer to deliver as well as cooking. She also runs all the errands either before she comes in the morning or after she leaves in the evening. She's not young either. Soon she may need to go into a nursing home which Papa will pay for, of course; she's family to us and we couldn't do otherwise.

The other woman Papa hired is Orella's niece, and that poor lady is doing all the heavy housework as well as caring for my flower garden. She does the laundry and ironing as well and helps Orella as much as she can. I'm almost useless these days. Even sitting on the swing wears me out. I stay in bed quite a lot. The medicines and iron don't seem to be any help anymore.

We kept one of Champion's pups which I named Dora. She is quite odd-looking; she is a Boxer with a French poodle hair-do. I do wish you could see her—seven months old and full of energy. She keeps Champion well exercised. Both, when still, stay very close to my side.

Champion leans against me if he suspects that I am off balance or about to fall. I use his strength to help get out of bed. Even when playing, he keeps a watchful eye and comes running even if I do not call. He just seems to know when I need him.

Please write. I do know how busy you are, but Papa and I are concerned. Do you need any money? Are you well and happy? Edith mentioned that you spoke about talking to a recruiter. Surely you aren't considering joining the Army!

The war is in Europe and we aren't involved! Please write and say you are not joining. That would be such hard work. Love you so much Darling,

And miss, miss, miss you!

Love,
Mama

Feb. 21

Dear Mildred,

I think you should return home very soon. Your mother is not well, and you will find her greatly changed. She is in a wheelchair now. I have not been able to persuade her to go to that specialist whom Dr. Parker recommended last year. Perhaps it is now too late for any help. I do not know. She can no-longer walk as she is so weak, and she has little appetite.

Dr. Parker suspects she has a perforated colon which means poisons are seeping from her intestines into her body. The blood may be coming from the damaged area. I know she is afraid that she has cancer, and that is why she won't go to the hospital or anywhere else for help.

Contact me soon and I will drive up to get you. I suspect your mother has only a short time left, and we both miss you very much. Come July, it will have been two years since you have been home or written. I am tired of seeing the disappointment in her eyes when the mail comes each day, and you have sent no correspondence. Surely a simple letter would not be a burden to you. Are you so busy with your life? She can no-longer even hold a pen to write to you. Make arrangements at the bank soon for a short leave of absence. Send a note stating when you can come.

The food won't be the best here. I am trying to cook as Orella has retired and may need to go to a nursing home soon.

Incidentally, if you are planning on joining the Army, say nothing of it to your mother. The worry could harm her already precarious health greatly.

Love,
Papa

April 3

Dear Mildred,

Your mother died last evening of a perforated colon so the hospital assumes. An examination will be made to be certain. If that is what she truly had, it could have been corrected with an operation had she not been so afraid it was cancer, had she not refused to seek help. She was so stubborn in her fears.

Make arrangements to come home for the funeral. I will drive up to get you, as soon as you are ready. Edith and Bob are already here as you know.

Dora and Champion sense that something is wrong and are walking aimlessly around getting underfoot. They are staying so close to Edith and myself that Dora tripped her two days ago. Orella will be here later today. I will put her in charge of those two dogs!

I wish that you could have visited your mother before she died. She asked if you were coming, then said she understood how busy you have been at the bank and how you just couldn't get free. She said to tell you she will love you always.

I'm sending this special delivery and hope it reaches you before I arrive.

Love,
Papa

Section Four

Trimmings of Henbane

She

There she was--
a small red-leafed maple
as tall as I,
no bigger,
no smaller.
Her mahogany leaves waved at me
each time we met,
so beautiful in the summer sun.
My parents shopped at her nursery
very often,
and we became fast friends.

Her yellow tag read five dollars.
I saved to buy her.
I was about to pay the man that day,
then mother slapped my hand,
"Money's burning a hole in your pocket,"
she sneered.
She forbade me,
and I went home alone.

We could have grown tall together
that tree and I.
I could have sat
under her spreading branches,
and told her my secrets,
or held her trunk when I cried.
She would have loved me
when I had no other mother.

Perhaps it's just as well
when I looked to the past.
Our house and yard were sold.
New owners cut down the twin maples
which shaded our front lawn.
They too came from that nursery

where she and I met.
Such would have been the fate
of my little tree.

Someone else surely bought her.
Maybe they loved her
as I did,
and planted her by their house.
I hope she lives there still.
She would have long since
forgot me,
but I have remembered her
these long many years.

Image

You know not me,
And I know not you.
Yet strange as it may be,
You judge me, you see.
And you do not notice that
As you form your opinion,
You hold up a mirror,
And within it is the portrait
Of Dorian Grey.

Black, White, and Gray

Blessed are the ignorant
For they shall sleep at night.
To them, the world and all they see
Is cast in black and white.

It is the old and hoary heads
That see the shades of gray.
This steals from them their worthy sleep
Until the break of day.

Sadness

The dusky silence of dying times
Presses onward unceasingly.
There was love—late autumn.
The unended rhyme .   .   .
Bitterness
      Numbness
           Apathy
                Bewilderment

Regret!

What good is hind-sight?
It is sorrowful, broken shoes
Fastened to an escaping bridal car.

Nursery Rhyme

Hickory chicory dock
The vine climbed up the phlox.
The phlox was bound
and both fell down.
Hickory chicory dock.

Fireflies

Meteoric lightning bugs
Rocketing through the May trees.
Florescent, luminescent life,
yet so evanescent.

Queen and Quean

Two spellings of Queen:
The wife of the King,
His second in charge;
The other means slut.
How strange that may seem
That one is exalted,
The other, faulted.

Life

Snow, you two-faced beauty,
And you, majestic trees,
Swirling planets, fiery sun,
What are you
But a small part of that vast cosmos
Which fills a formless void.

Then what am I?
I cast myself down upon my face,
Humbled and awed.
I am a tiny barge
Upon an endless river that flows
From eternity to infinity.

Two Dogs Chasing Cars

Suicide pugs,
Suicide pugs,
What is it about
Cars that you love?

Piper's Pied reed
Must cause this need.
Why be such minions
To gods you heed?

Leashes won't hold;
Wheels are your goal.
Has neither one heard
For you the bells toll?

Leaves

Stems of leaves carry life.
As months drift on,
The leaf crinkles and falls.
With the passing years,
Man wrinkles and dies.

The years are stems
Uniting leaf to tree.
The stems are years
Severing life from death.
Leaves spring again.
Do we?

Mama

How does a child
Gain its Mother's love,
Or can that never be?

What can it do
To make Mother smile,
And not stiffen if touched?

Must She reject
Her tiny newborn,
Saying it's too ugly?

Is it so bad
That it needs punished
With a thick stick each day?

Why must She sneer
When the child tries hard
To do everything right?

Is no success
Good enough for praise,
Instead of just ignored?

Why must She make
The child feel worthless
In all parts of its life?

Why at Her death
Is She so happy
To have disowned Her child?

Why must there be
This final revenge
As She leaves for heaven?

Sorrow and Love

They say animals feel no love or sorrow.
That they aren't as evolved as us.
Then why did my cat stand vigil
For one whole day
Next to his dead brother
On the side of the road,
Killed by an indifferent, rushing car?
He would not leave his side,
Nor would he eat or drink.
Neighbors told me when I returned from work.
When the burial was over,
He grieved for one week more,
Sitting by the grave.

I saw a dead chipmunk in my lane.
Another stood by his side
And touched its nose
To that fallen companion
Several times.
Then I watched it stroke

The dead one's fur
Gently
With its hand.
He pushed the body,
Perhaps hoping it would rise again.
But, it did not.

A squirrel eats seeds dropped from a bird bowl
On my back deck.
While his companion, a black cat
Eats canned food next to him.
They share a drink of water.
The cat, a prodigious hunter,
Protects his friend

From another, too-interested feline.
After the challenger is driven away,
They sit side by side, protector and protected.
Such behavior makes me wonder.
Was that sorrow which I saw
In the actions of cat and chipmunk?
How grew that odd friendship
Between hunter and hunted?

But surly animals are less evolved than we?
They feel no love or sorrow.
Many explanations can be offered
For their behavior.
Couldn't the same be said of us?
Many explanations can be offered
For our behavior.

The Sentinels

All night long the dogs will bark
Then sleep by day to rest.
But what *is* it that they see,
Which makes them sing their best?

There are those who say it's deer,
And creatures in the dark;
Thunder, water, groaning earth,
Or to the wind, they hark.

Is it messages they send,
Hoping to find their own?
After all, we do the same;
We call by telephone.

Are they noisy sentinels
Barking into the air,
Stating to all a warning,
"Trespass if you dare"?

And yet there are those quiet times
When nothing seems awry,
That they will growl and carry on.
What something snags their eye?

But at such times one wonders
Do they sense the other side?
Do they hear the fluttered movements
From spirits who have died?

Our old folks call them "cobblies,"
That dogs can see and hear.
So let them warn, don't hush them;
No danger will tread near.

Merry-Go-Round

It is amusing to me that a man who elicits help to cheat on his wife, will, after he is divorced, get a girlfriend and cheat on her, sometimes even with his ex-wife. It must be intrigue or challenge, not love, which fuels him. Woe to the ladies whom he calls his "soul mates."

Two Curiosities

If alcohol is so evil, why do we have wineries with names like St. James?

When I hear someone say, "That's the honest truth," it makes me wonder – is there a dishonest truth?

A Problem

It's a sad commentary that sometimes women who have had mastectomies lose their husbands or boyfriends because of the operation. This has happened to five women I know.

For a guy to refer to his girlfriend as "not marriage material" or to call his wife a "Cyclops" after having survived cancer seems terrible. Some women refuse the surgery for this reason, and resign themselves to a death sentence.

Too bad whatever spell was put on Hal in the movie *Shallow Hal* couldn't be cast on anyone who sees the outside and ignores the inside of people.

Times, They Are Emerging

Ι went to a movie at the library last night which was put on by the League of Women Voters. The title was *Iron Jawed Angels*. While I have heard the horror stories about what women went through just to be allowed to vote, the movie, while a bit Hollywood-styled, really brought those vague accounts to life.

I called my daughter later in the evening, and told her to find the movie and any others she could at the University Library or on the web, and have her friends watch it with her. She and many other women her age, as well as mine, take so many things for granted.

Our rights as women are still emerging. My mother served in the army during WWII; she was a tech-sergeant at Camp Crowder in Missouri. Her commanding officer would not give her a transfer or a promotion with a pay raise; he said she was too good at her job, and he didn't want to lose her.

It wasn't until two or three months before the war was over that she got the rank of tech-sergeant. She told me she was frustrated, but nothing could change her commander's mind except the threat of going over his head. That's the only reason she finally did get the promotion.

When the war was over, she went to college on the GI bill to be a CPA. She met and married my father. I guess her dream was still possible as a married woman, but then she became pregnant with me. She felt that she wouldn't be able to work at her chosen career because she would soon be a mother; maybe she felt no one would hire her. Instead she took some education courses to become a business teacher.

She never wanted to teach, and never really adjusted to it. She couldn't get a job while pregnant, and Mom and Dad needed two salaries to live; she and I stayed at my grandfather's while my father traveled with his job.

We moved to Ohio in 1955 as both my parents found good paying careers. Mom managed the family money, and paid all the bills, but she could *not* get a credit card in her name. Nor anything else, for that matter. The cards were only issued in Dad's name. So were the insurances and car loans. The house, at least, was in both names.

She had no credit and could get none. Believe me, she tried very hard everywhere, but was turned down. Even Dad couldn't help her.

Finally in 1965, a ladies' shoe store—Crawford's, located in Dayton, Ohio, gave her the first credit solely in her own name that she had ever had. This had been a bitter pill to swallow over the years, and when she got that little paper card with a $100 limit, her hands shook and tears filled her eyes. Mr. Crawford, the store's owner, bent the state rules to

178

allow her that credit as she had been a regular customer for 19 years, and they were good friends.

The hand-written card carried his personal signature. It was that little piece of paper which forced other stores to extend her credit until she finally got a MasterCard.

In the late fifties in Ohio, my parents taught with a couple who wanted badly to buy a home. The bank would not use the wife's salary when figuring whether they could purchase a cheap track house. The husband didn't make enough by himself.

Finally that institution agreed to lend them the money, but only if both signed an agreement not to have children—women were expected to quit teaching if they became pregnant. That document gave the bank the right to foreclose or demand a balloon payment if she did have a child. They got the house, but remained childless, to their great heartbreak.

I too have experienced such frustration. When I attended college in Indiana in 1967, my career counselor recommended that I become a teacher, nurse, or secretary. These were proper careers for proper young ladies. I had wanted to be a biologist, but chose to be a science teacher because of his "counseling."

Later, it was my Dad's strong-armed tactics that got my second car put in my name rather than his. It had been his car, and the BMV wouldn't change the title back in 1972. Finally in 1973, I had a car in my name alone.

After I began working in an Ohio public school in 1973, I was able to get a couple of charge cards in my name and had excellent credit. When I married in 1980, suddenly my husband had the right to use them even though I did not authorize him with the companies; however I alone was responsible for the debt which he ran up.

The bank automatically gave him the rights to my lock box too, and handed him a key. That's how he got those cards to use, and I knew nothing about it. When I questioned this, the bank manager just shrugged and said he had the right as my husband, and they didn't have to notify me.

My second husband was the vice-president of a bank in Ohio. Without my consent, he took the money from my savings account, closed it, and put the money in his. ATM's were just beginning, but without his okay, I wasn't allowed a card or pin number. I had no recourse as he was my husband. No, I didn't get an ATM card until I was single again.

My girlfriend was working at his bank and reported to me some of the things going on there. Women were not given the promotions that men on equal footing were given, and their pay was less. One man was hired in as a teller as that was the only available job at the time. In less than a year, he was promoted over several ladies who had been there longer, and had more training and experience. Suddenly he was a manager over the very women who had trained him.

I asked my husband about this, and he said, "Women just have babies and quit. Why should the bank spend time and money to train and promote them when they will just get pregnant? They're too emotional. Men run the bank. Women make pretty tellers, and pretty tellers bring in customers."

I have never forgotten his statement. I won't express my thoughts concerning this revelation, only that his attitude was a factor in our divorce.

I purchased a house in 1996 on Christiansburg Road here in Brown County. It was in my name alone, and I made the payments. However, because I was married, a local insurance company put the house insurance in my third husband's name.

I informed the agent that if the house were lost, I wouldn't get the money to replace it—my husband would. The insurance might not even be valid. He shrugged and said that was the way it was done. I canceled and bought my insurance at another local agency.

Times have changed and the rights of women are emerging. Still many problems exist. I found that, for me, I have more rights as a single woman than I did as a married one; and more rights in Indiana than in Ohio.

Even the divorce laws can be discriminatory against women in certain states. But because of our great Constitution, women have won more rights in America than have others elsewhere, and I wouldn't want to be born in any other country on earth. I thank the Founding Fathers for their forethought.

Synchronicity

When odd, mismatched scenarios happen together, some folks call it "coincidence" and others "synchronicity." Many say all things are connected and happen for a reason. I agree with the connections, but sometimes wonder about those TV commercials.

Somebody has to have a twisted sense of humor; I just can't believe that coincidence is involved with many of them. For example, my daughter and I were watching the scene in *Alien* where the baby monster is ripping its way out of the astronaut's stomach. Then it switched to a commercial. The first words spoken were, "Do you suffer from upset stomach?"

180

Another good combination was a Pampers advertisement talking about keeping baby dry; it showed all the parts of the disposable diaper. Then the very next commercial was for disposable cleaning cloths with a lady wiping up spilled orange juice on the kitchen counter – just rinse and reuse. Yellow orange juice? It conjured up visions of using a diaper for cleaning – just rinse and reuse.

There was a comedy where a sadistic female doctor was snapping on those white latex gloves to do a rectal exam. Then a commercial appeared with a woman scrubbing dishes while wearing gloves. Her smiling friend offered her a dish soap that cleaned up those tough, dirty jobs. The soap was so mild that she didn't need her gloves; it even softened her hands. Hummm.

Just the other day, one channel put two commercials back to back. The first one was cut off just as the sole actor swung his arms out and said, "I love..." the next commercial had part of its beginning removed. Instantly, a different man was now standing center screen saying, "male enhancement." Excuse me?

Another show had two cops getting lunch. The fat one was seen eating a salami sandwich. The commercial cut in with a man using a slicing machine on a large, long deli-case-sized salami and saying, "Who are you kidding, bigger is better." It was another male enhancement advertisement. I won't mention the images conjured in my head by that mix.

I should like to file such oddities under "coincidence," but I believe that all things are connected in this universe and have a purpose. I can't help wondering if someone is deliberately combining such lovelies or if the universe has a comic side. Such may be "synchronicity."

A New Chapter

The older I get, the more philosophical I become. I guess that's one of the benefits of age. I'm an empty-nester as my only child took off to college, and it's time to make some changes.

I look around me and see all the cages or chains I've put on myself, and I suspect most everyone has done the same. Sometimes I feel like Scrooge's friend Marley with all the baggage I'm dragging.

It's time to break free. I have too much stuff which requires my time, energy, and thoughts. I have longed to be free of such responsibilities. I can't keep cleaning folks because they gasped unintentionally when they see my house and began to find excuses not to take the job.

I decided to act upon my need to break these chains. I just recently sold some land that I don't want to manage. I sold my antique furniture and dust collectors to my good friend and trusted antique dealer. He's taking my "chains" right off my walls. And since I have much more packed away that I will bring out as I'm able, he will be coming back many times. Each cabinet, copper piece, or bowl he takes lightens my heart a little more. When he has taken all he wants, the rest will be sent to an auction.

Then the 20 or more pairs of shoes I never wear and the clothes crammed into boxes and cabinets which I saved for when I could wear them again will go to charity. Some outfits have waited for nearly 20 years. Even if I could wear them again, would I want to? I doubt it.

I have too much of everything – saved back for when I might have a need or want, but I know I never will. As these anchors on my freedom and future life began to leave, my sense of well-being increases. I'll be talking the money to pay off my bills and build a little nest egg.

I'm cutting up my charge cards; when I want something, I'll pay cash. But first before I buy, I'll be asking myself – do I really need it or am I just adding a new "shackle on my ankle?"

The pounds of catalogs that invade my mail weekly are being tossed at the post office. If I don't look inside their covers, I won't be tempted to buy. I'm slowly giving away my houseplants to friends who want them.

When I've pared my life down to just a few things that truly touch my heart and necessities such as a bed, a couple of tables, some lamps and chairs, and a few linens, pots, pans and dishes, I will truly be free. I remember a time in my distant past when all I needed or wanted fit into my car – including my dog and cats. I would like to be that care-free again.

All I want now is to enjoy nature and my friends, to travel to new sites, and to meet new folks. Somewhere out there is another chapter about to open. I'm ready!

Beauty

Having had more than one mild brush with moving past the veil, I've really come to appreciate nature and the life it contains. I love to be outside breathing the air and feeling the breezes on my hair. Listening to chattering hummingbirds eating from my feeders and flying within inches of my face fills me with calm happiness.

The beauty and diversity of life here in Brown County is amazing. Red foxes, red raccoons, opossums, mama deer with twin dappled fawns and males with racks wander my yard with no fear. Squirrels raid my birdfeeders and routinely stare in my kitchen windows as if curious about the human inside. The spring peepers pipe to me from the stream at the bottom of the hill, and whippoorwills call from the woods, behind the house.

Wildflowers abound and no one is yelling, "Weeds, weeds! Kill, kill!" Folks don't' want their trees topped by linesman and are upset when they see a rotten one slated for cutting.

Walking sticks are common sights on my outside walls. Large moths like the Luna and Sphinx flutter in the nightlight or linger on my screens, and multicolored butterflies cover the flowers by day. Noisy insects serenade me from the trees each afternoon and early evening.

Birds call and sing all day to each other or rob the cats' food bowl sitting on the picnic table. A pair of hawks sit patiently on wires across the highway by the park. Buzzards circle on air currents. I've seen their nests and wander how branches can support the weight when many such birds roost in the same tree.

Wild turkeys in groups of 10 or more often make me brake when they cross a country road, and I occasionally catch the males displaying their full tails to hens in the fields. Canadian geese honk when they fly in v-formation over the house. Wood ducks and mallards float on nearby lakes. A ring-necked pheasant flew in front of my windshield.

I even saw a golden headed pheasant walking alongside the road in a park a couple of years ago; he didn't seem afraid of the traffic that passed close by. I was amazed at how brilliantly colored he was.

All sorts of woodpeckers tap rhythms on the tree trunks and share the birdfeeders with finches, chickadees, Blue Jays, Cardinals, and other colorful winged friends. At night, bats take care of the mosquitoes.

The air is clear; no smog hangs low to block out the stars and moon. The sun's heat is mollified by the trees' leaves. Perfume from honeysuckle and black locust blossoms fills the air. At times, a purple haze wafts around the hills, compliments of our pines and cedars.

Blackberries, raspberries, eatable mushrooms, and ginseng abound. I found yellow Jack-in-the-pulpit, and have heard that there are pink ones also. There are purple trilliums lining my wooded drive in the summer, and my yard is full of flowering trees in the spring.

Brown County is unique – an oasis in a desert of surrounding cities. Because we have the Brown County State Park, Yellowwood, and the Hoosier National Forest all here, life is protected – even us two-legged variety. Every day is a joy to the senses, and a healing balm to the soul. I love it here!

Turning Point

Many folks can point to a specific book, person, fortune cookie, TV show, or whatever as the moment of enlightenment--the turning point in their lives. I do not have such a specific pivotal point in my life. For me things changed gradually over several years.

I was reared by two parents who had been tech-sergeants during WWII, one who prided herself on her strict discipline of me. I was told what to eat, when to eat, how much to eat, even what to wear, and what my favorite color was. In other words I had no thoughts of my own or even a real sense of self.

When I headed to Ball State University, mother told me that "everyone loves a baby" so I should smile and laugh, listen to others, and say little—just like a baby."

I remember thinking, *I'm more like baby Huey from the comic strips.* We did have a lot in common. I decided that her advice wouldn't work, so I re-made myself as an extroverted clown. The extrovert part worked but I wasn't clown material. I discovered that I did occasionally have a quick wit so that sufficed.

It was about this time in 1967 that I saw a "Look" magazine article about the scene in California—Height Ashbury, Mama's& Papas, Rolling Stones, The Age Of Aquarius, and the song "When you're going to San Francisco, be sure to wear some flowers in your hair" sung by Scott McKinsey.

All this created a stirring in my soul—a burning longing. But I didn't know what to do about it—I spent many afternoons walking like a crazy person trying to run away from that hunger, but nothing helped.

I started hanging in the hippy sector at the Tally-Ho—a restaurant in the administration building. I de-activated from my sorority.

I met Christanne Swain who was the first free thinker I had met. I started going with her to the rock services at the Catholic Church—she played guitar there. Then at a huge campus party, I met several other "hippy" folks who became lasting friends.

Over a period of 3 yrs., I changed from a super-conservative nerd to an independent, free thinker. I changed my looks to suit myself and relaxed. I no longer cared what others thought of me—they could like me or not for whom I was.

Suddenly I was a leader, not a mouse. I stood my ground with my parents, voted my own way, and lived my own life. I allowed my artistic side to come forward—not be suppressed by my scientific side—so there are now two people inside me. I can think logically about art and creatively about science. Soon I found that those two parts of me meshed very well. I already had a degree in science so I pursued another one in Literature. I have no trouble reconciling that right brain/left brain combination. Life is good.

Just My Opinion

Have you ever been given too much advice from family, friends, or people you don't even know? It seems as if everyone has an opinion and is very pushy about forcing it on others.

When my daughter was born, it was "suggested" that I get rid of my houseplants, my cats, and all my pretty knickknacks, and to stop wearing jewelry. Erin might eat the plants and die; the cats would suck out her breath; she would destroy everything in my house that she could.

Concerning the jewelry, my little one would rip out my pierced earrings, thereby damaging my ears, break my necklaces or choke me with them, and stick herself on my pins. That advice I ignored and all was well.

No matter what diet I'm on, no one thinks it's the right one. I must use the various other diets suggested. No matter that mine works well for me; I must instantly switch. I could have five people a day trying to shove their five different plans down my throat and denouncing my ideas.

How to decorate my house or even what paint to use is another sore issue. I've been told I have too much stuff and should get rid of it-- either through yard sales, eBay, or charity. I've even been told which items to remove, and what colors to paint each room. Some folks even offered to take the unnecessary items home with them.

What brand-name foods I buy or where I shop seem open to criticism, as are selections I make in restaurants. My clothing, hair, and entertainment choices, seem fair game for all. Now I watch others doing the same to my daughter.

I don't mind a gentle remark made by a dear friend. Sometimes I even ask for opinions or advice. However, it seems everywhere one goes, there are people who just have to literally force their suggestions on others even if those ideas cause hurt or anger.

Criticism should not be delivered with a rude anvil. Actually unless asked, one should refrain from offering any opinions. The old rule which states: "If you can't say something nice, say nothing at all," may seem outdated in our society, but it still works well.

185

Treasure

My mother came from a well-to-do family so her ideas of gifts ran to the expensive side. Unfortunately as a child and as an adult, I didn't have the money to buy her such items. I made do with what I had.

In second grade, we made Christmas gifts for our parents. We used popsicles sticks to fashion shadow boxes and glued ceramic fruit inside. Some of the fruit pieces were brightly colored and some were just painted gold. I made two shadow boxes and put gold cherries in one and gold grapes on the other; I knew Mom didn't like "gaudy" colors.

I was really excited when she opened her present because I thought that I had made a very classy gift for her kitchen—the wallpaper was green and gold on white. I was sure she would be pleased. She looked at my gift as if it were something offensive. Later it went in the trash.

Since I no longer received an allowance, I had to find ways of earning money. I worked at the fair and at a grocery store. I had been saving that money plus any other I could earn for Christmas.

I heard Mother say that she wanted a tapestry purse that year. I looked all over town and found a very nice one trimmed in black. However, it cost $25.00, and I didn't have that much.

I persuaded my father to help me out. He seemed a little dubious about my choice and tried to talk me out of getting it. In the 1960's, that $25.00 was a lot of money especially since the black trim was plastic rather than leather. It did make me nervous, but I bought it anyway. I should have listened to Dad's advice; after all, he knew Mother better than I did.

When I gave her the gift on Christmas Day, she smiled and began examining it. She looked closely at the trim and said, "That's plastic, isn't it," and lay the purse aside. She didn't even thank me, and she never carried it. Several years later, she put it in a yard sale for a dollar. I never did succeed in getting her a gift she liked.

When my own daughter was old enough to give Christmas presents to Mommy, she made me a macaroni necklace strung on yarn and colored with washable markers. It wasn't my idea of a perfect gift, but as I started to lay it aside that Christmas morning, I saw the excitement and hope in her eyes; it mirrored my own feelings so many years ago. I also remembered how hurt I had been because of my mother's reaction—a reaction I almost repeated. My hands shook.

Quickly I grabbed that necklace and put it on. Then I took her hand and we went to a mirror. I asked her how it looked, and she said it looked beautiful. I wore that necklace the whole day, *and* I wore it off and on over the next several weeks until it fell apart. Then I carefully stored it away in its box. She was so thrilled that I liked her gift.

Van Buren Elementary had a Christmas store each year where children could buy presents; my daughter shopped very seriously. Nothing cost more than a dollar, and I made sure she had money.

My allowance before I started school had been 25 cents and I was allowed to keep only 10 cents of it; Erin received a dollar each week and carefully saved it. I also paid her to do little chores for me throughout the year.

So when she went shopping, she had enough to buy presents for several people. Nothing gave her greater pleasure than to see the happy faces when her gifts were unwrapped. She wouldn't open her presents until the ones she gave were opened. She has grown into a very astute shopper who has a keen sense of what will please others. She still would rather "give than get."

I wish my mother could have realized that each gift bought or made by a child is a gift from the heart. That is the real treasure. Her rejection of my gifts only made me determined that whatever my own daughter gave me would never be tossed aside or considered "not good enough..." So of any gifts I receive, I treasure Erin's the most. I have kept and used them all. I will admit I finally threw away the macaroni necklace as it disintegrated after 15 years.

A Suggestion

A wealthy man, whom we will call Alexander, following the advice of a friend, sought out a certain expert. He confided that he thought his wife was cheating on him, and he wanted revenge. "She loves chocolates," Alexander said. He wanted a small poisonous box of these candies sent to her in the evening after seven o'clock. His wife always brought him hot grog to drink before bedtime; it helped him sleep. It would also provide an alibi.

The expert said the chocolates would arrive in two days' time. His customer paid and left. The expert then worked on his order for the day: a cheating wife wanted a tasteless poison to place in her husband's hot grog. It was to be delivered today to be used that very evening at seven o'clock.

The expert was a "poisoner", a Roman and Greek assassin for hire, if one could pay the price. Caligula had such a full-time employee living in

187

his palace: a woman. After he was dead, she was the next to die-- the soldiers beheaded her.

"Thou shalt not suffer a 'witch' to live," says the Christian Bible. It was written in Greek and/or Latin which did not have a word for "witch." The original word was "poisoner," and truly such an unscrupulous, paid killer deserved to die.

"Witch" is a Celtic word for "wise woman," a person similar to the Native American "shaman." Perhaps the mistranslation was an accident, or deliberate for religious reasons. These Celtic women were the local healers who had knowledge of plants and their medicinal uses; one example would be Willow bark-- chewing it reduced pain. Aspirin was the chemical inside. Unfortunately poisoners also had a ready knowledge of plants-- deadly ones, and such experts were both men and women.

The early Church took a dim view of women in general because of their creation story in which Eve, the first woman, was also the first sinner. Holy men dominated the Church. Celibacy for clergy was a way of remaining clean from women's sin as well as holding on to the priest's inherited money. They even massacred the Coptic Christians who had women as well as men for priests.

Strong, knowledgeable women—leaders--were a threat to the Church's idea of the order of the world. Midwives who eased the pain of their patients were killed because God wanted women to suffer. If a baby's umbilical cord wrapped around its neck while in the womb, and the child was stillborn, the mother was killed. The Church maintained she had murdered the baby. Even Joan of Arc, a great freedom leader, was burned as a witch.

Since the Church has finally acknowledged that Mary Magdalene was not a prostitute but a disciple, and since parishioners now openly pray to the Father and the Mother, shouldn't the idea that wise women or "witches" are evil be erased?

Cat Magnet

I have seen and heard a lot of commercials on television, in magazines and newspapers, and on billboards in my lifetime. I even attended a lecture on symbolism found in commercials and taught a class on advertising propaganda. I've spotted many odd combinations of ads juxtaposed next to each other such as a billboard stating, "don't almost give" right next to another one saying "feed the piggy" (meaning to save money). These cause me to chuckle. On the whole, I ignore most advertisements; maybe I've just seen too many over the years and have become jaded.

Still if I had to choose just one ad that affected me, I have to choose a billboard I saw while traveling Highway 46 toward Bloomington. It showed a cute gray kitty stuck to a large U-shaped magnet. The sign said "cat magnet." I really don't know what the advertisement was about, but as I looked at it, I wished to myself that such an item existed.

I have had many cats in my lifetime and have lost several of them. They simply went outside in broad daylight and never returned. The worry, the asking of neighbors, the ads in the paper offering rewards, and the final resignation that something unknown happened to them isn't easy to forget.

Even years later, I think that maybe they had tried to get home but were hurt or trapped, and if I had just looked a little longer or paid more attention, I could have found them. The unknown is what has always hurt the most.

So when I saw that cat magnet billboard, I envisioned myself using one and pulling Oscar, Tabitha, Freddy, Mittens , Jaxie, and Geb back home to loving arms and medical help if needed. Maybe such magnets could be invented to bring home other missing pets or even children.

These thoughts cross my mind every time I remember seeing that billboard. I always think, "wouldn't it be wonderful if...." No other advertisement, commercial, or sign has ever affected me as that one did. It reminds me to love each pet every day as I may not see that four-footed friend again.

Paradox

The day was Tuesday. I thought that I would sleep in, and then begin some housecleaning-- especially in my kitchen. My daughter left for college last week, and I had deliberately neglected the house all summer in order to spend time with her and to get her ready to leave. But it seemed that the universe had other plans for me.

The first phone call came early with information I needed to pass along to another. Then two more calls came in from girlfriends about going to Lotus Petal Cinema that evening. These three early calls ended my late sleep-in and were my first clue that my plans would be changed.

Next I tried to discuss some business over the phone. I was disconnected by a solicitor's call. (Yes, I have call waiting and that shouldn't have happened.) That was my second clue.

189

Soon after, my daughter called with a problem, and that call was also disconnected by a solicitor. That was my third clue.

Then, another friend called; he asked to borrow my car as his was not working. I owed him a favor because I had borrowed his vehicle when mine was being repaired. This meant I couldn't go downtown to run some errands I had planned. That was my fourth clue.

Looking outside I noticed the weather was very mild with soft breezes. The insects were wildly singing in the trees. It was a perfect day to sit outside at my writing table. That was my last clue. I gave up. Obviously I was only going to get into the kitchen for a quick breakfast and nothing more.

I grabbed my pen and paper, and sat down outside. Suddenly the frustrations of trying to do practical things fell away. I realized that a higher consciousness did not want me to clean, run errands, or handle problems; I was supposed to write.

I needed to compose an article for a magazine and only had a couple of days left before the deadline. This was what I was being herded into doing. Once I stopped battling against the interruptions and relaxed, my earlier writer's block disappeared; my article flowed freely over the paper in less than 20 minutes with no interruptions at all.

Folks are often frustrated by stumbling blocks when they feel they must accomplish some task. I have come to realize that obstacles are put in our paths to redirect plans. The more I battled against that redirection, the more frustrated I became. When I stopped fighting and listened inwardly, I knew what I was supposed to do. Once I redirected my plans, those obstacles melted away.

Paradox often means "above the ordinary "or "in contradiction to the norm, but may actually prove true." This was what was occurring. My "norm" was to do practical work, but the universe was contradicting that. It truly was a time to write instead. The more I tried to accomplish my plans, the more I was thwarted. When I quit trying, I got a lot done. Instead of frustration, I found satisfaction. Such, to me, is a happy paradox.

Age

When Mom was in her early 70's, she located an old friend-- a crony from her days at Camp Crowder. She was *so very* excited as she rang the phone number. When her buddy actually picked up the telephone, and they began re-acquainting themselves, I noticed a change come over my mother.

Suddenly her eyes and face were no longer that of a 70-year-old woman, but of a 20-year-old girl. Then she sat sideways in her chair with her legs dangling over the arm. She kicked off her shoes and swung her legs. She pointed her left foot up high as if trying to decide what color polish to paint her toenails. She laughed and giggled.

As I watched her transformation, I was awed. I had seen black and white pictures of my mother as a young woman, but here she sat in front of me. I actually saw that young Tech Sergeant sitting in the living room and plotting her schemes and fun with her partner. That happy, carefree girl had eclipsed the mother I knew. How wonderful to get a real glimpse of her!

Now that I am older, I see my younger self peeping out impatiently. It's time to let her out. I worked, retired, and gained my pension. My daughter is in college, and it's time to begin a new chapter.

The girl in me says travel, meet new people, have fun, write those books which I outlined at an earlier time. I am, and I will continue doing so. I think I'll just skip those three-inch spiked heels and *really, really* short miniskirts which I wore when I was in college. I like my comfort, and those things weren't very comfortable even then.

Flowered Trash

As I was leaving my drive today, I saw, across the street on the other side of the road near a church, a crumpled bouquet of yellow daisies, purple dahlias, and tiny striped pink and yellow lilies. The flowers were still wrapped in bright pink tissue paper covered with a plastic cone. Even the little packet of plant food was there. I picked up the limp, broken stems and stared. Questions formed in my mind.

These blooms were carefully gathered when they were at their prettiest and placed in a store for sale. Bright, beautiful flowers to make somebody happy, to be anchored in a vase and proudly displayed. The individual who bought them must have thought these particular blossoms were just perfect to give as a gift.

I could imagine the hopeful person picking them out and paying the cashier. Perhaps he or she was smiling at the thought of how these flowers might brighten the day for a special person.

But here they lay, heads ripped from broken stems, limp from lack of water, and dying. Ruined, useless, sad—why? Were they placed on top of a car and forgot as the driver left? Did they fall off and get run over, only to land near my driveway? Were they not wanted? Did the receiver mangle, then throw them out a car window?

If the gift was not wanted, either because the giver was unacceptable or had caused anger, hurt, or guilt, couldn't these beautiful gems have been given away to another or donated? Why destroy living beauty. Someone could have found joy in simply looking at them. After our past harsh winter, they were an early promise of warm weather and gentler days ahead.

And what of the person who broke their stems and ripped off their blooms? What did he or she feel-- deeply pained, vengeful, scornful, or just disinterested? Did the giver see the present destroyed or did he or she think the flowers were joyfully accepted? Were they given anonymously? So many possibilities.

Even in their saddened state, I loved them. I brought them home and gently scattered the broken blossoms so that their bright colors could decorate my March yard. Their deaths did not go unnoticed.

My nosey cats sniffed them, and as they were gone the next morning, I imagine the nine deer who graze my yard daily found themselves a tasty treat. I'm so glad I found those flowers. Now I anxiously await my own bright blooms to arrive as well as the redbuds and dogwoods. And the bouquet was just litter on the side of the road. How curious!

Laundry Mats

I have several friends who really like taking their dirty clothes to the laundry mat. They say they can get everything washed and dried quickly and do other work at the same time. They throw their items in a machine and go grocery shopping. When they return, they throw their laundry in the dryer and go run a couple of errands. Then they fold everything and head home.

I suppose it's efficient, but I prefer the convenience and privacy of home. I can take my time, do a load during the night or before I go away, as I please. But "privacy" is the key word here.

Men seem to think a laundry mat is a good place to meet women, a shopping heaven, so to speak. Magazines list these places as in the top ten for hunting since many folks don't like bars or churches. There was even a TV show about places that have music, food, drinks, and soft seats to make date finding easier. Not for me, thank-you.

Think about it: you begin sorting out your lacy lingerie, and the guys are gawking. They think they can learn what type of gal you are by your nightwear and underwear. Now I like pretty things as do most women, but having some total stranger hoping to see bikinis or thongs in a variety of styles, colors, and fabrics is most disconcerting. My bras and night gowns are no one's business; neither are my dresses, socks, body wear, altogether outfits, jeans, or blouses. My sheets and towels are even perused.

More than once I've been approached. One ugly guy with a pocked face and pimples came up to me while I was trying to hide behind a magazine, and said, "Do you believe in fate—our meeting this way?" He then proceeded to sit next to me and jabber. He thought he was a witty, suave fellow. I turned down his date offer.

Another started his line with, "Have you ever gone spelunking? I'd love to take you to a couple of places I've found." My mind conjured visions of a serial killer hiding my body in one of those caves.

A third man said he was a truck driver doing his laundry, but hadn't had a bath in three days (he didn't look or smell dirty) and could he come to my house to take a shower? Oh, yeah, a naked, wet, stranger in my house—should I offer to soap his back?

Then there's the usual, "What sign are you?" or "I'll bet you're a _____ "(put your own choice here.)

Occasionally a guy will act helpless and ask advice on the type of soap, water temperature, clothes sorting just to start a conversation.

However, the male who wants to help by grabbing your lingerie out of the washer or dryer without permission, is a real treat. Invariably he will hold up the panties, and say something embarrassing or sexual. This type likes the "hands on" approach and nothing short of a grenade hidden in the clothes will shake him off.

I often would buy extra undies just to stave off my dreaded washing trip for an extra week. Then I would drive by on different days or different times to see when the fewest men were there. That way I hoped to avoid such situations. I've tried going when I knew it would be crowded and there would be lots of kids were around. That seemed to work. Nothing appears to dampen a Casanova's ardor like running, screaming, crying, whining kids being yelled at by distraught mothers. It's about 95% effective.

When I started working, the first items I bought after my necessary car were a used washer and dryer. Talk about love at first home use! Hello convenience and privacy. Goodbye bad opening lines. No more singles laundry mats for me. My washer, dryer and I are living together very happily.

193

Section Five

Songs from Angel's Trumpet

Memories

(key of G)

Verse:

A child's in the kitchen,
Where's his mom and dad?
Six years old and searching
But no supper's to be had.

Verse:

Just cold corn and tuna,
He tries to open cans.
Hungry girl and brother,
Was hard for little hands.

Verse:

Mom's working at the diner;
Dad's drinking ain't no joy.
Life's lessons can be hard
For a frightened little boy.

Verse:

No one sang us nursery rhymes
Or tucked us into bed.
No loving family arms,
Just an empty house instead.

Verse/Chorus:

Lonely rooms and cold bed sheets
And no one ever home.
These memories still haunt me
Anywhere I roam.

Verse/Chorus:

My music keeps me strong
Each time life gets me down.
I'm a child of the fifties
From a backwoods little town.

The Diners' Café

Verse:

> It was quarter past two,
> Was hungry, couldn't sleep.
> Only one place open,
> A diner down the street.

Verse:

> Sitting at the counter
> Waiting for eggs and steak,
> She sat down beside me,
> Ordered coffee and 'cakes.

Chorus:

> I'm just a lonely man;
> I should be on my way.
> Fancy we should meet here
> At the Diners' Café.

Verse:

> I nodded a "Hello."
> She gave me a soft smile.
> Something caught in my throat;
> Couldn't talk for a while.

Verse:

> I said I was sorry.
> She said it was just fine,
> "Think nothing about it;
> Happens to me sometimes."

Chorus: *See above.*

Verse:

> She passed me the pepper;
> I handed her the cream.
> We talked about nothing,
> But I couldn't help dream.

Verse:

> I didn't want to leave;
> I wanted her to stay.
> I smiled into her eyes
> The words I couldn't say.

Chorus: *See above.*

Last Chance Angel

Chorus:

> She's your last chance angel
> About to say good-bye.
> She's your last chance angel;
> Don't you understand why?

Verse:

> You're getting older now,
> And have to face your fears.
> What's life going to be like
> In those long, later years?

Chorus:

> (last line) It's lonely when you die.

Verse:

> Who's going to be there
> When your star begins to fade?
> It's your bed, you made it,
> Will you like the price you paid?

Chorus:

> (last line) See the anger in her eyes?

Verse:

> What you've done to hurt her,
> The times you didn't show,
> That fighting and complaining,
> She might say, "Hit the road!"

Chorus:

> (last line) Don't make her sit and cry.

Verse:

> If you really love her,
> You'd better walk the line;
> Stop missing work and drinking,
> Or there'll be no ties that bind.

Chorus:

> (last line) Who'll find a different guy.

Whippoorwill

Chorus:

> I thought I heard a whippoorwill,
> Telling me to follow it home.
> Daddy rests in his front porch chair,
> Listening when he's all alone.

Verse:

> Chug my coffee, tighten my tie;
> Briefcase and meeting at nine,
> Company car is stalled in line,
> Cell phone's ringing at my side.

Chorus: *Same as above*

Verse:

> City noises and flashing lights,
> Everything's grey from the smog.
> Grind my teeth; don't sleep at night,
> I'm running through time in a fog.

Chorus: *Same as above*

Verse:

One last week and I'm heading home,
Taking off this suit I wear.
I found a job out in the air;
I'll have the whole woods to roam.

Chorus:

I'll get to hear that whippoorwill
Welcoming me home to stay.
I'll rest in my front porch chair
Listening at the end of the day.

Section Six

Jimsonweeds and Wolfberries

The Steel Mill

Dad was always looking for places to take me as a way of broadening my education. One such place was a steel mill. Somehow he talked the foreman into allowing the two of us to take a tour. Considering how dangerous a steel mill is, and how guided tours of such places are nonexistent, I don't know how my father managed to get us inside, but he did.

We put on hard-hats, and walked across narrow grid-like bridges to stare over the sides into huge cauldrons of molten metal. It hurt my eyes to look at the red hot liquid; it bubbled and boiled like a pot of soup on a stove. The walkways went right over the top of these man-made volcanoes. I could look down between my feet and see the bubbling steel and feel the incredible heat blasting my skin; that heat even partially melted my shoes. I could feel them sticking to the metal grid which left its pattern on the soles. There were many of these inter-connected bridges suspended in the air at different heights.

Our guide looked at some gage and said we needed to head to a lower level. We descended until we were below the giant cauldrons just as a siren went off. This signaled everyone to get away. Then those massive containers began to tip over, one by one, pouring the liquid out onto moving "roads" below. It sent hot sparks flying high into the air almost like firework displays. It looked like lava rivers on some wild planet. I was wearing special glasses to protect my eyes, but nothing protected my skin from the awful heat.

We followed the liquid metal down its path as various massive machines worked with it. I don't remember a great deal about what those machines were doing. I couldn't hear the guide, who was talking, or rather shouting, to my father, partly because I was behind them, but mostly because of the loud noise. I just watched.

At one point, the steel was formed into thick bars rather like very long bricks. I think these went to companies which melted them again and poured them into molds for engine or machinery parts.

Everything seemed anticlimactic after seeing those emptying cauldrons. I could have watched that part over and over, and I still do in my mind. It was one of the most impressive and dangerous experiences I've ever had, and I have the utmost admiration for the men who have the courage to work there.

Jane

Did you ever have a friend who could figure you out just from watching—no words needed? I've been fortunate (or unfortunate) to have a couple such buddies over the years. One such was Jane B.

After I finished Ball State in Indiana, I went job hunting. I substituted at Van Buren, and Trafalgar offered me a job, but Kenton Public Schools offered me $4,000 more to teach there. Kenton, Ohio was an hour and a half due east from Ft. Wayne where my college roommate lived.

It was a lonely, unhappy place to stay during the week. On Friday nights I headed back to Brown Co—I'd pick up my mail, general delivery, on Saturday mornings while Joyce, who worked at the post office, fussed at me for not getting a mailbox. I finally did--#14. Then I'd have to leave Sunday afternoon.

After about two years of this, Jane B. came to teach biology at the school. As I taught English and earth science, we often worked together on ordering materials, designing labs, and coordinating the lessons. We became friends, not just co-workers. However, she was married and did community work; I was single, and I left on weekends—so we weren't as close as we could have been—we only socialized at school. Still she could read me like an open book.

Since I wasn't from Kenton, all the other teachers just labeled me that "crazy person from Brown County," and ignored me. Because they did so, I often played "head games" with them until they didn't know what to make of me. That suited me just fine—the less they really knew me, the more my private life remained my own—those folks were critical and gossipy. Jane, however, would just laugh. She enjoyed the fun too.

She even made money betting about me against my confused co-workers. This is one of my favorite memories of her. Another English teacher had a party at her house in Mt. Victory, a town about five miles from Kenton. A childhood playmate had come up from Nashville, Tennessee to visit me, and I took him along to the party.

His mom and dad had warned me that after spending six weeks in a coma from a car accident, he had changed. I hadn't seen him in a long while, so I wasn't sure what they meant. I soon found out.

Maybe P.H. was uncomfortable and stressed, but he started drinking. He didn't eat anything but had a whiskey in each hand, and both were going down fast. Then he grabbed two more. It seemed he had lost the ability to control certain actions—he couldn't gage alcohol. We had only been there about an hour when I saw him start on two more. I didn't

202

want him to embarrass himself or me or upset the other teachers—I knew I'd hear about it later—many times.

I had only been drinking a Coke—no rum in the glass, but I could pretend to be drunk. Everyone there thought I was. I insisted that P. drive me home, because I was "not able to." I got the finished drinks away from him, and said our goodbyes. I had him lead me out the door towards the car which was parked just across the street from the front door and large picture window.

I shoved him in the back seat, climbed in, and drove us to my house where I managed to get him into bed in my guest bedroom. He had passed out in my car so it wasn't an easy task. He recuperated on Saturday and headed home on Sunday to my great relief.

I knew I'd have to face my colleges on Monday. I figured they'd be jeering that I had got drunk in only an hour. One teacher was the type who wouldn't let up for weeks; he never knew when to quit. I'd seen him in action over the past two years. He often laughed at fellow teachers over things from years before.

Oh well, I figured the ribbing I would get later would be better than their treatment of P. This was his first trip up, and he would be returning many times to look for a teaching job or a career change. He had been teaching biology in a prison near Nashville, Tennessee and really wanted to quit that. Also his fiancé lived in Columbus, Ohio. So he would be staying either at my house or my parents'. The teachers didn't need to know all that or about the car wreck and coma.

When I entered the teachers' lounge Monday to put away my coat and get a cup of coffee, no one said a word! That was a big shock. It was business as usual—the party was not even mentioned. I finished my coffee and headed to the bathroom to rinse out my cup.

Jane followed me. She had the biggest grin on her face. She told me she had won $65.00 off bets at the party because of me. I asked how she managed that, and she proceeded to tell me.

Now, I usually didn't go to the teachers' parties because I was always in Brown County on the weekends and because none of my colleagues were friendly. So no one knew much about me. They didn't know if P.H. was my boyfriend or not. They didn't know if I drank or not, and if so, whether I got drunk or limited myself.

I was being watched carefully that evening. I had felt that and maybe P.H. did also. They probably plied him with many questions as we had wondered off in different directions. Only Jane had seen him down six drinks in an hour and me drink only Coke. She knew I was just pretending so I could get him out of there. Everyone had been gossiping behind my back about possible "sleeping arrangements," and how drunk I was.

203

She had quietly taken bets with them about who would be driving whom when we left; she told them I wasn't drunk. It seemed everyone was peeking out the front window drapes and had seen me drop the drunk act, half-carry P. H.'s staggering body to the car, get him in, and drive off. After we left, she told them what I had done and why, and collected her sixty-five dollars.

That's why no one said anything to me that Monday—she'd proven them dead wrong, defended me, and cleaned their pockets. Some teachers gained a little insight and respect for me after that and started being friendly.

I remember smiling at her and just saying, "I can't believe you did that, but thanks." She bought me supper at the Elks that evening—said it was my part of the winnings.

Home Sweet Home

This evening I have decided to work on my taxes; for the moment, all my information is heaped on the kitchen table. My kitten Grim is sleeping on a large envelope of receipts beside me. I go to my office for a minute. When I return, Grim is eating the envelope. I chuckle and put him on the floor.

He jumps into a large potted plant and proceeds to throw dirt everywhere. I lift him out, grab the broom and dust pan, and begin cleaning. Grim jumps onto the kitchen counter and fishes an apple core out of the compost bowl. He bats it to the floor, dives for it, and slides on the rug. He's eating the fringe. I put up the broom and retrieve the apple core. He jumps onto the table, swatting right and left. My papers fly through the air. I set Grim on the floor and pick up the mess. He's got that apple core again. There goes the rug again. I get the fruit. He gets the dirt. I grab the broom again.

I *need* a drink! I get a glass of water, add ice, and set it on the table. I go to my office and open the file cabinet. Grim jumps in and goes behind the drawer. I pull him out and send him away.

I return to the kitchen. He's fishing ice out of my glass. I grab it before it turns over. Now he's back into the potted plant. I sweep up a third time.

I quit! I need chocolate! I need to rest! Forget the taxes! I grab a chocolate bar and click the TV remote. Grim chases another cat into the room and over my lap. They tear back out the door; I hear squawking in the hall. I am *not* going to investigate.

I sit quietly. Grim returns and jumps on my lap. He purrs, looks at me angelically, and settles down for a nap. I sigh, serene in my knowledge that all is in order and under control.

A Helper

Sometimes there are people who seem to be local legends during their lifetimes. One such person lives here in Brown County. I got to know him in the 1970's when my girlfriend and I were looking to buy a place together. We were going to split the down payment and mortgage fees.

This realtor took us all over the county trying to help us find a place which we both could afford. I had my half for the down payment, but my friend was short some.

He showed us everything from trailers in Bean Blossom, to land in Timbercrest, to houses in Helmsburg. He also steered us away from some places we had spotted on our own if he knew of potential problems. He tried to help work out all kinds of creative financing since my girlfriend couldn't come up with any more money when we did find a place. Finally however, she just gave up.

I had never known anyone to work so hard to help; most others would have just shrugged and walked away. In later years, he did sell me a house; I loved the land and location. Although I now live elsewhere, I grow nostalgic when I pass by those old haunts.

I've heard a few people speak badly about this man, but I've also heard others say that he helped many, and did so quietly. I tend to agree with that second group of folks knowing how hard he worked to help us two girls, years ago. Who is this guy? His initials are T.B.

A Day at the Doctor

Every spring, usually in March, I would leave my job as a teacher around 3:30 and rush twenty-five miles away to my gynecologist for my yearly appointment. Oh, how I loved that special day. RIGHT!

Usually there was a long time to be spent in the waiting room surrounded by several ladies, a few pregnant. It was interesting that these pregnant women were there without their husbands, while some of the single ladies, who were definitely not pregnant, were accompanied by their boyfriends. Why these poor guys were there, I won't venture a guess. The women, including myself, were not comfortable with men there, and the poor men looked as if they had been forced there under some dire threat to their lives.

They tried to be invisible behind magazines. These desperate gentlemen did not succeed, probably because the only subjects available for reading were those on gynecology, exams and problems of such, parenting, babies, and other materials so suitable for this type of office. Green was the color of most masculine faces present. They should have been awarded Medals of Honor for such courage. Instead, each endured the nervous, hostile, or amused glances of the ladies not accompanying them.

When each patient was called to enter the unknown corridor, her man, if she was there with one, would look as if he were being called to his death, only to be extremely relieved when told he couldn't follow. Each Atlas would collapse into his chair looking to all there as if the weight of the world were suddenly removed from his trembling frame. Usually a great sigh of relief would follow, and he would look around the room.

Then sheer terror would register on his face. He was alone. His Joan of Arc was not there to protect him from the other women present or from their eyes which now gazed openly upon him. Often grins or outright laughter at his plight would issue forth from carnivorous female mouths. As uncomfortable as the situation would be for all of us, it really was funny. Laughter can be the best medicine, and I was in an unusually giddy mood this one particular March afternoon.

For those not acquainted with the unknown internal workings of the examination room, I will elucidate. The nurse accompanies the patient to one room, asks a couple of necessary questions concerning health, hands the woman a paper gown or sheets of paper to wrap around her body, tells her to strip off all her clothes and to wrap herself in the paper.

Next this nurse has the patient lie back on a padded table while she pulls the short stirrups out from the end of said table. The patient is instructed to put her bare heels in these cold, hard, metal rings which are spread far apart, but are close to the table on short levers. This requires the knees to be bent almost straight up. Then the nurse leaves and one is left in this most comfortable and dignified position. Did I mention that the room is COLD? One or two little pieces of paper do nothing to alleviate that COLD. Then the next section of waiting begins.

Eventually the doctor, generally a man, arrives to ask more questions while the lady remains in said position. Next he calls a nurse in to help him and to rule out any impropriety.

He has the speculums in a drawer. Now these lovely implements of torture are made of metal and are at room temperature. Did I mention the room was COLD? The tormentor removes the object and insets it into the warmest and most private area of a woman's body, and then ratchets said area apart. Before it is inserted, the doctor globs on some lubricating slop which will continue to make itself known when the lady leaves and drives elsewhere.

After sitting down on a stool between those spread knees and shining a light on the subject, the doctor begins digging around inside for a minute, until he has a sample of said area to send to the laboratory for analysis, and the patient is allowed to get dressed.

Shivering, and feeling very lubricated, the poor distressed damsel may now attempt to regain her dignity, walk past the green-skinned gentlemen in the waiting room, pay at the front desk, and escape, hoping aforementioned lubrication isn't already manifesting itself. This then was my usual plight each March.

However for some reason that particular spring day, I was feeling rather mischievous. I left the mixed-gendered waiting area and reached the examination room directly across from the open front desk and close to the victims waiting outside. While I was waiting for my paper products, an inexplicable urge came over me. I had to act upon it. I opened the door, and called out as loudly and clearly as possible so that the words had maximum carriage, "Get the speculums out of the freezer, Ethel, Patrick's here." This seemed to relieve the tensions in every room.

The accountant managing the front desk snickered loudly and tried not to make a further sound. Then the men and women in the waiting room began giggling and outright laughing. One nurse walked by my opened door, saw me, and doubled over cackling so hard that she dropped her patient's folder. The place was in an uproar. Tensions were suddenly released.

The red faced, sputtering doctor, who had examined me for seven years, came charging out of another room and flew to mine. Not only was his face red, but his ears began to glow also. He started grinning as he stood outside my door. He shook his head as another laughing nurse saw him and leaned against the wall, holding her stomach. She nearly sank to the floor before regaining some solemnity and stumbling onward.

The doctor shooed me inside and quickly took care of my exam even though I wasn't next in line. He said he wanted to get rid of me before I pulled anything else.

The following March when I again entered his examination room, he personally followed me inside with his nurse and showed me his new heater located in the speculum storage drawer. He had had one installed in each room. He said he did not want a replay of the past year.

Before I left, one nurse informed me that he hadn't been able to live that embarrassment down for nearly a month. Nurses had teased him as well as patients, and so did his wife and several daughters when they heard about the commotion. He just HAD to be ready for me.

I believe he treated many happy patients for years afterwards. It feels good to know that I struck a blow for womankind that March day even if it was just a bit of spontaneous mischief.

Superstitions

My mother held a Master's Degree from Ball State with a major in business and a minor in guidance counseling. However, she was very superstitious about many things, and I have logically tried to figure out why over the years. Papa King wasn't and neither was the rest of the family; but she was.

For instant she would not allow an opened umbrella in the house, and she would not go under a ladder. I figured that going under any ladder wasn't safe because tools or paint could be dropped, or someone could accidently jiggle the legs and cause the ladder or person on it to fall. But....the umbrella, well, maybe the reason was because of its size; those spokes that hold the fabric could poke out an eye in the close confines of a room, or at least hit someone in the face. If on the floor, it could be tripped over. At any rate, I learned to live with Mother's idiosyncrasies.

Then my daughter Erin was born. Mom stayed with me for three days after I returned home from the hospital, and among other problems she caused, her superstitions concerning babies came out.

I had had a C-section, and Erin was having trouble keeping her food down, but my mother insisted that I climb up on a ladder to remove four hanging plants, the pots being situated about six feet from the floor. She was afraid Erin would eat them and die.

No amount of logic would prevail; after a heated argument in which I reminded her that Erin was only a few days old, that it would be a long time before she could get near those four ivy plants, and that I was in no condition to climb, Mother stomped off.

She returned, dragging a three-step folding stool out of the basement, took down the plants, and threw them out in the yard. Luckily she did not hurt herself or break my expensive hand-made clay pots.

Next she turned on my four gentle cats, saying that they were going to suck Erin's breath away and kill her. I believe that old wives' tale came from not understanding crib death, believing that cats were transformed evil witches who killed babies, and from cats licking milk from sleeping children's mouths or sniffing their faces.

Now, my cat Casper had lain on my lap as I slept in a recliner the last four months of my pregnancy and purred. When Erin was very fretful, he would lie next to her on my bed and softly purr to her. His warmth and purring seemed to soothe her, and she would sleep, gripping his fur. I think they knew each other; after all, she had heard him when she was inside of me, and he recognized her smell as being my "kitten." Sometimes he was the only thing that would help calm her.

However, my mother, who hated cats, would scream and knock him off the bed, nearly rolling Erin onto the floor in the process. Once she almost hit me in the stomach while trying to get to him. He would hide under the bed and continue purring as loudly as he could; Erin would hear and go back to sleep.

Mother did manage to lock the other three cats in the basement, but couldn't catch Casper. After three days of her insisting that Erin was going to die because of my evil white cat, I told her to go home. I had had quite enough of her superstitions.

Only one other time did her unfounded beliefs rock the household; I was in high school. That was when a poor disoriented bat got in my parent's family room. It was early afternoon when the little creature flew through the opened sliding glass door. (Why it was out in the daytime, I haven't a clue.) Mom was scared to death. She slammed the outside door shut and also the other one leading to the rest of the house. The bat was trapped.

She began screaming that the blind thing would get tangled in her hair. Dad tried to explain that bats have excellent echo-location skills and weren't going to get anywhere near her short hair. I tried to explain that they aren't blind. She wouldn't listen to anything we said.

She grabbed a tennis racket and ordered Dad to knock the bat out of the air and kill it. He wasn't about to do that even if he could have; that frantic little creature was very fast and easily dodged the lamps and us.

Mother jumped on the couch, then the chair, and waved her hands in the air. She screamed, "Kill it, kill it before it bites us!" She then ran to the bedroom to tie a scarf around her hair.

While she was gone, Dad re-opened the sliding glass door to the outside, and he and I sat down. The little bat immediately flew out when his "radar" reported the opening. We went outside also, and Dad shut the door.

The look on his face was one of long suffering. He took a deep breath and sighed. Mother returned, opened the door, and came out. She demanded to know if the bat was dead, and my father simply said, "It's gone," and gave her a look that said, "Don't ask anymore." She took the scarf off and went back inside.

Now, my father was a patient and gentle man who did not believe in hurting any animal—he even gave up hunting when he killed a mother squirrel and two of her three babies. He was in tears over that, and he and I raised that third baby. So Mother's hysterical screaming, "Kill it, kill it!" did not sit well with him. He was very angry.

We left for ice cream, and did not return for a couple of hours. Dad didn't talk much while we were gone except for a small lecture about the worthlessness of superstitions and the harm they can cause. Maybe he later had a talk with her. I don't know.

I never told him about her behavior when Erin was born. I thought that it was best to "let sleeping dogs lie." Perhaps she complained to Dad about the cats and plants, and he stopped the craziness. I know that that was the last time I ever had to endure her superstitions.

The Velvet Tapestry

While Papa King was in the nursing home, my mother kept his house intact, but when he died in June 1967, she had the sad task of emptying the cabinets and closet, and selling the furniture in his two rooms. He had closed the part where we had lived and no longer rented it.

My father was taking care of some legal matters in town, so it was mother, Uncle Claude, and me that went to the house to begin the work. I was eighteen and could have been useful, but as usual when my mother was nervous or upset, she was very volatile and preferred to be alone. She was just hanging on by a thread and didn't want me around. She told me to get out of the house.

Actually that was a good thing. I was feeling Papa's loss also and needed some time to manage my feelings of being back in a house which held such strong memories. (Mom and I were feeling many of the same things that day. Mine were just bottled up.) I walked down the gravel driveway and stood a while looking at the back yard.

There was the tree where Daddy cut his fingers deeply when he shinnied up two stories to hang my swing. It stood just to the left of Papa's garage where we sat on sunny afternoons officially shooting rats—but not really.

There was the meat house where I used to play and where we took our weekly showers. It still smelled of the old smoked hams. To its left were the vegetable garden and fenced yard that held our Bantam hens.

Further back was the old outhouse and the grassy field where I helped Peggy hang clothes. The big weathered, leaning barn with its croquet set still survived.

I walked to the back steps where our dog Champion and I had sat eating cereal and ice cream together so long ago. That was also where I ate his Milk Bone dog biscuits behind Mom's back. Champion was gone now just like Papa.

I climbed those stairs and imagined that large cage sitting on the covered landing which held my father's beloved pair of Mynah birds. He was very upset and hurt when they escaped. Mom had been cleaning their cage, and they slipped out the door.

She claimed it was an accident, but cleaning their cage didn't involve opening the door--just sliding out a bottom drawer. Whether deliberate or not, and I have always believed it was deliberate as she could lie when it suited her, Mother was very glad they were gone. The only pets she liked were dogs and horses.

I opened the door and entered the section of the house where we had lived for most of my first five years. It had been our bedroom. These three rooms had no furnishings now as they had been rented for a while after we moved. It gave Papa some money and provided company.

In time, it had been too much trouble, and he closed that part off. He only used the other two rooms. My crib had sat in the left corner. There was just enough room for it next to the doorway which led into the living room. Heavy dark green, loosely woven curtains covered the entrance right behind the high-backed crib.

Often I stood up in my bed and peeked through the panels to see what the grown-ups were doing; I listened to many of their conversations or radio programs instead of going to sleep.

The side of my crib blocked the closed door into Papa's. Sometimes I would reach through the rails and open that door to wave at him. I wasn't supposed to bother him, but he didn't mind.

The kitchen was to the right of the bedroom. We didn't eat in here much except for breakfasts; we cooked in Papa's room. It housed my fish bowl filled with two black Mollies and two Goldfish. I had been a little too over-zealous in feeding them or so my mother said; I only know they disappeared. One Molly did survive—for a short awhile.

The room opened out onto the L-shaped verandah with the green porch swing. I headed that way after each breakfast as Papa usually was out there chewing his cherry tobacco. He carried a little compressed brick of it in his shirt pocket, and I loved the smell of it on his clothing.

I walked into the living room which had held our Christmas tree each December and where I first saw Jit-it bear. That's where I listened to the many radio shows and played my Little Lulu records. The big picture

211

window once held a television turned to the outside. My family and passing neighbors sat in the grass and watched.

I stood there awhile just looking out the front door. The giant Maple tree still stood off to the right where Papa and I would sit in old metal yard chairs. Teams of mules pulling buckboards and driven by Black farmers used to clop down the street heading out of town toward the cemetery and their farms beyond. The mules' huge shod feet and rigging could be heard for quite a ways. As there was little traffic back then, the farmers would leave their wagons in the street and come sit for a spell, sharing a plug of Papa's tobacco.

Then I opened the living room door which connected to Papa's half of the house, and entered the cold room. We had used it as a bedroom/living room when the other half was rented.

Here, long ago, stood the infamous Naugahyde couch. This room still had its large wool rug, Mom's steamer trunk from WWII, a table with its stained glass lamp, and the two iron beds. The upright piano was long gone. Only two antique pictures hung on the blue flowered walls, and...a velvet tapestry--a hunting scene with a large dog in the foreground.

That rectangular piece of cloth always hung just above the side of my bed. I stared at it each night when I slept there even as a visiting teenager. I couldn't be afraid of the dark or my mother with that dog acting as a sentinel.

I loved that moth-eaten scrap for no other known reason. It just symbolized Papa's house more than anything else in my memories. It never changed or moved like the rest of the house. Even the wallpaper behind it was brighter from being protected so long from dirt, sun, and time.

Mother never allowed me to ask for things—not food, clothing, or anything else. I was expected to take what was given. That was all. But...I thought that, perhaps, just this once, maybe I could ask for that tapestry—something by which to remember my Papa. It was worthless and dust-covered, and Mom wouldn't want it.

I went into Papa's large bedroom/kitchen/living room and sat on the bed for a while. Mom was emptying the chunky tiger-maple dresser and putting the clothing into a trash bag to be given to charity. She had already emptied the small closet in the corner. Uncle Claude was just sitting in the oak rocker; even he wasn't allowed to help. No one was talking. I looked around.

This room, more than any of the others, held a bushel of memories; this was the heart of the house—Papa lived here. I remember Mom cooking on the narrow four-burner green enameled stove. Two tall pressurized gas tanks which fueled it and a heater sat just outside the back door. Papa would throw water on them occasionally. The way the water stuck, told him how much gas was left.

The Hoosier kitchen and its companion cabinet were next to the stove. Everything for fixing meals was found there; food was prepared on the pull-out enameled shelf or on the old black-varnished, square oak kitchen table. The sink did duty for washing dishes, brushing teeth, spit baths, or shaving.

Papa's old razor strop hung on a nail nearby. His shaving mug and brush still sat on the narrow counter which ran from the sink to the corner—a homemade three-foot piece fastened to the wall with one leg underneath. The wastebasket/overthrow bucket sat strategically under the sink.

A refrigerator sat across the room next to the dresser. It didn't have a freezer, just a small ice box for two trays of cubes.

The high-backed walnut bed where I was sitting held cherished memories. It wasn't terribly ornate, but to me, it was made for a princess, and I often begged to be allowed to sleep there with Papa. He had to keep a rubber doughnut-shaped pillow between his knees because of his damaged leg, and sometimes I'd accidentally kick it away. I know that must have hurt, but he never said anything. He'd often read the newspaper funnies to me there if not in the swing outside.

I didn't know the history of that bed until later. Papa had been sheriff many years before and had been friends with Jessie James' mother. That was the bed Jessie slept in when he came home to visit, and Mrs. James gave it to my grandfather. I wouldn't have cared at that young age; it was Papa's bed. I thought it was interesting when I found out—it gave me insight into my grandfather, that's all. I suppose it should have gone to a museum, but it, as well as the rest of the furnishings, were already sold to a used furniture dealer—everything for sixty dollars.

I managed to get the courage up to ask about the velvet tapestry. I figured since Uncle Claude was there, I'd have a buffer. I was wrong. Mother simply exploded like a grenade. I don't remember many of her cruel words, but the gist of the diatribe was that I had no right to ask, that I was being greedy, and that I was very selfish to only think of myself. She slapped me twice across the mouth.

The tapestry was to be given to charity or thrown in the trash—I'm not sure which she intended. Uncle Claude simply stared at the two of us and said nothing. I think he was shocked at Mother's behavior. That was not a side of Mildred he had ever seen.

I said nothing, but turned and walked through the cold room and out the door to the green porch swing. Its chains were rusty now and squeaked as they moved back and forth on the large eye hooks screwed

213

into the roof above. But then, as always, it was my solace in many a cruel time with Mother.

I heard Uncle Claude say, "Mildred," as I left. I sat there slowly swinging for some time. When they finished in the late afternoon, she came to the door and told me to get in the car.

No one spoke to me even when we arrived at Uncle Claude's house a few blocks away. He cooked supper when Dad arrived. My father may or may not have known something was wrong; he too was reeling from Papa's death and the logistics afterwards. And he had to cope with my mother.

I'm sure Uncle Claude wasn't feeling well after losing Moten—now he was the only one left and he had no one to turn to, but he was everyone's rock during those days. I stayed to myself the rest of the evening; there were too many emotions battling for my head to be around others.

No one went back to the house the next day as they had to go to the lawyer's office. I stayed behind and walked back the few blocks to Papa's. It was my time to say good-bye. I spent some time walking the neighborhood up to Uncle Erten's old house, the cemetery, Cheryl Leech's empty store, and then turned down the other way to town, past the Methodist church, courthouse, and Casebier's Restaurant. Every place was close together back then. We left the following day and didn't return until Uncle Claude died.

Sometime after I began teaching in the '70's, Mom pulled out a plastic bag and handed it to me. She simply said, "I saved this for you. I thought you might want it."

Inside was that velvet tapestry. All I could do was look blankly at her and say, "Thanks." She seemed disappointed with my reaction. However, better that emotionless response than what I was really feeling.

When I returned to my place, I broke down and cried so hard that I had to sit down on the floor. I held that rotting rag as tightly as possible to my face without shredding it. Everything bottled inside poured out that late evening. I don't know how many times I said, "Papa" over and over as I swayed back and forth. I finally had something of my beloved grandpa that I could hold.

I know now that Uncle Claude had had a talk with my mother after I left the room. But, I'll never know why she waited so many years to give the tapestry to me. Maybe it took her that long to get up the courage, or maybe she really didn't want me to have it, but had to because of a promise to Uncle Claude. My deceased relatives have been known to return to set some things right, so maybe she received a visit.

It really didn't matter then or now. Her gesture came too late for the two of us. If she were disappointed at my blank reaction, she would have been horrified if I had reacted. There are just some deep, dark doors that should never be opened.

Alice Weaver

I began my love affair with antiques while in high school. I bought two tables for seven dollars at a neighbor's auction and kept them for almost a half-century. I've combed shops, auctions, and flea markets since I started making my own money. So naturally I discovered Alice Weaver at her Ferguson House shop. In Brown County, Indiana that place was one of a kind!

Upstairs behind locked gates was almost a museum. There were caskets and skeletons, fabulous furnishings, and an odd assortment of bric-a-brac. The downstairs was jumbled, dark, and dusty but no less interesting.

Mrs. Weaver was in my opinion, an icon. She almost always sat in one spot off the left of the main entrance. If you asked her for something she usually sent her husband to help you. She had a reputation for being cantankerous if she didn't like a customer and would refuse to sell anything to whoever aggravated her.

I saw this happen once when some pushy man demanded her attention. Alice didn't even speak to him; she just glared until he left. (Actually I didn't blame her—I didn't think much of him myself.) To those she liked, she was loving. I was sometimes nervous around her because of that reputation, but she must have liked me.

Once I asked her about a birdcage I saw upstairs. She sent Mr. Weaver with me to unlock the door and let me inside so I could see it. It wasn't just a cage like I thought; inside was a mechanical bird. He sat it on a plant stand and wound it up. The bird opened its mouth, turned its head, and flapped its wings while it chirped a song.

Mr. Weaver told me the price—I think it was around $2000. I dropped my jaw. Then he told me it had come out of the French court back when they still had kings, and the bird and cage were not brass, but gold. It was definitely a beautiful piece and quite a buy, but more than I could have afforded. My MasterCard only went up to $500 back then.

I was able to buy a couple of items over the years; I still have a lamp Mrs. Weaver sold me. She had several in a building next door which she unlocked to let me take a look. I bought a pretty one with an amber glass shade.

I remember her smiling and calling me "Honey" when I was looking. Maybe that's why that lamp is so special these days. She could be formidable, but she called me "Honey."

Her shop is long gone now as is she. I think Nashville really lost something special when she died and her many unusual antiques were gone. There's just never been anything like her shop or her since.

Mrs. Ferguson who originally had a hotel in the Old Ferguson House had a reputation too—she wouldn't allow women in who didn't wear skirts. It just seems fitting that Alice Weaver owned that house, because she's a legend now too.

Just A Shakin'

It's said that you can't teach an old dog new tricks. I beg to differ with that statement. I have three dogs—a German Shepherd with hip dysplasia and cataracts, a 10 yr. old Dalmatian/lab mix, and a three-year-old bouncy "pup." They have a large straw house in my heated garage filled with pillows, but they have trained me to keep them inside since a year ago.

Now that garage is heated to 60 degrees in the winter, and since it's partly underground and made of concrete blocks, it remains very cool in the summer. I usually get my shepherd's thick fur shaved in early June so she won't get too hot. Since the heat wore on last year and her fur grew quickly, I had her shaved again in August.

For some reason her usually fast growing fur didn't grow in fully that winter. This was ok as it was really mild (I wore shorts and sandals through December) until February. Then it really got cold.

Cookie showed up at my kitchen door shivering and looking pathetic. I immediately let her in. I kept her inside all during the cold weather and brought Maggie and Grace inside also since they have short fur. Now, all three would rather be in than out, but not because they're cold. In fact, Cookie begs to go outside as she gets too hot. They just like the companionship.

Maggie, my 10 yr. old, is a quick learner, and she taught Grace this routine. Whenever either wants in, they stand at the door looking as pathetic as possible and shivering so much that I could attach paint cans to them to stir the pigments!

The first time they pulled this shaking routine was in July! No way were they cold. Maggie had just watched Cookie shivering that past winter. Can't teach an old dog a new trick? I don't think so!

Halloween

October is a special time of year for me, and not just because it's my birthday. I like the cooler weather, which doesn't have the winter chill in the air as yet. The maples, sumacs, and oaks are brilliantly cloaked in oranges and gold. Burning bushes are bright red.

Fall mums in many colors from purples to whites are in every yard, garden, and planter. Great big pumpkins are carved into fanciful faces with candles inside. Colorful gourds and multicolored ears of corn are grouped on tables and decorate bare areas. Autumn is an artist's painted canvas.

The fall harvest is in; food is plentiful. Apples are everywhere and are great for munching or baking into pies. Hot spiced or cold cider can be found in grocery stores and open air markets. Pumpkin pies and persimmon puddings abound. It's time for fall parties, hayrides, bonfires and of course, Halloween.

Celtics called it Samhain and other places called it the Day of the Dead. This celebration of life and the remembrance of the dead are celebrated in many places around the world.

One legend said these remembrances started after Atlantis sank because of a large comet or meteorite which crashed into the Atlantic Ocean setting off storms, earthquakes, volcanic activity and tsunamis. The world drowned except for a few who could read the cosmic signs and escaped (with their families or not) in boats. It supposedly happened around this time of year. The comet came from the Pleiades and the meteor shower we have each fall was part of its tail. The exact date is not known so celebrations vary by a few days.

The ancient stories have long been forgotten unless one searches dusty volumes in huge European, Egyptian, or Mediterranean libraries. These days Halloween is a time of parties and fun. Children of all ages love to wear costumes and prepare for "trick or treat" night.

I remember taking my daughter, Erin, door to door to get candy on her first Halloween. She was 2 1/2, and was wearing an Augie Doggy mask, a white sweater, and blue-jean overalls. I would take her up to a house and tell her to say, "Trick or Treat," and hold out her bag for candy.

After three or four houses, she sat her bag on the ground, took off her mask, and appeared very thoughtful. She looked up at me and asked, "They give me candy, Mommy?"

I smiled and said, "This is Halloween. Everyone wears costumes, and the children who go up to lighted houses and say, "Trick or Treat" on this night, get candy."

Then she asked, "Do I get to keep it?" I nodded.

It was as if she had just now figured everything out. A big smile lit up her face, and she laughed. "I get candy!" she said, grabbed her bag and began running toward the next house and the next and the next. I couldn't keep up with her.

She said, "Trick or Treat" at each house and "Thank-you" when she got candy or an apple, or a small bag with a caramel popcorn ball inside.

I didn't know a 2 ½ yr. old could move so fast. She only waited for me when we had to cross the street. In the time allotted, she made it to every house in the neighborhood. I'd never seen her so excited. When we returned home, she dumped her loot on the floor and began dividing it into two piles.

She said, "Nobody gave you candy, Mommy, so you can have some of mine." I told her that Halloween was for children. Adults passed out the candy and often went to parties after trick or treat hours were over.

She asked if I were going to a party, and I said, "No, you and I are going to have one." I had borrowed Charlie Brown and the great Pumpkin and Garfield's' Halloween from the library. We had a great time that evening and she was a happy little girl when she went to bed that night.

It became a tradition for us to watch *Garfield's Halloween* each Oct. 31st. As she got older, we added the movie *Hocus Pocus* with Bette Midler. Even as she grew older, she still insisted that I go with her and her cousins or friends when they "Trick or Treated."

She's sixteen now, and is going without me tonight. It saddens us both, but I thought it best that I didn't go. Some new neighbors have a problem with our religion.

Ours is a nature based religion similar to that of Native Americans. We respect all life--plant, animal, and human--because the Creator made it. Many of our faith are vegetarians and will not even wear anything made from animals. Conservation and recycling are very important to us to protect our planet. We are Wiccans, but there are those who feel we are satanic.

That's strange since many members of our armed forces are Wiccans, and a Wiccan priest or priestess services their needs just as Catholic, Protestants, Jews, Buddhists, Islamic, and others have their spiritual leaders who are serving the needs of their faithful. But to prevent any problems which might affect my daughter's favorite night of the year, I have decided not to accompany her. Hopefully, she will have a happy Halloween his year as she has had for the last thirteen. Blessed Be to all on this lovely harvest Sabbat.

Boots

I first met Boots through my father when he and my mother had a vacation cabin on Long Island at Indian Lake, Ohio. Dad was a very sociable person who always managed to turn a stranger into a friend. I don't know exactly how my father became acquainted with the old, disabled man across the street, but as always, he soon had Boots talking away about his life. But then, Dad did something a bit unusual.

Often he introduced me to his new acquaintances, and that was that. However this time he worked hard to get this neighbor and me to connect. He knew something I didn't—at the time. I figured the reason behind my father's attempts involved pity or compassion for a lonely old man with no family, and I trusted Dad's judgment.

Boots and I really did become good friends; I made it a point to go visit him whenever I was over at my parents' cabin. Sometimes we sat on one of his two concrete and wood benches next to the lake and talked. Other times we walked around his yard, and he would show me his plants or yard ornaments.

He seemed to love the colors of gold, silver, and copper. Most all the objects that inhabited his property were painted a modernistic mixture of all three. If he had a new birdbath or concrete rabbit, out would come the three colors of spray paint. They would be sitting on the patio until I came over. Then he would hand me the cans, and we would walk to where he had arranged the new item. The spraying would begin, first with one color, then with another, and finally the third. He always asked me which area should be what color and whether enough paint, especially copper, had been applied.

I remember his buying a large concrete owl which he sat on a tree stump. He patiently waited until I came over that Sunday afternoon so that he could get my advice about the decorating. We decided to paint the stump all copper before we were finished. The owl was an abstract arrangement of all three colors. He had purchased the owl to scare off the critters that were eating his flowers and few garden plants.

He also had several twirling brown and white plastic owls which he, of course, repainted, and then asked Dad to hang near the roof line. I don't know what the hungry, local denizens thought of their multicolored enemies or even if they were scared of those owls, but the property was colorful.

Learning from Dad that I needed a new refrigerator, and his having a spare one on his carport, Boots offered the machine to me. It was in excellent shape except for a small dint on the front edge where Boots had grazed it with his car when pulling in to park. I was thrilled to get it, as mine was a used one on its last legs.

When I went over to inspect my appliance, Boots promptly brought out the three spray cans. It took all the tact that I could muster to stop his spraying it. The dinted spot had a little rust where the enamel had flaked off, and Boots wanted to protect the metal so it wouldn't continue rusting when I took it home. He was sure I'd love to have it customized. I finally convinced him that basic Rust-oleum white was the best color for my apartment.

I thoroughly enjoyed those afternoon talks, and we discussed many things. I learned much about his life and interests. He never saw his estranged family, so he truly was all alone except for Mom, Dad, and me. It turned out he was even more alone than I could have imagined until he opened up about his psychic abilities. The folks in the neighborhood thought that Boots was "just plain odd" and avoided him as much as possible.

Since Dad knew I had some psychic abilities myself, I suddenly figured out why my father worked at getting Boots and me to become friends. Dad understood that I needed someone to talk to who was a kindred spirit. If my father had any "powers," he never spoke about them, and Mother just brushed such things off as intuition. Only once or twice did she mention in passing about their being such things in the family, but wouldn't elaborate; she'd just shrug and change the subject.

Even she was cordial but cool towards Boots. So that gentle old man and I formed a close bond, and one day he began telling me some minor details about things he had seen. Then he dropped a bombshell on me which explained why he was avoided by the neighbors as if he carried a plague.

He could see when people were about to die! He would dream about someone lying in a casket, and that vision would occur two weeks before the person's death. There were five neighbors on Long Island whom, over a period of time, he dreamed about. Boots had spoken to each man about what he had seen, and had begged him to go to a doctor for an examination.

I don't think any of them did or maybe there wasn't enough time for them to get help. They died, and their widows sent up the alarm throughout the island. Each had accused him of causing her husband's death.

Then I found out from Boots that my father had stood by him and held the neighbors at bay when they wanted to burn down his house or have him arrested or committed. Ever the diplomat, Dad found a way to defuse the situation. How? I haven't a clue, and neither parent said much. That information explained why my mother was polite but chilly; possibly she was concerned about my father's involvement with the volatile situation.

I do know she worried that Boots might see Dad in a casket. She nagged him into going for a complete battery of tests and only relaxed when all such tests showed nothing wrong. Mom loosened up after the doctors' reports and occasionally invited Boots over to eat or took a plate of food or ice tea to him. I made Boots promise to tell me immediately if either one of my parents was in danger, and he agreed.

He told me how frustrated he was because his ability to foresee death didn't include *how* a person would die. That particular lack seemed to anger or scare folks even more than the prediction, so he had become very lonely and retiring after this ability manifested. He didn't tell me when it had started, so I don't know. I do know that he spoke of having several fishing buddies in the past, and I met one who came to visit. So either some friends weren't worried, or the predictions didn't arrive until much later in his life.

I think his psychic abilities weighted heavily on him because he was taking many medications. I remember seeing some twenty bottles (I counted them) of prescriptions sitting on his kitchen counter. Dad and I both asked him repeatedly to discuss the necessity of all those pills with his doctors. He never did. Somewhere along the line, he seemed to just give up.

Shortly before he died, he insisted that Dad and I take his two concrete and wood benches which sat by his dock. We did, and they sat by my parent's retaining wall until Mom and Dad sold the cabin and moved to Florida. One bench was left there, and one was given to me. It still sits in my front yard today as a reminder of him and of a lesson learned.

The Peony Bushes

My ability to see rather mundane future events appeared to be growing. Now instead of visualizing orange flames or glows around significant objects, I began dreaming whole scenarios. One in particular stands out.

221

I lived in a house which had three apartments in it. Mine covered most of the first floor and opened out onto a large back yard. To the left of my back door on my side of the property line was a row of beautiful pink peony bushes. These were the only flowers in either of two adjacent back yards.

My girlfriend and her family had lived in an apartment in the house on the other side of these large plants, and we had tended them together in the past. When they moved out and into a house across town, some new couple moved into their apartment. They weren't friendly.

I came home one afternoon after work, and my eyes were drawn to those bushes. They were worth admiring, but they appeared to glow faintly, I think, when I look back on it. Whatever held my fascination, something seemed disturbing.

Shaking my head to toss off the feeling, I went inside. The evening was quiet and uneventful until I fell asleep. In full color, I dreamed that the neighbors were digging up and destroying the bushes; then, I heard angry voices arguing. The dream seemed particularly vivid, and I remembered it the next morning. It troubled me whenever I walked outside my back door or came home from work and saw the large pink flowers.

Approximately three days later when I returned home, I saw the neighbors digging out the roots and chopping up the stalks. It was what I had seen in my dream exactly. I went inside and called my landlord to tell him what was happening. Then I went outside to tell the couple that those bushes were on my side of the property line, and that they were destroying private property. They informed me that they had their landlord's permission to tear out the bushes and put in a vegetable garden. They proceeded to pile up the destroyed plants and attempt to burn them.

Then their phone rang; I could hear it through their opened door. It was their landlord telling them to stop. Shortly thereafter both house owners arrived, and those angry voices I had heard in my dream were now shouting in my back yard. It was a property line dispute.

It took a surveyor to decide the problem. The peony bushes were indeed on my side. I assume that the other owner had to make some restitution, but the beautiful flowers were gone.

The unfriendly neighbors never apologized or even spoke to me. They simply moved over some six feet, and proceeded to dig up the grass. I'm not certain if they ever planted anything in their garden plot. If they did, nothing appeared. It was just a long narrow scar where neither vegetables nor peony bushes nor friendships grew.

Route 66

This fabled highway spawned a song and a weekly television show. I've traveled on many of America's roads over the years and seen lots of unusual or amazing things, but Route 66 always has me shaking my head.

First of all, for anyone wanting to find antique cars, traveling between Indiana, Kansas, and Missouri is the place to find them. Old lots and repair shops have all sorts of vintage autos for sale. Most are just rusting away on either side of the highway. I can't imagine that any would be expensive.

Gasoline stations still have their old logos up. When was the last time a Sinclair Gas sign with its green dinosaur hanged over a pump? How about the old Texaco sign that resembled a pentacle with a "T" in the middle? These can be found as well as the old semaphores along still-used railroad tracks.

There's a wigwam motel where tired travelers can sleep in individual concrete tee-pees complete with a hole in their tops. I was told the cement was plastered over the original canvass to make each more durable.

Then there's the unbelievably tall metal cross very close to the road. Benches encircle its base, and considering the types of storms that roll across that flat land, it must attract a lot of lightning bolts. Unless it's heavily grounded, anyone sitting below contemplating the afterlife would soon be traveling there.

Also there are churches everywhere on both sides of the highway. Unfortunately, or fortunately, depending on one's point of view, just about every one of these is accompanied by a pornography store close by. I saw a church, liquor store, motel, and "adult" store clustered together. Then I saw an L-shaped mall which contained a church, a tattoo parlor, Big Louis' exotic dancer club, liquor store, and an adult bookstore all together. It gives new meaning to a "strip mall." Several billboards sport only the name "Jesus" in huge letters. One had an adjacent billboard advertising a pornographic store nearby.

I often wonder if there's a practical side to the combination. Does the sinning and saving need to be together perhaps? Or maybe billboard owners along the famous route just don't pay attention to what ads sit side by side. Another pair was equally unusual. One said, "don't almost give" and, its partner said, "if you save, it will pay you back someday." Seems to me they nullified each other.

Antique stores are everywhere, and most seem to have old, rusty advertising signs fastened to their sides or roofs. Any still existing

223

Phillips 66 gasoline sign in America must be found exclusively along this highway.

Many concrete statue places can also be found on route. Most seem to love angels, the Virgin Mary, trolls, and geese, but a couple are rather large; they have more unusual offerings. I think I spotted some classical style statues and mystical creatures in one.

A lot of local roads cross Route 66 and many have single or double letters instead of names. My favorite is ZZ. I can just hear the jokes now: "Want to catch some Z's?" "Was this named for ZZ Top?" "This road is so boring it puts you to sleep!" There're probably many more quips that folks have chuckled over.

There are also lots of unusual names for establishments or such along the way. I ate at Ma Gooche's Restaurant. Breakfast was tasty and hardy. Other names I've spotted are Satisfied Frog, Horney Toad, Salty Iguana, Frogg Mortuary, Deluxe Budget Motel, Cooking from Scratch (a restaurant with a scratching rooster for a logo), and Rustic Motel of Rolla (say the words fast and it comes out "rusty Motorola"). One person in our car spotted a junction of roads "8" and "69". I won't mention the connotations conjured up over that combination.

There's a Saint James winery along the way. It has several billboards announcing that a driver is approaching it. But before these advertisements come into view, there are some saying alcohol ruins families. If it does, then why name a winery after a saint?

As I said, Route 66 is very entertaining. I've only mentioned a few interesting things seen along the way. Every time I travel it, I spot more sights to bring a smile to my lips. In this age of speed, road rage, and long interstate drives, at least this famous asphalt stretch seems to try hard to make traveling enjoyable. I definitely recommend trying it out.

Through Thick and Thin

I'd heard of M.D. as a realtor for several years but when I needed to look for a house, I got to know her. I had broken my right leg in May 2000 when I stepped into a hole my dog Maggie dug in my shade garden. That was right about the time I was involved in the finalizing of my mother's estate. One of the provisions was to buy or build a house. The trust set up wouldn't fix our old one. I went to T.B. for help, but he was out of the reality business at the time; he referred me to M.

I had had a variety of mishaps over that broken leg which kept me in a cast unnecessarily until November. I changed doctors at the time only to discover that my leg had been healed for five months. I was not pleased to find that out, but sometimes problems can create silver linings. Such was the case with M. and her co-hort B.L.

When I first went to the reality office in July, I was dragging a foldable wheelchair with me. I used it to balance on my left leg and hop up the stairs. Then I plopped down and wheeled in. The loud banging of the door against the chair certainly let everyone know I was there. I wasn't wearing a walking cast and my fold up walker which wasn't recommended for stairs or great distances was hanging on the back of my chair. I'm sure I was a strange sight.

In addition to the noise, equipment, and my antics, I was out of breath, my clothes were every which way, and my hair looked like I had been electrocuted. I have no idea what M. or B. were thinking, but they calmly acted as if this happened daily. Their eyes didn't even widen.

Over the next five months, M. showed me fifty-four properties, both houses and undeveloped land. Some she showed me more than once. She would make the appointments with the home owners; I would meet her in her office parking lot, and transfer the folding wheelchair into the back of her vehicle. I'd use the walker to get into the front seat and hold it on my lap while she drove. We had this "down to a science" after a couple of times.

Usually we went to two places in a day but sometimes we would go to three. Whenever we arrived, M. would watch me reverse the above process to get out, then I'd drag the chair to the entry steps, use the walker to get up them and pull the chair up as I went. Then we would go inside.

I'd use the chair to move around the main floor and to rest. To go down to basements or up to second levels, I would get out of the wheelchair, sit on the floor, and raise or lower myself on my rear while again dragging the walker. Then I would have to stand up to get from room to room. The whole process would have to be reversed to get back to the main level. I wouldn't let her help me, because she is about half my size, and if I fell on her, she could have been hurt.

I did let her help me once. I had crawled to the second story bedrooms but could not get off the stairs and on my feet. M. pulled an upholstered rocking chair over to me and held it steady while I tried to pull myself up. My arms slipped and I took a nose dive into the cushions. I was on my knees with my rear protruding over the top of the stairs and my face buried in the back of the rocker. She cursed me out which started us laughing and cracking some unprintable jokes.

That evening we went out for a bite to eat. We were back on the hunt two days later, and I saw her house which she had just remodeled and put up for sale. I ended up buying it, out of all the ones I had seen, and

I haven't changed any of her decorating as I discovered we have similar tastes.

Next we needed to free up the money from the trust to buy the house. She went through all the paperwork, set up the lawyer, and was there in the courtroom to present the reasons for this particular house.

That accomplished, she took on the job of selling my old house. We found a buyer, but his bank was causing problems—at first the lending committee wanted the house painted white—M. convinced them that cedar siding shouldn't be white. Then the committee was unhappy that the foundation under an add-on laundry room was ugly. M. and B. went out to my house on their day off, made a raised bed around the foundation, and planted flowers. Finally the bank folks were happy and the loan went through.

Then when I wanted to buy a piece of land adjacent to the new house, M. again went through hoops because of two difficult sellers. They even tried to back out of the deal 30 minutes before closing. She worked it out and we signed the papers.

I don't have a clue if these two ladies go to the extreme for other customers as they did for me (I suspect they might.) But since they worked with me so much for almost six years, I guess we didn't have any choice. We *had* to become friends.

Dad's Vomit Shirt

My father had been battling lung cancer for almost two years; it was temporarily in remission. Mom had tried for twenty years to get him to take at least one trip overseas, but he had always resisted. He had had opportunities to work in colleges in South America, Spain, and Thailand. The University of Thailand wanted him to spearhead the entire agricultural program for the country, but he refused all offers. He even refused to learn a foreign language for his doctorate.

It all stemmed from his experiences during WWII when he was part of the Army Air Corp stationed in England; there was some lingering anger. Maybe my mother knew what it was all about, but I was not told. I did know he was in special ops and crossed enemy lines at night to string radio lines. He had no trouble with anywhere in North America or Mexico.

But I guess faced with his own inevitable death, he relented and agreed to go on a trip to Europe. Dad sent me some post cards, so I know many of the places he and Mother visited. One card had a camel on it.

226

He mentioned that he had ridden one and didn't think much of it as a form of transportation. He had to either hook one leg or cross both legs around the camel's hump, and he told me that that position was very uncomfortable.

I know they went to Spain because he mentioned in another postcard about people running from bulls in the streets. He wouldn't go see a bullfight because he said it was bloody and brutal. The next card he wrote came from Italy; he said there were statues and relief carvings everywhere.

My parents went to Ireland and to St. Patrick's Cathedral in Dublin. This was where our Patrick family originated. Mom had wanted to see the Book of Kells which our ancestors would have used long ago. Dad said the tour guide was so busy talking about the church itself that there was no time to see the famous bible. I guess my mother was terribly disappointed but had been afraid to slip away from the group to walk over and take a look although she was in the same room with it.

Then Dad wrote me about the Rock of Gibraltar and the monkeys which lived there. I also know that my parents went to France, but Dad was strangely silent about that part of the trip. When they returned home, Mother called and told me what had happened.

Dad's cancer had returned while they were traveling, and he was really sick and weak in Paris. He had been very cold and had stopped at a shop to buy something warm. He picked a burgundy and grey hooded sweatshirt with a depiction of an ancient carving—two cherubs on dolphins and a god-like face between. The picture was printed in shades of grey on the front.

My parents had then ridden on one of those double-decker busses often found in European cities. Mom said he was shivering and nauseated. Sometime during the bus ride, he vomited all over his new shirt. Mom and others cleaned Dad up as best they could, but he was now wet, weak, and cold. They had to get off the tour bus and return to either their hotel or ship, I'm not sure which.

When my parents returned home, Dad went back to his doctor. He had to start chemotherapy again. He often wore his "cherub" sweatshirt when he went to the hospital; it was his favorite. He had purchased it and now wore it over Mother's constant protests.

She did not like that piece of clothing at all; she had always picked my father's clothes, and his choice did not please her when he bought it. She said he completely ignored her when he picked it out. Over that last year whenever he wore it, my mother would say to both of us, "I *hate* that shirt."

She later told me that she had tried to throw it away, but Dad had become very upset. He *fought* her to keep it, and wore it sometimes days in a row until the last three weeks before he died. When he was confined at home to a hospital bed and only wore pajamas, Mother never relented in her dislike of it. After my father died, she was quick to throw it into the trash. She wasn't happy with me when I dug it out and kept it; now I was the recipient of her complaints.

But why did she dislike that shirt so much? Maybe it was because he asserted his independence when he bought it, and Mother definitely liked being in control. I'm sure that initial defiance triggered Mother's intense dislike for the sweatshirt, but logic would say she should have got over it especially since my father was so sick. He had never been so stubborn before over a piece of clothing.

But knowing my father, he bought it because of the depiction. He must have thought it was pretty, and it must have also affected him emotionally. He knew he was dying, and I think the print gave him a sense of peace and faith in an afterlife. Maybe that's why Mother detested that sweatshirt—she couldn't and never *would* accept Dad's dying.

She kept thinking she could save him with the right foods or care. She had been in denial when she was told he only had two or three weeks left; she convinced herself he had six months. Maybe that burgundy "cherub" shirt was just too vivid a reminder.

I took it because it *had* meant so much to my father, because he stood up to Mom, because he bought it himself, because it came from Paris, because he vomited all over it, and because it symbolized his cancer and his three-year-long, hard-fought battle with it.

Silly how that piece of cloth could mean so many things to a family. I feel close to my father when I wear it, as if his loving arms are wrapped around me. It's threadbare now, so I seldom wear it; I couldn't stand to see it damaged. Still, I'll put it on for a few hours now and again before I carefully refold and put it away.

The Roach Motel

Whenever we travelled, Mom carried along a bottle of Lysol to disinfect the bathrooms—toilet, counter, sink, floor, and the entire shower curtain included. Then we had to wear shoes on the carpet. Now Lysol back then was a thick, dark, liquid concentrate resembling pancake syrup. It had a strong scent, not an unpleasant one—just one which made you know that if you could smell it, the area was very clean.

Mom didn't trust the various places we stayed in. These privately owned motels were off the beaten path, and sometimes they could be rather run down. Mom always inspected the rooms before we elected to stay, and there were times we went elsewhere. Sometimes my mother even packed our own blankets and wouldn't use the ones provided. She examined the towels and the sheets.

I thought nothing of it as a child, but as a "knowledgeable" adult, I felt this wasn't necessary. After all, most places had to meet certain health standards by then, and such caution was too much work. I learned my lesson the *hard* way.

It was my 35th high school reunion in Greenville, Ohio. The two-story motel I called had been the same place I had stayed in on my 20th reunion. It was right down town and very convenient because I was taking my daughter along to show her the various sights. The town was part of the old Fort Greenville where an Indian treaty was signed and has a lot of history. I had heard that the motel had new owners, but I figured things hadn't changed. Wrong!

The building was three sided; all rooms were on the inside with the parking in the middle. Erin and I weren't given one of those rooms— we received a room on the outside. There was a decrepit privacy fence, a dumpster, and a pot holed sidewalk to our chamber of horrors. We had to turn sideways to avoid bashing our faces into the rusty, dripping air condition which stuck out over that walk-way. We parked by the office door because we couldn't get a spot on the street.

The owners weren't ready for us even though we arrived later than scheduled. Erin and I waited while we thought they were cleaning. All they did was make the bed and change the towels. Since Erin and I sat on the bed (no chair or table), I thought the sheets were wrinkled from our sitting on them. In reality, they hadn't been changed. The carpet was dirty, thread bare, and musty; I told Erin, shoes at all times; no bare feet—even in the shower. There was a refrigerator in the room; it ran but didn't get cold. That rusty air conditioner was noisy and dripped inside as well as out. To top it off, the room was dark. There was just one lamp. The TV worked but only had two channels. I would have left after seeing the room, but nowhere else had a vacancy for 30 miles. It was the weekend of Annie Oakley Days and the Eldora Speedway races. Something else was also going on, but I forget what, plus the high school reunion. We stayed.

I wished at that point in time to have had a bottle of Lysol. The dirty, musty smell was very strong. I ordered a pizza for Erin as I was eating at the reunion. I paid the delivery boy when it arrived, sat it on the bed and went to put on make-up. Erin opened the box. We had ordered a pepperoni pizza; this was anchovy. It was also jumbled, upside-down, had a bite out of it, had hair or fur or fuzz on it, and was cold.

I called the pizza place; they sent over another one and returned my money. I made the guy wait while I inspected it. It was fine, but we both had little appetite after that first one. It was too late for me to take her to the Maid-Rite down the street, so she gingerly ate the pizza. I finished dressing and went to the reunion.

We stayed there two nights. Erin slid off the bed, and just for a minute her foot touched the floor. That's all it took. We were back in Brown County about a week when she began complaining that her foot hurt and her head itched. She had picked up a planter's wart which our doctor had to cut out, and we both got head lice. One louse I picked off my head was big enough that I broke it in half with the thumb and index finger from both hands; it was a quarter inch long. Yuk!

Neither of us had ever had lice before so it was quite an ordeal to get rid of them before Erin's school started. We managed—I bought something called a Robocomb. It sent an electric current through the metal teeth which killed nits and adults alike. Thank goodness it worked. Nothing else did in those huge bugs, not even kerosene.

I learned my lesson. I only stay at AAA approved places now, and I inspect the sheets and bathroom. Even so, Erin and I wear swim shoes all the time we are in the room. We usually take our own pillows and extra pillow cases. I guess we earned the right to be paranoid.

The Maid Rite

Lots of towns are known for some special food or restaurant, and Greenville, Ohio is no exception. It has the Maid Rite. This little place has been in business since the 1930's, and is located on the edge of town near a railroad, cemetery, and historical museum. Places all around are empty or have been torn down. But the Maid Rite thrives—standing room only. It's a narrow and not-so-long brick building. Along one side of the interior are booths, and on the other side is a long counter where customers stand in line to give their orders and pay. Just behind this counter, workers make the Maid Rites—you watch the whole process. They sell beer, sodas, and chips.

The only thing on the menu is the Maid Rite sandwich. It is crumbled, steamed ground beef with onion, heavy spices (no ketchup or sauce), and put on a steamed bun. You can get cheese and pickle. That's it. No other condiments are available and no other food. BUT—there's nothing like a Maid Rite once you've tasted it. That place is always packed when it opens for lunch and supper.

When we were in school, everyone went there after the Friday and Saturday night ball games. If you couldn't drive, parents took you. The restaurant is located three blocks from Fountain Circle, the center area of town.

I've seen cars backed up around the circle waiting to get to the drive through. Even during a Monday afternoon in the summer, long lines of standing people go all the way out the back door into the parking lot. Since there's not much room inside, people will sit on lawn chairs beside their cars to eat.

It has become a tradition to stick chewing gum on the outside brick walls. And those walls have been covered by all the school kids whoever graduated from Greenville High. Ever ten years or so, some of the mess is cleaned off, but not all. Then it quickly gets coated again. Yes, my boyfriend and I chewed gum just so we'd have some to mash into the bricks when we went by the drive through.

I've taken Erin there during the last two reunions I attended. She can't get enough of those sandwiches and often wishes we could pop over there on a weekend just to eat some. My 45th reunion is coming soon, and I promised to take her along again. If she can't go for some reason, I said I'd bring back a sack full in a cooler to be microwaved. Also she wants a tee-shirt from there. Yep—once you eat a Maid Rite, you're hooked for life! I know I am.

Section Seven

Stella d' Oros

The Tufted Titmouse

A little tufted titmouse
now sits upon the rail.
At first she looks for this,
and then she looks at that.
There's pet food on the table,
but underneath, a cat.

I know she sees me sitting
so close by in my chair.
I think she wants to trust me,
and feels she needn't care,
'cause all these cats around
won't touch her if I'm near.

They're lazy and so fat,
and chasing birds is work;
they'd rather nap in sunlight
than stagger from each berth.
But prudently she watches,
in case she needs take flight.

Thus when it's very certain
all caution's been applied;
no danger is a'lurkin',
toward that bowl she'll glide.
With little wings so quiet,
she'll land upon the food.

She takes one dainty piece
as quick as quick can be.
She won't stay there to feast,
but flies up to a tree.
Her tiny morsel's eaten,
Oh, there is plenty more.

Thus she repeats this process

each day of every week
until the bowl is empty,
and cats have none to eat.
That pretty tufted titmouse,
the boldest little thief.

Goddess

Golden Isabella,
Ra's eye watches above.
The wind whispers gently,
Rippling the tiny curls
On an alabaster neck.
And the tall new-green grass
Parts before tender feet.

Beloved one.

Gods vie to give blessings;
You are perfection born.
Flowers lean to be touched,
Birds sing to give pleasure.
Soft laughter, precious smiles
Are most treasured rewards.

Trees offer quiet shade,
Branches straining o'r head,
Lest the gentle spring warmth
Prove too much for thy brow.

Bare feet touch the damp ground,
And the living Earth yields,
Drawing down the hard stones,
Leaving softness above.

Gaia will nourish you
Throughout this chosen time.
Anubis and Bastet
Will send their sacred ones
To guard through every hour,

And be staunch companions.
Life will hearken always.

Run free now through the fields,
Then sleep in father's arms.
For such, may the world woo
Tiny girl child of two.

Marmalade Jelly

There's a Marmalade cat
Sitting on my lap,
And she shows no signs of leaving.

I am trying to write;
She is deaf to my plight,
And lies on my hand to halt me.

With an eye dripping tears,
And crinkly right ear,
She's alert in her 17th year.

Her tummy's so tender;
Nothing can mend her;
She vomits whatever she eats.

With a healthy loud purr,
Wears clumps in her fur;
She doesn't take time to groom it.

I can see all her bones.
With Amber she roams.
They zoom from one room to the next.

She'll walk over the dog,
Who sleeps like a log,
To nap on her favorite pillow.

She just lost her daughter.

Sadly she mourned her.
She's matriarch to all the cats.

The Weaver

The weaver is poised at her task,
Surrounded by years of her craft.
Since dawn she dyed the cotton and wool
With onion, tea, blueberries,
And bright dandelions plucked from her yard.
The vats stand empty now;
Their colors exhausted,
Transferred to the yarns now hanging
In bundles on her clothesline
Some still dripping their excesses
On the ground below.
Her fingers stained from the pigments
String the heddles and harness
Drawn from last night's drafting.
She works the treadles with bare feet,
Not from necessity.
She wants the familiar touch
Of the worn wood.
The low drifting air currents
Chill her body through her feet.
A fever races within
And only the cool air can numb it.
The movement of the warp and weft,
The up and down, the up and down,
The rhythm. Its rhythm.
The shuttle carries the fill back and forth
The beater presses the twill weave tight.
The years at her craft have schooled her fingers;
They work without her.
She surrenders to the hypnotic movement.
Her eyes do not see the pattern.
Her thoughts fly to the past.
She is happy there.
She stares more deeply into her hypnotic dream,

Where she and her grandchild
Play on a blanket she plans to weave.
This blanket.
Now it will shroud the small body
As it sinks into the Earth.
The loom is her solace.
Its hypnotic weaving comforts her.
She is lost in its spell.

Teachers

Two people,
So different.
One gave horsey rides,
Squeezes, hugs, kisses,
Seats on the lap, stories told.
Tucked into bed, find bear.

The other—" No, don't touch!"
No hugs, squeezes, tickles.
Frozen kisses, no tucks in bed.
Separate chairs, flash cards and spelling.

One said, "Let's build a doghouse—together."
Other said, "Go iron the clothes—alone."

They taught me well.
Two ways--so different.

Green Bottle Fly

Have you ever heard
The buzzing
     The buzzing
          The buzzing
Of the green bottle fly?

The iridescent,
Incessant,
Corpulescent,

     Effervescent
Green bottle fly?

Sky Puppets

The sky puppets
Dance with the wind.
Blue ocean above
Flecked with cloud islands.
Octopus, jellyfish,
Yellow dragon, black bat,
Diamond with rag tail.
The trees are jealous.
Tattered remnants
In the branches,
One that flew too close.

Some laugh with the clouds;
Others flirt with the trees
Or beckon to the birds,
"Let us go up, up!"
Knifing back and forth
Through the currents,
Higher and higher.
Gracefully flitting,

Waving from beyond,
Sending encouragement
To puppets near the ground.

First published 2010, *The Wishing Well: Discoveries*

The Cat with the Flashlight Eyes

It was my cat
I saw last night
That glided up the hill,

And when I gazed
About his face,
It gave me much a thrill.

His flashlight eyes
Were all aglow;
Night's beacons, if you will.

I'll go to bed
And know I'm safe;
He's watching out there still.

Bedtime

The sighing night wind,
Misty moon in the sky,
Soft murmuring owls,
Feathers hushing by.

Quiet child's giggles
In a darkened room,
Nightlight on the table

Soaks away the gloom.

Tired cat on the bed,
Teddy's holding tight,
Covers soft and warm,
All is safe tonight.

A Writer's Blessing

May the Dream catcher hold
Your dreams safely entwined
Until the time is ripe
For you to give them life,
And the ethereal
Becomes reality.

Mother

Golden red hair,
Rosy cheeks,
Silver-blue-green eyes,
Outstretched arms
For hugging,
Cherry lips,
Soft voice,
Kind heart,
Love.

My daughter gave me this poem as a Mother's Day card when she was 10:

Jax

Dead cat on the tall clock,
Moon face chimes the hour.
Black striped tail ropes down;
A sigh,
     A stretch,
               Leg drapes over,
Did the time telling disturb?
10 o'clock,
Pendulum swings,
Lulling you to sleep again.

Genius

Squirrel on the tree trunk
staring at the birds.
Four foot food feeder
too tempting for words.

Squirrel on the tree limb
known for his misdeeds.
Partners on the ground
eating the dropped seeds.

Squirrel on the long cord,
silly little clown,
how to reach that treat—
tail up or tail down?

Squirrel on the long tube
closer to his goal.
Little paws slide passed;
can't get a handhold.

Squirrel off the long tube,

tumbles to the ground.
Thinking while he falls,
a new idea's found.

Squirrel on the tree limb,
steady gnawing heard.
Four foot food feeder
no longer for the birds.

Squirrel on the soft earth,
happiness abounds.
Lots of seeds to eat,
quiet munching sounds.

The Lady

Fine boned,
tiny,
her face more beautiful
than any that could have been formed
of porcelain.
Gentle spirited, well mannered, unassuming,
a dainty lady.
Soft and loving,
she sat next to me
as I wrote my poems and stories,
my muse and my comfort,
never judging, steadfast and true.

It was her wont in summer
to lounge on the deck's railing,
sleeping perhaps.
The heat seldom bothered her;
when it did,
she retreated to a pillowed,
white-wickered,
Victorian chair
on the shaded porch.
At night she slept on my pillow

and purred me to sleep,
her soft paw stroking my cheek.

She was the age
of my daughter.
They grew up together,
having met when both were two.
Over the years,
she weathered the loss of companions
and her only daughter of 16 years.
She adopted another
to fill the loss,
if such a loss could be filled.

Yet she played and groomed
the once abandoned, starved, half-dead,
calico kitten who knew no mother
before her eyes were opened.
Her heart was filled with generosity
which she gave freely and quietly
as befitted the lady she was.

When my daughter and she
were 18 and two,
she tried to leave
so as not to concern us with her dying.
I would not allow it.
I laid her on a pillow beside my chair,
and kept vigil throughout the night.
She slipped away
silently at five
with only a soft cough or two
to let me know.

If only I could as quietly mourn and live
as she's so quietly left;
but I fear I'm not quite the lady
that my calico Marmalade was.

Little Birds

All summer I watched
the tiny hummingbirds
fly to and from my feeders,
chattering at each other
and at me
when the glass cylinders
were empty.

Often one or both would hover
in front of my face
as I sat at my writing table outside,
then zoom over my head
and perch on an overhanging branch,
watching and waiting, impatiently,
until I would do their bidding.
And they,
drinking even as I placed their lunch
on the hangers,
seem to have no fear of me.

Then two babies joined them,
testing their wings,
flitting about my head as I wrote,
their mother chattering
fearful of their boldness.
Were they being taught
that I was another mother
and there was nothing to fear?

Soon,
all will leave until next summer.
My own little bird has been testing her wings
these past three months.
She left my protective nest today,
and has flown away.
I cannot follow her
in her migrations;
I must stay behind.
This is the way it should be—

the way of nature.
But I, like the other mother,
am fearful of her boldness.

With the hummingbirds,
she will return next summer,
and we will chatter at the table
as the little birds chatter above us.

A Child's Memory

My little black inflatable cat,
which held my soap for me,
floated along in my bathtub pond
and kept me company.

Gracie June

Thunder crashes.
Gracie runs to me,
Shaking, whimpering,
Tail between her legs.

She wants my lap
For comfort,
Hiding her head under my arm.
Being held
Gives security.

She had been a young stray,
Accompanied by
Two half grown pups,
And pregnant again.

She must have had a home
Once,

Or she wouldn't be
So loving, friendly,
Seeking humans.

Did she have to hunt?
Dry pellets from a bag
Confused her;
It wasn't food.

Did frantic owners
Search for her?
Was she dumped by those
Who no longer cared?

Her pups were friendly.
Surely they too knew kindness,
Once.

A mystery.

Thunder still crashes.
She sighs and wags her tail,
Contented and safe.
She knows
I won't let go.

The Glassblower

The glassblower toils long hours in place.
Propane and other tanks litter his space.

A hot blazing torch heats glass at his bench;
Big things and little he shapes inch by inch.

Dragons, dolphins, and dachshunds he creates,
And shimmering toppers for wedding cakes,

Hummingbirds and fays with pink golden wings,
Octopi, bottles, pipes, jewelry, and rings.

247

He fabricates colors and knows their ways
To mix with clear glass and not crack or craze.

Cinderella's coach he forms with glass lace
While sweat travels down his weatherworn face.

His shoulders are aching; his arms are all burned
From creations fair he's fashioned and turned.

"An angelfish please, but make it all clear.
I'll paint on color; your price is too dear."

"Give me your secrets and teach me your skills.
I'll leave you no cash to give to your bills."

He carries his cases from store to street.
His wholesaled wares sellers want too cheap.

Been forty-some years of hard times and ease,
Now sadly his art's remade overseas.

"I'll send a check later," shopkeepers say;
They'll take a long time if ever they pay.

With credit he buys more glass for his art.
It's filled his whole life, so deep in his heart.

The glassblower works long hours in place,

While sweat travels down his weatherworn face.

Dragons and dolphins and Dalmatians he makes,
And shimmering toppers for wedding cakes.

Homecoming

There's hustle and bustle
With spaces to play,
When Gracie the kitty
Comes over to stay.

It's upstairs and downstairs
With Gebbers she'll race.
Lame Maxwell will groom her,
She's back in her place.

Old Marmie, the eldest,
With calico fur,
While mourning her daughter,
Adoption occurred.

Big Jaxie, she loves him,
So tiny and sweet,
His arms wrapped around her,
They fall fast asleep.

Surprise

Faceted glass trees
and crystalline ground,
bits of diamond dust
fluttering around.

A blaze of color,
sun's shining so bright.
The fairies' gemstones
magically delight.

Crocus and jonquils,
their heads bending low.
Birds searching for seeds
on the deck below.

The world is crunchy,
a glistening sight.
We had an ice storm
rather late last night.

Lullaby

A fairy's in the window;
She's winking all to sleep.
A gentle, soft, and starry night
With pillows warm and deep.

She sings a silken summer song
Of kittens curled in bed,
Fat lop-eared hares and panda bears;
Such dreams fill up the head.

Playful stars shine in the sky,
A theater in the round,
Acting out their nightly script
With fireworks shooting down.

The fairy's left the window.
All eyes are sound asleep
With gentle, soft, and happy dreams
On pillows warm and deep.

Vampires

My daughter asked, "Are vampires fact,
And will they come into a flat
Through unlatched panes and unclosed doors,
Or search for those outside at play
In darkened light near end of day?"

"Such surely are, oh yes, my dear,
But those which cause all folks to fear
Or make them quake within their beds,
Are not the souls on movies' screen
And aren't the ones who make us scream.

"Into our chambers these will creep,
On silent wings and tip-toed feet,

And while we think that all is safe,
They steal among us in the night
To pierce our flesh, to suck and bite.

"Elvira plies hypnotic charms
While Varnie gasps with steely arms.
Such cunning tales until we meet:
Mosquitoes, bedbugs, fleas, and lice,
With gnats and chiggers, flies and mites."

Section Eight

Daylilies and Petunias

A Fairy Wedding

Serenades from insects in tree heights,
Strings of fireflies cascading soft lights,
There'll be a fey wedding soon tonight.

All through the day small hummingbirds flit,
This way and that, invitations sent.
A starlit sky, the sun is spent.

Down in the woods, a fey circle glows,
Made of white mushrooms; quickly it grows.
Its proud purpose, a sacred enclose.

Outside the circle, covering the ground,
Pearly shell platters with foods abound;
Silver cups of wine for toasts are found.

The gentle low breezes ruffle the air,
Wafting perfumes of the night flowers fair;
Nicotina's a favorite, all are aware.

Guests are arriving by two's or by one;
Faces are smiling, ready for fun
When vows are said and ritual done.

Small owls in white suits usher them in;
Rabbits, raccoons, and even a wren
Mix with fey folk, anxious to begin.

Rev. Brown Sparrow nods to the choir.
Night birds start singing, insects up higher.
Comes the best man, playing his lyre.

The groom's men follow, voices in song,
All in harmony, no note is wrong.
Then sudden silence; now sounds a gong.

Pixies above drop silvery dust.
The maid of honor in dress of rust
Leads the ladies, similarly trussed.

All now are waiting, facing the aisle,
Down walks the groom, solemn all the while,
Ring bearer, flower girl wave and smile.

The blushing bride's a beautiful sight—
Beaded, shimmery, silvery white,
Long flowing veil behind her so bright.

Bride and groom together, hands interlace,
The Celtic goddess will grant them grace.
By two rings joined, a pledge face to face.

Light the marriage candle, man and wife.
Strike up the band; play bagpipes and fife.
They are one through happiness and strife.

Up they fly now in the night air.
Fairies and pixies all join them there.
Magic dust, fire lights, a sight most rare.

Silver cups with wine are passed to all.
Loud toasts spoke round, shake the forest wall.
Laughter, merriment, so grand the ball.

Let the songs began; dance, feast and drinks.
An owl circles left, holding two minks.
Revelries won't end 'til the moon sinks.

Wedding cakes are cut and passed around,
Then all is eaten except one's crown.
The bride and groom stand upon its mound.

Bells are ringing; folks shout to the pair,
"May your lives be long; your children fair."
Next, bawdy jokes started by the hare.

Ah, the food is gone; the wine is spent;
A pixie sleeps, o'r his plate is bent.
The guests are yawning; it's time they went.

Now in the forest a silence grows.
The fireflies' light just barely glows.
A fairy wedding is at its close.

The Gargoyles of Shadows Glade

Up high on a ridge
O'r looking the leas,
There stands a strange house
Surrounded by trees.

By architect built,
Designed from deep dreams.
Eyes watch the hill's side,
A raptor, it seems.

An icy cold night,
No cats are on guard.
Two orphaned gargoyles
Collapsed in the yard.

Wind-slapped and weary,
Broken winged elder
Helped by his brother,
Desperate for shelter.

Mistaking the house
For Mother they lost,
Some comfort they sought.
Must stay at all cost!

"Stone lion we beg
(Alert by the door)
To grant us consent,
We cannot fly more."

"Permission I grant.
It's here you may den.
For this night will bring
Much ice, snow, and wind."

"Young gargoyles, I ask—
Forsake ye your home?
Uncommon it is;

Your kind does not roam."

"They carried their crux,
Those Cassocks from town.
Destroyed our fair nest;
Burned all to the ground."

"We've traveled this week
With nowhere to rest.
All chase us away;
We're not welcomed guests."

Then smiled the old guard
And wisely he said,
"The ladies within
Are differently bred."

"You'll have a new home;
My words will prove true.
Rest there on the ledge
till tempest is through."

Each chose a safe berth.
Assumed their old stance.
Outstretched broken wing
Held only by chance.

Long dragged the dark night,
As banshee wind howled.
Ice flogged without care;
Wild snow devils yowled.

By noon the next morn,
The fury expired.
Two brothers sat firm,
Though grated and tired.

Then clamored 10 cats;
All tumbled outside.
Their ladies behind

To see what arrived.

"All praise to our Gods,
These sentinels sent
To shield this lone house
From evil intent."

Thus spoke the wise dame,
Her daughter agreed,
"Yon broken winged one
From pain must be freed."

Together they healed.
From stone came his aid;
Fine powdered, then steeped,
A poultice was made.

"The limb shall be weak;
Yet it will still hold,"
Thus spoke the women,
"Be cautious, not bold."

"Now give us your names;
This house will be blessed.
We ask you to stay,
Here guard and here rest."

"I'm Fang, the first born,
My brother is Spike.
We'll stay at this hearth
And guard day and night."

The cats gathered round,
Began their low growl.
Crescendo it rose,
Became a long howl.

Allegiance was pledged
To each and to all;
To stand side-by-side

If given the call.

The lion observed.
He closed his tired eyes;
No longer alone
To watch the night skies.

This guardian gleaned
Dark clouds were at brew;
The ladies saw not
A reason to rue—

What happened before
Would happen again:
Irrational fear
With evil within.

Mild pagans they be.
"Harm none" is their creed.
Concern for the land;
Aid creatures in need.

This offered to God:
Sweet cakes and good ale.
No flesh or the blood
Ingested; they'd pale.

Say those who will hate,
"Destroy them we shall;
To differ is wrong,
Send sinners to hell."

The law of the land
Says freedom for all.
Accept it, some won't;
It's bitter as gall.

In borough below
There housed a sly quaint.
A deil in her dwelt,

But none saw the feint.

Quean Rachel, her name,
Gave succor to men.
Clan of the Waters.
To women, no friend.

Rosemary, she loathed.
(A personal grudge)
"You dare see a man;
He's mine, I do judge."
That male found it fun
To stir up her ire.
But Water runs deep,
The consequence dire.

"The pagan's a witch—
Such lies I will weave.
Some cultists will fear.
With this I'll deceive."

Old Guardian watched
The drama unfold.
His Rosemary shunned.
Her champion ran cold.

"Leave town," said her knight,
"You have no friends here.
Tartuffe all abhor;
I'll not have you near."

Bewildered and hurt,
Young maid at her side,
They thought themselves safe.
At home they would hide.

From small things, grow big;
And such be this case.
Control was all lost;
Now fiends showed their face.

So neighborly met,
A leader they chose;

When Luna grew dark,
The witch they'd oppose.

To stone or to burn,
Which did they desire?
Their plans were all laid.
All wanted a fire.

They gathered their ranks
To ready the deed.
This night seemed pitch-black.
Each carried a gleed.

But high on the ridge,
Kith gathered around.
All harked to Niguere:
(None uttered a sound.)

Commanding the cats,
Grey gargoyles beside,
Grimalkin's his aid—
A pale ghostly glide.

Cimmerian born
Of darkness and mist,
This guard by the door
Unlocked the stone cist.

This sacred old box,
Protected for years,
Had objects within
T'would quiet their fears.

A magical rock
Of hematite born,
A glamour will make
If carried or worn.

Clear crystal of quartz
Burns day in the night.
It mirrors the sun,

Increasing its might.

Beryl horn from the Gods:
So lordly its sound
That all within range
Collapse to the ground.

These only he chose
As best for the ruse.
Although there was more
He deigned not to use.

The shape-shifting ore
That Rosemary holds
(Red ocher or iron)
Wild nightmares it molds.

Sweet Corwinn commands
Black wings of the sky.
Bats, ravens, and crows,
On these she'll rely.

Of battles and blood,
They're seasoned and hard.
Black swans sing of death.
Great cormorants guard.

The gargoyles sharp claws
Lift quartz-searing light;
Niguere holds the horn,
Cats scream for the fight.

Tartuffs tramp the ridge;
Some laugh as they run.
Most chant, "Burn the witch!"
Remorse is in none.

Dark screaming wild wings
Dropped stones from the skies,
Attacked with their beaks;

Claws sliced at the eyes.

Grimalkin, the White,
With banchee-like wail,
Flew over hunched backs,
Flogged heads with his tail.

The ground underfoot
Turned slimy with mud.
Nine panthers attacked,
Fanged mouths dripping blood.

Niguere blew his horn;
Earth quaked in reply.
Men fell to stiff knees,
Thought judgment was nigh.

Rose glamoured each mind
And twisted the sight.
Each way people turned
Huge snakes blocked their flight.

But books dare not say,
And legends won't tell,
That gargoyles can shriek
Like spirits from hell.

Protectors of homes
Their voices cause fear.
A gift from Bastet
Men flee when they hear.

Bravura all gone,
Most leave in great haste.
A lesson is learned,
No longer so chaste.

Each safely escaped,
Though naught had gone well.
The Adams blamed Eves—

All femes' fault they tell.

This happened before
In Eden, the same.
Accused God did Man;
Denied his own blame.

On top of the ridge,
Relief was fourfold;
They had not been sure
The glamours would hold.

Some folks are immune.
But strength lies in need;
Mind's sight will hold true,
And helps hone the deed.

Loved wings were her pets.
Brave Corwinn risked all.
These birds she owned five,
Well trained to her call.

Those panthers were cats;
They clawed at each shin.
Grimalkin climbed trees
And jumped on the men.

Vibrations are notes
A horn can well play;
But sing it just so,
All things become prey.

And yet without help
From Powers above,
Each knew she'd be lost.
The Heavens sent love.

The pets all ate treats.
The ladies drank ale
And shivered with thoughts:

What *if* all had failed?

Tired Rose and her child,
The Great One they praised;
Gave thanks to be freed
From evil so crazed.

In town, there's a tale;
It's only a wisp
T'ween those who were there,
And those who shout, "Whist!"

Sharp mirth and the law
Have quelled the dazed mouths.
Though Sunday each week
Affirm their vows.

Black witches they weren't;
No magic was there.
The gargoyles' dread shriek?
Wind, women, night air?

Yet here stands a fact:
On Shadow's Glade wall.
Two gargoyles perch proud,
One big and one small.

The Fairy Church

Far down a paved road,
All broken and patched,
There stands a lone church,
All clapboard and thatch.

And by it, a well
That runs alongside,
A door in the rock,
There fairies abide.

They're head-sick and sad,
And some are just dour,
At what they must hear
On each Sunday hour.

"Why me?" men all wail,
"Give riches and fame."
"A husband for her."
All curse and complain.

No thanks in their hearts;
No gladness found here
Or neighborly love,
Not praises nor cheer.

The fairies heard all;
No more could they stand.
Turn moans into smiles,
Together they planned.

Now fey folk aren't sour,
They do like their fun.
For all's peace of mind,
A change must be done.

They called a town meet,
And most had their say.
Decisions were forged
Throughout the whole day.

With lists of their needs,
Then scattered fays all.
A family of bees
Were first to the call.

Next aphids and ants
Arrived at the scene.
Each offered her aid;
All sent by their queen.

Much nectar was brought
From flowers most sweet,
A mixture to make
of dew, hops, and wheat.

The ants brought fresh grains,
And aphids gave dew.
All bees had the task
Of making strong brew.

Fays saved for themselves
A secret not told,
Their making of bread
From recipes old.

They ground up the seeds
Of hemp in the dough,
Its leaves and fresh yeast,
Then let it all grow.

Now flattened and baked
And cut into squares;
One bite, and good folk
Forget all their cares.

Into the old church
Fays slipped the sixth night,
With wafers and brew,
Before the sun's light.

The kitchen was found
And all put in place.
They had too much drink,
To toss was disgrace.

Oh what could they do?
To store was their wont;
One fairy then spied
The baptismal font.

No better a place
The fairies all hail!
They climbed up its leg
And poured in their ale.

Then downward they climbed,
And rushed out the door
To hide in the trees,
And listen once more.

Soon shuffling and slow,
Came Reverend McVeigh;
Worn down from complaints,
He dreaded church day.

He pulled on the rope
To bells in the tower
Which told to his flock
That now was the hour.

Soon true to their ways,
No soul did they greet;
They cursed and complained
As each took a seat.

McVeigh closed his eyes
And prayed for the while.
He called out a hymn,
Then baptized a child.

The font with the ale
Was used in this case.
The frown disappeared;
A smile crossed her face.

She clapped her young hands;
This babe laughed and cooed
As soon as her lips
Touched magic just brewed.

Then after a hymn
Came personal prayers.
Such selfish demands
The fays could not bear.

Soon came the time
To taste wine and bread.
Each came to the front
And knelt to be fed.

The magical feast
Had barely touched lips;
The priest stood in awe
As men did back flips.

The women kissed men,
Yes, even the priest.
All danced on the pews,
High kicks to the east.

One sipped from the font
As dancing gave thirst—
Not water but ale!
He dived in head first.

As others found out,
Great gulps each one took.
Warm slaps on the back
And hardy hands shook.

Soon all had light hearts
With nary a care.
There're smiles all around.
No wails of despair.

"Red Rover," they called,
"Send over the priest."
He played the game well;
He sure wasn't least.

The fairies can't help;
They must join the fun.
They rushed in the door,
Before all was done.

The organ pipes blast
As feys danced on keys.
A bagpipe's sweet sounds
Were heard from the trees.

All joined in a line
And weaved through the pews.
Feet moved to the beat;
They danced with the muse.

They played through the day
And laughed through the night.
They're dancing there still
At dawn's early light.

So they all agreed
That each Sunday hence
To serve bread and ale.
It just made good sense.

Then fey folk and men
Each year after year,
No cursing or cries,
All were of good cheer.

Long times have gone by
Through trouble or mirth;
A heaven be there,
This small patch of earth.

The place can be sought,
But only if lost.
It's hidden so well,
And there is a cost.

If found, do not leave;
You cannot return.
It's placed out of time;
So listen and learn.

You'll fade from our world
Of sorrow and woe;
For time here is fast,
And there it is slow.

This legend I've heard
Since I was a girl;
Yet still I may go,
And leave this mad world.

The Bones of Old Radnor

By the fire's low light,
As the sparks flair bright,
Sits a tall old crone.
In a sing-song drone,
For a child's delight,
Tells a tale tonight.

Some enchanted stones,
Called the Giants' Bones,
In a group of four,
Sit at old Radnor.

Ancient legends say
That when dark ends day,
They shall rise at will
For to drink their fill
At the Hindwell Pool
During winter's Yule.

Any soul so bold,
Who can brave the cold,
If he wants to see,
All the wise agree:

He must hide away
As they walk and sway.
One should not be seen
By these granites green,
Or with angry tones,
These most ancient stones
Will evoke this curse,
Long ago rehearsed:

All his sense will freeze.
Down upon his knees,
He will crawl toward
Where the slabs were moored,
And descend inside
To be crushed alive,
When they come all four

Back to Old Radnor.

But a goatherd's boy
Found his greatest joy
With those rocks of yore.
All his heart he'd pour
To these granite friends
While they blocked the winds
From the cold-washed air.

During summers fair,
In their shade he'd rest
From the sun's hot quest.

During five full years,
He had felt no fears
Of a winter's Yule,
Or the Hindwell Pool.

He would disappear
When the time drew near.

To those granites green,
Most polite he seemed,
Not to watch them sway,
In an uncouth way,
When they rose at will
To drink their fill.

Then a dark man came
To the Highland plain,
With a story, told
From a legend old:

'Under Garr, the Big,
(If one were to dig)
Is a treasure hold,
And "tis filled with gold!'

'But the digging's hard

In this stony yard.
There's a better way.'
(He was wont to say.)

'On the marrow's night
Will be Lune's full light,
And I hear there's talk
That the stones will walk.'

'So while they're away,
We must not delay.
You climb down the hold
To retrieve the gold.'

'I above will stand
To aid with my hand.
On my trust, I pledge,
Raise you from the edge.'

'Then we must retreat,
Ere those bones we meet.
They will speak the verse
That shall cast the curse.'

'Said the goatherd's boy
To the dark man's ploy,
'I will not yon night
From my friends take flight,
Nor betray their trust.
So do what you must.'

Then the dark man smiled;
But by all the while,
There upon his face
Could be seen a trace
Of the hateful side
He was wont to hide.

Though he feigned to leave,
It was not his creed
To quit plots undone;
He had always won.

Thus the youth did know
He should loyalty show;
To Old Garr he'd turn.
For his friend must learn
Ere he slacked his thirst,
He need call the curse,
Or he'd lose by stealth
His long-guarded wealth.

The next night he stayed
And the scheme relayed.
All the bones took heed;
They would thwart the deed.

Then he felt Garr say
Not to run away,
But to stand nearby
With an opened eye.

The Old Four agree
To allow him see
As each leaves his place
With a lumb'ring grace.

When Yule time was right,
The fair moon full bright,
A low rumbling roar
In the earth's deep core
Grew more louder still;
Then cried thunder shrill.

Next that ground did quake;
The rocks heave and shake,
And from the hallows' fold
They unfast their hold.

With a lurching step
Old Garr boldly crept;
He was first to lead
As his mates concede.
Came his brothers 'round.
The lad heard the sound
Of a runic chant

In a secret cant.

Granites cast the curse
In that ancient verse,
By a mystic wrought
From a time forgot.

To his wonder still—
He so kept his will;
On his feet he stayed,
Though he quaved and grayed.

The dark man appeared;
With his eyes, he leered.
He deemed by his stealth
T'would soon gain the wealth.

He would hold his stance
Till the slabs advanced;
Their thirst to slake
At that distant lake.

He'd not heard the rhyme
Which withdrew his time.
That most ancient rune;
It bespoke his doom.

All his sense did freeze;
Downed upon his knees.
So he crawled behind
Their towering line.

Then that desp'rate knave,
With his eyes, he craved
From the goatherd's bairn,
To be saved from harm.

Yet that gentle son
Could not be the one
To release the fool
On that fateful Yule.

Aye, the culprit crawls,

(His confusion palls)
Not to Old Garr's docke,
But the Hindwell lock!

To the rogue's dismay,
He is going to pay;
But not crushed inside
Old Garr's pit alive.

He begins to muse.
Oh, where leads the clues?
Opens wide his eyes,
As the thoughts arise—
In a watery crypt,
He will soon be dipped.

Then ahead he moved.
Not his plight he rued;
Only hatred seared.
At the lad, he sneered.

The old knars agree
That the youth not see
As the villain die,
Or his mind awry.

But the screams he heard,
And his ears were gird;
Then the sounds expired.
He, no longer mired,
In his heart rejoiced.
His great gladness voiced.

When the boulders came,
Old Garr breathed his name:
'A rare gift for you,'
As he claimed his pew.
From his treasure horde,
Rolled a golden orb.

The lad touched the sphere,

And could suddenly hear
The old menhirs' speech;
He knew each from each.

He learned hist'ry true
Of this granite crew.
They are gods of old,
And all chose this mold
To guard evermore
This charmed treasure store.

Of each golden bit
Were great stories writ
Of their powers great.
But dire be earth's fate;
Without wisdom's helm,
Men would blight their realm.

Aye, these boulders knew
Blair was wise and true—
He sat proved when tested,
Now with globe invested.

T'was called Odin's Eye,
For which, kings would die.
If such force command
Like a god he'd stand.
But a wise man knows
From such, madness grows.

Blair would understand,
From the small or grand,
All their language spake,
And such knowledge take.

He must guard it well,
But to no one tell
How he 'came this year
A young magus seer.
He would use his life
To ease others' strife.

So he thanked them well,

Then returned to dwell
In the town below,
Where he eased each woe.

In his goatherd hut
With the front n'ere shut,
By this way, he heard
From each passing bird,
And young doe so fleet,
Or the grains of wheat,
All of nature's lore
In those times of yore.

Then by far or wide,
The increasing tide
Comes to find his door,
For his help, implore.

He so many saves
From untimely graves;
Thereby grows his fame.
They all know his name.

Yet three days each week,
With his goats he'll sneak
Out to travel far,
Still to seek Big Garr.

O'r old times they talked.
Aye, on solstice walked
To the Hindwell Pool,
All the five at Yule.

In life's twentieth tide,
Where he wed his bride,
T'was at Old Radnor,
With the granites four.

When his twinborns died,
With the bones he cried;
All their hearts were torn,
And they sat forlorn.

But the days do wind;
Then at harvest time
His small girl was born.
A resounding horn
Heard upon the lea
Told the One and Three.

She was Garra named
For the stone so famed.
Those three days each week,
She would sleep and crawl
In their shadows tall.

O'r the years she grew.
Learned the stories true,
At her father's feet
'Bout that dark man's cheat.

Then her mother died;
These two softly cried.
They entombed her near
Their old boulders dear.

Three score years flew fast;
Nothing mortal lasts.
Now young Garra grown,
With a child her own,
Laid her father down.
The gold orb she found.

This she knew not what.
It was in the hut
Wrapped in silken tulle;
Just a comely jewel.

She recalled a time,
In her childhood's mind,
When it was a toy.
She would laugh with joy,
As she rolled the ball
To her father tall,
And then with his child,
He would play awhile.

All alone and lost,
As if tempest tossed
A small ship aground.
With that toy she found,
She so felt the need,
Took her goats to feed
At the menhirs' side.
There she thought to hide.

Ere she reached the stones,
Garra heard soft tones.
As her name-sake said,
'Aye, your father's dead,
Yet we four are here,
And we hold you dear.'

I'll your father be;
You may come to me.
I will always heed
When you call in need.'

With that golden sphere,
All life's' speech you'll hear;
As it was with Blair,
'You can earn your fare,
As a healer wise.'
It was her surmise
That the stones had talked
When her father walked
There within the glade.

Now this grateful maid
Stopped awhile with Garr.
He became her dar
To her sire's long past,
And she found at last
Where her future lead—
In her father's stead.

Soon an ancient seer;

She is long of year,
But has daughter fair
As her seasoned heir.

While her grandson ages,
Crone tells him of mages;
She, his int'rest hails
With her bedside tales.

In this way she trains,
And some day the reins
Will be given him,
Lest the orb grow dim.

Now the story's done,
My small precious one.
It is time to sleep;
Let your dreams go deep.

'Granny Garra please,
You are such a tease!
Was this telling true?
Was the lady you?'

'Not another word;
T'was a yarn you heard.'
She tucked quilts up tight.
Though her eyes shone bright
From a thought of four
Up on Old Radnor.

Section Nine

Tales from the Mandrake

Two Victims

The little cat looked hopefully out the window waiting for his beloved mistress to return. She left every morning and returned each evening when the sun began to set. It was almost time for her to return. He began to get excited. He couldn't wait for her to open the door, scoop him into her arms, and administer hugs, kisses, and head rubs. Then he would help her fix supper. He always got a canned cat food treat when she sat down to eat. Then they would play.

But tonight she didn't come. He sensed she was late. The last blue jay left the bird feeder outside the window. Where was she? It was getting darker. He began to get nervous. His food bowl was empty, and it usually was filled again by now. He wanted her; he missed their playtime. The hours ticked by-- he heard a car. Was it her? No, the car didn't sound right. A man came to the door and put something on the window. Then he walked away. Mittens was nervous and curious. What was that thing on the window?

Other cars drove by, but none pulled into the driveway. It was very late. He slept. When he awoke, he heard a mouse rattling the cabinet door. He watched and waited. The mouse came out cautiously, and Mittens was ready to pounce when the sound of a car horn blared outside. The sudden loud noise scared the mouse away. He sighed hungrily and tried to sleep.

When he opened his eyes later, she still wasn't home and the sun was rising. Did he miss her? Did he sleep right through? Did she come home and leave again? He resolved not to sleep when it became time for her return. He would bat his cloth ball and chase it to stay awake. For now, he slept.

He kept his sad eyes and alert ears to the window all afternoon. Would she be home soon? He found a large paperclip on the floor and began batting it around just to while away the hours. Still she didn't come and the time grew late.

He was thirsty now as well as hungry. He had drunk all of his water because of playing. The clock on the wall ticked away the long hours, then the next long day. He couldn't sleep. He was too hungry and too thirsty.

His bag of cat food was on the kitchen counter. He jumped up and tipped it over. He knew it was wrong, but he was *so* hungry. He clawed and chewed at a corner until it tore open and some food fell out. He gobbled it greedily, looking over his shoulder every minute or two, expecting to be told he was a "Bad Kitty!" He couldn't help it. He tore the bag more, and more food spilled out. He was having trouble swallowing the pieces; his mouth was very dry.

He needed water. He jumped off the counter and padded to the bathroom. The toilet had water in it, but the seat was very slippery. He almost fell in head first. He couldn't reach the liquid. He balanced on three feet and carefully lowered a paw down until his fur was wet. Then he licked the moisture off. He did this many times until his thirst lessened.

Then he took his toy mouse in his mouth and jumped onto the bed. Her smell was on the pillow; it comforted him. Somehow he sensed she wasn't coming home, but he refused to believe it. His hope failed over the next few days. There was still food but no more water. His sadness was deeper than his thirst. He refused to eat, and he wouldn't leave her pillow. He felt so weak, so tired. She filled his fitful dreams as the clock in the hall ticked away the hours.

Soon the band in the seven-day clock wound down, and the pendulum stopped.

Her Father's Cologne

It had rained heavily. The wind and lightning had been frightening. When the frozen rain, or rather pea-sized hail, covered the deck, Molly was sure another tornado was nearby. Although the television had warned of a tornado watch, no actual touchdowns were reported. She breathed a relieved sigh when the storm passed.

She needed to go to her parent's house to start sorting through family possessions accumulated over the years. Dad died first, in December, then Mom, last March. She hadn't been able to even go to the house in three months, but she told itself she had to get started this evening. The storm relieved her of the responsibility temporarily, but now she needed to go. She wished she could give into her temptation of wanting to stay home another day, but, she told herself, the work had to be done soon if she planned to put the house on the market in July.

Another sigh, then Molly grabbed her umbrella and hurried out the door before she could think of another excuse. The clouds were clearing but left a haze on the moon. The warm sticky air promised a foggy night later. She climbed into the car and backed out of the driveway. It was a 30 minute trip to her childhood home. Molly stared at the road ahead. The monotony of the white lines in the middle of the road helped to numb her mind, and she watched them hypnotically. She rolled the windows down and breathed the sweetness of the air. She loved the way

285

the air smelled after a storm—"ozone," a teacher from high school called it.

Even the skunk aroma wafting on the evening breeze made her smile sadly. She remembered when she was little and riding in a car. Both parents had gagged when they smelled skunk, but she told them it reminded her of goldenrod. Her mother had had her nose buried in a Kleenex and rolled her eyes, but her father had just smiled as if he understood.

That thought made her pull to the side of the road and stop. She started crying and leaned her forehead on the steering wheel. Was this some descent into madness? How could smelling a skunk make her so sad? She *had* to stop this. The teardrops on her jeans stood out like ink stains. They'd dry soon Molly told herself and wiped her eyes.

Carefully she put the car in gear and moved back onto the road. She refused to think until she pulled onto the gravel drive that wound to her old home. A large limb from the maple tree had fallen on the bluebird house her father had made eight years before.

There had even been a little erection ceremony when he dug the hole, poured in the concrete, and set the pole. He carefully measured to make sure it was the right height and used a level to get it straight. Molly had been given the job of holding it steady until the concrete set. Dad had started the charcoal in the grill while he waited to fasten the birdhouse to the pole. When the grilled hot dogs were eaten and the birdhouse set, Mom produced blueberry pie in celebration. She remembered it had only been a week later that her mother had spotted a bluebird inspecting, then claiming the handmade house.

"Something else gone," she thought and parked in front of the garage. She unlocked the side door and went in. Hanging in the corner over her dad's workbench was a dusty birdcage made from straws and yarn. Inside was a peanut glued to a dowel and hanged from the top like a perch. She had made that thing in fourth grade art class. Since chickadees had fascinated her at that time, she had painted the peanut to look like one. Molly didn't think that that white peanut with a black glob on one end looked much like a bird, but her dad declared it perfect, and after all these years, it still hanged where he could see it when he worked on some home project.

She crossed over the smooth concrete floor, up three steps, opened the kitchen door, and flipped the light switch. She quickly circled from room to room turning on lights. Molly wanted the darkness gone; the silence was too much. She called, "Mom, Dad, I'm home."

Molly knew there would be no answer, but she couldn't help herself. It was what she always announced when she entered. To stop the tears, she roughly turned on her father's radio. It was still on the golden oldies station he loved. Refrains of "Mama's Got A Squeezebox" blared in her ears. For some reason she started giggling. Then she doubled over laughing hysterically at the idea of her mother playing accordion. Maybe that's what she needed to shake off her feelings of loss, abandonment, and fear. She felt a small measure of tranquility. She could almost hear her father lecturing her about life and death after the doctor said he had lung cancer.

He had said, "*We* may never be able to accept this view, but I think other religions were right. There is a life after death that does not involve punishment, but reincarnation. I've tried to talk to your mother, but she won't listen. Perhaps you will?" he asked. For the next three hours, she and her dad had discussed such issues and his impending death. He said he'd leave her a sign if he could. He joked that maybe he'd knock over a glass to say he was alive. She looked around hopefully, but saw no changes which might signal that her father was nearby.

She shrugged, and walked to her parents' bedroom. She began opening drawers and placing clothing on the bed. In the bottom drawer of the dresser, she found two old Halloween costumes-- a pinstriped Zoot suit and spats that her father had worn, and her mother's silver-fringed flapper's dress with a pink feather boa. She had been 18 when her parents wore those costumes to a neighbor's party.

Molly and a boyfriend had gone as Gomez and Morticia Addams. She wondered what had happened to her outfit. To her surprise, that long tight dress was under an Indian costume in the same drawer. She pulled it out and held it up to her body in front of the mirror. It looked like it would still fit.

"I think I'll save all these outfits. They're pretty elaborate, and I can use them," she thought, making sure all the parts were there. She went to the kitchen to retrieve a sack to put them in. The radio was still on, and a five minute show on stargazing had just started. She and her dad had loved to listen to the announcer tell about constellations or planet conjunctions, or various astronomers like Galileo or Copernicus. Tonight he was telling about a lunar eclipse coming tomorrow night. Molly smiled and made a mental note to watch it.

She grabbed a sack and headed back to the bedroom. On the way, she thought she smelled her father's cologne. "Must be from those costumes," she suggested to herself. Then she entered the room. The boa was draped over the chair, not on the bed where she had left it. She shook her head. "My emotions are making me tired and absent-minded," she thought. Carefully she folded the outfits and put them in the sack. Her father's Zoot suit was the last one in.

She sat the sack by the door so she wouldn't forget it and continued to empty the drawers, putting everything in neat piles on the bed. Again she thought she smelled her father's cologne. Her fingers shook as she opened the closet to start removing its contents. Her father scent overwhelmed her, and she set down on the chair.

"Daddy, is that you; are you here?" she asked hopefully. A slight draft brushed her face, and she closed her eyes. She could almost feel his presence in the room. Molly kept her eyes closed because she knew nothing would be there if she opened them. She just *knew* he was there because of the cologne. "You said you'd come back, and you have. I love you so much." The smell disappeared as quickly as it came. Tears stung her cheeks, but she smiled. "Thank you, Daddy, thank you," she said as she opened her eyes. She felt at peace. "I can do this now. I'll get an early start tomorrow morning."

She got up, gathered the sack of costumes, turned off the ceiling lamp, and headed toward the front of the house, clicking off lights and she went. When she reached for the radio, the song "Toot Toot Tootsie, Don't Cry" began playing. She laughed and turned off the radio. "I won't, Daddy; I won't anymore." Then she headed out the kitchen door and to her car. Molly was actually humming when she started the ignition.

Luna

He sat in his car, forehead resting on the steering wheel. On the seat next to him was an expensive box of chocolate turtles tied with a pink satin ribbon. He raised his eyes and stared at the waning gibbous moon filling the sunset--a Goddess clothed in robes of orange, gold, and magenta. He pretended indifference, but it didn't work. Past experiences had warned him to expect little, and he wanted so badly for Luana to care for him. If only for a little while-- if only for another month, before he again became a werewolf. He slammed his fist into the dashboard.

"Life sucks," he yelled. The pain from his knuckles made him testy. "I hate you, moon, I hate you! There's nothing beautiful about you. You're like quicksand; one wrong step and you get another victim! How many more horrors have you made? How many more monsters--like me?" Tears stung his eyes. He knew no amount of screaming at the inflexible Goddess would make her loosen the chains around his neck, not even for one cycle.

Then he heard a car coming up the old, half-forgotten fork in the road. It had to be her Chevrolet. No one else knew it really was a road-- that there was asphalt and gravel underneath the weeds that had taken over years before. He was surprised when she suggested it; surprised that she knew about it. Even he hadn't been here often--at least, not in a car.

They hadn't seen each other for the last several days. So they had planned this tryst away from others and especially away from her overly protective father. It was a chance to just be alone and to talk. He didn't want to tell her what he was, but honesty compelled him. She had said she needed to talk to him also.

He could see the headlights now. It had to be her. He opened his door, grabbed the candy, got out, then thought better of it, and dropped the box back on his seat. He went around to the back side of his car. He put his shaking hands in his pockets and leaned against the fender. The lights flashed, then went out. The signal-- it *was* her.

Steady, he told himself. *Don't let her see how nervous you are. Smile.*

Her car pulled alongside of his. She cut the engine, and he fumbled for the door handle. She slid out of the car in one long easy motion, her muscles moving like liquid. That's one of the things he admired about her. Other girls' movements were jerky at times, but she always flowed.

Her hazel eyes, flecked with green, crinkled as she smiled at him.

"Isn't the sunset beautiful," she said, "and the moon is pretty too."

Luana seemed a little haggard as she opened the trunk and pulled out a flowered tablecloth. She handed him the cooler and a picnic basket, then reached back for another cooler and the bug spray. They found a spot that was less weedy and organized their supper. He noticed that there wasn't any meat-- just bread, peanut butter, chips, celery, radishes, tomatoes, bananas, and oranges.

"I didn't think you were a vegetarian," he said. "I bought you a cheeseburger last week."

"Oh, I'm not. It's just sometimes every month I need a break. I hope you don't mind. My father taught me to make peanut butter and tomato sandwiches. They're delicious. Peanut butter is also a good coating for celery and bananas. I brought salt and chip dip. You have your choice of spicy tomato juice or sweetened iced tea to drink, and brownies for dessert."

It was an odd meal for him, but he enjoyed it immensely. "Maybe it's the company," he thought. But he liked the idea of no meat for change, just the same.

Both ate voraciously and silently as if they were starved. He liked watching her eat; she didn't pick at her food as if she were on a diet. That was something else different about her. She could eat as much as he could with no apologies; she liked food.

There wasn't much left when they finished. He helped her put everything back into her car except the drinks. Then since the mosquitoes were ignoring the bug spray, they climbed into his car. The sunset was gone, the stars were out, and Luna was higher in the heavens.

"I'm glad the moon is smaller now," Luana said. "Sometimes it seems to overpower the sky."

"Sounds like you don't like the moon so much," he said, watching her with a dreamy, full-stomached ease.

"Oh, I like it most of the month. It's just too bright when it's full. The night should be dark so you can see the stars. It's waning now, and soon it will be a crescent—'a Cheshire cat smile, holding lots of secrets,' Mom always says."

He grinned, "You're so different from other girls. I really, really like you." He reached under his seat. "Here, for you. I think I sat on the edge of it when we got in the car. It's sort of a happy three-week anniversary present."

She grinned as she took off the pink bow. "Did you tie this ribbon?"

"Pretty bad, huh?"

"No, but you're a spendthrift. We've only seen each other for two weeks. We missed this last week, you know. And you've got a tuition bill coming up. Kelly's Hardware doesn't pay you well enough to blow 20 bucks on me."

"I don't care. But maybe you'll give me a chocolate turtle, if I'm a good boy."

"I'll give you three. But we need to talk… about this past week." She was watching him like a cat watches a bird.

"I know; I'm sorry I didn't call or see you. Sometimes I'm tied up--you know—work, college, parents. It'll happen. Seems like every month something takes over for two or three days."

"Oh, I don't mind. Same thing happens to me every month. I *am* a girl, you know. I just had a bad three days. That's why I can't handle meat for a few days afterwards. Sometimes it happens twice a month, if there's a blue moon," she said sadly. "It's cost me a few boyfriends over the years. No guy wants a gal who's sick three days each month and won't see or talk to him.

He had noticed earlier that there were dark circles under her eyes. She hadn't slept much lately!

Could it be, he thought as excitement shivered down his spine. He put his arm around her shoulders.

"Luckily blue moons don't happen very often; once a month is plenty. I'll bet you grow the cutest ears when she waxes full." He tried to look nonchalant, but couldn't help grinning from ear to ear.

Luana's head snapped towards him, her mouth and eyes frozen wide-open; she forgot to breathe. Defenses up, she started to say she didn't know what he was talking about. Then one thought raced through her head,

He's like me! She breathed again. His goofy expression made her laugh.

"Do ya think?" she asked quietly, cocking her head flirtatiously to one side, exposing her ear.

"Yes, I think," he said.

Not knowing what else to say, both stuffed chocolate turtles in their mouths and stared out through the windshield. Then David pointed toward the gibbous moon. "I guess the old Gal can toss a straight ball now and again, after all," he said.

Luana nodded.

Sandra

Adela preferred the hourglass to a modern clock, at least, in her studio. This was a large three-hour one, especially commissioned for her by Sandra, her lover. The glass was a bittersweet, but impossible to give up, memory of a happy past, only one month lost. Each morning when she turned it over to start time anew, she thought of Sandra – her beloved one – the sparkling one, as glistening as the glitter within the blue sand.

Today she couldn't shake the memories – Sandra's silver slippers dancing silently on the studio's hardwood floor as her gauze skirt swirled around her. She sometimes played a carved flute as she moved. Adela mused, *No, Sandra isn't beautiful in the standard sort of way. She's too thin for that.* But she was beautiful in Adela's eyes, none the less.

Something about her movements reminded Adela of a young fox from her childhood – a silver one which ate the food put outside for a feral cat. Her father had been exasperated and threatened to throw a lug wrench at it the next time it came around.

Adela persuaded him not to – after all, the fox was hungry too. Her father had just looked at her as he ruminated her arguments, then lowered his eyes to the empty food bowl and poured out another helping.

She smiled at that memory. *Daddy couldn't stand the thought of any animal going hungry.* Maybe that's what attracted her to Sandra --she had a thin, hungry look.

Adella looked around her studio. She hadn't been able to paint for a month, not since her lover left. She could still hear her voice saying, "I love your street scenes, your landscapes, your impressionistic faces. Your work gives me inspiration. There's a whole novel on each canvas!"

There's no writer to interpret my paintings now, Adela thought sadly. She took a deep breath and stretched. *I need to get outside away from these morose memories. Now would be a good day for a picnic in Garfield Park. I'll take my paints and a canvas along. Something might strike me.*

Having a direction, she busied herself in the kitchen. Two sandwiches of Braunschweiger and mayonnaise on rye paired with a thermos of hot cinnamon-laced cider brightened her mood considerably.

I should do this for as many sunny fall days that are left. A different place each time. She grabbed her supplies and fairly skipped to the bus stop.

Forty minutes later, Adela had her short easel set up. She sat on the ground munching a sandwich and watched a woman do a Tarot reading for a customer. She tried to be discreet, hoping that the pair wouldn't notice her sketching them. She could add details later.

Right now she needed to get the general poses done before the customer left, or they changed their positions. Then she would add the park's setting and the skyline as that wouldn't change. She already knew the title for this painting: "Reading in Garfield Park."

Adela was close enough to hear the Tarot reader exclaim, "Ah, you've drawn The Lovers!"

"The Lovers! It looks more like a vampire's card – he's sucking her life out. Just like the bastard did me!" said her customer.

"No, no, you don't understand. This card means sexual attraction, beauty and love, a moral choice to be made. It's a drawing together of opposites with difficulties overcome. This is a good card – a card of healing or moving forward. Let's see what the card next to it says."

The reader's words slammed into Adela's head and heart.

"There are no single coincidences in this world. Everything has meaning and a purpose, a direction needed taking." She remembered Sandra telling her that last summer.

Well, this is just such a "coincidence", she thought.

Adela finished her preliminary sketch and briefly outlined the background she smiled to herself, feeling full of hope. Tonight when she returned home, she would call Sandra and apologize. She'd been so blindly stubborn. She was determined not to let five happy years disappear because of her fears.

It had been such a silly argument that split them apart. Sandra wanted them to go to Tokyo, Japan...just for a year. She would write and Adela would paint. They would do a book together – have a showing with Sandra's writings next to each painting which inspired them.

Adela hadn't wanted to leave. She told Sandra that it would be too expensive and stressful. She wasn't sure she wanted to sublease the apartment to her brother for a year; things might get damaged. Who would want to see their work over there? Where would they stay? How long would it take for them to find an apartment? Who'd ship their belongings to them? The list went on and on.

There had been angry words, accusations, hurt feelings. Her lover had stormed out. That was only a month ago. They hadn't been apart in five years.

The real problem was that Sandra spoke Japanese, and she didn't. She would feel isolated, helpless, scared – like a small boat tossed in the water with no wheel or rudder.

Adela had never been out of the country; Sandra had, many times. She had been too afraid to let go and allow Sandra to take care of her for a change. She was afraid of failure.

"Yes, I'll call her tonight," Adela said out loud. "She'll be sleeping now – the time difference. She's already in Japan and has an apartment, so going there will be easier. I won't have to be afraid. Sandra will be waiting for me at the airport. Two weeks, Babe, two weeks."

The "Reading in Garfield Park" went quickly.

No Way Out

The movers came yesterday. They packed glassware and toted furniture into the large van all day long. Today Abigail cleaned the house like a sleepwalker. She didn't know what to do. She had nowhere to go. Her daughter Karen was moving to North Caroline to start her new job. The town house was sold and the money used to buy a small condominium. There was no room for Abigail.

There were plenty of places she could rent here but none would allow more than one cat or one dog. She had six cats and two big outside dogs. Two of the cats and one dog belonged to Karen but she didn't want to take them to Charlotte.

"The animals won't be happy in a small place. They're used to going outside and I won't be home much. They'll be a lot happier in familiar surroundings. You keep them, Mom."

Abigail had tried for weeks to find an affordable place—houses, apartments, even a couple of trailers. She had hoped to buy, but no bank wanted to loan a sixty-eight-year-old woman money for a house.

"After all," as one loan officer said, "you would be ninety-eight before your thirty-year mortgage would be paid off. What are the odds of your

293

living thirty more years? It's not practical for a bank to risk its money on a person your age. You could get sick and default. No, Mrs. Baker, you should consider renting instead."

She had taken his advice. She poured over the want ads, called agents who handled rentals and checked the internet. Some places asked more for rent than what a mortgage payment would have been: first and last month's rent plus damage deposit. Then deposits to turn on the utilities. No matter that she was a long-standing customer with excellent credit. Now she would only be a renter and utility companies had their policies.

She had the money. The town house belonged to her daughter, a gift from Grandma years ago. Karen was only a child then, so Abigail had sold her country place, invested the cash and moved. She maintained it through Karen's school years and while she went to college.

Now her only daughter was leaving to start a new life. An east coast condominium cost a lot of money, so Karen had had to sell the place that had been their home for fifteen years. The furniture and the daughter were traveling east today.

All that remained were cleaning supplies, a vacuum cleaner, some snacks and juice in the refrigerator, cat and dog food, pet dishes, litter boxes, cat carriers, the pets, and Abigail.

That evening after the house was cleaned, and the animals all cared for, Abigail sat on the floor leaning against the kitchen door. She literally felt "up against the wall." She couldn't give the old animals away. They would be euthanized at the shelter because of their age; the manager told her last week that they were not adoptable.

"No one wants an old dog or cat—potential health problems would be costly," he said "Better to put them to sleep."

Abigail began crying as she remembered how callous the man's words had been.

Maybe she was too old also, she thought. *No bank will give me a loan because I might get sick or die. No one will give my "babies" a home for the same reason.*

She fell asleep still sitting on the floor. There was no bed, and she didn't feel like leaving her already stressed animals in an empty house to go to a motel. Sometime during the night she rested her head on the German shepherd. The others grouped around her for comfort.

The next morning after everyone was fed, Abigail made a decision. She held each pet in her arms for a while. Then put the cats in their carrier and put the carriers in the garage. She led the dogs in also. She pulled her car inside and closed the bay door. Then she started the engine and sat on the floor.

She grouped the pets around her and wrote a letter as the toxic fumes filled the garage. She finished her writing before her tired arm fell to her side.

Several days later a concerned daughter had the police check the house because she hadn't been able to reach her mother. They opened the garage and found the bodies.

The letter simply said, "Karen, I couldn't bear for the pets and me to be separated just because we are old. We were together in life, please see that we remain so in death. I love you. Mom"

The Rocker

The little rocker with a caned seat had belonged to her great grandmother, Agnes Carson. The fact that it had no arms made it perfect for Great Grandma to rock her infant son over many a happy hour. When Grandpa David became a young boy, he delighted in holding onto the seat and rocking back and forth as fast as he could. It became his horse Tom-tom, and many were the cowboy battles they won together.

As he grew old, he needed a bigger rocker with sturdy arms to help him get up and down. He gave Tom-tom to his daughter Belle. She had the light oak refinished and buffed to a high sheen and found an expert caner to duplicate the pattern of the worn-out seat. She proudly kept her restored heirloom in the bedroom and allowed no one, not even herself, to sit on it.

Sometimes her own daughter Angela would slip into the room when Belle was gone and gently sit on the forbidden seat. Then she too would begin to rock faster and faster until Tom-tom rode the wind. She became a Bedouin princess sailing her carpet across the Egyptian desert to a hidden oasis and cave filled with jewels and magical objects.

Sometimes she would forget the real world around her as she rode. Then her mother would catch her in the rocker and give her a lecture on its age and history. She wouldn't punish her, however, because she remembered the Tom-tom tales her father had told her.

In time, Belle moved the rocker into the family room and allowed her daughter full reign over Tom-tom. She realized the little antique needed to be loved and used, not hidden away. When Belle died, the rocker came to live with Angela.

She too gently cared for it, but her own daughter Fay was too old to enjoy it, and it held no magical attraction for her. So when Angela needed money to pay her cancer bills, Tom-tom and many other valuables were sold. Before it left the family in the back of an antique seller's truck, she penciled "Tom-tom" and the family names on the bottom of its seat, then sealed it with urethane. Angela cried when her old friend left.

A year later in another town, the little oak rocker with its spindled and knobbed back sat in an antique store's display window. It caught the eye of a pretty pregnant brunette.

She walked past the window every Saturday for several weeks. She just knew that rocker would be perfect for rocking her newborn-to-be to sleep. Finally she had saved up the money to buy it and resolved that today was the day. She didn't haggle over the price with the dealer, and he agreed to have his son deliver it to her apartment at six o'clock that evening.

She paced all afternoon. It seemed an eternity until her rocker arrived and was carried upstairs to the baby's awaiting bedroom. Eagerly she tipped the young man and sent him on his way. Then she sat down on the caned seat, pushed back, and released her knees. It moved forward with a silky motion. She smiled. She rocked in it often over her last trimester. It helped ease her back from the baby's weight.

When her son Dan was born, she enjoyed rocking him over the hours. As he grew old enough to sit in the little rocker, he named it "Horsey", and they thundered over the western plains racing the wind.

After he grew up and married, she gave Horsey to him for his pregnant wife. She hoped her grandchild and daughter-in-law would feel the same gentle, comforting motion she had felt during her pregnancy and mothering years. And, she hoped Horsey would still have many long rides left.

However, Anne didn't like antiques and resented having the old thing in her house. Dan tried to get her to sit on it; he knew she would love it when she did. He said there was just something magical about the way it rocked. She refused. She wanted an overstuffed, rocking chaise lounge. She bought one in gray, and relegated the old rocker, over her husband's protests, to the front porch for not-so-welcomed guests to use.

It endured the wind and rain, cold and heat for three years. Its luster was now gone and its caned seat had a crack or two. Still Dan would sit outside many evenings and rock.

In time, Frank, an acquaintance of Dan's from work, began stopping over regularly. He always sat in the little rocker even when offered a large cushioned lawn chair. Sometimes Dan even felt a little jealous of another person sitting on Horsey.

Frank confided that Horsey reminded him of his Grandmother Angela's old rocker Tom-tom. She had rocked him in it when he was a toddler, but had had to sell it. He still had a picture of himself sitting on it back in a family album.

Dan told him that Anne never liked the rocker and wanted to get rid of it. Then both men laughed over women's likes and dislikes, and changed the subject to car racing and basketball.

Two weeks later, Frank returned and spoke to Anne. He begged her to sell the old rocker to him, and after a short pretense of not wanting to sell a beloved, family heirloom, she allowed herself to be persuaded to let it go for $50.

The excited man quickly transferred the rocker to his car's back seat before she could change your mind, and making his getaway, took his treasure home. His wife Julia met him at the car when he pulled into the driveway. Proudly he revealed the perfect little rocker to her.

She smiled gleefully and exclaimed, "It's perfect for the family room. I can rock little Mark to sleep on it, and read Janet's bedtime stories while she sits on my lap. The caned seat is still good and will be comfortable."

Frank helped her carry it inside and up the stairs. As he did so, he noticed some penciled words on the seat's bottom. He saw the family names and the word "Tom-tom." Tears filled his eyes as his puzzled wife read the words. She smiled and touched his shoulder.

"Welcome home, Tom-tom," she said.

The Great Hat Contest

Millie Jo Hanson and Lou Lou Belle Bradley were constantly in competition with each other. If Millie had a pretty picket fence, Lou Lou had to have one with hearts cut out of each picket. If Lou Lou had a beautiful calico cat, Millie had to have a magnificent calico main coon. And so it went.

It all started their junior year at prom time. Since those two gals were the prettiest in high school it was only natural that they both expected to have the handsomest boy for their date.

Luckily for the high school, the best looking guy was a pair of twins—Terrance and Jerald Carlyle. Terry and Jerry were so identical that their mother had had to have each one's left palm tattooed with his name.

When she wanted one son but not the other for some household task, she'd say, "Left hand up!" She would then read the palm to locate the chosen boy for the task.

Both Millie and Lou Lou had landed one of the twins for the prom, but each girl felt she needed to outshine the other, and twin dates, no matter how handsome, were still just equal.

Each had tried to find out what the other was wearing. What those dresses looked like was a more closely guarded secret than Area 51.

Terry and Jerry didn't even know what color their vests and ties would be that went with their tuxedos. These articles of clothing matched the dresses and were hidden until the boys arrived at their dates' houses to finish dressing. Even the corsages they'd paid for were a complete mystery.

Lou Lou and Jerry arrived at the prom before Millie and Terry but only by two or three minutes. Then the entire junior and senior class saw the fabulous dresses the girls were wearing—Millie wore an amethyst gown that enhanced her beauty to goddess stature. Lou Lou's was peridot colored that was pure awe inspiring next to her red hair and green eyes. Trouble was, other than color, those dresses were identical! Matching dresses and matching dates were just too much for those girls. The war was on.

The whole town, being small, knew about their struggle. Some folks even had on-going bets as to who would finally top the other. Both girls became engaged to their prom dates and were planning on out doing each other's wedding.

Luckily Terry and Jerry, sensing trouble ahead, insisted on a double wedding. The girls' parents gratefully agreed. The on-going wails of protest from Millie and Lou Lou caused the local coyotes to howl nightly for months.

Everything was to be shared so the only chance the girls had to out-do each other was with their wedding dresses. Lou Lou and her mother drove to New York City to get a tour of the bridal shops they had seen online and to have a custom dress made.

Millie begged her mother to take her to Paris, but Mrs. Hanson said, "Absolutely not."

Instead they flew to Hollywood to look through the stores where the stars bought their dresses and vintage clothing shops where the stars sold their dresses.

Lou Lou chose a white lace design and Millie found a dress worn to the Oscars at an exclusive used store called Star Threads.

All the decorations were in white, so the girls' dresses and bridal bouquets would be the only color.

Lou Lou was the first to walk down the aisle. Hers was a stretchy lace and seed pearl halter dress that fit tightly against her torso, then flared to a long train behind. Her see-through, white lace gloves hooked over her middle finger and went all the way up her arm. The veil was woven into her red hair and flowed ten feet behind. She carried copper and yellow lady slippers and purple lilies. All that white, tight lace and red hair made everyone ooh and aah. The organist even lost his place and stopped playing when he saw her. Her fiancé became weak kneed at the sight.

Then Millie followed in a pastel yellow, low-cut back and front, tight fitting satin gown with a tiny strap on one shoulder and the other arm covered to the wrist. She wore yellow lace gloves—one short and one long. Her flowers were yellow and orange daylilies. She wore a wide brimmed straw hat with yellow lace trailing down the back. The shoes were also pastel yellow and tied around the ankles.

Folks didn't just ooh and aah, they clapped. The organist hit a couple of sour notes; then his fingers shook so badly that it seemed like he was playing chop sticks rather than the processional. The minister and the bride groom on the alter steps wiped their brows before they could do their parts. Clearly Millie won this round.

Lou Lou vowed the day would come when she would totally beat her. Equal and second place did not sit well with her.

Over the next four years, they were bitter rivals for the tour of homes award, the studio and garden tour award, most authentic Victorian costume for a Christmas Carol award, best Halloween Theme award, and most beautiful floral arrangement made with one's own garden flowers award (documentation required).

Sometimes Millie would win and sometimes Lou Lou would win. It was six of one and a half dozen of another, but Lou Lou had never forgotten that yellow wedding gown worn by a star to the Oscars. It festered in her. How could she ever top that? Her dress had been custom designed for her and cost twice what Millie's had, but that yellow dress went to the Oscars and just had to have been photographed on television. In fact, she saw a DVD showing the dress at the Oscar awards and drooled over the star wearing it. Somehow she had to top that. Somehow, Somehow…..

Then along about late February, "The Daily Bugler" advertised an Easter Hat contest sponsored by the Hat Fanciers Club. It listed the prizes and other pertinent information, but Lou Lou paid no attention. All she saw was "Hat Contest"—a chance to beat Millie maybe for good. She figured Millie would see that article, but just to make sure, she circled it in red, and taped the page to her rivals front door. Yes, she saw it. The contest would be held April 6, the day before Easter.

Millie located a milliner online in Paris to design her hat while Lou Lou went to the State Historical Library to do research. She found a hair-do with a bird-cage in it, complete with bird.

That's it! she thought. *Millie will go for beautiful. I'm going for unusual. I'll beat her this time for good!*

She copied the picture, drove home, and purchased a ticket online to Los Vegas. Her patient husband took her to the airport the next day. She was headed to Dame Edith's, a designer costume shop she had seen on the clothing channel. The store specialized in outrageous, one-of-a-kind costumes for professional drag queens.

It took three days for the owner Mr. Edith and Lou Lou to design the hat, and choose colors to go with her red hair. She was so excited when she flew home that she was almost bouncing in her seat.

Three weeks later it arrived at her house. It was even more fantastic than she had dreamed. Lou Lou modeled it for her husband that night at dinner. He was so taken aback that his jaw dropped and his spaghetti slithered out of his mouth and back down to his plate.

"You've got to be kidding," was all that he could muster.

"Oh, no, I'm not," she said, "and I promise this will be the last time. I'm using a different strategy, and if this doesn't top her for good, then I'll admit defeat. And, Dame Georgia from the show 'All Decked Out' is going to have this hat, outfit, and me on his show. Mr. Edith arranged it. Even if I don't win the contest, I'll still win because I'll be on television and only her wedding dress was on TV. We'll get a vacation out of it, and I get paid $5000 to tell my story. You'll even get to tell your thoughts on this feud. Just don't tell your brother, or Millie will find out and want to be on the show too."

"Well, I guess you do have a new strategy. I'll go along with these shenanigans one last time if it means peace in this family, and for my brother too," said Jerry.

"I promise, besides if I refuse to compete with her again, I still win!" Lou Lou shook her beautiful red hair, dimpled, and kissed her husband.

Whatever reservations he had about that wild hat melted.

She just might finally pull it off, he chuckled, *and if this stops the competition, I'm all for it.*

The morning of April 6 finally arrived, and Lou Lou rushed off to the pet shop to purchase a green parakeet for her hat. She bought all the bird accessories and a "How to Care for a Parakeet" pamphlet also because she was giving "Beaky" as a birthday present to her younger sister the following week.

Beth had always wanted a parakeet, and now she'd get a soon-to-be-TV-star bird for her apartment. Then Lou Lou rushed home to get ready.

The contest was at 2:00 on the Village Green. The judges would be in the gazebo and each contestant would parade by. Those watching would have chairs or blankets or just stand.

Jerry took the van so Lou Lou could hide in the back until it was her turn. He parked on the street next to the Green so she could watch.

Quite a parade of beautiful lacey, flowered, and beribboned hats floated by on proud heads but everyone was waiting for Millie and Lou Lou. Bets had been placed as to which of the two would win.

It was Millie's turn first. Everyone ooh'ed and ah'ed over her black and white, asymmetrical straw. It was cocked on the side of her head. The brim was short on one side, and very wide on the other. It dipped and covered one eye partly for a very flirty look. There was a very large black and white silk flower attached to the white band. She wore a black suit trimmed in white, and black and white spectator shoes to compliment her simple but elegant hat.

The "Daily Bugler's" photographers took many pictures of her. Two judges whispered that unless Lou Lou could top that, Millie was definitely the winner.

Lou Lou was the last contestant. Just as she was carefully getting out of the van, a small orange kitten close by attracted the attention of a dog in the audience. He was leashed, but tried to lunge for the cat, barking loudly.

The lab was quieted quickly enough, but no one saw or cared where the kitten went. He had jumped up on the fender, then hood, then top of Jerry's van. He saw Lou Lou's parakeet and hopped onto the stiff hat. He lay down in front of the cage and watched the bird intently.

Lou Lou couldn't see that there was an addition to her headpiece or feel the weight difference because it was already twenty pounds.

She removed her cover-up and stepped toward the cat walk in front of the judges. Everyone's mouth dropped open. The judges dropped their pens and their collective eyes bugged out.

She was wearing a green iridescent spandex long-sleeved unitard. Starting at the bottom of the left ankle, an orange and black banded snake wound around her leg, torso, and over a shoulder. The neck of her unitard had a stiff cut away high collar like Dracula's cape. The snake wrapped around this collar like a fastener and moved up the side of her face to her temple.

The parts of her outfit not surrounded by snake were wound in vines. The ivy wove through her long red hair and up into the hat and then cascaded down. One eye had a leaf painted over it. Her nails were green and her shoes were ivy covered thongs.

But the hat! It was over 2 feet tall! The back of it was a golden sun disc surrounded by gold wire rays. In front of the orb were two colorful Egyptian figures. The man held a golden birdcage with Beaky inside and the woman held a bowl of fruit with grapes dangling down as if she were about to feed the parakeet.

Smaller golden birds with upturned wings were at their feet, and flying ones encircled the hat's brim. Right in front, watching the figures, dangling grapes, cascading vines, and moving bird, was that small orange kitten.

As Lou Lou promenaded, music played from the van with voices singing "She's a Cold Hearted Snake." The title on the judges' list was "Summer Solstice," but they hardly noticed. It was the most outrageous hat and outfit that Mr. Edith had designed so far that year, and everyone who saw it on Saturday was stupefied. Obviously Lou Lou had won. But the gods of contests weren't finished yet.

There was a long table set up to one side holding various refreshments for all after the contest, and a table to the other side holding a victory cake and trophies. Five of these trophies for the runners-up resembled Easter bonnets with large looping metal bows. A larger winner's trophy was a sophisticated art-deco lady sporting a hat with a metal-lace flower. One of her hands held her brim, and the other rested on her hip.

As Lou Lou promenaded by s and near the tables, the little kitten chose to stretch—paws out front, rump up, and tail held tall and curled. Then it batted at the grapes. Everyone went, "aah, how sweet," but that dog on the leash lunged loose from his sitting owner and made a dash for the small tabby.

He jumped up on Lou Lou, barking, then ran around and around her feet, tying her legs together with his leash. Then he jumped again. The kitten fled onto the refreshment table and the lab charged after it, yanking Lou Lou's legs out from under her. The leash slid off, carrying her shoes in its loops. They flapped along slapping the dog in the side, on the rump, and over the head.

The dog thought his owner was beating him so he began yelping when hit and barking when not. He jumped upon the table, knocking over the large containers of drinks. All went crashing to the ground, sending a tsunami of punch, lemonade, ice tea, cookies, sugar, sliced lemons, and ice into the crowd.

All the folks sitting nearby were soaked in different flavors and sprinkled with sugar. Many wore their new lemon or cookie hair decorations very well. The lab's owner grabbed for the leash but got Lou Lou's thongs instead. The leash whiplashed and smacked the black dog on his rump. He squealed, ran two blocks to his doghouse and cowered inside.

His owner threw the shoes towards Lou Lou, but missed, and tore off after his dog, yelling, "Bad Chuckles, bad dog!" The flying shoes landed end up in the middle of the large single-layer cake forming a V-shape right above the words, "Winner, Circle County Easter Hat Contest."

The little orange kitty ran back to Lou Lou and quickly climbed up the snake to her shoulder. It didn't realize that its refuge was in the process of falling onto the trophy table. Lou Lou crashed, the birdcage opened, and Beaky flew out. The table turned over. Trophies flew into the air. The cake slid off onto a stunned spectator's lap. The shoes flipped out and smacked him in the face leaving globs of white icing on his forehead and cheeks.

The poor terrified kitten jumped into the birdcage, which flipped shut when his tail fur caught on the latch. The flying trophies came raining down onto Lou Lou's hat. The sun-rays speared the first-place statue by her arms, second-place landed right-side-up in the fruit bowl, and the wings of the encircling birds caught the other four trophies by their big bows.

Beaky was so nervous that he flew 'round and 'round the hat, pooping uncontrollably in Lou Lou's hair, then settled on her wide collar.

Lou Lou rolled off the edge of the table and gracefully landed on her feet. The man, holding the cake and shoes, handed her thongs back, righted the table, and placed the cake on it. Still wearing the trophies, she carefully continued her promenade as the music from the van finished, "Snake, hisssssssss!"

Everyone jumped to his and her feet, even the judges, and clapped wildly. The bird-poop only frosted her hair beautifully. The kitten in the cage and bird on the collar were her crowning glories. She was awarded all six trophies that Saturday.

Millie, green with envy, had to endure countless pictures and reports of Lou Lou in the papers, on the radio stations, and on television. Then there was that interview with Dame Georgia on the Clothing Channel!

Author (Mary) Deborah Bowden

first developed a love of story-telling and writing from her father, Bradley Garrison Patrick, when she was very young and began creating her own tales in the 1970s. She especially enjoys writing about animals for children.

She taught English and creative writing in the public schools and college for 25 years before retiring to rear her daughter, Erin Bradleigh, on whom she honed her talents.

She has been in love with Brown County, Indiana since her college friends enticed her here in early 1970; she knew she had found her home.

She is a member of the Columbus Writer's Group; Mill Race's Senior Scribes in Columbus; and the Writers, Readers, and Poets Society of Brown County. When not writing, she enjoys the trees and hills around her Brown County home.

She is the author of other adult books: *Dandelions and other Weeds: A Collection of Musings, Memories, Songs, Poems, and Stories; Pat and Little Pat: A Slightly Unconventional Cookbook from a Dad and Daughter; Little Lestoil Ladies: the Cream of Premium Dolls and How to Identify Them, Kudzu Beyond Control, 30 Hydes* (two horror novels) And now, *Daylilies and Nightshades,* a sequel to her *Dandelions and Other Weeds.*

Her works for children are The Mr. Bramble Bones Series: *Mr. Bramble Bones and Grimmy in The Case of the Missing Blue Blanket; Mister Bramble Bones and Grimmy Share a Home, Mr. Bramble Bones Is Too Cold to Play, Mr. Bramble Bones and Grimmy Clean Up; Mr. Bramble Bones and the Ghost Hunters; Mr. Bramble Bones: A Christmas to Remember,* with more coming.

The Horus the Misunderstood Buzzard Series: *Horus, the Misunderstood Buzzard: Horus Has a Problem, Snickers Has a Toothache,* with other books in the series.

The Sack Lunch, a children's book illustrated by her talented daughter. Coming soon is the first in the series: *The Many Misadventures of Felicia Brown: Groundhog's Day.*

Ms. Bowden has contributed articles and stories to *The Reflection Rag,* a quarterly publication, *Pen-It Magazine* for writers; and *The Realm,* an online magazine of the paranormal.

Her writings have appeared in *Kairos:1970; Midwest Poets from Pen to Paper; Treasured Moments, Hillsounds III,* and *The Wishing Well: Discoveries,* three anthologies.

Her books can be found on Penitpublications.com, Amazon.com and Barnes and Noble and other sites.

She's available to speak at writer's conferences and to entertain groups with her storytelling at rosemarycoven@yahoo.com.

www.ingramcontent.com/pod-product-compliance
Lightning Source LLC
Chambersburg PA
CBHW060523180626
46817CB00002B/468